THE BELL FORGING CYCLE, BOOK IV

Gleam Upon the Waves

K. M. Alexander

THE BELL FORGING CYCLE, BOOK IV
Gleam Upon the Waves

Print Edition ISBN: 978-0-9896022-8-0
eBook Edition ISBN: 978-0-9896022-7-3

Published by K. M. Alexander
Seattle, WA

First Edition: March 30th, 2021

Cover Design by: K. M. Alexander
Cover Lettering by: Jon Contino
JONCONTINO.COM

Did you enjoy this book? I love to hear from my readers.
Please email me at: hello@kmalexander.com

BELLFORGINGCYCLE.COM
GLEAMUPONTHEWAVES.COM
KMALEXANDER.COM

1.0.6

For Pat & Carol

The sea can bind us to her many moods, whispering to us by the subtle token of a shadow or a gleam upon the waves, and hinting in these ways of her mournfulness or rejoicing.

— H. P. Lovecraft & R.H. Barlow, *The Night Ocean*

GLEAM UPON THE WAVES

PROLOGUE

Decay lingered on the air; fetid and cloying as if some ancient grave buried beneath the city had opened and from it rushed a corrupt perfume. It permeated everything, imbuing the bricks and asphalt with its stink like a spreading stain.

It had arrived a few weeks earlier, riding into Level Two on the back of the early King Tide. For a while it remained near the Sunk, flirting with odors of ruin and refuse that never dissipated in Lovat's lowest levels. Then, as if it had a mind of its own, it slowly drifted upward past Level Three, then Four, until even the wealthy in their gilded tower far above had begun to complain.

The shoalta—an ordained priestess of Deeper—moved with purpose through the stink, head down, her black eyes alert. She imagined it swirling in her wake like a mist. The odor made her lightheaded and giddy. But below those feelings was a knot of conflicting emotion. This had been foretold. This was the first sign. A prophecy etched into the senses.

Look west! Look west, oh, children!

She should be glad. But she wasn't. The moment was lost. There was danger. The Guardian had not fulfilled their duty; the cycle was broken. As much as it pained her to admit, her golden master was correct. Now wasn't the time.

Adjusting her salt-stained robe and straightening the chain of her office, the shoalta rounded a corner and moved along the broad thoroughfare that ran along the western edge of Haliaetus Lake. It wasn't a true lake, not really. Just an open patch of seawater centered above a flooded basin and surrounded by the streets of Level Two.

Hundreds of small stands vied for space, each offering identical merchandise with baskets full of clams, crates brimming with muscles, and bins filled with geoduck. The smells of seawater and shellfish should have overpowered the stink, but it lingered even here.

He was close now. Like the city, she too had heard the rumors. Missing boats. Coastal communities disappearing. Sightings of something unknowable and indescribable from cephel farmers along the Gorda and Blanco. Her heart thumped in her chest.

Fisherfolk, stevedores, buyers, merchants, and farmers mingled and lingered along the edges, living their small lives in this crowded city of lost souls, unaware of what was coming. Could she convince them? Her heart ached for these people. But she'd be disregarded, brushed off as just another crazy street mystic. What shoalta preached Hasturian words? Could she even call herself a Deeperist anymore?

She pressed among the throng. Eight-armed cephels and squat anur were the majority—the true aquatics of the lower levels. But an occasional swarthy human or pale maero bobbed through the crowd in their ungainly way. No umbra or dauger however—shadows and masked labored elsewhere in Lovat's nether regions. She saw at least one dimanian with mean eyes and curved tusks that sprouted from his cheeks. There were stocky kresh as well with their vaguely avian heads and dark eyes—her people. Usually ignored, mostly forgotten, always treated as simpletons.

Everyone moved with a nervous energy that had become more common in recent weeks. The ordinarily boisterous crowd still hummed with discussion, but it was suppressed, muted. Strange weather had lingered along the coasts. Riptides had taken whole fishing villages. Sailors had reported seeing huge waves out in the channels.

Then there was the King Tide. It had come early without the full moon. Parts of Level Two had flooded, and Deeperist Shoals scrambled to prepare for the usual celebrations to mark its arrival.

The shoalta continued her journey, leaving the hustle of the shellfish markets behind. She passed through several of the lower warrens, moving deep into Lovat's recesses. She passed unlicensed centipede breeders, pitch dens, and seedy casinos outlined with gaudy neon that flickered against the shadows. She saw neighborhoods of hovels where starving people gazed with hollow eyes, and some nicer warrens where the stumps of grander buildings rose and the poor managed to eke out a semi-decent life even this far down. The stink lingered—the sweet rot punctuated with the base smell of death.

She stopped before a narrow, unassuming door along a narrow, unassuming street in a narrow, unassuming part of Lovat. The warren was named Myrtle, and it was a decent place a few levels up. Down here in Level Two, it was a rougher warren. The remnants of a crematorium stood to the left. An abandoned automat sat to the right, and a sign above it read WHATELEY'S, or it would have if the letters weren't half-missing, leaving a rusted "What" behind like a question with no answer.

A pair of dauger with oxidized brass masks leaned against one another inside the automat. They breathed shallow breaths and occasionally twitched in their sleep, two souls lost in the ecstasy of a pitchfork high.

This was the place. She had been told to look for those land-marks. A dull glow emanated from beneath the door's jamb. It lit the tips of the claws at the end of her toes, and she wiggled them, smiling at the play of light.

Her smile was short-lived. The smell grew stronger, as if reminding her of what was to come. *Look west*, it urged. *Look west, oh children, oh servant.* It was both a promise and a subtle warning. A will, bound in stench.

The golden king's words tickled at her mind. The hot air of the desert filled her lungs. She mimed the dusting of ash from her shoulders—knowing full well it wasn't actually there.

She took a deep breath and could almost feel the stench tickle her insides. Then she knocked, the rap of her claw louder than she expected on the door's metal surface. She looked toward the pitch users, expecting one to stir, but neither did.

In response to her knock, a sound echoed from within. A shuffling. A murmur of a voice—a deep and resonate voice. Someone was talking to themselves.

The door swung inward, and a pool of light and the pungent scent of pine spilled out onto the dirty narrow street. The light and this new fragrance washed over her. Clarity sparked within her mind. She almost gasped. She was here for a reason. She was here to make things right.

A medium-sized dimanian stood in the doorway. He had small black horns sprouting from his forehead and long hair pulled back and worn in a loose topknot. He was dressed smartly, much smarter than most Level Two citizens: a white button-up shirt with double cuffs, pressed black slacks over glossy pointed shoes. No tie.

He regarded her with a slight tilt of his head. He had a notebook in one hand and a half-finished bottle of beer in the other.

"Help you?" he asked, lowering the bottle. His voice was as slick as his appearance.

"Um, hi. I…" the words were there, but the shoalta had trouble making her tongue say them. This smartly dressed dimanian was intimidating. She wasn't used to interacting with his sort down here.

Realization sparked behind his eyes. "You the Deeperist shoalta?"

She nodded and felt a pang of guilt pierce her heart. She was here, after all, going through with this.

"Been expecting you. Trust you found the place okay?" He didn't wait for a response. "Come in."

They left the stink behind, and her nostrils were assaulted by an overpowering scent of the forest. She blinked—stunned to be removed from the stench that had haunted her for days now.

He led her down a hallway into a medium-sized room. It was an ordinary kitchen. A counter ran along the far wall, split by a stove and a rusty icebox. A thick table sat in the center, surrounded by four chairs.

Along the room's edges, sitting on shelves, counter space, and atop stacks of boxes, were jars filled with sand. Stuck into them were burning sticks of incense—hundreds of them scattered around the room. Wisps of fragrant smoke drifted into a dense cloud that settled against the low ceiling.

Two doors opened further into the building. One was open, and from it came the buzz of neon and a dull-pink glow. Somewhere water dripped. Distantly a band played an old swing number. Somewhere else, perhaps floors above, came the muffled sound of people arguing. Or maybe that was just in her mind? It was hard to tell anymore.

A single lantern hung suspended from a cable in the center of the room, its glow hazy in the cloud of incense. Now, removed from that sickly sweet stink, the shoalta felt alone, removed from reality. The room felt oppressive. She began to sweat, and she hugged her robes close, resisting the urge to shiver.

"Drink? Wine? Beer?" the dimanian offered, his voice pulling her back. She turned, saw him standing there, waiting. Through the pink door came a third figure. An enormous bok, its deep-green scales color of canopy moss on a cloudy day.

The shoalta stepped back, blinking at him. She had met only a few bok, and most of the interactions had been brief. They were a long-lived species who rarely interacted with anyone, even their own kind. They had a reputation for being temperamental, but this one presented himself as casual, perhaps even friendly.

The bok regarded her in silence. He didn't look aggressive. He wore a gray button-up shirt and cut-off shorts, both damp as if he had recently come from a swim in the Sunk. He held a delicate glass of red wine in his head-sized claw.

"I'm okay," she managed. She just wanted this over with. First this slick dimanian and now a bok. If she thought too long about it, she'd abandon her plans altogether. If she did that, everything would fall apart. The master would be angry.

"Suit yourself," the dimanian said. "I'm Allard. I don't need your name, Shoalta'fhalma."

She stared at him, stunned at his use of the old tongue.

He smiled. "Grandmother was a Deeperist."

They all watched each other: her with caution, Allard with cool indifference, the bok with what seemed to be a silent amusement.

"You know why I'm here," she finally said, shaking off her shock.

Allard nodded. "Sure you can go through with it?"

"I'm sure," she said.

Allard's brow raised. He scratched behind one of his glossy black horns; they matched his shoes. "It's risky business. Especially now."

She tilted her head, regarding him, her question clear.

"It's a new Lovat. A post-riot Lovat. Security firms are on edge. The LPD ain't messing around anymore. Magnez is coming down hard. Showing her strength. Making up for the lost time." He grimaced as if pained and then repeated, "It's a new Lovat."

"If there was another way…" she began. She hated being here. She hated talking with these men. She was a shoalta. She was supposed to be here to guide, lead, and prepare. Not to make backroom deals in a Level Two alley with criminals. But she had no other choice. The master had warned her. If it happened now… all was lost.

Allard held up a hand. "Don't need to explain. Just saying there's time to turn back from this. My experience is ladies like you are good people. We'd understand if this was too much. Sometimes a soul gets this far and can't go through. Wouldn't fault you any."

"I have to do it." She had stressed this before, through the many contacts they had sent. She had explained where and why so many times it hurt to think about. She didn't need to explain it again.

"On the *Gamble*," he emphasized the name.

She nodded. Thoughts of the vessel made her sick to her stomach.

"During celebrations."

She nodded again.

"We love this city. We want what's best for her. Something happens to the *Gamble* while she's in port, and something

happens to the city. Something happens while she's away...."
He let the sentence drop and gave a well-practiced shrug. "Hence our willingness and generosity. But we need promises."

"I don't have any money."

"We know."

"Then what?"

The dimanian tucked his notebook into a pocket and set his beer bottle down on the counter. He leaned back, folding his arms. "We see ourselves as silent partners. We're essentially financing this operation. Like the... like..."

"Camalote," said the bok. His voice was a rumble, a grinding of stone.

"Right. We're a charitable organization. Think of us like the Camalote Group. But the thing is, we don't want nobody to put two and two together. We like remaining anonymous. Follow? We need to be kept separate from this. If it goes down—" He raised a hand before she could interject. "—I believe you're capable, I do—but if it goes down and the LPD is going to start asking questions, well, we want to make sure there's no trace. Protect ourselves. Protect our investment. You acted on your own. We ain't a part of this."

"I am acting on my own," she said. It was true—sort of, the master was also involved, but she couldn't explain that to this dimanian. She had sought them out. They didn't find her, she found them, asked for help. Truth be told, she hadn't expected anything to come of it. But it just happened that their desires aligned.

"We have your word?"

"On the body of Deeper himself, sir."

Allard smiled a sleek, snake-oil smile. Behind him, the bok flashed a grin filled with rows of sharp teeth. It was a wicked expression on such a fearsome face. Some deep instinct sent small blips of panic sparking through her belly. She felt like she should run, but instead she smiled back.

Before she could say anything, the bok turned and shuffled to a cupboard, pulling out a blue half-sized duffle from a lower cabinet. He set it gingerly on the table between them.

The shoalta's chest seized. It was happening. Celebrations would begin soon, on the night of the full moon, when the King Tide was scheduled to ebb. Shoalta from shoals all over the city were planning to convene at Our Father of the Obscured Atoll, the church on board the *Gamble*. They'd anchor above the sunken Looff Fields just off the West Lovat shore, and perform the necessary rites. It would be a wild affair. Deeperist revelers from all over Lovat would come. The mayor was even sending a proxy to attend the celebrations.

She should have been excited. For decades, this was what her mother and grandmother had hoped and prayed for. But they hadn't seen the world beyond. Neither of them had spoken with *him*. They didn't know what she now knew. If the cycle were intact, she'd have joined them willingly. But the cycle was damaged, off-kilter. Years ago, a Hasturian sect had acted the fool and failed in their summoning. The process was upended.

"Ten hours. No off switch," the bok explained. "Chemical mixture. Press the button. Vials break."

"Once that happens, there's no going back," said Allard.

The bok nodded. "It'll mix. Smolder. Get hot. Then…" He made a silent gesture, the webbed fingers of his claw unfurling and expanding.

Allard smiled wickedly. "Good luck, Shoalta'fhalma."

The title stung her soul like a bee sting. She swallowed. It was all she could do to shuffle forward, giving both creatures a curt nod before taking the duffle and quickly walking back the way she had come.

Allard and Hank—the bok—watched the Deeperist priestess disappear down the hallway toward the exit. The dimanian scratched his jaw with a finger and didn't move until he heard the narrow door close. Then he let out a breath he hadn't realized he was holding.

"Guess that's that," he said to the room. He rarely spoke directly to Hank.

The bok settled after the shoalta left. He pulled himself to a sitting position on the counter, his broad tail hanging to one side. He and the dimanian wrinkled their noses as a waft of the wretched stink attempted to penetrate their cloud of pine and cedar incense.

"Thinks she'll pull it off?" Allard asked.

Hank said nothing.

A woman appeared. She was shorter than both of them but moved with a self-assurance the shoalta would have noticed. Her tweed suit fit well and gave her the look of an ancient hunter, the sort of person who'd tread through the swamps pursuing fowl with a faithful hound. Allard had seen similar characters on fantasy serials, and it was impossible to shake the comparison.

The woman had a sharp nose and full mouth that gave her a vulpine appearance. A cigarette hung from her lips. Its pungent scent paired oddly well with the odor of the forest. Her shifty eyes darted around the room, taking in everything in a heartbeat. Her eyes turned to the two men and then toward the exit where the kresh had disappeared, parcel in hand.

"So, our little soldier marches off to war." She gave a mock salute in the direction of the exit.

Hank nodded in silence and took a drink of wine.

"You sure about this, El?" asked Allard, picking up the remnants of his beer. "I mean it's the *Gamble*, for First's sake. Ain't no one been this bold in a decade."

"Oh, I'm sure," said Elephant. Her eyes narrowed slightly, and a subtle smirk moved across her lips.

"We get caught…" Hank said with a rumble of thunder.

"Chen ain't the forgiving type," added Allard. He paused, took a swig of beer, finishing the bottle. He scratched his jaw with a thumb. "Neither is Jurer, thinking about it."

The woman waved a hand, disregarding Allard's concern with a wave of her cigarette. "Ain't no getting caught. That was

Syringa Militia ordnance in that satchel. Someone catches that little sister there, they ain't going to come sniffing around here."

She took a long drag from her cigarette, blowing the smoke toward the single lamp. "If she manages to finish what she started, then Chen, Jurer, even damn slack-jawed Shelna will be at the bottom of the sea." The smoke swirled, then joined the incense haze. "It's business. Nothing more."

"Business is business," the bok rumbled.

Elephant gave him a side-eyed glance, and echoed his words, "Business is business."

ONE

A city has no memory; you come to her to be forgotten. It's not difficult. The city is entropy, and entropy cares little for the past. Each person is a hurtling meteor drifting on their course, reacting to the gravity of others. Lives, events, and demands swirl in an uncaring maelstrom. The vortex moves this way and that as personalities and powers direct it. But that never lasts, and eventually the city returns to a state of unrelenting chaos. If one scrapes out space for themselves, they can hide in the disarray.

Lovat sits on the western edge of the Territories, gazing out like a sentinel at a vast ocean and the scattered islands of the western archipelago. To describe the city adequately is impossible. She's too large to comprehend, too immense to explain. Lovat is a mass, a heap, a jumble—millions upon millions of souls living on top of each other. Nine labyrinthine levels constructed of steel, iron, asphalt, and cement rising from sea and stone, each a tangle of warrens.

She's a city of tunnels lit by halogen, sodium, and neon. A city of stairwells and lift shafts. You can live your whole life within her depth and never see the sky. You can spend years wandering her passageways and never realize a fraction of her reality.

She's a place of contradictions and a place of change. She rises from the shoulders of a ruined civilization and reaches toward the heavens with an air of misplaced optimism.

The only constant in a city like Lovat is yourself. Learning to embrace that is the key to survival. In a world where private space is limited, the safest place is usually within your head.

No one knows who originally built this city, or why. No one knows what it was before. Most of our ancient history disappeared after the Aligning. Occasionally someone managed to eke out a living within the in-between places, and that attracted folks like me.

The small piece of chaos I currently inhabited was called Cedric's. It's a diner that sits in between Level Three and Four, in one of the city's entresols, a sort of non-space usually reserved for machinery, not people. City services—electrical, sewer, water, that sort of stuff.

Cutlery clinked and clattered against flatware, and the noise mixed with the purr of conversation. The coffee tasted burnt, but I drank it anyway. Vile coffee is a diner's constant. Spend enough time in the city, and one learns to appreciate whatever steady beat you can find.

I liked Ced's. Discovered it after a harrowing journey on the Broken Road. It's unpretentious and simple. It has a full bar. I can bring anyone here, and I can stay as long as necessary. The staff knows me. It's nice to be known. The high-backed wood booths provide a calming sense of privacy.

The long counter lined with stools was lined with the backs of hungry work-a-day patrons in various stages of eating, drinking, and conversation. Their presence added a din that made talking easy.

Four of us sat in our booth—the three partners of Bell Caravans and Taft, our occasional chuck. Across from Taft and myself was Wensem dal Ibble, the co-founder and the guy who thought it'd be funny to name the company after me. Wensem is a maero. They're a pale and long-limbed species. They look a lot like us humans but are generally taller, usually stronger, and they live longer. Their pale skin and seven-digits on their hands and feet are their defining feature. Wensem said it makes them good at handshakes. He's not wrong.

Beside him was Hannah Clay, the newest partner and our scout. Hannah is human. She's small of stature but tough as leather. We've been through a lot together.

"So let me get this straight." Hannah leaned forward, her green eyes sparkling.

Wensem took a drink from his coffee and watched her.

"Mayor Magnez is looking for security."

"Yes." Wensem nodded.

"And she reached out to you."

"Ah-ah," I said, holding up a finger like I was correcting her. "You mean she reached out to the 'Hero of Destiny.'"

A small revenge, but one I enjoyed inflicting from time to time. Wensem slumped slightly and blew a heavy breath. His dejected expression made both Hannah and Taft laugh.

A few months earlier, Wensem had led a group of citizens south in an attempt to break a blockade that had been starving the city. No one had expected much of the Blockade Breakers. But they had been successful.

Lovat had heralded them as heroes. The papers ran stories profiling them. Being their leader, Wensem had gotten the majority of the attention, something he didn't relish. The papers even gave him his fancy 'Hero of Destiny' moniker, as I didn't mind reminding him on a near-daily basis.

He hated the publicity, but it had been good for the company. Most import-and-export businesses liked teaming up with a maero regarded as a civic hero. Brands sought him out as a spokesperson. Plus the newly elected Mayor Magnez—the first dauger mayor in Lovat's history—had gotten real chummy with him. Which was also handy.

"Yes, she reached out to me," Wensem said. I could tell he was a little exasperated by the repetition.

"Okay," said Hannah. "But this is a security job on a boat."

"The *Gamble*," Wensem added.

"Right, the biggest damn boat in the Territories."

"Yes." It was both an agreement and an admission.

"We're a caravan company," Hannah said. "We caravan."

"This is like caravanning."

"No, it's not. It's sitting around on a floating piece of Lovat looking grumpily at people. Security duty isn't anything like caravanning."

Taft took a drink from her coffee. "Not much work on the *Gamble* for a chuck."

She was a large human with short brown hair and dark skin. She liked to say she was as big as a barn and twice as heavy, and it was probably true. Everything about the woman was enormous, from her personality to her opinions. Originally from Syringa, she had worked the trails between here and there for decades, flipping hash and slinging advice. A roader's roader.

"You're good with a gun," I said, leaning back. "You want a job? You got one. Always do."

Technically we saw Taft as an associate of Bell Caravans. She always had a gig with us, regardless of our need for a chuck—it was up to her. If Taft was interested, we were interested.

Taft shook her head. "I can be menacing, but I'm not good with a gun. I'm good with gravy and grains."

"No guns," Wensem said.

Hannah, Taft, and I all turned and stared at him.

"So it's a security job with no armament." Hannah sounded dubious. She narrowed her eyes at my partner.

Wensem spread his hands. "No guns. Look, I don't like it either, but the *Gamble*'s Council of Captains doesn't allow guns or knives—any weapon really—on board. They're real strict about it. Checkpoints, searches, the whole deal."

"They make most of their money from the casino trade," I said. "Every day there's thousands of lira and gallons of liquor flowing all over that boat. Makes sense why they'd want to eliminate weapons."

Hannah looked from me to Wensem. "How exactly are we going to provide security?"

"We can hold our own in a fight," Wensem said. "We have keen eyes for trouble."

"If we take this gig, we're the security detail on a boat for Magnez."

"Pays well," said Wensem. His crooked mouth twisted into a sheepish smile.

"How well?" Taft asked.

"Imagine the money we'd get from a handful of Big Ninety runs," said Wensem.

Taft rubbed her hands together.

"Then double it," Wensem said. "And throw in an opportunity to bonus."

Taft sat back, eyes wide as pie-plates. A low whistle escaped her lips.

"Damn," Hannah said. Her wood hand tapped softly on the table, counting out the figures that were running through her head. She had lost the hand on the Broken Road, a botched job. The circumstances surrounding it was something she still didn't talk about. For months it hung about her like a pall, but now, a few runs into the season, she was starting to seem like her old self. Falling into a relationship with Veata had also helped.

"That sort of money could put us in a good way. Coffers are getting empty. We need the lira. We could hire a second crew. Start running multiple jobs," I said, looking at Hannah.

Wensem had told me earlier that the mayor wanted our help, but he hadn't gotten specific. I'm not sure he knew the specifics.

Hannah leaned in. "It'll give Bell Caravans a bit of cachet. Swagger. Workin' for the Mayor like that."

Taft leaned forward and narrowed her eyes. "What exactly are we providing security for? It's not like City Hall doesn't have their own army for that work."

She was talking about the Lovat Police Department, the LPD. Part municipal police force, part militia. City-states like Lovat have to make do somehow.

"They can carry guns," I added.

Wensem ignored me. "First, it's not Magnez. It's a diplomat of some sort. Don't know much beyond that. If we're interested, we talk with the mayor. Second, if we're not, we can walk away. We already have two runs done, and there are more contracts open."

The flow along the Big Ninety had exploded as spring had crept into the world. We had taken easy gigs. The first run was a group of settlers looking to find work in Hellgate. We escorted them as far as Syringa. The job back had been even easier and less talkative: a shipment of wheat.

It was all trouble-free work, but the pay had been meager, and the runs were dull. Still, even with my bum knee, it was good to get out of Lovat for a while. Walk the roads. Clear my head. See the mountains and the tablelands beyond.

Wensem liked to say, "a good walk will clear out any troubles." It was advice he believed. Since returning from the blockade, he had begun taking long solitary walks around the city. Said it gave him time to refocus.

"The money's good. The work is honest," I said. I was sold.

This was something new. Something interesting. The only hurdle was to convince the others.

"Something still feels off about this whole thing," Hannah said. "There are hundreds of security firms in the city. Maybe thousands. Companies better equipped to handle this sort of work. Why hire a caravan company to do what they do every day?"

"They don't have the Hero of Destiny," Taft said.

Wensem made a face, and we all chuckled.

"You know she's right," I said.

"Doesn't matter," Wensem said. "What matters is deciding if we are willing to hear her out."

TWO

City Hall sat on Level Eight. Technically it began on Six, but years of constant construction had forced it upward. It burst through the streets like a sprouting seed, and the scaffolding on its roof suggested that it was prepared to go higher. The monorail deposited us at City Hall Station and together my crew and I made our way inside.

The main Level Eight lobby featured an artificial waterfall and broad open stairwells that climbed up and down through a vast atrium in the building's core. Designed in contrast to the cramped style of the warrens below, the atrium harkened back to an era in Lovat when great public works benefited only the privileged. An era that, with the recent transition in government, I hoped was coming to a close.

"Never been inside before," said Hannah. "It's… impressive."

Wensem crossed the atrium and quietly spoke to an aide dressed in a simple business suit. Before I could fully take in the waterfall, reflecting pool, and the acres of glass, we were whisked upstairs in a glassed-in lift that played pleasant chimes whenever it stopped and opened its door. A pair of carpeted hallways later and we were deposited inside a conference room to await the mayor.

The room occupied space on the building's highest floor. Enormous floor-to-ceiling window gave sweeping views onto a wide-open plaza below. Beams of sunlight streamed through the open superstructure of the perpetually under-construction Level Nine, creating little dappled pools of golden sunshine along the paving.

The King Tide stink was present here, less pronounced this far up but strong enough that a cone of incense burned along a side table near the room's entrance. It helped, somewhat.

The stink had not been the most welcome addition on our return from the last job. When we had left the city, it was still cold. When we returned, spring rains had begun to fall, and an early succession of King Tides had rolled in, bringing with them the atrocious smell. Getting out and away from Lovat had an olfactory as well as monetary appeal.

"Nice digs." Taft gave a low whistle.

"Different then I remember," I said.

Months ago, throngs of protestors had demonstrated on the plaza below. It was a turning point for the city. Hunger had gotten to everyone. You push a people far enough, and eventually they'll break.

The protestors had demanded an end to hostilities with Syringa—the hostilities that had shut the city off from the Territories and allowed the Purity Movement to make their move to the south. Lovat had been starving, and that had made its rage all the more ravenous. Pitted craters and scorch marks from the protests still stained the stone of the plaza.

I had been too busy to join the crowds. I was another floor up, chasing a First through the construction of Lovat's newest level. Now the plaza was mostly empty. A human street mystic in a salt-stained robe braved the rain. He shouted while he marched in a circle waving a sign that read: ARE YOU READY FOR THE NEW ALIGNING? The ink had begun to run, the rain slowly turning the Strutten letters into esoteric glyphs.

Camilla Magnez, a dauger and the newly elected mayor of Lovat, entered the room. She wore a sharp suit, and nodded in greeting as she moved to sit across from us at the dead-center middle of a long oak conference table. Flanking her were a pair of aides. One was a pudgy umbra, a living shadow wearing a baggy suit. The other was a human, with a broad jaw and small eyes pressed together.

Dauger society is caste-based—or was once. These days, castes are usually ignored. However, the precious families at the top—the Golds, Platinas, Argentums, and whatnot—had to be stewing over the fact that someone from a "lesser" family now held the most powerful position within the city.

Personally, I've had an odd history with dauger. I've known good dauger, and I've known evil ones. I've had dauger seek to kill me, others betray me. Some have worked for me. I once dated one. As far as I could tell, the mayor was one of the good ones.

As her name implied, Magnez wore a mask of polished magnesium. Hers was form fitting and wrapped itself around her oval face with soft lines. Intricate raised vines laced their way around the wide openings for her eyes and mouth. Through those openings were wide bright-blue eyes and soft red lips pulled back in a politician's smile. The mayor's dark hair was pulled back into a ponytail. She looked powerful, and she knew it.

Her presence and confidence immediately set me at ease. I liked her. Hell, I had voted for her.

Wensem introduced Hannah and me. "This is Taft. She's our chuck."

"Chuck?" The umbra aide asked. "What exactly is that?"

"Roader slang for cook," said Taft. She tapped her chest. "I can make a six-course meal out of just about anything."

"Pleasure to meet you all," said Magnez. She looked at my maero partner. "It's good to see you again, Wensem. How's Kit?"

"She's fine. Back to work. Writing another book. Pregnant again. Expecting this summer, actually."

"Two! That's unusual for maero," Magnez said.

Wensem smiled, nodded in his usual way, but said nothing more.

I leaned forward. "My partner said you have a job offer for us, Madam Mayor?"

"Right to business," she said. "Heard that about you."

"Hope that's a good thing."

"It is," she said. "Rest assured."

"What is it you need doing? Security of some sort?"

"We live in interesting times," the Mayor began, almost as if she had practiced this. She leaned back in the chair and steepled her fingers before her, pondering them a moment before continuing. "My predecessor ran this city like a fortress.

Rich on top, poor on the bottom, insular and isolated despite our diversity. We had enemies, and he was quick to exploit the population's fears despite trading with Syringa and Victory on a regular basis."

"Excuse me, ma'am," Taft said. "Did you mean to say Victory?"

Magnez smiled, showing a row of white teeth behind her mask. "I did."

Taft shook her head. "Victory ain't traded with nobody for years, ma'am."

"I'm afraid we'll have to disagree," Magnez said. "Lovat has been trading regularly with Victory."

"How?"

"The *Gamble*," Magnez's smile looked so vast I half expected her to crack her mask.

"The *Gamble*," Taft repeated.

Magnez nodded. "She's been the sole channel between the two nations for a long time now. Dragged back and forth, Lovat to Empress, Empress to Lovat. The Council of Captains has a special relationship with the hermit nation, and that has given them an opportunity with the more progressive portions of its government. That's where you come in."

"How?" I asked. "We know you need security. Wensem filled us in. But we'd like a few more details before we agree to anything."

"Understandable." She took a deep breath. "The Czanek administration nearly killed this city. His strong-arm policies and positions put us in a perilous situation. When the blockade happened, Lovat was ready to burn herself down. I don't want that to happen again. I want to restore relations with Victory. I want to reopen free trade."

"You're sending an emissary," I said flatly. She had already done that with Syringa, and it was working. The Syringan embassy in Lovat had been reinstated, and one was being built for Lovat within Syringa. Bilateral talks were looking positive. Tensions had eased.

"I am," Magnez agreed. "Ambassador Castaigne, a dimanian."

"She ran against you," Taft said.

"She did," said Magnez with a smile I couldn't read.

The campaign to replace Czanek had evolved rapidly over a month. Nearly three hundred people had run. Most of them didn't have a chance. A few had small pockets of support—warren heroes and neighborhood personalities, mostly. Some had bought their way in.

But toward the end, four candidates had floated to the surface. Magnez had been the clear frontrunner throughout, populist and progressive, with a mind for finance and an eye for business. She had drawn a lot of attention.

Constance Castaigne was a former prosecutor and an up-and-comer, but her ties to the Czanek administration had sunk her appeal toward the end. Samuel Danforth, a Level Nine socialite, had the backing of the Camalote Group and a few other elevated charities, but was seen as too out of touch by most of the population living in the span. Finally, there had been Conrad O'Conner, the cadaverous preacher, founder, and leader of the speciesist Purity Movement. His message of hate and fear was as old as the earth. He longed for and campaigned on a pre-Aligning order where humanity came first.

The Purity Movement had been responsible for the second blockade that had cut off the city. O'Conner had been quick to distance himself from their actions, calling the Movement's action the fault of a "rogue faction." Some people bought it. Others didn't care. Wensem called him a liar. The fact O'Conner had even been in the running just showed that Lovat still had a long way to go.

The city had been caught up in the excitement of the campaign. Until now, elections had been a rarity. People proudly wore buttons bearing the faces of the politicians they supported. Colored bunting hung from the ceilings in many warrens. You could still see the political posters hanging on walls, in stairwells, and within the lifts. Most were capped with strong Strutten letters proclaiming all manner of slogans and promises. Others were written in Cephan and Elano.

When the vote came, it had been chaotic. But the vote *had* come, and Lovatines turned out for it. Magnez won but Castaigne had made a good show, coming in as a solid second.

"She's smart," Magnez said. "We need public servants like her working for the betterment of Lovat. I don't harbor any ill will toward her or her campaign. Politics are messy. Pettiness doesn't serve the common good."

I leaned back, nodding. "So what's the plan?"

"The *Gamble* is our link to Empress. Up until now it's only served as a go-between—cargo mostly. No unloading of foreigners. That's changing. Victory is opening up Empress for the first time in living memory. Bridgetown is sending a boat, as is Hellgate. Five hundred visitors coming from each city. It's not a lot, but it's a start."

Taft gave a low and somber whistle.

"As I'm sure you're aware, this is a big deal," the mayor said. "I have spoken with the *Gamble's* captains, and they've agreed to ferry Castaigne to the city. I want you to make sure she gets there safely. My hope is there aren't any problems. But I want to be sure."

"This *is* the Territories," Hannah said.

"Right. I'd rather be prepared than surprised. But there's more. If all goes well—and Victory tends to be jumpy and irrational—Castaigne is staying in Empress, and you'll be bringing the Victory Ambassador with you on your return. On the return, the boat is scheduled to stop off West Lovat for the Deeperist's King Tide's Ebb celebrations—"

"Wait, Victory is sending someone *here?*" Taft interrupted.

Magnez nodded. The can lights above reflected off the edge of her mask in shimmering sparkles. "The accords they propose offer more than I could have hoped. But we need to be careful. As I said, they're jumpy. Smallest hint of trouble and they'll close their boarders and shut us out. I'm sure you're all aware of the, uh, tenuous peace between Victory and Syringa."

Taft leaned forward. She had served in the war—fought on the Syringan side in General Bowles' brigade. Came away from the conflict with plenty of stories and no love for the hermit nation. Yet she'd also understood the foolishness in her home-town's aggressive posturing. The tough-guy act doesn't get you very far in politics, especially national politics. It's too easy to manipulate, and in the end, you come out on the wrong end of history.

"They ain't going to like that," Taft said.

"Exactly, but we can't allow Syringa the sole control of trade into our city. We're planning on easing them into this. But until that happens, it's paramount that no one is aware we're talking. Things are tentative enough—if word got out, there'd be threats, and if there were threats…" Magnez let her words drift. "They're not above closing their borders and ejecting foreigners. They've done it before and would do it again."

Her words hung in the air, and somber silence fell on the room.

"Why us?" I asked, breaking the stillness. "Why a caravan company? Why not one of the security firms? Merck has a security division. Hassler. Waite."

Magnez tapped the jaw of her mask and then pointed at me. "You're tenacious. You're fighters. I've talked with Wensem. I know about the Broken Road—and I know what you managed to keep out of the papers. I admire that. I don't just want security. I want subtlety. I want tenacity. I want passion."

Her lips turned up in a smile, and her eyes met mine.

A buzzing bloomed at the back of my skull.

Then I wasn't even in Lovat. Once again, the wasteland swallowed me.

I stood on endless hardpan; the ground had cracked from lack of moisture. It was a place I had visited many times before. I could still feel myself sitting at the conference room table, but I wasn't in the conference room. I was in the wasteland. Above, a broken sun radiated with a warped heat. The wind hissed madness in my ear. The warbled song of a coyote carried across the vastness. But there were other noises as well. Noises from another reality. The hum of the air recycler in the corner and the buzz from the lightbulbs. Conversation.

In the far distance was a ruined city—the corpse of another Lovat, its levels and towers shattered and broken. Past it, beyond even the horizon, was something else. Something immense. A crashing moan filled the sky—a sound I had heard before. It carried through the air like the trumpets of distant angels.

The bones of ancient monuments scattered the tableland—broken fragments of a dead civilization. Strange inhabitants peered out from crevices, their pale faces just visible among the shadows—the locals.

I looked down at my dust-covered boots, the revolver at my side. I was clearly outfitted for caravanning. Then I noticed some of my tattoos were missing.

The twin wain wheels were still on my forearms, but the rose tattoo on the back of my hand was gone, as were the apple and oxen skull on the insides of my wrists. That was odd. I rubbed my thumb absently against my skin. Why were only some of my tattoos gone?

I puzzled over this as I looked out at the ruins and wondered how long I'd be here. Rusted girders stretched for miles, like the bones of an ancient titan. They reached towards the broken sun far, far above.

Something moved. Rocks clattered against rocks. I turned, nervous now.

An elongated figure, familiar to me, stood in the distance. I remembered its shadow from when I had visited the wasteland before. That had been on Level Nine, with Ashton. What was left of him had scoffed at the figure, called it a "pretender." Was it the reason I was here? Was he?

I stepped toward it and wondered what my body was doing in the conference room. The thought made my brain hurt. Wensem was saying something. Then Taft. Then the mayor. The jumbled mix of spaces made my brain hurt. Why was this happening again? Why now?

The realization of conflicting truths warred inside me. This place was real. Lovat was real. I was in both and yet in neither at the same time.

The creature had made the clattering sound, I was sure of it, but as I moved closer, I noticed that it wasn't touching the ground. It hovered a few inches off the hardpan. Yellow robes the dirty color of sweat stains drifted around it, ignoring the wind and moving like fabric caught in underwater currents. Its legs weren't visible, but it had long thin arms and pale hands with long fingers. They looked stretched out—too long.

"Who are you?" I demanded.

It said nothing in return. Just tilted its head. Beneath the shadowed cowl of a heavy hood, it wore a pale mask, the shape based on the form of an elongated human face. It had no opening for a mouth, and none cut for eyes. A lone hole sat in the center of the brow. A single line rose from the hole and split the forehead before disappearing amidst the cowl's gloom.

The figure remained silent. Its placid expression unnerved me. I couldn't suppress the frosty tingling that traced a line down my spine.

"Who are you?" I repeated.

For a long moment, silence fell between me and the creature. The wind whipped between us, carrying bits of ash and dying embers.

Ash and embers. That was new. I could smell sulfur on the wind—also new. Most of the time, the wastes usually smelled like dust and sun-scorched earth—but the stink of sulfur was almost inviting compared to the putrid scent that had attached itself to Lovat.

"Who are you?" I said again.

The voice that responded was a hiss—a whisper, but spoken from the mouth of a titan. It came from the figure but surged in from everywhere. It rushed forward, moving between worlds like a hiss of steam. I stumbled under its sound, my eyes going wide as the words registered.

"Look west," it said. "He is coming."

THREE

"How long has this been happening?"

My response wasn't quick. I processed the question—unsure for an instant if it was even real. "Started on the Broken Road. Dreams. It's become more frequent since fighting with Ashton. More real."

Lovat—my Lovat—was returning to me in fits and flashes, breaking though the tar of vestigial memories which offered a competing overlapping reality. A wall was a wall, then it was a vast expanse of dirt and dust, then it was a ruin before it reverted into a wall again. Had I even said those words? Had I replied at all? My mouth felt dry, my breath muffled and stalled. I opened my mouth to either respond or repeat myself, but Wensem interrupted me.

"Carter's cross, Wal! You ever consider telling someone?" Wensem said. He rarely raised his voice, and hearing him do it now was unnerving. I turned and looked at him. He seemed real enough.

"You know, we do *actually* care about you," said Hagen Dubois. He leaned with his back against the inside counter, his arms folded across his stomach. Behind him several scented candles burned, filling the room with a fragrant odor of sandalwood, musk, and moss that pushed away the ever-present stink.

Wasteland. Meeting. Magnez. I had been talking with the mayor, in the conference room at City Hall. Everything slipped back into place. Reality—this reality—took a firmer hold.

"What did you tell Magnez?" I asked. That time I knew I had said it.

I barely remembered leaving City Hall. The lift ride was still a blur—I was struggling to process my return to reality. All I could remember was a poster bearing the mayor's mask and the words MORE WITH MAGNEZ written in thick letters below her magnesium chin. It had grown larger and larger until it was finally obscured by blowing ash.

It wasn't until we passed through the door to Saint Olmsted Religious Antiques that I began to feel grounded. It was like returning home. The old counter. The stools. The shelves lined with artifacts and trinkets. Hagen's greeting. The smell of musty books and oiled hardwood. The squeaky floorboards. The bell at the door. The old jazz records spinning on Hagen's ancient player. Everything made sense here. The world felt right. Each detail lingered reminding me of my reality until the fogginess had begun to lift.

Why was this happening? Which each subsequent return from the wasteland my feeling of confusion and detachment grew stronger. Before it had a hazy faded quality, like daydreaming. Now I confused the actual reality and the dream. It was like being trapped in the space between wakefulness and sleep.

"Magnez?" I asked again.

"Told her you were concussed from a fall on our last run," said Taft.

"She was fine with that?" I raised my eyebrows.

"Don't try and change the subject," said Hagen, perturbed. He was dimanian. His prominent horn was a single wild spike that rose from his right temple, rolled back across his brow, and tangled itself in his nest of dark hair. The horns grow fast and are usually shaped by dimanian barbers. Hagen didn't care about that. I smiled as my eyes passed over it—another constant, another beat in this city, another anchor that drew me back and held me here.

"Not changing the subject," I said. "It's related."

Hagen didn't seem to buy my excuse. I looked at Wensem. "How'd she take it?"

"She understood. She was concerned—rightly, but she understood," he said. His voice had lowered, and his expression was serious. "She's still interested in hiring Bell Caravans. Hannah hung back. She's still up there going over the contract, reassuring Magnez we can handle this."

"I should be there," I said. I leaned forward to rise. My body ached. My joints hurt. My right knee throbbed.

"No," said Wensem. He pushed me back down gently. "No. You shouldn't. You need to relax. You were a mess. Hannah's got this. She's a full partner now. You sit down and tell us what's going on."

A mess? I had always assumed my trips were unnoticeable. Guess I was wrong.

Embarrassment swelled inside me. The world became a bit clearer. I rubbed the side of my head. "It's nothing, I—"

"Hell no, it ain't nothing," said Wensem. "I need to know you're okay. Not just because I care about you. But because I need to know you'll have my back on the trail. We're partners, Wal. You, me, Hannah. We need to be open and honest about shit like this. If something happens, if you collapse again…" The words faded. He shook his head, ran his seven-fingered hands through his stringy shoulder-length hair. "Someone could die. It could get one of us or one of our clients killed."

His words resurrected bitter thoughts and ugly memories. Our eyes met and then separated. Both of us still felt the sting from our failure on the Broken Road. I let out a long sigh and held my head in my hands, slowly rubbing my eyes with the heels of my palms. He was right. My little trips were a liability.

I looked up at the three of them standing across from me—Wensem, Taft, Hagen—took a deep breath, and began to explain. I started with the dreams. Then told them how I had first visited the wasteland while fighting Curwen in the burning church all those months ago, how it happened again when we met Kiver, how it continued to occur throughout my confrontation with Ashton. I told them about the endless flat expanse, the ruined city, the strange faces that peered out beneath the shadows of broken monuments. I even told them of the thing that moved beyond the horizon itself.

I held a little back—they didn't need to know about the conversations I had on the other side or the more recent changes of sulfur and ash. Not yet. I was still mulling those over, still trying to ferret out a meaning. Perhaps in time.

Look west. The voice echoed in my mind, and I shuddered. Words I had heard before.

When I had finished, I ventured a glance at the others. They each wore similar expressions of concern mixed with stunned disbelief. The way they looked at me made me feel like a pariah—they didn't mean to, but it was there, lingering behind the fear. I was describing something they could barely comprehend, and speaking gibberish. Hell, *I* couldn't understand it, and I was doing the traveling.

"It's getting worse. The coming out of it, I mean. It used to be quick." I snapped my fingers. "When it happened with Kiver, it was like a memory. In and out. Like a moment had passed. A murmur. Now it's… it's *heavy*. When I come out—return, whatever—I feel sluggish. Hungover. Sore. Exhausted."

"We should talk to Samantha," said Hagen. His tone was solemn. His eyes narrowed in thought. He held a hand to his chin, thumb perched below his lower lip in contemplation.

I opened my mouth to tell him otherwise, then closed it. If anyone could grapple with this situation, it was Hagen's younger sister, Reunified Priestess Samantha Dubois. Ever since I met the pair, they had been stalwart friends. Sam and me… well, we might have been something more as well, but life—and whatever I am—got in the way. We were close once, really close. But the Broken Road had shaken all of us, and now there was a barrier between us, one as broad as Victory's wall and twice as high. Something constructed from failed communication and half-hidden emotions and a little dishonesty. Talking with her had once been easy—now, it was awkward. Uncomfortable.

"Okay, so you occasionally get whisked away to this other world or something," said Taft. "But you said you can still feel this world? Your body doesn't leave?"

I thought about it. At that moment, I realized I felt the other world as well. The wasteland was still there on the edge of where I sat. A wind howled along the rim of my perception. Blowing sand scratched at my skin. Sun beat down on my shoulders. The only constant in both realities was me, and I wasn't much of a constant.

"When it happens I can feel both worlds equally," I said. My skull buzzed with warmth. I spread my arms. "I can feel the wasteland now. It's… there. Here. But it's also nothing—nothing but a memory."

A silence fell in the room. Somewhere a clock ticked. Outside a baby cried. Two people traded obscenities behind layers of walls. Water trickled down in its endless flow to the Sunk. Lovat droned on, unmindful and uncaring.

"I sound crazy, don't I?" My smile was bitter.

"Damn," Hagen said, breathing out.

"Heavy," Taft mumbled.

"Wal," Wensem looked at me coolly. "Can we talk? Alone?"

We walked in companionable silence through the narrow streets of a quiet dimanian warren called Martello. These days it was home to apartment complexes, private one-room school-houses, and small manufacturing facilities. It wasn't far from the Bonheur Seafoods cannery, and many of the union workers employed there lived here. The streets were cramped, brick and cement walls, the roof above low. It gave street sounds a muffled quality you don't find in many other warrens.

Recruitment posts were plastered along the street's walls, with Hellgate Mine's continual encouragement to any able-bodied workers to GO TO HELL. I'm sure some copywriter thought they were *real* clever with that one. Seafood boats advertised their desire to find fresh greenhorns, reclamation workers were sought for the crater, and there were even a few aquatic conglomerates offering work to anyone willing to spend extended time below the waters—with, of course, underwater breathing required.

We passed down narrow alleys and onto fuller streets with ceilings that extended higher and gave the neighborhood space to breathe. Here the gloom of interior Lovat was broken by flashy glows of pink and purple neon cut by bright beams of golden fire from more radiant sources. Cart merchants sang out for their wares. Dogs barked. Distant sirens wailed and faded. Jazz music, both live and recorded as well as new and ancient, mixed and echoed through corridors of cement and brick. All the noises added to the raucous din of Lovatine life. Scents of cooking combined with the baser stink that lingered within every corner of the city like the untimely tear in a favorite shirt, ever present, ever lurking to ruin the perfect moment. Despite the smell, I could feel my stomach rumble.

There's all manner of food scattered across the city. If you aren't picky, it doesn't make much sense to ride the monorail for twenty minutes to get yourself a bowl of noodles. But there are noodles, and then there's Pernet's, easily one of the best dimanian-style noodle joints in the city. I'm a fan. Dimanian food meant fiery spices, fermented vegetables, and breaded meats.

Pernet's wasn't large, but it operated under the radar, so there were never lines of hungry people outside waiting for a bowl. It still turned a decent profit—especially from the delivery market. Like most places in Martello, it was long and narrow, only allowing for four two-person tables that ran along one wall. Faded photos of family members and semi-famous visitors hung along the wall. A speaker near the back was warbling a trumpet rendition of "How Deep is the Ocean?" as we entered.

We ordered at the counter near the back and took seats at the only open table in the middle of the long corridor of noodle-eaters. Pernet's worked fast. We hadn't even had a chance to sit and make small talk before our food was brought and sat before us, steaming.

"I forget how fast they are," said Wensem, lifting a pair of chopsticks and clicking the tips.

The smell from my bowl was fragrant. It pushed away the stink and kept the narrow space lively and fresh. Chilled wood ear and sawtooth mushrooms tossed in vinegar and chili flakes sat atop picked water chestnuts and cabbage that had been flash-fried. This small salad rested atop a piece of breaded whitefish, which in turn crowned a bowl of dry-fried noodles sitting in a cloudy broth. Small pockets of bright red chili oil formed tiny islands in the liquid. It was a masterpiece and made my stomach rumble.

Wensem bobbed his head to the music while he sipped room-temperature whiskey and fiddled with his noodles. He went plainer than I had, opting for a bowl with crumbled pheasant sausage and noodles soaked in a thick and tangy gravy.

Beyond the counter, an umbra chef and his assistant argued in clipped Lindintin—the tongue of shadows—while we ate. Occasionally a teamster—another umbra—rolled through pushing a battered hand-truck stacked with boxes overflowing with partially wilted vegetables. A shadowy delivery boy with glowing green eyes came and went, sending the bell above the door swinging as he rushed in and out with to-go bags packed to the seams with paper boxes of noodles.

I speared a mushroom with a chopstick and held it up, staring at it. Bits of breading, orange chili oil, and several red pepper flakes clung to the dome.

"I'm not an invalid," I said, diving into the conversation I knew Wensem wanted to have.

Wensem gave me a weak smile around a mouthful. "I know you're not. But I'm worried."

"I've lived through three Firsts," I said, popping the mushroom in my mouth. It was tender without being rubbery. It began with a deep earthy base—soil and moss and forest—but finished with the fiery chili oil that stung my tongue and lingered long after I swallowed. I had to chase it with a sip from my vermouth to keep my eyes from watering. "What's a few weird dreams?"

The pronounced shrug I produced didn't impress my friend.

"It's more than that," said Wensem. He fiddled with his glass absently. The tips of the chopsticks in his other hand clicked together in an irregular rhythm. Maero have an odd way of using chopsticks. Their extra digits allow them to manipulate the bottom stick in ways we five-finger folks never can.

"Explain," I pointed my chopsticks at him, and then at his chopsticks. "And stop that."

He stopped but didn't set his sticks down. "It's just... everything you know? Kit's pregnancy. Little Wal. You. These vision... uh, *things*. Bell Caravans. Family. It all has me thinking." He pushed some noodles around. I waited for him to continue. "It has me thinking about what matters. Why we keep doing this."

I wanted to laugh, not mockingly but with reassurance, but for some reason I held it in. Distantly, I could hear murmurs. Somehow I knew they emanated from the skittering things that lived in the ruins of the wasteland. An echo of a reality beyond the one I sat in currently. My brain flipped as it tried to make sense of it all. Doubt once again sprang into my mind. What if *this* was the dream?

I pushed the confusion away and glanced at Wensem.

He looked pained, his food largely forgotten, his expression distant. It was best I didn't tell him. Not now. Not yet. We work well because one of us is strong when the other is weak. Despite our troubles, it was my turn to lift him up.

"We're about to take our most lucrative job offer ever—one of our most prestigious—and you're worried. It's natural. But I think you're overreacting. Look, I'm nervous as well. It's strange to find ourselves here about to become sailors and security, me dealing with… everything." I waved my hands. "I always thought we'd be walking the Big Ninety until arthritis did us in. I still think that. No reason to be worried."

"But I *am* worried." Wensem turned his elongated face up at me and set his crooked jaw. The worry was evident in his blue-gray eyes, and I could hear it clearly in his voice. Something was chewing at him. "But not about the company. Not about Magnez's job. Hell, not even about your little trips to wherever."

Something about his tone changed my approach. An old line from my personal code surfaced in my mind. *Trust no one but your company.* Wensem was more than just my best friend, business partner, and travel companion. He might as well be my brother. We had fought and struggled together since we were young. That code existed for a reason. If something was bothering him, then it should be bothering me. My flippant attitude had brushed aside his concerns. Instead of being comforting, I was the asshole.

"What's up?" I asked. I set the chopsticks down and leaned back, folding my hands across my stomach.

Wensem sighed, looking at me, and returned to pushing around his noodles. "It's just…"

He looked away.

"Wen," I said.

He let out a long breath and looked back. Meeting my eyes. The dust-brown of the road met the blue-gray of the sea. Finally, he spoke. "I'm tired of seeing you tear yourself apart. I'm tired of you carrying the blame about Maggie Shaler and Kiver dal Renna and Peter Black as if this isn't a partnership—"

"Wen," I interrupted. "It's—"

He held up a hand, silencing me. "Ever since the Wilem, Black & Bright job. It's been bothering me. You know there was a time when we walked the roads, and I always knew you'd be okay. But then..." Silence passed through his words like a creeping fog. His eyes grew distant. For a moment I thought he had gone to the wasteland.

Then he was clearing his throat and continuing. "Sorry. When you and I fought in that tunnel together. You held my son, kept him safe. Then, when you returned him to me, and you turned to follow Black... I could see the determination in your eyes."

"We had to stop Black—"

"No, it was more than that. You were willing to *die*, Wal."

A lump formed in my throat.

He went on. "You were willing to put yourself on the *line*—not for just me and little Wal, not for Lovat. Hell, you were willing to die for *everyone*. That disregard for yourself... it scares me. We can't walk the Big Ninety until arthritis or whatever does us in if you're dead."

I placed my palms down on the table, unsure of what to say or do. I wasn't sure if he was right. Perception can taint someone's reality. Sure, a part of me felt that drive to stay here and defend the Territories. But a part of me thought I should surrender to the wasteland. Both were there, and both pulled for my attention. Both felt as real as this conversation.

"I don't know what to say," I said.

"I don't know what I want you to say," he replied. "Been on my mind is all. You're the namesake for my son. You're a member of my kinship, my family—if not by blood than by deed. I can't keep sitting across from you and wondering if it'll be our last drink together."

"I'm still not sure what this whole Guardian thing entails," I said. This time I couldn't stifle the chuckle. It had been nearly two years since Black's cult named me Guardian. Two years, three Firsts, one bum knee, an arrest, several escapes, and so many cuts, scrapes, and bruises that I had lost count. "But I promise you: I will do my damnedest to keep myself alive so I can watch you get old. No more stupid risks."

I held up a hand as if swearing. Wensem smiled a weak smile, but it didn't reach his eyes.

"No more stupid risks," he repeated.

I raised my glass of vermouth, to which he clinked his whiskey. It was the Bell Caravans handshake if it was anything— an agreement between brothers. I wasn't sure if it eased his mind or not. Not quite sure if it eased my own.

"Guess we're becoming sailors," I said.

FOUR

Contemplating the future, I stared down at the waters below from an open perch on the edge of Level Four. It was evening now, a clear night. From this high up the sea below had a softness. Moonlight glinted on the evening's waves. A thousand sparkling diamonds rolling against a black canvas, reflecting multitudes of indescribable colors. Black-rainbow waves. Waves I'd soon be riding upon.

The overlook was a familiar place to me. A bench. An open view. A burned-out sign that once advertised denim overalls. It was the border of Edgewater, a warren on Level Four, and one of the few not crowded by windowed apartments trying to grasp at those ephemeral million-lira Lovatine views.

The air might not be so fresh these days, but you could breathe free here, see the sky and feel real wind against your skin. I had stood here before, in darker memories, after my confrontation with Ashton. In happier ones, I was half-drunk and smoking with Essie after being threatened by a faux-assassin named Argentum.

Oddly, that had been a good night. It had ended in Essie's bed, and the pair of us had found a bit of comfort in each other.

That felt like a long time ago. Before Ashton. Before Elephant. Before the riots. Before Essie had disappeared.

A piece of me still pined for her. I worried over where she had gone. She had been afraid—Argentum had masqueraded as a Collector. His whole schtick had been a ruse to finagle lira out of me, but I hadn't found that out until later. When I told her about him, it frightened her. Her voice still echoed in my head. *You can't stay here. You can't bring those people here. You shouldn't have come here.*

She kicked me out, then disappeared. Left her job, maybe the city. I had considered looking for her but thought better of it. Still, I always hoped to see her come out of a storefront or emerge around a corner. It's a fool's hope—in a city this large with this many people, it's easy to hide. It's easy to be forgotten.

A cold breeze blew in off the water—it stank, as all wind did these days. I wrinkled my nose against it. Tried to push it out of my mind.

It's been said that you can get used to any smell. Whoever said it hadn't smelled something like this before. It wasn't that it was foul. I could handle foulness. It was that it changed. Some days it would be acidic and sharp, and on the next, it would be base and pungent. But it was always there, always reminding you of its existence. It was persistent.

My keff—the scarf we caravaneers carry—was back at my apartment where it did me no good. I would have to bear the brunt of the stink until I returned. I made a mental note not to leave it behind again. Wensem had been pouring peppermint oil over his, said it kept the smell mostly at bay. It was a good idea. I made a mental note to ask him where I could get peppermint oil.

Gripping the rail, I leaned over the edge and tried to catch a wisp of fresh air. The motion allowed me an excellent view, and I glowered down at the bay nestled in the curving hook of Lovat, between the city proper and the warren of West Lovat.

The *Gamble*—my ride to Empress—floated far below, the largest vessel in a bay filled with all manner of patched-together craft. It was a bright festival of lights. Noises and music rose from its decks, audible even from this high up. A cavalcade of colored bulbs danced and flashed as they reflected off its bulkheads and the water surrounding it. A fleet of small boats swarmed around it like cleaner fish, ferrying goods and people back and forth from the city's wharves.

Enormous in scale, it looked less like a ship and more like a part of Lovat that had broken free and set itself adrift—the city in miniature. It looked blocks long but couldn't be more than a single level high. I had heard it contained seven or eight cramped decks, each about the height of a tall maero. Stairwells, ramps, causeways, and catwalks connected each. Corridors wormed their way through atriums, stalls, nightclubs, taverns, restaurants, and homes that were smaller than my studio flat—a knot of wood and steel. If Lovat was cramped, then the *Gamble* was claustrophobic.

It was built around three ancient ferries from the pre-Aligning day—eons old by all accounts—set end-to-end. I doubted much of the original structure remained. So much had been replaced and patched that whatever floated in its place was more homage than anything genuinely historic. One of the tugs that dragged the monstrosity back and forth between Lovat and Empress bobbed near the bow of the first boat, with another amidships and the third near the aft. All three were running silent this evening.

I'd never been on board—never had the capital or the desire—but I'd heard stories. The casino trade was the primary money maker for the *Gamble*, hence her name. High rollers from every level would find their way out to her decks to play high-stakes games or waste lira playing pachinko in cramped parlors. It was strange to imagine sitting on that vessel for a week solid. Carter's cross, I hoped I wouldn't get sick. I doubt a roader like me would do well on the water.

I checked my watch—twenty minutes late. He was supposed to be here by now.

Typical.

This was a power play—or an attempt at one, not that it mattered much to me. He had so little influence now, it was sad watching him hungrily grasp after anything resembling power. Still, it'd be his fault if the food was cold. I was the one doing him the favor.

No one else knew about this, and I wasn't sure how to tell them. It was easier to keep our meetings clandestine and away from places my friends frequented. What could I say if Samantha or Hannah found out?

Distantly I could hear the drone of a monochrome, the talking head rambling through the late-night news. Somewhere a couple sang an old jazz hymn, their drunken voices muffled. Further off, yet one more LPD siren wailed. The bumping rhythm of bass-heavy music was a faraway heartbeat. Closer were the always present sounds: the endless drip of water, the buzz of lights, the hum of machines, and the rumble of pipes, all combining to form the quiet din of a Lovat night.

At last there were footsteps on the pavement.

"You're late," I said without turning.

A noncommittal grunt, half-dismissive.

"We agreed midnight," I said, finally turning around.

"Yeah, yeah."

He had once looked young, but that—like everything else—felt distant. Now he was frail and withered, face marked with age spots, his hair thinned. Wrinkles starburst around his bulging eyes and emanated from corners of his too-wide, inhuman mouth. Folds danced across his forehead in a mimicry of the waves below.

The clothes he wore were plain and simple—earth tones, mainly, thin at elbows and knees, dirty. I'd found them for him in a second-hand store. The shoes on his feet had holes near the toes. I had no idea how he procured those—charity, perhaps. Theft, potentially, though he wasn't the type to take risks, especially for a pair of worn-out shoes. There was a time I'd have commented on his sour-sweat stench, but the whole city smelled rotten, and in comparison to *that*, he was almost fresh.

"I've heard your names at meetings," Ashton said. "You should be careful."

He waggled his index and middle finger at me. He wasn't really Ashton. Not the Ashton I had faced. Not wholly. He was human, or as human as a First could get. This wretched little creature was nothing more than the severed avatar of a titan, a walking carcass left to wander in a city he hated. His old form had died, leaving him behind—lost and adrift.

I had found him several weeks earlier playing a one-sided game of checkers in a park with a maero pitch addict. It had been an odd reunion.

I didn't hate him.

That's an odd thing to say about a man you watched murder people. But was it him? You could also argue that the Ashton standing before me was just a tool. The knife, not the hand that wielded it. A costume, not the actor inside. In this state he was pitiful. Sad.

If anything, I felt a little sorry for him. He was trapped. There was no way out. Lovat didn't care about what you were. The city only cares about what you are and how you can be used. A city devours. It's survival urbanized. The worthless are discarded and replaced.

Ashton was now a part of that cycle. He had no job, no source of income. He had no skills, and our fight had ruined the body he had inhabited. Lovat had no use for that.

He had tried to find a congregation of those wayward souls who worshiped him as a First. But you can imagine how that went. How many lunatics have claimed to be a returned deity? It's not exactly an uncommon scenario, and his 'followers' reacted as you'd expect. He still attended, though. Maybe it made him feel connected to something, maybe he got a bit of charity. I'm not sure.

"You stirred up my followers." He waggled his fingers at me again.

"Followers?" My eyebrows rose, and I made a point to gaze over his shoulder as if I spotted a column of devotees behind him. "To have followers you'd actually need to be followed."

Ashton looked over his shoulder, grunted, and then turned back, frowning slightly. "You know what I mean."

I handed him a small paper bag stained with grease spots and some coffee in a paper cup. I had picked both up before coming here. He took them and mumbled a thank you before settling on a nearby bench. He set the bag beside him and took a sip from the coffee.

"Lukewarm," he said.

"You're nearly half an hour late, Ash."

"Monorail was late."

"Right," I said.

"It was," he said. "What's this?"

He rolled the brown paper bag back and peered inside. Within the bag were several orders of kikiam—ground shrimp tossed with spices and wrapped with sheets of bean curd before being deep-fried. They're delicious. Ashton tucked into them immediately, using his fingers to pluck them out of the bag. We stayed that way for a while, him eating and drinking his coffee, me looking out over the water.

"These are good."

"I love 'em," I said, scratching at my beard. I was keeping it closely trimmed these days, which meant it was itchier than when I let it grow wild. "They're best fresh."

A murmur. Barely a response.

"Next time I'll bring you pierogi."

"Thanks," he said. Sincerity had leaked into his voice, pushing away the snide attitude.

I stood, still leaning against the rail, staring down at the *Gamble* as Ashton ate in silence behind me. Life is weird. I ran through explaining this to any of my friends and drew only a blank. Out of any of them, Sam might be willing to come around. Reunified Priestesses were all about charity and kindness. Then again, she had been with me in the Shangdi Tower.

Finally, I broke the silence and broached the reason I'd asked him here. "I've been going back."

"Back?"

"Returning. Traveling. I don't know what to call it. To the wasteland."

Ashton wiped his hand on his shirt and looked up at me from the bench. "Same wasteland we stood on together? *The* Wasteland?"

I didn't like what that implied. Were there others? Multitudes?

"Yes. I think. And no. It's different now. I smell sulfur and ash. I see a figure in sweat-stained robes, yellow robes, wearing a blank mask with a single hole. That's new—it was there with you, but distant and blurry. Now it's *there*—you know? Present. It's been trying to tell me something."

"*Him,*" Ashton considered himself for a moment. "Screw him. He's a son-of-a-bitch. He's a rat bastard. Only his shadow lingers there. A ghost. A damn ghost."

He swore like someone who just learned to swear. Odd for a man who was once a creature so old you could consider it removed from time.

Ashton wasn't looking at me.

"Why?" I asked.

He didn't respond, just returned to eating.

"How much do you remember?" I said. "From before."

He thought about this, his eyes narrowing. "Enough, but at the same time not enough. I had access to knowledge that I know is unknowable now"—a sneer—"not that you'd understand."

"You told me to 'look west' before. And warned me. 'He is coming.'"

"Did you look west?" He gestured with his chin toward the distant isles.

"I'm going west. I'm leaving the city for a few days on the *Gamble*. I want to know what 'look west' means."

Ashton laughed, a weird eldritch tittering that started at the back of his throat. It rose as he continued to laugh, holding his belly and rocking on the bench. His eyes leaked tears. "You're riding the waves? Now? Oh, Waldo. You fool. The King Tide is only here so long, and then it will retreat."

"What's out there?" I demanded.

"You haven't figured it out yet?"

"Help me figure it out! Dammit."

It took Ashton a few moments before he stopped laughing. "Oh, Wal. Just because you ply me with food doesn't mean I'll betray my people—my *family*—for you. Even if I wanted to, this body won't let me. You're a man of *two* worlds now, Guardian.

That might not be easy to comprehend, but you'll either figure it out or go mad in the process."

I sighed. "You have to give me something, Ash. A bunch of gibberish isn't going to help me."

Ashton smirked. "You remember what I told you I was—before, I mean."

"The Herald," I said.

"Indeed. The Herald. A messenger. I have had other duties at other times. But here and now I am, or was, a messenger." He gave me a side-eye glance. "No one is ready for what's to come. This city isn't ready. The flock isn't ready. My followers aren't ready. Even that piss-stained pretender who visits you in the Wasteland cannot stop what is coming. He moves his pawns. He wins his small battles, proclaims victory. But the war was decided long before he tried to interfere. We—" He scowled. "No, *they* have had a few setbacks. But everything is on course now."

"What? What does he want to stop?"

"The High Priest," Ashton said, as if it was the most obvious thing in the world. He balled up the paper bag, rose, and walked to the edge to stand next to me. "I know you smell his perfume. Everyone smells it. That's the fragrance of a corpse-city, sealed away for eons. But the seal broke and the King Tide carried the smell here. It flickers in and out, the way he flickers. But eventually the flickering stops. Eventually, the flame burns whole and bright. He'll remain. Not much time left. Tick. Tock. Tick. Tock."

Ashton inhaled deeply and patted his chest with his long hands. He smiled a too-wide smile with his too-wide mouth. It had a ranine quality to it—like he was part anur.

"Who are you talking about?"

His mouth turned into a wide, almost manic smile that showed rows of stained teeth. Then he pitched the crumpled paper bag over the edge and watched it fall, wincing slightly as it bounced off the extended arm of a crane and dropped somewhere below unseen.

"You're the Guardian, Waldo Bell. You figure it out." He turned and walked away, sipping his coffee and giving a wave of his hand. "Thanks for the kikiam."

FIVE

Give me the dirt. Give me hardpan beneath my feet. The gravel of the road. The creaks of a rumbling wain. The sing-song calls of drivers. The hot breath and grunts of oxen. The sun beating down upon my neck. And a comfortable pair of boots.

The road.

Give me the road. Leave the sea for those who are called by it.

Legs planted, I precariously rooted myself on the bow of the small launch that crawled across the water toward the *Gamble*. Behind me stood Wensem. Taft and Hannah sat conversing to one side among a few other passengers. Hagen sat nearby, reading a leather-bound tome with softened tooling. Blackened brass corner pieces and open clasps added to its important if not somewhat archaic appearance. As he read, he scratched in a notebook with a stubby pencil. In the inner pocket of my jacket were the visa documents I'd need to get into Victory. The Mayor had given them to all of us. It was our key to Empress.

I wore a suit. I hate suits. The last time I wore a suit, I attended a stuffy Auseil party for a client. This time I wore one to play the part as security for a politician. Simple colors. Black pants and jacket, white button-up shirt—the wealthy's concept of nondescript. A fool's concept. In a sea of beige, the crisp monochromatic colors were a beacon. They drew the eye and attracted attention. Perhaps that's the point?

The suit was uncomfortable. The jacket was too snug. The pants bunched in odd ways around my crotch. The belt was constricting. And the shoes—by the Firsts, the shoes! Did the devils themselves make these? The patent leather was shiny, but the soles were slippery and the uppers rubbed my toes the wrong way. I was bound to end up with blisters before the day was over. I felt hobbled.

My crew wore similar garb. Dark suits, shiny shoes. Most had even combed their hair. We came unarmed. No guns. No knives. No weapons of any kind. The *Gamble* didn't allow weapons. Technically, Lovat didn't either, but unlike Lovat, the *Gamble* had an easier time enforcing it. There were only a few ways to get on board, and every passenger was manhandled while their gear was thoroughly searched.

The rest of our crew—there were four more, all security, Wensem's guys—would come over on the next boat. They were cross with me and I couldn't blame them. After all, I was the cause of our uncomfortable dress code. Well, technically it was our client, but it was my job to take some of the pressure off Castaigne. They'd watch her furiously and curse under their breath at me. I could handle it.

The *Gamble*'s open aft rose before us. It lifted from the water like a craggy cliff face. In ages past gasoline-powered fourgons and motor-coaches rolled through this mouth and into the vessel's vast stomach. Once secure, they were carried from island to island, the boat regurgitating them upon distant shores. It was hard to believe, looking at it now, rusted and barnacled, with smaller vessels lashed alongside its hull—more flotilla than ship.

A floating dock as broad as the vessel's beam sat just below the cavernous mouth. Our small boat pulled alongside. It bumped against worn white fenders marred with black skid marks. A human woman stood on the dock wearing a white linen uniform trimmed with black and gold—one of the boat's stewards. She leaned on a long metal crowbar with a hooked end. Its opposite end had been wrapped in leather, turning the tool into a makeshift club.

With a flourish and a *ker-thunk*, she swung the hooked end up and over and embedded it in the launch's gunwales. Then, with a twist, she used the crowbar to hold the small boat steady. A broad smiled crossed her face as she greeted and helped each of us off the launch and directed us up a set of stairs. Other boats were landing as well, delivering all manner of people.

The stairs carried us off the rocking wooden dock and up onto the more substantial metal decking of the *Gamble*'s super-structure. The area here was clear, save for a snaking line that led to a single security checkpoint. You could laager a whole caravan here, oxen and all, and there'd be room for more.

Beyond the mouth, the throat of the vessel was clogged with the makings of a city, so thick it was impossible to see beyond the external layers. It was a haphazard labyrinth. Walls, awnings, windows, balconies, and doors plugged the vast central deck—

a tangle of wood, iron, and steel. A pair of side shafts flanked the central space, each crammed to bursting. Casinos, bookmakers, pachinko and massage parlors, dice and dance halls occupied tiny hovels and vied for attention within the central chamber. Theaters, cafes, restaurants, taverns, liquor stores, brothels, and pitch dens clamored for customers among them.

Dense and haphazard, the makeshift city made it impossible to sort out where the *Gamble* began or ended. Narrow passages served as thoroughfares between the businesses. Buskers. Prostitutes. Street merchants. Stalls of food. It all reminded me of any other busy warren, only the spaces here were tighter and more cramped. The crowds pressed against each other as they jostled to and fro.

Occasionally sets of stairs would rise, sometimes a ladder, each leading to another level. Catwalks crisscrossed above the makeshift streets and alleyways.

The *Gamble* was a raucous furor of color and texture—an assault on the senses. Strings of lights stretched across passageways and dangled from balconies, forming sparkling webs of light. Lines of laundry drooped lazily from awnings. Brightly colored banners hung above businesses. Neon throbbed from behind windows. Painted advertisements spread across walls like lichen.

People were everywhere. Some were passengers like ourselves, others were clearly more permanent residents. Music filled the air. The smell of smoke and cooked meat was prevalent closest to the dock—the stink that had plagued the city was present but distant. It was almost refreshing.

Rowdy laughter drifted from the labyrinth. The *Gamble* was a pleasure barge, a passenger transport, and a cargo vessel all in one, and it relished its existence to the fullest. Below me, the deck shifted ever so slightly. My stomach lurched. Any good nature I felt was snatched away.

"I hate boats," I said to no one in particular, moving with my crew to stand in line behind a kresh shoalta—one of the Deeperist priestesses. She wore the salt-stained robes of her office and was carrying a blue half-sized duffle that looked enormous in her small claw. "Humans weren't meant to stand atop the water."

The shoalta turned and gave me a bemused smile that caused her black eyes to narrow.

"You're just saying that because you get queasy," said Hannah. She wore a white button-up, dark pants, sport coat, and over it all a new oil coat that ended just below her waist. She had its big collar turned up. Black leather gloves covered her hands, both flesh and prosthetic. It was a striking look, that of an assassin—or perhaps a chauffeur.

"Nice coat," I said.

"Veata bought it for me. Like it?" She twisted in display. "Nice, right?"

I could hear the longing in her voice, see the way her lips turned up as she spoke Veata's name. I had only met the maero woman once, at a feast-party just after the first shipment of food had flowed past the blockade and begun to full the shelves of the city's bodegas. She was tall and stately, with a relaxed demeanor and an easy smile. We had talked for a bit, enough to feel like I had gotten a good read on her. I hadn't seen her since, but hell—I had hardly seen Hannah.

"Makes you look like the member of a security detail." I could hear the admiration in Taft's voice.

"Or a chauffeur," I added.

Hannah punched me lightly in the shoulder.

"I'm kidding. I'm kidding. It fits." I laughed and pulled on my own coat, tugging at the lapels, mimicking the way I had seen monochrome actors dress. "Guess we're now Bell Caravans and Security."

"How about Guardian Security?" Taft asked.

"Oh, I like that," Hannah said.

I made a sour face—Ashton had already reminded me of my place in this whole… what did he call it? *Cycle*. The last thing I wanted was my job to remind me—or my friends.

Wensem laughed. Hagen joined in as well. I gave them a mock scowl.

"Next!" the man in the security line said, and the line shifted forward. The shoalta struggled with her half-duffle. It was an unusual piece of luggage for a Deeperist. They tended to prefer sackcloth bags or steamer trunks—luggage that took several grumpy porters to move.

"You need a hand with that?" I offered.

The kresh turned and flashed a nervous smile with the reverse V-shaped beak of her mouth. Her claws gripped the duffle's strap tighter, her arm hooked in a casual posture that reminded me of folded wings. "Oh, I'm okay. Thank you, sir. Thank you."

"Well, let me know. It's a big bag."

She nodded but said nothing in return. Not everyone wants a conversation. She turned around and dragged the duffle forward as the line shifted.

We were drawing closer to the front now. I wasn't expecting any trouble. Our gear had been sent over last night; we were just showing up to join it. Made the trip a lot easier. That had been Taft's idea.

The checkpoint wasn't much, just a small gate in a tall chain-link fence that separated the dock area from the rest of the boat. The gate was open, and a table sat to one side. Four well-muscled maero stewards flanked the opening, two inside and two outside. They wore the same white linen as the others. In their hands were long leather-wrapped crowbars with hooked ends identical to the steward's at the dock edge. Guess the *Gamble's* weapons rule had exceptions.

"Ticket?" the human steward behind the table asked.

The shoalta handed over the paper stub.

He glanced at her and then back at the stub. "Here for King Tide's Ebb celebrations?"

"Oh, I live here! I assist Shoalta Sander with preparations at Our Father of the Obscured Atoll. Normally I stay on board, but we needed someone to disembark for supplies."

The desk steward didn't seem to particularly care. He checked the stub, stamped it, and then looked down at the duffle. "Bag, ma'am?"

"This? It's so heavy. It's, uh… it's full of delicate items."

"What sort of items, ma'am?" the desk steward asked.

"Carved shells, driftwood effigies, dried seaweed, and krill, among other things." She unzipped the bag and opened the top. "All for Ebb celebrations. I'm taking them to—"

The man looked bored. His tone was exasperated. "Still need to look through it, ma'am. Ship's rules."

The shoalta pulled at her robes. She turned and gave me a pained smile. No one likes being the person who is holding up the line. I smiled back, hoping it'd help ease her—what could I do? I wasn't going anywhere. Kresh tended to be more anxious than other species—I always assumed it was the side effect of being the smallest of the sentient races. They tend to get bullied more than others. Rightfully, that'd make anyone jumpy.

"Okay," she finally said. There was an air of pitiful surrender in her tone. She swallowed, wiped her claws on her robes, then strained as she struggled to lift the bag.

"Here," I said, "I can help—" I stepped forward and gripped the handles and pulled. It was heavy. The contents inside moved. My hand brushed her claw. My skull buzzed. Unreality shifted around me.

"What the—"

A desert wind blew outward, emanating from inside the vessel. A broken sun beat down upon my neck. I stumbled, reeling from the profound shift in reality. Whispers filled my ear. My shadow played across the deck. It spun around me like I was the center of a sundial and the sun was flying across the sky.

Hannah's hand gripped my forearm and kept me upright. The touch pulled me back. The wastes retreated, cool air rushed to fill the void. I blinked. Breathed in. Straightened. When I opened my eyes again, Wensem, Hagen, and Taft were leaning in close.

"It happened again, didn't it," Hannah hissed.

"I'm okay, I'm okay," I planted my feet. My head swam. I expected to see everyone staring, but a commotion had started on the floating dock. We all turned.

A long boat with a belching engine had pulled up to the dock. Fuel-powered vehicles were uncommon—an extravagance, since no refineries operated within the Territories anymore, which made fuel expensive—so it was already drawing a crowd. I had forgotten how loud a vehicle like that could be.

The driver—a stout anur—was arguing with the human driver of another launch. Apparently one of the boats had collided with the other, and both pilots blamed the other. I wasn't able to tell who was at fault. Both men had leaped onto the dock and were already angrily shoving one another. The crowd was backing away, and a couple of unlucky souls were pressed off the dock, landing in the cold water with a splash.

The splashes set off something within the two pilots, like a gun going off before a race. Someone threw a punch, and a true fist-fight broke out. Both pilots were pulled away from the other. I instinctively stepped toward the chaos—but seeing the fray devolve, I quickly thought better of it. Besides, I was still feeling woozy from that mini-trip I had just taken.

Two men in slick suits stepped off the fancy launch and stood to one side. They brushed dust from their jacket shoulders as they watched the tussle unfold. One of the men reminded me of someone—like an actor you recognize but can't name. There was an air of authority about him. His eyebrows were raised; a grin of bemusement crossed his lips as the anur sucker-punched the distracted human pilot.

"Hey!" the desk steward shouted. "Stop! I mean it! Stop, dammit!"

The four maero stewards abandoned their post and rushed past the line, leaping down to the floating dock. Four enormous maero landing on the dock at the same time shook the platform. Everyone stopped and looked at them. The anur, the human, and their cadre of temporary disciples all stepped away from each other and retreated to their vessels.

"Who's the high roller?" Taft asked.

"Not sure," I said. "Looks familiar."

The unfortunate folks who had fallen into the water were being helped back onto the dock by several eight-limbed cephel rescue swimmers. I had once read that the *Gamble* had a small army of them to patrol the waters around the vessel. It prevented drunks from falling overboard and drowning, and kept the boat safe—one less way for people to sneak on board.

"Fighters can go back. We don't want them here," said the man at the desk. A few people began to complain, holding up and waving tickets, but their complaints were silenced when the maero stepped closer, his seven-fingered hand wrapping around his crowbar. The long metal rod looked like a small billy club in his hand. The *Gamble* was serious about security. This job would be easier than I expected.

"Dirt-cursed tourists," the desk steward mumbled.

Two of the guards remained behind, making sure the brawlers left, while the others returned to the entrance, flanking the gate just inside. The desk steward waved me forward. I had nothing on me, just my clothes, billfold, and a few knick-knacks in my pocket. I wanted to make a smarmy comment about the fight as a way to show him I was on his side, but decided that would annoy him further. Sometimes it's smarter just to behave and keep your head down.

We all passed through with relative ease, though Hagen got a bit of side eye when the desk steward noted his choice of reading. It wasn't until we were through that I realized the small shoalta and her duffle had disappeared. My mind had been so preoccupied with the fight, I hadn't even seen her slip away. Strange how her touch had nearly pushed me over the edge. She didn't seem the type. But what was the type? Ashton and Curwen were both Firsts, Kiver a wealthy patrician, Magnez the Mayor, and now a lowly shoalta—so if there was a pattern to this… thing, I certainly couldn't figure it out.

Besides, I couldn't blame her for running. Most folks don't react well to threats of violence. She must have rushed away when the commotion started. The desk steward didn't seem to care, and the shoalta was kind enough, so I said nothing. Wensem tapped my shoulder, pulling me from my ponderations, and pointed to an umbra in a pinstripe suit and fedora who glided out from the crowd and moved towards us with a smooth gait.

My back went rigid. I've had run-ins with umbras, and it made me untrusting, nervous, and wary around them.

"That's Evans. Be nice," Wensem whispered as the umbra closed the distance.

"Bell Caravans?" asked the umbra. "Master Bell?"

I forced my hand out. Smiled. Hope he didn't notice my initial reaction. "Mister Evans?"

A chill flowed up my arm as the shadow man took my hand in his and gave it a firm shake. His eyes glowed a bright purple that brightened as we touched. A smile. Umbra are living shadows. They're well aware that their strange form unnerves those of us bound to more corporeal forms, so they try to blend in as much as possible. As far as I can tell, they can maintain states of either solidity or something more aeriform—though most preferred the former when in public.

"Call me Byron. Glad to meet you. Your partner"—he nodded to Wensem—"had nothing but praise. I serve as Ambassador Castaigne's secretary. We've been waiting for you. How was the ride over?"

"Uneventful. Pleased to meet you," I said. I introduced Hannah, Taft, and Hagen. "The rest of our company will be coming over on a later boat. Should we wait—"

Byron turned to the desk steward. "Henry, will you send the rest of Master Bell's company to Chee when they arrive? I'll be taking these five there now." He didn't wait for a response. "Thank you, Henry." Then, to me, "Such a dear."

Palms meeting palms, the pressing of the flesh, broad smiles followed by understanding nods, cleared throats, sensible chuckles at unfunny or witless jokes—this was politics, I realized. The great game. It was awful. I suppressed a shudder.

Ambassador Constance Castaigne was in her fifties. Quick-witted and clearly whip-smart. The horns that marked her as a dimanian started just behind the tips of her eyebrows and curled along the side of her head, turning up just past her ears. They gave her the appearance of speed. She wore a dark blue suit, white shirt, and dark tie. A small gold lapel pin glinted in the deck light—the Great Seal of Lovat.

"Good to finally meet you, Master Bell."

"Call me Wal," I said. "Master is just the job—not really a title."

"Okay, Wal." Her golden eyes widened, and she laughed a bright, bubbly laugh. A striking woman and a born politician. "As long as you call me Connie."

"I can do that, Connie." My smile came easily.

We stood in yet another conference room. This one was built at the peak of the *Gamble*, near the bow. It was nice if not a little dull and worn down. The windows set into the walls were much smaller than the floor-to-ceiling stretches of glass in Lovat's City Hall, but these afforded a better view. I stopped myself. Was I comparing conference rooms now? Is this what happens—the more successful one gets, the more time one spends in committee meetings? My whole life was becoming conference rooms, and I didn't see the appeal.

The room was crowded. Besides my two partners and Taft, there were Castaigne, two of her staff, the *Gamble's* Council of Captains, and a few more stewards in their white linen uniforms.

Our trip from the dock here had been uneventful but enlightening. Passing through the vessel allowed me to better understand the ship.

The *Gamble* was composed of three districts. The aft district, where we had boarded, was named Yallup; the central district, smallest of the three, was Kaleetan; and the forward section, where our buzzing conference room perched, was called Chee. Of course, all of this would be reversed on the return trip, with the Yallup leading and the Chee bringing up the rear. Apparently, the *Gamble* wasn't keen on turning itself around. It relied on a pair of ancient tugboats to drag it through the water, with a third tug keeping its aft in line. On return trips the whole process reversed. The tugs simply tied up on the opposite ends and pulled the other way.

Castaigne's staff was Byron Evans, her secretary, whom we had already met, and a communications director named Platina—a dauger. The ambassador also had a ten-year-old son who traveled with her. He was currently spending time in one of the *Gamble's* many child-friendly arcades with his nanny.

"First time on the *Gamble?*" asked one of the three captains, a stout human woman with a broad face and a forced smile that never reached her eyes. She had been introduced as Denise Chen.

"Yes," I said. "Different than I expected."

"Well, we hope you enjoy your stay. You're VIPs here, so you have the full run of the sundeck—off limits to regular passengers. If you're looking for gaming, I'd recommend heading to the Kaleetan. Better odds and the casinos are newer." Captain Chen folded her hands before her.

"Speaking of," Taft said, "we were told we'd be assigned rooms when we got on board."

"Yes! Yes, indeed." This from a kresh named Eeoshi Jurer, another co-captain. "We have cabins for you in Chee. Just down the hall actually."

Wensem glanced at me, concerned.

"But the Ambassador's staying on the Yallup," Taft said.

Captain Chen smiled. "I told the Mayor we didn't need extra security for this trip. Besides, there's plenty of access between the Chee and the Yallup—most of the upper deck is open and serviced by a promenade. A five-minute walk and you can be knocking on her door. Enjoy yourself. Let my crew do their work. This will be the easiest money you've ever made."

Somehow I was beginning to doubt that. Wensem met my eyes. He was thinking what I was thinking: a five-minute walk was too far. Much too far.

Hannah, sensing our exchange, touched my arm and stepped forward. "Beg your pardon, Captains, but we're here at the request of Mayor Magnez. We have a job to do."

"We're aware," said the third captain—a maero woman named Shelna wen Oshen.

Jurer interjected. "We told the Mayor there's no need on the *Gamble*. Violence isn't tolerated here. You were boarding when that fight broke out earlier, correct?"

"We were," I confirmed.

"You saw what happened then?" Captain Chen asked.

"Be that as it may, we have a job we were hired to do. We intend to do it," I said. "We can't do it a district away."

"There are no rooms on the Yallup," said Captain Shelna. "They're taken."

"By who?" I forced a smile and tried not to show my annoyance.

"Customers," Captain Jurer said.

"We're customers," I said.

Jurer spread the talons of his claws. "We got a better offer."

The air went out of the room.

"A better what?" Hannah spat. I could feel her rage growing. "A better *offer*?"

"Easy, Hannah," Taft said softly.

"I don't believe this," Hannah said. She looked at the Ambassador, who was standing awkwardly to one side. "I'm sorry, ma'am."

"Care to explain?" Wensem said.

Chen feigned exasperation. "Look, we're a business, not a ferry service. Camalote had the money. We accepted it and shifted a few things around. You can set up a watch or whatever. You'll have access—your room will be just across the way."

"Camalote?" I said. "As in the Camalote Group? The charity? What do they have to do with this?"

The Camalote Group was a powerful foundation that operated from the elevated levels within the city. The sort that had their own tower. Much of their focus was on health and education, but as of late they had been making plays into other parts of city infrastructure as well, and had gotten cozy with the police department. Much of their membership was kept private. Only the names of the board members were public. The list was who you'd expect—a who's who list of society types, the sort of people whose billfolds served as buttresses for their hearts.

The door to the conference room opened and in walked the slick man in the dark suit I had seen on the dock earlier, but this time he was alone. His sunglasses were in his hand, and I could see his beady eyes flick from beneath thick eyebrows. Recognition dawned on me. This was Samuel Danforth, former candidate for Mayor, and Camalote employee—I wasn't sure where he ranked within their vast hierarchy, but he wasn't on the board.

"Samuel!" The Ambassador embraced the man, and they kissed each other on both cheeks.

"You're Samuel Danforth," Hagen said. He looked stunned.

The man laughed and flashed us a perfect white smile. He shook Hagen's hand. "One and the same. Apologies for my tardiness. Takes a bit to navigate this boat."

"I was happy to hear you were coming along," Castaigne said.

"Power that be willed it—so, I am here," Danforth said. "I only seek to serve. It's good to see you, Connie."

"And how is Giselle?" asked Castaigne.

"She's excellent and surly—as always. Drives that son of hers up the wall. She's wrapped up in action items from the last commission report. You know how it goes." Danforth turned and regarded us. "This the crew Camilla hired? Bell Caravans, right?"

"Guardian Security," Hannah said her voice was flat, but she shot a sly smile in my direction.

Danforth's eyebrows rose slightly as he nodded. Castaigne introduced us all and the Council of Captains. There was another round of shaking hands, clapping shoulders, and grinning grins. Hannah looked wary through it all.

"Hope you don't mind that Camalote is tagging along," said Danforth. "It's not often we get access to Empress."

"You do good work," I said. "Don't see a problem."

"We must all prepare Lovat for the future," Danforth said, pressing his palms together. Camalote people always had lines or slogans they liked to rattle off. The thought was it kept them on message and united.

"Just wish we'd known about it earlier," Hannah added.

"You and me both," Danforth said.

"Any particular reason you want to come along?" asked Taft. I could tell she was suspicious, but the easy smile on her face and the spark in her eyes would have masked that to strangers. She had a way of asking questions that put people at ease. It's what made her a good chuck. Out on the trail, all roaders needed someone to talk to, someone who could listen and understand. Chucks often filled the duty of cook and trail therapist.

"Ah. Good question," Danforth crossed the small room and poured himself a glass of water. "We're all interested to see what goes on behind Victory's walls, and Camalote is no different. It's been several generations since any Lovatine representative has been inside. The *Gamble* was the meeting point for any communication. Now that they've opened their borders, we want to know what's going on. See if they could use our help. We've been eager to reach out to Victory for some time now." He paused. Looked at me, then Hannah, then back at me. "Mayor Magnez didn't tell you I was coming, did she?"

I didn't know what to say. I looked at my friends.

"No," Wensem said, crossing his arms. "She didn't."

"Took us by surprise, is all," I said.

"Well, this is embarrassing," Danforth said. He ran his hand through his short hair. "No wonder you're putting off the whole suspicious vibe." He looked bothered. "Maybe she just had too much going on. Look, I know this is supposed to be secretive. But Camalote talks with the Mayor's office frequently. We've been pushing for an embassy for some time now. The more trade Lovat has, the better it will be for the economy. A rising tide lifts all boats, after all."

"Okay," I said. There wasn't much I could do. Danforth had the cabins—which meant we'd have to improvise. We'd figure something out. "Way I see it, Mr. Danforth, you're now a part of this job. Consider yourself under the protection of"—I winced as I said it—"Guardian Security."

SIX

Once, i was in love with Samantha Dubois. It was an awkward love, born half out of gratitude, honed in the fires of danger, and tempered in tragedy. It was a desperate sort of infatuation. A hunger of a sort. It never went anywhere. That's not the meet-cute story people like to hear, but that doesn't make it any less accurate.

I'm still not sure if that love was ever reciprocated. Sam's smarter than me and has a better head on her shoulders, she's less dramatic and quicker on the uptake. Also better looking— but you can be the judge if that matters.

Further complicating things, I drifted as I'm wont to do, and hooked up with Essie Cove. Fell in love there as well. More danger, more tragedy, more of the same. I'm not sure what it says about me, but I really need to meet someone during a dull point in my life—not when I'm in a life-or-death struggle to stay alive.

I think about this a lot. Usually when I'm bored. Or tired. Or sad. Or distracted. Maybe all four. I distract myself a lot.

It's often easier to observe details, reflect on history, or dwell in memory than face reality.

Hagen Dubois—Sam's brother—interrupted my thoughts. "You seriously don't remember seeing this?"

He sat across from me at a table for two in a tiny four-tabled dim sum restaurant called Golden Market, holding up yet another black leather-bound book. The tooling on its cover had softened from generations of use, giving it more of a textural quality than any defined design. It looked like every other esoteric tome to me. We had been underway for almost two days.

He claimed Samantha had read it and had given it to him. She wanted him to check her notes. His adamancy had been the fuse that triggered the explosion of memories.

I missed Samantha. She was a good friend. We had been through a lot together: the Children of Pan, the Broken Road, the whole Ashton affair. She was off—somewhere in the south at a conference with their father, the Bishop Dubois, and wasn't due back for a month. I hadn't seen her in weeks.

"I don't remember, honest," I said. "Wait, is that the Keziah book?"

"*A Treatise on the Writings of Keziah?* No, it's not, thank God." He set the book down and speared a chive dumpling. "Pass the chili oil."

I handed the jar filled with bright red oil to Hagen and stared down at the collection of round bamboo steamers on the table between us, each filled with various bites glistening atop their wax paper. Shrimp stuffed har gow, siumaai wrapped in yellow egg pasta, sauce-coated rib tips, charred turnip cakes, and sweet tofu—a feast on most occasions. I'd typically had devoured them all by now. Hagen had eaten—was still eating—but my stomach was upset that I had decided to spend a few days on a boat.

"So, what is it?" I asked, taking a sip of my tea. That went down easy enough. I hoped it'd settle my stomach.

"This book was mostly written by a human named Freddy Junzt, eons ago. It was originally called the *Unaussprechlichen Kulten*," Hagen said, his Strutten breaking and becoming hard and throaty as he pronounced the title. He took a bite of his dumpling and talked around the mouthful. "Hope I'm saying that right. It's ancient. This is a translation of a translation. Sam had to fish it out of the basement of St. Mark's. I don't know what language that is, and I'm probably saying it wrong anyway. These days most scholars call it the *Black Book*. It's quite rare."

"Okay," I said. My stomach, always the traitor, rumbled. The food looked appealing, but the inevitable puking of it over the side of the *Gamble* did not. I stuck with my tea.

"So, why are you and Sam interested in this *Black Book?*"

"Well," Hagen said. He inhaled and let it out slowly. His bright green eyes met mine. I could see him swallow. "In most of it, Junzt details the cults that have worshiped various Founders throughout history. It's quite thorough. Locations, names, and various rituals are described. Even old Keziah Mason—from the *Treatise*—is in it. But toward the end there's a shift. Sam thinks this translation is actually two books—the first *Black Book* and its sequel."

Books aren't usually my thing, but in the past my friends and I have found a few answers in esoteric pages. So I nodded and continued to listen.

"The second part is much different. Makes me wonder if Junzt didn't go mad while writing it. Most of the time, it's hard to follow. But there's a particular section toward the end that got Sam interested."

Using my fingers, I plucked a piece of siumaai from its basket and popped it into my mouth. My stomach threatened a revolt, but as I chewed, the unsettledness subsided. Stomach be damned.

Hagen continued. "The latter half is almost a warning. Not sure who it's for—perhaps the Founders? It describes a group of people whom Junzt refers to as adversaries."

"So why did that interest you and Sam?" I asked.

Hagen lifted and handed the book across the table to me. I reached for it, my fingers brushing the hard leather cover.

"Well, we think it's about *you*, Wa—"

Wasteland overwhelmed me. Hot air filled my lungs. It was like drowning, the ocean swallowing you whole as the world you left faded away into muffled nothing. The smells of the dim sum stall lingered, as did the sound of the *Gamble*.

Realities warred, and my mind was the battlefield.

I struggled to sort through the conflict, but that it only made my head throb. Below my feet the ground was solid, but my soles vibrated as the *Gamble* passed over the waves. I stood once again where I always stood, only this time I was alone. No yellow-robed man, no ash, no sulfur, no coyotes, no black-robed gargoyles. It was just me and the weird faces among the ruins.

"Hello?" I called out. Why did this keep happening? Was this some side effect from my fight with Ashton or was this something else? These forays had to be connected to me being the Guardian.

When Peter Black had hired me to protect the mummified remains of his dead wife—look, I had no idea at the time, all I knew is that I was hauling a big crate—he marked me as Guardian, bound me to her with some ritual. When I signed the contract, I had agreed to it. Not to be a protector of the living but the Guardian of a corpse. I was supposed to have died in a ritual to bring her back. Instead, I became something else—an obstruction, a barrier, a problem.

An adversary.

I was all that stood between reality and the incomprehensible machinations of the Firsts. I had faced three: Cybill, Curwen, Ashton. And now the fourth was looming—this nameless High Priest that former-avatar-Ashton had warned me about. Fate had put me on the path. Hooray.

Something in me waited. There was nothing here, and I half-expected this vision or trip or whatever it was to fade. But it didn't. The wind howled, the distant city stank, the dust danced across the bone-dry ouklip. So, with nothing better to do, I began to walk.

Strangely, my bum knee felt better here. In fact, it didn't hurt at all. The *Gamble* was all stairs, and stairs, in particular, are a killer. Over the last few days, the knee had become bothersome again. The *Gamble* had lifts, but they were crowded and expensive. Spending money felt like a loss of profit, so I stuck to the stairwells and ramps. My knee had been aching something fierce. Now it didn't. Walking pain-free felt good. I couldn't remember the last time I had walked without some glimmer of pain haunting me. Before the Wilem, Black, and Bright job—but that was ancient history.

The wasteland moved around me. Ash and dying embers drifted by on air that had gone sulfuric. I passed ruins, spying the faces of the small shadowed people who always peered out at me. They wore expressions of shock and awe, never changing. Their black eyes were hollow circles, eyeholes of masks, the flesh beyond lost to darkness. When I drew close, they scattered. When I called out, they scurried away and disappeared into the darkened recesses.

In the distance, I heard the howl of coyotes—first one, then two, then a cavalcade. But I also heard music, and realized the Golden Market was playing an old song I recognized. Someone was asking me how the food was. The desert wind howled. Someone else was asking me if I was okay? Was that Hagen?

"I'm fine," I said to no one, and yet I said it to Hagen as well. The coyotes went silent. Hagen didn't seem reassured. Another group of the ruin-dwellers scattered. How did I know Hagen doubted me? He wasn't in the wasteland. He was there in the dim sum shack on the *Gamble*. With me and without me.

The buzzing at the back of my head turned into a throbbing ache. I set the book down on the table, but I also rubbed at the back of my head in the wasteland.

Murmurs. Whispers from the ruined city on the horizon. Something moved beyond the sky itself. Something vast and huge and somehow… angry. The architect to this madness, an unknowable shape that shifted and twisted ever so slowly. This was the creature that pulled the strings. I was looking at my enemy, and he was staring back.

"Really," I insisted. "I'm fine."

"Are you fine?" asked a voice—this one I recognized.

I turned, putting my back to the dead city and the thing beyond. Behind me stood a gargoyle. The creatures had haunted me ever since the Broken Road. Its tall pointed head listed as it contemplated me. Its billowing robes moved, trapped in a cycle of rhythm that reminded me of fabric billowing underwater— the same motion as the yellow figure's robes. It drifted rather than walked, and tittered a creepy edge-of-your-seat laugh that rattled around in my skull. I *hated* that sound.

"The Guardian is in over his head."

"Is he now?" I said.

"Wal?" said Hagen, but Hagen wasn't here. "Waldo Emerson Bell—you there?"

I wish I had my gun, and when I looked down I saw that I did. The five-shot Judge was in the holster at my hip, fully loaded. Its wooden grip had dried in the desert air. I pulled. The sound of steel on leather was a familiar one. It echoed across the wastes. The weight of the revolver in my hand reassured me. The wood was soft against my palm. I lifted it, aimed it at the gargoyle. It cackled its maddening laugh.

"Whoa, Wal. Where did you ge—"

"You're starting to get the hang of this," said the gargoyle. It tilted its head, looking at me like a confused puppy, or maybe I was just projecting. Hagen was looking panicked. His hands had gone white where he pressed them on the table. The spurs on his knuckles were little mountains.

"Wal," he said softly.

There was a cry of panic, a shout for security, the howl of coyotes, and the roar of a ceaseless wind.

"Wal, people are looking."

"I am," I replied to the gargoyle. I had watched these things kill people. Watched their hands pass through a man's chest like it was nothing. I hated them, and I refused to be their next victim.

"Put the gun down," said Hagen.

"I'm not pointing a gun at you."

"Yes, you are," he said, his voice a forced calm.

"Yes, you are," the gargoyle repeated. There was a shift in pressure. My ears popped. One instant the gargoyle was there, the next it was gone. Poof. As if it had never existed in the first place.

I blinked. Rubbed my eyes. Lowered the gun. In one reality I set it on the table, but in another I holstered it. Both made sense. Both were real. Totally and absolutely real. But at the same time, neither were real.

"Carter's cross, Hage…" My head was woozy.

"Wal? Shit, it happened again, didn't it?" He pushed up from the table. His hand was on my shoulder. "Dammit. They called security. Wal! Can you hear me? They called security!"

My world was spinning. Strange blurs shifted in the air around me. A hand was on my wrist. Sand scoured my cheek, and I winced, turned my face, and squinted my eyes. I was a dust-colored man in a dust-colored world. My stomach felt vile.

Sour bile rose in my throat. I couldn't stop blinking. The world was a merry-go-round of images and places. Dust and wind and water and dim sum.

"Hagen," I managed to say. It came out weak and pitiful. Yet I felt neither weak nor pitiful.

Then *he* was there.

"You again," I said.

The yellow-clad figure with his sweat-stained robes, his face that same pale mask with the single hole drifted before me. It reminded me of the skittering dwellers in the ruins. It reminded me of the gargoyles. And for the first time, it reminded me of the dauger.

He regarded me in silence.

In my other reality, Hagen gave me a concerned look.

"Why do they call you the usurper?" I asked. "The pretender?"

Hagen said something—it sounded muffled. Far away. Underwater. My head swam. I blinked. Everything felt fuzzy and distant, covered in moisture. The world sparkled. The sand, my skin, the dim sum. Tiny pinpoints of starlight blinking, glimmering, on and off, on and off.

There was no response from the creature.

"Who is coming?"

I paused, waited.

"Who is coming?" I repeated. My voice was stronger.

"Wal, maybe we should leave?"

My knee was aching again.

"The High Priest," hissed a voice. The smell of sulfur rose. It stung my nostrils—sharper and more wicked than before.

The voice came from everywhere and nowhere. It reverberated around the man in the robes. My stomach lurched. I might have cried out. I'm not sure. I'm not sure of anything anymore.

"Wal, come on." A hand on mine—pulling. My shoulder wrenched. My body unmoving, but also walking. Moving towards the masked figure in the yellow robes.

"What do you want from me!" I demanded, my voice rising to a shout. The wasteland became sharp. It was just him and me. The fuzziness cleared. Everything was bright and in focus, except for him. He flickered like a monochrome with a lousy signal. He shook his head. It was sad, almost pitiful.

"They will call," he said. "He will answer. Stop them."

I woke up in the brig.

SEVEN

Y ou had a gun."

"I did."

"Weapons of any kind are forbidden. You knew our rules."

"I'm well aware." I folded my hands on the steel table. They had placed manacles on my wrists, connected by a chain that looped around a metal bar bolted to the surface.

I was somewhere below deck. Old pipes covered a wall. Everything wore dull-gray enamel paint. The hull creaked and moaned as the *Gamble* was pulled through the water. It smelled damp and briny down here.

The ship's three captains sat across from me.

"How'd you get a gun onto the *Gamble*?"

"I'm not sure." I was sure. I just didn't want to say it. No one would believe me, not these captains, perhaps not even my friends.

"What does that mean?"

"It means I don't know."

Displeasure. Annoyance. Frustration. I could see all three play across their faces. I understood. I felt the same way.

"Look, I didn't bring the Judge with me. Your own security can confirm that. I came unarmed. My gear came before me. I assume you search all of that."

They exchanged looks. I could see them wondering if their security had lapsed. Did my bags get searched, or did someone slip up? Regardless of what had happened, someone was going to get chewed out later.

Captain Chen leaned forward. "How did the gun get onto our boat?"

"It appeared in my hand," I said flatly. I wiggled my fingers for effect.

"That's impossible," said Chen.

"Believe me, I know," I said. "But that's how it happened."

Captain Chen scowled and leaned back. She thought I was lying; I could read it on her face. She extended an open palm in my direction—a can-you-believe-this-guy gesture, rooted in suspicion.

"I'm serious. Last time I saw that gun it was on my dresser back home."

"So it *is* your gun?" Shelna asked.

"Yes," I said. "I told you that. Wensem can confirm. He was with me when we left it."

"I don't believe you," Chen said.

"Will you believe Wensem?" I asked. "If I brought my revolver on here for some nefarious means, why would I brandish it in a dim sum stall?"

"Maybe you were trying to impress your friend," Shelna said.

"You've met Hagen. You think he gives a crap about guns? Besides, I'm not a child. I wouldn't bring my gun on a boat to show my buddy over breakfast."

Shelna scowled. Chen looked away.

"I know your rules," I said. "I know what's at stake. It'd be idiotic for me to violate them."

"And yet you violated them," said Captain Shelna. She leaned in close, blew sour cannabis smoke in my face. It curled around my head and hung below the lamp that rocked above us.

"I did," I agreed. Shelna sat back and stared at me in silence. She seemed annoyed that I admitted to having the Judge. But what else could I say? A mess of crew members saw me with the weapon. It was on the table and in my hand. There was no use trying to lie my way out. I leaned toward her. "But not *intentionally*."

Hannah emerged from the shadows behind me. I caught her in my peripheral vision. Her long dark coat billowed in the thick air. I had known she was in the room, but I hadn't known where. "He's been having, uh… *incidents*."

"Incidents?" asked Captain Chen.

"Yes. Incidents," said Hannah. "Episodes."

"They're hard to explain," I said.

"What kind of incidents?" said Chen. She squinted at me with one eye.

Mania? Insanity? How did I explain the wasteland to her? My friends were having a difficult enough time believing me. "Problematic ones. I'm in the process of trying to figure them out. Believe me when I say this, your passengers and crew will be safe. You have my guarantee. You can take the Judge. Dispose of it. Whatever."

That gun and I had been through a lot, but right now I wasn't sure if it was even the real Judge. The way I saw it, my willingness to destroy the weapon worked in my favor.

Jurer's face appeared in the light. His fleshy beak worked at a toothpick. Did kresh even have teeth? "When you came on board you gave us a guarantee that you'd be unarmed. So, I apologize if I find your guarantees to be bullshit, Mister Bell."

"That's understandable." There was no reason to be defensive about this. I had brought a gun on board. That was against the rules. It was better to capitulate than struggle against their demands. "Punish me how you like."

"What if we send you to the shore? Leave you on an island? Maroon you."

"I'm at your mercy, Captains," I said. I spread my fingers—the cuffs prevented any elaborate gesturing. I glanced at Hannah. Could see her tension. Strangely, I didn't feel tense myself. If anything, I felt in control. Honesty and humility were working in my favor.

Silence flowed between us. The captains traded a few hushed words—conversation low enough that I couldn't make out what they said. Finally, Captain Shelna leaned back into the light. Light from the hanging lamp poured down her face, each overhang mirrored by a heavy shadow. It made her look older and angrier. "We're going to take a break. Converse. Then we'll issue our verdict."

"I'm at your mercy," I repeated. "Can I talk to Wensem?"

More hushed conversation.

"Yes," said Jurer. "You can."

Crooked jaw set, eyes serious, face expressionless, Wensem hadn't said anything, just came in and sat down. He was frustrated. Beside him sat a nervous Hagen. The dimanian looked put out and a little stressed. He didn't meet my eyes.

"Castaigne?" I asked.

"She's fine. Taft's shadowing her."

It's an odd turn of phrase, that. Taft was as much Castaigne's shadow as I was Wensem's. I wasn't used to all this security talk. Whenever we led caravans, Wensem handled the security aspect; my focus was on navigation, repairs, and the logistical side. All this slag still sounded strange in my ears and heavy on my tongue, but I relaxed knowing Taft was with her. Taft was tenacious and trustworthy. Still, I'd have appreciated having her here. I could have used her advice.

"Good," I said. I flexed my hands. "At least something's going right."

Wensem gave me one slow nod.

"It's nice to have a little sliver of normalcy right now." I looked at Hagen. Whatever happened on this side clearly disturbed him, and I knew that I was responsible. "Hey, Hagen. I need to apologize. Didn't even see you on the other side. I was there. Not here. In the wasteland my gun was pointed at a gargoyle."

"A gargoyle? You saw a gargoyle?" said Hannah before Hagen could respond. She leaned against the table, arms crossed. Her voice was sharp and edgy. The Broken Road had done a number on her—gargoyles always disturbed her. She associated them with Curwen, and her experiences on the trail were hard to shake. She chewed at the inside of her cheek and stared at me.

"Just one," I explained. "Not here. There. The wasteland. It wasn't as aggressive. I think it was only there to bring me a message."

Hannah didn't look eased.

"How you get the gun, Wal?" Wensem asked.

"I don't know," I said. "I mean, I *do*, but it doesn't make any sense—I was carrying it in the wasteland. When I saw the gargoyle, I pulled. Instinct. It was just there."

"You brought it out from under the table," said Hagen. "Pointed it right at me."

"I'm sorry," I said.

"I know, but Wal, but… damn," Hagen looked away.

"I mean it, Hage. I'm sorry."

He nodded, stared at his hands in his lap.

"Thanks for your help, even with the whole… you know."

Another nod.

Wensem leaned back, folded his long arms across his narrow chest, and sighed an exasperated sigh.

"I'm a liability," I said matter-of-factly. "I know it."

"You are," Wensem said flatly. He seemed relieved that I had been the one to say it.

"You need to relieve me of my duties."

Hannah shook her head. "Look, I don't know if—"

I tried to hold up a hand but was stopped by the cuffs. "No argument. Think about it, Hannah. Imagine if trouble happens, and I go traveling again? I'm no good if my mind is somewhere else."

"This is crazy," Hannah rubbed her eyes. "You realize how crazy this all sounds? Traveling. Wastelands. Gargoyles. Guns appearing out of thin air."

I nodded. "Yeah. I do."

"Wal's right," said Wensem. "We can't have him working the job."

"What's he going to do in the interim? We're two days out from Lovat—two more before Empress."

"I'll hang out. Pal around, maybe see if I can't figure out why this keeps happening—or at the very least understand if I can control or stop it."

"The *Black Book* might help," Hagen offered. "I've only just started digging in."

"I don't want to touch that thing again," I said.

"You think it sent you traveling?" Hannah asked.

I nodded. "I'd also like the find that kresh shoalta— remember when I nearly slipped away at the dock? It happened *after* I brushed her claw."

"Touch?" Hagen mused. "Interesting."

"You sure this is safe—you walking around a ship when you keep getting whisked away?" Hannah asked.

"Don't have much choice," I said. "I need to figure this out now or find a new line of work."

"All this is dependent on one thing," said Wensem.

"The Council of Captains," I said, finishing his thought.

Hagen breathed out heavily, his eyes flicking to mine and then shifting to Wensem's. My partner's expression had gone grim.

The door to the room opened and in walked the three captains. Chen led them, with Jurer and Shelna flanking her. Both Wensem and Hagen stood and offered their chairs. Chen waved them away. Now six people stood looming above me. It was unnerving.

I spread my fingers. "Going to maroon me?"

Chen waited for a long moment before responding. "You're not going to be marooned or imprisoned. You gave the weapon over with no resistance—although, I should add, none of us buys your story of the gun magically appearing. Some of us believe there's something else going on. Personally, I think you're hiding something."

I nodded once but said nothing. Now wasn't the time.

"We're taking the gun," said Chen.

"I'm fine with that. Going to throw it overboard?"

"We'll return it to you when we're back in Lovat," said Jurer.

"Some of us want to keep you locked in here. But we decided not to do that for now," Chen said. "We're going to talk with the Ambassador. Determine if she wants to keep you on as sec—"

"He's already stepped down," said Wensem.

"Good. That makes this easier. We can't have you mingling on the sundeck," said Jurer. "The *Gamble* press core has already run special editions with your face on the front page of the *Gazette*. You're going to be very well known around here, and we don't want our guests nervous."

"I'll stick to the main decks," I said. "Keep your VIP section free. I'll rent a room down on the main decks, as long as my company can remain in their cabins. We're still on the job for Magnez."

The captains all looked at one another, and each nodded in agreement. Chen turned and regarded me for a long moment, her left eye squinting. "Okay. That'll be fine."

Shelna strode around the table and unlocked the cuffs. They clattered on the stainless steel, and I walked out of the brig as a free man.

EIGHT

everal other fishers report that the town of Rialto vanished
from the coast overnight. Some claim to have seen ruins,
others say only a muddy swath remains to stand vigil over a once
vibrant community. Where this finishing village has gone, no one
can say. But some still hold out hope on this cold spring evening.
Reporting for 191.9 AZAH, this is Denish Ahomiro…"

I didn't hear the rest. The radio voice dwindled away as soft
jazz replaced the dead air. A light breeze blew across the deck. It
kept the stench at bay and freshened the air. If it wasn't for the
subtle rocking below my feet and the sour feeling in my stomach,
I could almost believe I was still in Lovat. Sure, the buildings had
a more haphazard quality and everything was more cramped, but
the interior of the *Gamble* wasn't too far removed from my city. I
closed the door behind me and the radio grew even more muffled.

We were due to arrive at Empress in a day, so I had found a
cheap room in Yallup on the *Gamble's* port side. It wasn't much.
Nothing here was large, and the front office of the place served
double duty as a tattoo parlor specializing in inking flash for

drunken tourists during the day. I wasn't even sure if it had a name. The hotel couldn't have had more than three rooms, perhaps four, but I didn't spend much time exploring to get an accurate count.

The room was clean but cramped. A small single bed pushed against the wall that ran the length of the space. A wash basin and a mirror next to the door. A painting of a dog above the bed. No bathroom. There was a public restroom down the street, and the hotel manager-cum-tattoo artist instructed me to use it if I needed to relieve myself. Public showers were on the deck below. There was a three-stool tavern next door—not one of the pink-lit high-roller cocktail bars that sat up top, but something more stalwart. Something more my speed. This worked for me. I deposited my bag, locked my room, and decided to wander.

The plan was for Hagen and me to meet up later—after a good night's sleep and some breakfast, alone this time. Wensem was going to take a walk to clear his head—*remember*, as he often said—and Hannah was off to relieve Taft and fill her in on all that had happened. They were also going to break the news to the rest of the crew. I was sure they weren't taking it well.

For years I had been seen as the de facto leader in the company, but lately Wensem was proving himself better suited to fill that role. He was calmer, more collected and level-headed. Perhaps my fading into the background was a necessity. Let him be the Caravan Master, and I could become a partner. It didn't matter. Not right now. We could have this discussion over drinks after this job was done.

I was still reeling, trying to wrap my head around the circumstance with the Judge and the paradox it presented. Bringing objects across was a new one—and why did my knee feel better over there? Knee pain was another of my constants. It's worse in cold weather, but it's always uncomfortable. But in the wasteland it had felt whole and undamaged.

Currently, I was standing on the edge of the Chee, the opposite end of the boat from my rented room. Evening had fallen, and the Rosalia Mountains and surrounding islands were lost to the night. Only the occasionally flash from light-vessel lamps warned of treacherous waters along the shore. Throughout the day the sky had filled with angry gray clouds, and now they obscured the stars and the moon.

Off the bow, I watched one of the two enormous tugs drag the *Gamble* across the ocean toward Empress. The rumble of the tug's engine rolled across the water, and its form was nearly lost to the gloom. Lights on its hull blinked on and off in a slow rhythm, reflecting white and green across the water. Even now, at night, it was easy to spot the white foam that billowed from its prow and rolled along its flanks before merging into the wake.

None of this felt real.

If two realities existed, then what we perceived as real was just subjective. Everything was a single viewpoint on one plane of a faceted existence. But even as I doubted the reality I stood in, I didn't believe in the reality of the wasteland either. It felt just as dreamlike, just as surreal. And if both realities were a dream, then what about the Judge?

The gun was in the wasteland, but it also sat on my dresser in the Terraces, and I knew it was currently sitting above me in one of the captain's offices. I knew this because it was true. But I also knew they were lies. The revolver was only sitting in one place—upstairs. That was the only logical conclusion. It had been in my hand, and I had given it over. It couldn't inhabit all three places, could it?

I breathed in a big lungful of sea air. Struggled to clear my mind. I blinked against the wind, even as it pulled tears from the corner of my eyes. The wasteland pulled at me as if it was a living and breathing thing. It prodded at the edges of my sanity. If the gun was real here, then it was real there; if it was real there, that meant the wasteland wasn't a dream and reality wasn't a dream.

The broken sun warmed my neck. I pushed back. Not now. It wasn't time to return. It wasn't time!

The prodding stopped. Peace flooded me. The heat from the sun faded. The warm wind shifted and once again became cold. Scents of the air and the sea intensified—the pungent aroma of brine, and beneath that the lingering stench of—what had Ash called it? The fragrance of a corpse-city? Something like that, anyway.

The pain in my knee flared like a small bright star. I almost laughed, welcoming it back.

The echoey notes from the Monk crept their way from a small bar a few yards away. The piano player inside was doing a decent job with a rendition of "Round Midnight," and the accompanying tenor sax was nailing its role. The music made me feel a bit better. It splashed some pigment into a world that felt as if it was slowly being drained of color. The toe of my shiny leather shoes tapped on the metal decking with the rhythm of the bass.

It had been my mother who taught me to appreciate the Saints and the songs they had given us. I'm not religious—not the way she is—but even I can appreciate the music of the church. In the years since the Aligning, the world had shifted and changed. But the music of the old world had never faded from humanity. It clung to us like a symbiote that demanded attention but still energized us. It filled us with something beyond ourselves, a shared experience, never the same and yet always familiar.

Memories of music brought back other memories of home—the smell of sawdust and the sound of small-town council gossip, plum bread and tobacco smoke. I hadn't seen my parents in over a year. We traded telegrams, and they were okay, I knew that much. Merritt isn't too far from Lovat, but life had been a whirlwind since the Broken Road.

Those memories were real. I could doubt the reality of the present, but those memories of home were solid as stone.

Or were they?

It's too late.

The gargoyle's words hissed through my head. I reached out to steady myself against a bulkhead. Pain careened through my skull, shattered any memories and dragged me like the tug hauled the *Gamble*—unrelenting, undaunted, back to the present. Back to this half-reality.

Too late, it had said. *Too late.* For what? For whom? Even with Ashton out of play, something lingered. Something always lingered. I might have stopped him, but he had achieved something—something worrisome. Dread had followed me for the last several weeks. Our conversation in the wasteland. His warnings. His pleasure at seeing me writhe. It gnawed on me, worked at the corners of reality.

The yellow-clad figure had only confirmed what I already knew. Whatever was happening was already in play, and here I was looking west and seeing nothing.

NINE

Sleep came fitfully. Dreams of wastelands, disappearing guns, and gargoyles only further muddled my mind. My sweat flowed freely and chilled in the cold air, making me miserable. My room behind the tattoo shop was the biting sort of muggy that crept into your bones. When I roused, it was mid-morning, and I ached all over.

Skipping a shower, I washed my face and hands and dressed in a clean button-down shirt and my suit trousers. I skipped the tie. I wasn't technically a part of security anymore. The shiny leather shoes made me yearn for my road boots. I grabbed my suit jacket, nodded to the tattoo artist at the front desk, and pushed my way out into the *Gamble's* tight boulevards.

Breakfast was dimanian bao the size of my fist stuffed with peppers, crab, and a spicy cheese that numbed my tongue. It was delicious. I ate it as I made my way to a spot on Kaleetan's third deck called Shantak Coffee. It had been where Hagen and I had agreed to meet.

I melted into the traffic within the *Gamble* like I was a natural. Even my stomach didn't feel so sour now. Perhaps I was getting used to the rocking sea? One could hope. I had heard plenty of rumors about the food to be found here, and if the bao was any indication, those rumors were absolutely right.

The pain in my knee was bright and familiar—grounding— as I climbed the stairs from the main deck and up two flights to the low-ceilinged avenues of the third deck. Here the stalls ran floor to deckhead, and the passages in between forced the citizens of the *Gamble* to press against each other as they jostled to make their way fore or aft.

Bits of daylight leaked in from cracks in the port-side bulk-heads, outshining the dull yellow of incandescent bulbs and giving the interior of Kaleetan a mottled appearance. Passenger and citizen alike would occasionally squint as a shaft of daylight played across their eyes.

Smells of grilled meat, pungent liquor, and toasted grains hung heavy on the air. I heard jazz and drummers and the cries of a street mystic preaching from around a corner. A small crowd had gathered near him, and I had to turn sideways and shuffle to pass through.

My stomach was growling again by the time I arrived at Shantak Coffee.

The spot had a more substantial appearance than other locations on this deck. Its walls were solid bulkheads, and it had its own door that led into a dark interior. The sign above was neon, the glass twisted to illustrate in blue glowing tubes a creature that was a hybrid between bat and bird, paired with an ugly horse's head. The glass was animated to give the bird-thing a herky-jerky appearance as if it was in flight. A white fabric sign below read LOVAT'S OLDEST OPERATING COFFEE SHOP in red Strutten letters.

I passed through the door and into the haze inside. The smell of tobacco and cannabis was heavy here. A single bar ran along the back wall, most of it dominated by a large machine made of tubes and steel. Behind it—much to my surprise—was a Lengish man.

The Lengish are bipedal, and perhaps could be considered hominids. They have two arms that ended in hands, and two legs. But their heads are goat-like, and piebald fur covers most of their body. Four horns jutted from this one's head—two curved up and out, two more curved downward. This Lengish wore a tee shirt with the bird-bat from the sign and a black apron that covered him from the waist down. Try as I might, I couldn't help but stare. I had never met a Lengish man or woman, though I had been told a few lived in Lovat.

"Help you?" he asked in perfect Strutten. His lips rolled strangely, and the eyes on either side of his head twisted to lock into me.

"Uh, looking for a friend."

"Oh! Hey, Wal, over here," Hagen called from a table in a corner. A creeping feeling of déjà vu washed through me. The damn *Black Book* was sitting in front of him. Atop it was a wide bowl-shaped mug filled with something beige. Both he, the book, and the beverage were mostly lost to haze and darkness. Shantak's interior walls were painted black. The only light came from another blue neon sign burning behind the bar, a twin of the one outside. Lilting music was playing from somewhere— soft horns above a low and steady beat.

"Hey," said the Lengish man in perfect Strutten, before I could step in Hagen's direction.

"Yeah?" I said, pausing and trying not to stare.

"You gotta buy something. No freeloaders."

"Uh, this is a coffee shop?"

"What else it look like?" He spread his arms. His hands were unusual—the first two fingers were long nearly twice the length of my own, and then they quickly tapered back. The palms were black, and backs were covered in stiff hair.

"Um, black coffee?"

"Think this is a city-side shop?"

He waved me closer and pushed a paper menu across the countertop. Strange titles of various beverages I didn't recognize were written in bold letters with descriptors below. I ran my finger down them, passing a 'flat-white' and a 'cappuccino' before arriving on something that sounded more my speed.

"I'll take a long black," I said, the term clumsy on my tongue.

"Excellent choice. Three lira. It'll be up shortly."

I pushed over some bills and tucked a single into a paper cup with a small sign that read BOATS CAN TIP. SO CAN YOU. The Lengish man began to work at the machine, pulling levers and twisting knobs. There was a hiss of steam and the gurgle of water. The process fascinated me, but I pulled myself away, crossed the small shop and sat across from Hagen.

"Odd place," I said as I slipped into the chair.

"I love it. There's a few coffee stands like this in Lovat, though none this old. A few enterprising folks have begun rebuilding the espresso machines—it's been exciting to see their resurgence. They do make a better cup of coffee."

"Espresso?" I asked, still groggy and a little confused.

Hagen waved towards the machine on the counter. "Essentially, that machine uses pressure to push hot water through a powder of finely ground beans. It's good." He took a sip of his drink. "How'd you sleep?"

"Awful," I said. I rubbed my eyes. "Nightmares, among other things." I eyed the *Black Book* warily.

"Wasteland?"

I shook my head and lied. "No. Thank God. How's the crew?"

Hagen breathed out loudly and leaned back. He sipped from his beige beverage before answering. "Taft was upset. She wants to talk with you later today. The rest of the guys came across as more annoyed. They don't like change."

"No one does," I said absently.

"Wensem got them squared away. He, Hannah, and the Ambassador were in a meeting until late last night, and they started up again this morning. Something about the switch with Empress and the logistics surrounding it."

I squirmed in my chair. Removing myself had been the right call, but it still hurt to know everyone was upstairs making decisions and working without me. I was a dead weight holding the company back. I'd always be on Wensem and Hannah's mind— they'd never be truly focused. Wensem especially, I knew how he worried. His words from our conversation echoed through my memory: *I can't keep sitting across from you and wondering if it'll be our last drink together.*

"I didn't delve too far into it. I'm just a tourist," said Hagen.

"Long black!" shouted the Lengish man.

"Your coffee is up." Hagen pointed toward the counter.

I rose, grabbed my cup, and returned to the table. The coffee was served in a tapered glass cup with a handle atop a matching saucer. Inside, the liquid was pitch black, with a foamy top the color of dust. When I brought it to my lips, I could smell the roast of the beans. When I sipped it, the flavor was a stunning departure from what I had been expecting, deep and creamy with a nutty base followed by a dark chocolate bitterness. It was silky on the tongue and went down smooth.

"By the Firsts." I smacked my lips. "Damn!"

Hagen grinned and lifted his cup to his lips. "Told you it was good."

Before we continued, I rose and dropped another lira into the tip jar. The Lengish man gave me a nod, and his lips moved, but beyond that I found it impossible to read into the expressions on his caprine face.

"Any luck on the shoalta?"

"No," I said. "But I haven't started looking."

"I'd check below deck. There are a few shoals down there, including Our Father of the Obscured Atoll—that's the big one. Deeperists like to be close to the water."

"Our Father of the Obscured Atoll," I repeated. I didn't know much about the faith, only that they worshiped some aquatic god and called their congregation shoals. Deeperism was popular among the cephels, anur, and kresh—the non-humanoid species. "A moving church, huh."

"It's not abnormal, actually. Many Deeperists prefer boats, since you can get below the waterline without being submerged. Used to be the feasts and services took place underwater, but that made it hard to proselytize us humanoids. These days it's more a metaphor than true submergence.

"Most Deeperists are probably here for the Feast of Recession—King Tide's Ebb. Victory won't let them in—well, the aquatics—but the *Gamble* likes to cater to Deeperists. The boat passes over some of the ghost forests that were once used for tidal rituals—place called Looff Fields, just off the point of West Lovat. Makes the repeated trips holy to them." Hagen had slipped into a lecture.

"When does that start?" Magnez had said something about a celebration on the return.

"Won't happen until the King Tide recedes. It's a several-day affair—should be on the return if everything goes according to plan."

"How long does a King Tide last?" I asked, taking another sip of my long black. It's helpful to have friends well versed in Lovatine faiths and creeds. Hagen knew a lot—his shop catered to many sects, which gave him first-hand experience with the religious side of the city.

Hagen bobbled his head back and forth. "Week? Maybe two? According to historical accounts, King and Neap Tides were more predictable before the Aligning. Since then... well, let's just say they're harder to forecast. The moon is her own master, after all."

It was a dauger saying. I leaned back and glanced at the book. Hagen followed my gaze and pushed it toward me. The inky black cover made my skin crawl.

"Don't take it to the wasteland," he said half-joking.

"I'm not touching it," I said, holding my hands up.

Hagen opened it, and slid it toward me. The interior was layered with letterforms. Some I recognized, others I didn't— some ancient progenitor of Strutten? I knew our language was a hodgepodge, born from the remains of the civilizations that came before. But spending time with Samantha and Hagen and seeing some of the languages in ancient books made me realize how complicated that blending was.

"What's this language? Aklo?"

Hagen shook his head then leaned forward and peered down at it, as if upside-down it would somehow tell him. "Early progenitor of Strutten, actually. Don't know its true name. I'm using a few sources to translate it. Actually, it's more sources for sources, layers of language. Sam and I call it Armini."

"You can take it away now."

Hagen nodded and shut the book and tucked it into a bag that hung off his chair. With the book out of sight, I eased slightly.

"Discover anything more about me?"

"Honestly, not much. The adversaries mentioned fit you perfectly—they're all created from a failed ritual. Like Peter Black's. They can resist the Founders. Which you've done a few times now. It's a dense book, but as I said, I think Junzt went mad while writing it. He seems to circle around a single Founder in particular. A founder of founders, as it were."

The thing on the horizon. I swallowed.

"I'm still trying to translate the name. I don't think the original names are rooted in Armini. Anyway, I'm hoping you can help me out with that. There was a reason I was so... uh— out of it yesterday. In the brig."

"Well, I had just pulled a gun on you. I'd say being out of it was a valid emotion."

Hagen sat his cup down and started to laugh. It grew in intensity until he was holding his stomach. "Wal, Carter's cross, I don't give a damn about that. I trust you. Hell, I *still* trust you. If anything, I'm glad we didn't follow my advice. I was trying to get out of there. Running would have looked terrible."

"What was with the—"

He didn't let me finish the question. "I was processing something. Trying to wrap my head around the Judge."

"You and me both."

"I feel like something is missing. Not that you're lying to us, mind. But that you're not telling us everything. Or you're forgetting something. I mean, I know the wasteland, the ruined city, the creature beyond the horizon. I know the *place*. But there has to be more to your traveling. There needs to be a *reason*."

Old conversations—that's what he didn't know. Ashton's warning. Then the masked man in yellow robes. Then the gargoyle. Shadows on hardpan. I swallowed again. I'm sure it made me look guilty, but it was born out of nerves.

Hagen narrowed his eyes just slightly.

"What happened there, Wal? What aren't you telling?" His voice faded.

I looked away, studied the texture on the black wall. The lilting music swayed softly, and the haze had begun to make me feel lightheaded. That buzz was back—part noise and part vibration at the base of my skull. The wasteland pulled at me, but I ignored it.

"Wal," he pressed.

"It's not just visiting. It's not just observations," I said.

Hagen said nothing, just leaned forward. I could see the earnestness behind the eagerness. He cared, but he was fascinated by all of this. Could I blame him? He was a researcher at heart.

"It's conversations," I said. "Well… it wasn't before. It is now."

"Conversations?" Hagen's brow wrinkled. "With who?"

"Ashton mainly—before. But more recently there's been a masked man in these stained yellow robes. Also a gargoyle."

"Mind if I take notes?"

"Go ahead."

Hagen pulled out a small notebook and flipped it open and began to scribble as I spoke. I told him about my tête-à-tête with Ashton, how he introduced me to the shadows of the others. I named them as he had called them: the mother, Cybil; the uncle, Curwen; the robed man, the Pretender; and another. Then I delivered the same message he had given to me: *Enough prattle. Look west, Guardian. The High Priest comes and on his heels… a new Aligning.*

"Look west," Hagen repeated. His pencil scurried across the page. "A new Aligning. Fascinating."

"Terrifying," I added.

Hagen didn't seem overly bothered.

"There ain't anything there. I've looked." I said, then took a drink from my long black. "A lot."

Hagen drummed the spurs on his knuckles on the table. He did that when he was thinking. "Maybe it's a metaphor."

"Yeah? Maybe. Anyway, the masked figure repeated the same thing. Look west. Look west. Always look west."

"He a dauger?"

I thought about it. "Maybe? But he doesn't seem dauger-like. He's more ephemeral. His mask isn't a metal I recognize. It's pale but tarnished. Matches his robes. Oh—and during his visit I smell sulfur and the air is filled with ash and embers. That's new."

"When did he manifest?"

"After—during, I guess—the meeting with Magnez. He's been around since then, actually. There. Dim sum." I had dreamed of him as well. Thinking about that eerie blank expression made my hands go all clammy, and I fiddled with the hem of my shirtsleeve.

"Could be a warning." Hagen considered this. "Or a threat, I suppose. The west is more than just one of the cardinal directions. It used to be used as an indicator of forward momentum, progress. Ancient religious considered it the direction towards enlightenment, the afterlife, or the godhead."

"What does it mean to a First?"

"That's the million-lira question." Hagen waggled a finger in the air, then checked his notes. "Is that everything?"

I waited a bit before I responded. Part of me wanted to tell him about the Ashton-avatar I had been seeing. But I kept that to myself—I was still unsure how he'd handle knowing that Ashton was alive. I wasn't sure how it all worked out anyway, with forms and avatars and bodies and so forth. I was still trying to come to grips with it.

"Yeah, that's everything." Once I could explain Ash in a way that made sense, I would.

Hagen nodded and slipped his notebook into his bag.

"Taft's planning on coming to see you. Wants to chat—maybe grab a meal."

The *Gamble* had no directory agents, no telegram offices, and since I was forbidden from walking the upper decks, it was challenging to communicate with my company. I scratched my chin. "Have her come to my room. We can meet there."

"Where you staying?'"

I told him about the tattoo shop/hotel and roughly where it sat. "It doesn't have a name. Just says 'Tattoos' above the door next to a drawing of a smiling cat."

We finished our coffee.

"I'll come find you when I figure this puzzle out," said Hagen. "Want to explore Empress together when we arrive?"

That sounded good, and I said so. We both rose, embraced, and walked out of the coffee shop, giving the Lengish man a little wave. Hagen veered off and climbed a set of stairs that rose to the upper decks, and I decided to take my time wandering back to my room. The afternoon crowds had thickened. Taft was on duty until five or so, which gave me a few hours to kill. I considered stepping into one of the *Gamble's* casinos, but I don't really enjoy gambling. The risk never resonated with me. They all had bars, but it was too early to drink.

The humming at the back of my skull continued. But I ignored both it and the hot wasteland sun on my neck. There was nothing there. Nothing to interest me, no draw. Just vague signs and potent. I could do without that right now. The *Gamble* had several ramps that arced down to the main deck, and I opted for those instead of stairs. The walk was a bit longer, but stairs do a number on my knee, and here in this reality, it was throbbing.

On the main deck, I stopped among a large crowd to watch a Bleeding James street mystic perform tricks. Bursts of fire would leap from his palm and from beneath his cape. He grinned through a beard of flame that smoked and crackled before disappearing altogether. It was impressive, and the crowd clapped and tossed coins into a hat that sat at his feet. Once he had drawn his crowd, the mystic began to preach.

"Listen to me, good people. Listen to the Bloody Gospel. The end times are a-comin'! Fire will sweep this earth. A New Aligning! Too long we've allowed the repression of the true faith. Too long have the priests, bishops, and preachers conspired together to repress the truth! Listen to the word of Bleeding James! Hear the voice of the martyr!"

I left him to his bloviating. I didn't know much about Bleeding James and the Bloody Gospel. I knew the name, and I knew he had some vague connection to the Hasturian faith. But my understanding stopped there. Apparently, he was a popular enough figure to draw magic-performing street mystics.

I bought a bag of roasted chestnuts from a cart and chewed on them as I made my way to my hotel. The street preacher's comments on the "New Aligning" had taken root inside my head. It was an eerie echo from the mystic's sign I had spotted outside of City Hall. Were there preaching trends passed from mystic to mystic, or was this something else? It reminded me of a shift in the weather—subtle changes that everyone recognized but couldn't ever put their finger on. A pressure in the world—a hint that something was coming. Even the hustlers could feel it.

I took a side street that ran along the exterior of the boat. Cafes and taverns ran along one side, stomach-high railing on the other. Outside, rain came down in torrents. The peaks of the Rosalias were lost in a gray haze.

I had just crossed over from Kaleetan to Yallup when someone shouted my name.

"Hey! You Waldo Bell?"

"Who's asking?" I said, turning toward the voice.

The flat of a shovel connected with the left side of my head.

TEN

My face hurt. My left eye was swollen shut. My knee ached. My stomach groaned. My balls felt like they had receded. Someone had kicked or punched my left kidney, and the pain there was like a tight knot. A slight moan escaped my lips. It bubbled against a pool of saliva that had leaked from my open mouth. I was lying on the cold metal floor of a dark room, head throbbing.

Odd that whoever had assaulted me hadn't tied me up. It took some effort to peel myself off the floor. I wiped my mouth with the back of my hand, and it came away bloody. My head throbbed with each motion, and the dim light blurred my already hindered vision.

Where was I now? And who the hell hit me?

For a moment, a haze of rage blotted out all my pain. I rose, pushing myself off the floor with my good knee, hands balling into fists. I was itching for a fight.

The rage passed and the pain returned. All I wanted to do was slump back to the floor.

I tried to remember: coffee with Hagen; the Bleeding James street mystic; the voice; then here, a dark room.

I had to be below the main deck. But where? The paint here was similar to the brig—pipes along one wall and in a tangled maze on the ceiling. Unlike the brig, though, it was clear this section of the *Gamble* wasn't used often. A thin layer of mildew coated much of the room, and it had a musty smell. I could hear rats scurry along the walls, disappearing with echoing squeaks.

"Hello?" I tried to call out. It came out as more of a wheeze. I bent over, hands to my knees, as I coughed. Blood from my mouth spattered my pants in dark drops. Maybe it was better I stayed quiet. My attacker could be nearby.

What time was it? I was supposed to meet Taft tonight—or was it already tonight? I could picture her tearing apart the *Gamble*, hunting for me.

As the coughing receded, I took a moment to find an exit. The room had a door, and it was unlocked. I fiddled with the handle, still half-muddled, until it swung open silently and I stepped through.

"I'm sure," said a voice. *The* voice belonging to the person who had called out to me earlier. It was calm, collected. A tenor, if I heard correctly. Not the sort of deep growl I'd expect from a person who assaulted people with a shovel.

I squinted through my right eye.

The room beyond was larger. Rusted machinery occupied one side, and a fire burned in what had once been a boiler. The flames cast the room in shifting hues of oranges, reds, and yellows. Six people stood with their backs to me around a central table. A shovel lay on the surface between them.

They were silhouetted in the glow of the fire. Two humans. Two dimanians, one with large curling horns like a ram's. A stout anur. An umbra, crisp white eyes glowing. Tendrils of black mist drifted off his exposed form, slowly shifting from black to a thin white before they dissipated, like ink melting into water. Not something I'd seen from any umbra before.

A few large pieces of machinery were set at intervals into the decking beneath my feet. I ducked behind the nearest and listened to the hushed conversation.

"I'm sure. He turned."

"We need to be sure."

"He turned, Clarissa!"

"That doesn't mean anything," the voice belonging to Clarissa replied. "That's not good enough."

"It means he recognized his name. I know it's him. His friend called him 'Waldo Bell' in the Golden Market—before security led him away."

"If security led him away, why would he be wandering free?"

"I don't know, but it's *him*."

"If you're wrong, we're killing an innocent man."

My breath tightened in my chest.

"Hey, let's not fight." A new voice.

"I'm not wrong."

"The Sleeper deserves justice. We can't let his killer wander free."

The Sleeper—one of Ashton's many names. A term most folks wouldn't bandy about, not with that sort of reverence. These people had to be his disciples. Ash had said I'd stirred them up. Warned me to be careful. My face was evidence that he wasn't kidding. These psychos weren't messing around, and now I was listening to them calmly plot my murder.

"Do you want me just to ask him?"

"Yes!"

"Like he's going to give us a straight answer."

"We're damned no matter what we do," said a new voice, this one flat and impassive. "If he's the wrong guy, we can't just let him go."

"What do you mean?"

"He'll see our faces. He'll turn us over to the stewards," said that third voice.

Outside of the machinery, much of the room was empty. There was a closed door behind the group and an open hatch about ten or fifteen feet away. If I moved quickly, I could leapfrog from behind the pieces of machinery and slip through. But where did it lead? All I could see was the black shadows of the *Gamble's* underbelly. I had no idea where I was—it could be a dead end, and I'd be trapped. The cultists were so engrossed in arguing over my murder that it'd take them some time to realize I was gone. I had little choice—stay here and die, or flee and hope to find an exit. I chose the exit.

"Beek's right. We can't just let him go."

"We're not going to let anyone go.

I moved, slipping from the shadow of one man-sized machine to the next.

"How did you plan on killing him anyway?"

"With the shovel."

Moans and other noises of displeasure followed.

"That's disgusting."

I agreed. I took the next step, slipping closer to the hatch.

"What do you want to use?"

"I can get a knife from the shop," someone suggested.

"I wish you'd have spoken to us earlier. We could have planned this better."

"Didn't think we had time. I saw him and I reacted. Simple as that."

My next move put me through the open hatch and into the darkness on the other side. Thrums and metallic moans issued from the bulkheads around me—the pressure from the water pushing in on the hull. My vision swam. I blinked my good eye and struggled to focus. When I shook my head to clear it, a crashing headache nearly dropped me to my knees.

Breathe. Just breathe.

"I'm not going to kill an innocent man."

"What do you want us to do, Clarissa?"

I was definitely below deck. The air here was cold and humid. Most of the old machines that had rumbled down here in eons past had been removed. Only their bones remained—monuments to another time. As best I could tell, the space below deck had split into an upper and lower layer. I was most likely at the very bottom.

The now muffled conversation continued behind me as the hapless cultists tried to figure out the best way to dispatch the guy who'd killed their god. I moved quicker now, slipping from one black room to the next, half-feeling my way around in the dark, half-seeing only shadowed shapes, my fingers drifting across timeworn iron. There had to be stairs around here.

The conversation faded as I kept moving. Another door, another room, this one filled with crates. The next space had two doors. I kept going, walking along a straight line. The *Gamble* had stairs everywhere. I'd eventually stumble across one.

As I came through the door, I smacked my head against a pipe. It nearly laid me out. A hollow gong echoed throughout the room. For a moment, I stumbled around, hand pressed against a quickly rising lump. Then I realized the racket I was making. I froze and held my breath. My eyes watered. A headache surged. Would the sound clue the cultists into my disappearance? Carter's cross, I hoped not.

One heartbeat. Two. I didn't hear any commotion behind me.

I was reasonably sure I was moving along the length of the boat, and if I wanted to find a stairwell I'd need to stick to the edges. I forced myself to keep going. I passed through yet another hatch and into a large chamber that had a pool of standing seawater on the floor. It wasn't deep, only a few inches, but it made the whole room smell like the sea. A long table sat against one wall, and candles flickered atop rugged candelabras carved from driftwood. Above the table on the wall was a symbol with three rippling lines.

There was no one here.

Three doors led away from this room. One forward, the way I had been going. Two others flanked the table.

The seawater flowed back and forth. It would pool near the legs of the table before shifting and then crossing the room and gathering around my uncomfortable shoes. The *Gamble* tended to roll more than pitch, and the movement of the water helped me get my bearings.

"He's not in here!"

The shout sent a wave of terror through me. Panicked voices rose, followed by feet slamming against the decking. I splashed forward, moving across the room and throwing my weight against the level on the door. The metal moaned as the hatch dog flipped upward.

Beyond I found a room similar to the one I'd left, only this one was filled with people. Anur, cephel, and kresh mainly, but there were a few dimanians and humans in the mix. They were singing a hymn, and most had their backs to me. Water rolled around their feet and pulled at their salt-stained robes—a Deeperist shoal.

I pulled the hatch shut, throwing the latch and looking for another exit.

I hadn't been moving fast. The cultists would be getting close.

"Welcome to Our Father of th—oh, it's you," said a small voice.

The voice came from the kresh shoalta I had met when we boarded the *Gamble*—the same one who had sent me traveling when our hands touched. Seeing her standing in the ankle-deep water made my skull buzz, and my stomach flipped in response. Not now. I didn't need to trip out now, dammit.

"Uh, hi," I said, taking a step back, hoping distance would help.

The kresh touched her chest and whispered. "Amaia. Shoalta Amaia. I didn't think we were properly introduced. I didn't realize you were a Deeperist—oh, what happened to your face?"

"I need to hide," I whispered as I looked around. The other members of the shoal were still half-way into their hymn, their songbooks clutched in a variety of appendages. "Is there a way out of here?"

"What happened?"

"Trouble." I didn't have time for an explanation. "I need to hide."

Shoalta Amaia must have seen something in my face. She turned and moved to a collection of trunks and bags atop a pallet that sat out of the water on four cement blocks. Her little blue duffle sat among the pile, resting below a few other bags. She pulled out a substantial piece of dark fabric and rushed over to me. It was a robe.

"Put this on."

Her claws poked me through the rough fabric as she pressed me forward into the crowd. "The hood, don't forget the hood. Move here, stand here."

I was shoved between two Deeperists, a cephel, and a burly bufo'anur, as I pulled the hood up and over my head, keeping it low to shadow my face. With one eye swollen and a bloody lip, I didn't want to startle my fellow laics. The bufo'anur either didn't notice or didn't see my ruined face—she smiled and turned her hymnal so I could see, even going as far as pointing out the passage so I could join in.

Behind me, I heard the hatch whine open, followed by the sound of people splashing into the room.

I didn't turn. I sang louder. Lifting my voice as we sang of the coming of sleeping Deeper and his glorious ascension to the surface and the atonement he'd grant for all those who call to him. The words were overly flowery, the way all hymns are, and filled with oceanic metaphor. But I sang. Beneath the robe, cold sweat trickled down my back.

Shoalta Amaia was having a hushed discussion, and some of the shoal were turning from their song to glare at the troublemakers. I allowed myself a cursory glance. Three of the six followers were there, standing in the back and engaged in a lively discussion with the shoalta—a human man, a dimanian woman, and the white-eyed umbra. They weren't what I had expected. They had the look of academics. Historians, researchers, or perhaps professors from Portage City University—the sort of people Hagen would thrive among. They didn't look like brawlers, much less murderers. No wonder they were so manic—they were probably entirely out of their element.

The conversation continued. The hymn ended. An awkward silence fell on those at the rear of the gathered as Shoalta Amaia continued her hushed argument with the murderous academics.

"Keep it down back there," a voice called out in thickly accented Strutten. Murmurs, grunts, and clicks of agreement from the others in the crowd.

"Mind your business," growled the man.

Two people pulled away from the crowd—a human and another bufo'anur. Both were enormous and broad-shouldered. They slowly walked through the water to stand just to the side of Shoalta Amaia. There they folded their arms like bouncers outside of a nightclub.

My throat ached. I wouldn't let these folks fight my battles, but I also didn't want to see what the cultists had in mind with their shovel. For a tense moment, there was a standoff. Cultists staring upward at Deeperists, Deeperists looming over them.

It was the cultists who broke first, the umbra pulling on the man's sleeve, the woman urging him to leave.

"I apologize for the interruption," the man mumbled, then they turned and left.

The hatch door swung shut behind them. The tension drained from my body, and I nearly collapsed. Luckily, it was an appropriate time.

"With that distraction out of the way—" began a shoalta standing in front. He was a thickly set anur with a narrow ichthyic face bordered by heavy jowls and topped with bulbous eyes. He held his hands outstretched, a scallop shell in each hand and the sleeves of his robe bunched in his armpits. "All shall kneel."

"All shall kneel," echoed the shoal.

The crowd knelt. I was too far into it to break away now. So I joined them. My knee was unhappy with me, but the cold seawater on the floor eased the pain slightly. I heard the anur shoalta's words, but they didn't stick in my head. I was too distracted.

"May we, transitory shoal of the Mighty Deeper, keep the faith as we embark on this the greatest of our journeys…"

The pain from the assault was constant and distracting. I looked around, seeing each gatherer's head bowed, eyes closed, lips moving as they repeated the shoalta's prayer to themselves.

"…one that Deeper in all his majesty has led our kind—his followers—from one world to the next, and under his…"

As the anur shoalta guided the crowd in prayer, my tension ebbed, and with it the panic. Ocean water soaked my pants and filled my shoes. Foam collected around the fabric of my borrowed robe. Here among the Deeperists, I was safe. I had found a moment of peace.

It's a shame that peace was so fleeting.

ELEVEN

Thanks," I said. "For what you did."

Shoalta Amaia smiled a kresh's smile with her fleshy beak and took a sip of her tea. Behind us, the clank and clang of pachinko machines emanated from the parlor, adding to the sounds of the open deck.

I pressed the cold compress to the side of my face. The woman at the counter had been adamant, and I wasn't about to turn down charity. It had worked out swimmingly so far.

"Nice place," I said. "Good tea."

"Yeah?" She turned and regarded the parlor. "I like it. Reminds me of home."

"Where's home?" I said.

Her black eyes narrowed, and her mouth pursed into what I could only assume was a pucker. "Lovat."

We were outside a pachinko parlor and tea shop on the port side of Yallup, not too far from my hotel room. Amaia and a few of her shoal had offered to walk me back, concerned that my attackers might try coming after me again. I didn't think that likely, but I appreciated the added safety. When I offered to buy them a drink as a way of saying thanks, Amaia had politely turned me down and suggested tea instead. She knew a place.

I bought rose-and-brakendale tea for everyone and the others had left, returning to the small chapel in the *Gamble's* hull, which left Shoalta Amaia and me standing at a small counter on the exterior of a narrow parlor. It was the perfect height for Amaia, but I had to stoop slightly. We must have looked a sight—a kresh holy woman and a filthy security goon. Grime had made its way into my clean shirt and pants, but at least they had dried.

"Ah, yeah," I said. "I figured. I meant, what warren?"

"Stadium," she said.

Not far from Hagen's place. It was a kresh haven, especially the low levels. A lot of them worked shellfish farms in the Sunk.

I drank my tea. It was good. Warm, with hints of rose and that bright lemony flavor of brakendale that tended to linger.

"I know the neighborhood."

Her eyes widened a bit but she said nothing. For a while we drank tea and stood in silence.

"You know, charity is one of Deeper's teachings," Amaia said, speaking as if responding to a question. Her eyes were jet black and tapered, looking like a heart or a teardrop on its side. Occasionally they'd compress—the kresh way of narrowing your eyes, I supposed. "Helping the downtrodden is what we were told to do."

She quoted some scripture—not bothering to translate it. I recognized its nature only by its poetic cadence and the shift in her tone. I smiled, hoping it was the right reaction.

"Well, thank you. I mean it. You and your shoal saved my life."

The shoalta nodded graciously. "That man—"

"I don't know who he was," I said, holding up my free hand.

She dismissed my slight defense with a wave of her claw. "He said he was looking for a *murderer*." She had whispered that last word. "Are you a murderer, Mister Bell?"

I blinked, then coughed slightly, taken aback by her directness. "I told you, it's Wal. And..." How should I answer her? I had killed. But was I a murderer? What was the difference? Where was the line? Self-defense might fly in some communities, but many maero Dulodists would vehemently disagree. To them, to take any life was wrong—it shattered the bonds of community and family. Reunifieds were a bit more forgiving. They believed that killing in self-defense or for a noble purpose was acceptable. How 'noble' was determined was the subject of some debate. How did Deeperism approach the subject? I wasn't sure.

"Well?" Her tone wasn't suspicious—more curious.

"No," I said, not sure if I was lying or not. "I'm no murderer. They got the wrong guy."

For a long moment she just watched me, occasionally taking sips of her tea. I found it difficult to shrink away from her gaze, and I found it impossible to read emotion in her features. Kresh aren't as animated as the anur, nor are they as alien as the cephel. They come across as cold and impartial to many—it's not true, of course. She probably found it just as challenging to read me.

I rubbed the back of my neck and gave her a sheepish smile half hidden by the compress. My face hurt. The swelling had receded in the last hour, but the pain was still present. Shovel to the face—Carter's cross, yet one more bizarre injury to add to my growing collection. At least it wasn't permanent. Hopefully. I should probably find a bonesaw and get a professional opinion.

"So," I said, starting to make conversation. "I was told you have a feast coming up? Something on the return trip?"

"Oh!" She sounded stunned that I knew about this. "I… well, yes. King Tide's Ebb."

"Is it only for Deeperists?" I asked. "Or can anyone attend?"

"Aren't you staying on Empress?" she asked. There was a slight shift in her tone.

"Just visiting. I'll head back with the *Gamble*."

Her mouth pressed together, and she looked away. Then she turned and looked at me with a fierce expression. "I don't think the *Gamble* is safe for you, Mister Bell. I think you should find another way back to Lovat."

I laughed and sat forward. "Look, I was jumped. Just a misunderstanding. Now that I know those people are around, I'll be fine. I'll be more careful. Although I appreciate the concern."

"It's more than just those beasts—" Shoalta Amaia began. Were her claws shaking? The base of my skull began to hum. There was a nervousness in the kresh's tone, something that went beyond my attack. When she met my eyes, a rush of hot wind tickled my skin—wasteland wind mixed with the smell of sulfur and ash. I could hear the howl of a coyote. Whispers drifted to me from that other reality, and the heat of the broken sun played across my skin.

I shivered. Amaia did as well.

For a moment we both froze, watching each other. Had she felt that? I leaned forward, wanting to ask her about the wasteland. Eager to find someone else experiencing the same little trips. Excited at the notion that there were others.

I never got to ask.

A loud klaxon sounded. Lights around the boat came on and flashed in alert. Captain Chen's voice echoed through the *Gamble*. "Ladies and gentlemen, Empress is currently sitting off our starboard. All passengers disembarking, please prepare to queue for launches."

"I have to go," Amaia said. She rose and knocked her tea over in the process. The cup shattered on the deck. There was no pause. She didn't even turn.

"Wait, I—"

The shoalta fled, moving through the crowd at a half-trot. I watched her go until a pair of dimanians passed between us and cut off my sightline. By the time they had passed, Amaia had disappeared.

My head spun with questions.

"By the Firsts, what happened to your face?" Hagen asked. His hand rose as if he was going to touch my swollen eye. Instinctively, I jerked back from the sudden motion. The contraction of my cheek muscle made me wince again and I let out a small groan followed by a curse.

"You look like seven shades of shit," Taft said.

I scowled and pressed the compress against the left side of my face. Before meeting with them, I had returned to my hotel room and changed into my previous set of clothes. My two dress shirts were already ruined, and this trip wasn't half over. Give me a roader flannel any day over white shirtsleeves. But hey, better sweat stains than blood stains. I hadn't brought anything else with me. Maybe I could pick something up in Empress?

"Taft's right. You look awful," Hagen said. "What the hell did you do this time?"

We shifted forward, drawing further from the security checkpoint. The line between us and the bumboat launches grew shorter. Like Lovat, Empress had no port for a ship the size of the *Gamble*. Instead, passengers and freight were ferried to and from the ship by small crafts called bumboats. About half were powered by teams of strong stewards armed with long oars; the other half were powered by electric motors coupled with a battery system. Each were sizable craft on their own and could hold a great many, but with everyone crowding to go ashore, the queues grew long.

"Ashton's people," I said. "Wanted to kill me. Tried."

"Carter's cross!" Hagen nearly shouted. A few people in the queue turned to look at us. One lady glowered.

"I'm fine," I said. "Just bruised."

"We need to guard you as well?" Taft asked.

"No," I said.

"Wal, I think you—" Hagen began, stopping as I held up a hand.

"I'm fine," I said. "The Deeperists helped me out."

"We could put a roader with you," Taft offered. "Eli seems uncomfortable in the VIP section, I'm sure he'd be more than willing to—"

"I said I was fine," I said. The launch line shifted forward.

"I don't like this," Hagen said.

"Look, I'll give you the full rundown later. Can we just talk about something else?" I argued.

Hagen narrowed his eyes and stared at me. I glared at him from around the compress. It had warmed in the last hour but was still cool, and pressure felt good. I let out a long, performed sigh. "You're not going to let this go, are you?"

"My friend shows up with half his face swollen, tells me he was attacked by cultists, and you expect me just to let it go?"

People were looking at us and I didn't feel like explaining the whole situation to the crowd. The bits with Ashton were uh, tricky, to explain.

"He said he'd tell us later," Taft said, one of her eyes squinting at me.

Hagen shook his head. His mop of hair shifted with the motion. "Yeah, no. Sorry. Not going to let that go."

"Hagen," Taft admonished.

"You're a bastard," I said, forcing a grin that probably looked more like a grimace. My insult diffused the tension between my friends. Hagen didn't know Taft, not the way his sister did.

Hagen clicked his tongue and raised his index finger. "Correction. I'm a *concerned* bastard."

"You both are holding up the line is what you are," said Taft.

Turning, I realized just how far the column had gotten ahead of us. We all moved forward until we stopped just inside the doorway that led to the bumboat boarding ramp. In a brief instant, the people ahead of us disappeared into the daylight.

"Next," came a call from a small booth erected next to the door. There was a level active gate in front of the booth, and inside was another steward, a tall maero woman wearing the white uniform of the *Gamble's* staff. She looked bored. She didn't even mention my face or the compress held against it. "How many?"

I turned and looked at my friends. "Three."

"Sixty Lovatine lira," said the woman. "Or twenty Victory marks."

"Sixty!" Taft groaned.

The steward rolled her eyes and exhaled. "Twenty apiece. For three, that's sixty. Fare covers the return."

"What if I'm staying?"

"Then I suppose it's a twenty-lira one-way ticket, ma'am."

Taft grumbled something about robbery, and I slid the money across the small table.

"Here's your tickets," said the maero. She handed me three tickets and flipped the lever that opened the gate. The whole process felt mechanical and impersonal. The entire exchange hadn't even fazed the steward.

Beyond the gate, the *Gamble* had a small platform with extended metal stairs that ran down the side of the outer hull and attached to a bobbing floating dock. From there, passengers would transfer to bumboats. One was idling there now, its outboard motor humming pleasantly.

I ducked, passing through the door and into the light of the open deck where I got my first glimpse of Empress. Whatever I had expected, it wasn't this. For my whole life, all I knew of Victory was an enormous cement wall, watched over by soaring gun emplacements and black-clad guards wearing masks. Tall tales swirled about, passed from roader to roader, which had further muddied the vision. Depending on who you asked, Victory was everything from a utopian paradise to an authoritarian police state, and it only got more bizarre from there.

The city before me was not what I expected. It wasn't a massive nest of layers like Lovat. Nor was it the broad sprawl of Syringa. It lacked the sleepy prairie town feel of Robber's Roost. It was coastal, but it wasn't like the small island communities that made up Bridgetown.

It was familiar, despite being foreign. Peering into the water, I could see the remnants of a city below the waves, ancient buildings swept under after the Aligning. Not dissimilar from the Sunk back home. A few were tall enough to still rise above the water, but most were broken, pounded down by years of surf and weather.

Boats were everywhere. There were a few larger vessels like the *Gamble*. Several sported the flags of Bridgetown and one displayed Syringan colors, but most of the others were small personal craft. Buoys in a wide variety of colors and patterns bobbed above the sunken city, indicating all manner of things below. It was a common language the aquatics liked to use—one I hadn't taken time to learn.

"Watch your head," said the steward. He tapped the top of the hatch with his crowbar. Ducking, I stepped off the *Gamble* and onto the bumboat and found a seat near a window. Hagen sat behind me, Taft next to me. Her mass pressed me against the bulkhead.

Once filled, the bumboat slowly drifted away from the *Gamble* and towards Empress.

Beyond the sunken city, waves crashed against what I thought was a reef. It took me a moment before I realized it was artificial. A colossal wall—pre-Aligning by the look of it—had been erected underwater and was attempting to hold the sea at bay.

If the builders had intended for it to stop the water, they had failed. The area beyond was flooded. Ancient towers once erected on dry ground were surrounded by the smooth ocean waves of the artificial bay. The towers were remarkably well preserved. Was this what Lovat would have looked like if not for the levels? My city conquered the sky. Here the sky was a part of the sprawl.

The sea had turned Empress into a city of canals, each block its own little cluster of islands. Vegetation grew from every conceivable corner and added a lush verdancy to the place. It was as if the city floated on isles of leafy green clouds.

"I didn't expect it to be so pretty."

"You ain't kiddin'," Taft said. Her voice was hushed, almost in reverence.

"I'd heard stories, but they don't prepare you for this," said Hagen. He motioned out the window.

The bumboat slowly made its way through a gap in the artificial reef and into the tranquil waters beyond. The city grew up around us. It was my city reborn—as if Level Two didn't have the rest of Lovat sitting on its shoulders. Most of the buildings were twenty or thirty stories. Enormous blue banners bearing the golden sun and crown of Victory hung from roofs and shifted in the ocean breeze.

Most of the vegetation was evergreen fir and pine, but thick deciduous trees were mixed among them. They leaned out over the canals, the spring buds just forming on the tips of their naked branches. Mossy tendrils hung down and reached down to stir the brackish waters. The gray clouds far above were less dark than they had been in previous days. I wondered if we might get a glimpse of the sun before the day's end.

Shaded walkways and bridges connected each building to its neighbors. Crowds of people—mostly human and umbra—milled about. Others pushed their way down the canal-streets on narrow boats. The pilots used long quant poles decorated with colored ribbon to propel their crafts through the canals.

Beyond the canals, and slowly disappearing from view, was the upper city. High Empress, as it was known. The buildings there were rooted on dry land, with paved streets that curved in tight switchbacks up the steep hill. The same leafy green vegetation puffed up around the buildings there as well, though they had an air of solidity to them that the buildings along the canals were missing.

Hagen leaned between Taft and me and pointed to the upper city. "Apparently, before the Aligning, the Empress city fathers decided to move the Parliament building brick by brick into the hill above the canals. Parliament is still there today. Most of High Empress is erected with it at the center."

"Why'd they move it?" I wondered.

"Not sure. But it'd be underwater now if it had remained in its original location. So the decision was prescient. We passed over its original location as we entered the city."

The bumboat pulled up next to a long dock near an inner harbor that in turn led to a small building built on piles that sat above the water. CUSTOMS was written in enormous block in Strutten on the outside, and below it ALL VISITORS MUST REGISTER.

Inside, we found ourselves in yet another line. This one snaked through guide ropes that ended at the custom agents' stations. More signs dotted the area: ENTRY was apparently NOT GUARANTEED, and we were encouraged to HAVE PAPERS READY. I hoped my recent incident with the cultists and the shovel to my face wouldn't prevent me from getting into the city.

"How's security duty?" I asked Taft. Black-clad Protection officers moved around the edges of the crowds, their faces obscured by full-faced featureless helmets. No one paid them any attention. The line was moving rather quickly despite the sudden influx of visitors. Only the humanoid species of Lovat were represented.

"Easy," she said. "Boring. There's plenty of high rollers up on the upper decks, but they're generally uninterested in the VIPs— more concerned with losing their lira in the casinos or finding one of the high-priced escorts for the evening. Crew don't like the suits, though."

I ignored the last comment. "Feels odd being separated from everything."

Bell Caravans was my responsibility. Being decoupled from my crew and caravan ached. So much of my identity was tied up with my occupation. The tattoos on each of my forearms were wagon wheels, a symbol of my career and my father's work as a wheelwright. Caravanning had been one of my constants, and for now that had been snatched away.

"Wensem and Hannah are overseeing the exchange. They didn't want the full crew, so it's just them and Pascal."

Eli Pascal worked on-again, off-again security for Bell Caravans. One of Wensem's preferred hires. A wiry dimanian with stubby devil-horns and a cool relaxed demeanor that made him easy to like. He was also one hell of a shot. A born drifter, Eli was tough to pin down. He was a regular inasmuch as he always had a job with us if he wanted it, but there was never a guarantee he'd be in town. Last we worked together was the Wilem, Black & Bright job, and that felt like a lifetime ago.

The custom line rolled forward and we with it.

"What do you want to see?" Hagen asked.

Taft rubbed her chin. "I'd like to find a spice merchant. Empress has a wide variety that's tough to find in Lovat. Green flower pepper, cassia, cardamom—plants that don't grow local. Rare it gets to us. You?"

"I'm up for whatever," said Hagen. "I never expected I'd be here. Empress! Of all places." He chuckled, then rubbed the back of his neck and flashed a sheepish smile. "I mean... I'd love to stop in at any trinket dealers, of course. Oh, book shops, too."

Eventually, the line deposited us at its head, and then we were called forward. Several custom stations sat side by side at the top of a broad set of stairs—small boxes, no bigger than a directory agent booth with glass windows and a shuttered opening. Behind the custom stations was another row of black-clad Protection people lined up along the back wall. As visitors entered, one would peel off and follow at a short distant. Victory wasn't taking its security lightly.

We approached the small box. Inside sat a stern-faced human customs agent with a drooping mustache. His skin was dark but his hair ruddy. Redheads were incredibly uncommon among humans, though the trait had begun to reappear in pockets. The redhead wore the black leather uniform of Victory militia, the sun-and-crown patch above his left breast. A small scar was visible on his forehead.

"Papers." His voice sounded tinny. He glanced at the three of us.

We slid our papers across the small counter and through a slit below the window. The man picked them up and regarded them suspiciously.

"Names?" he asked.

"Waldo Emerson Bell," I said.

"Taft," said Taft.

"Just one name?" the agent narrowed his eyes.

"It's what my daddy named me," said Taft.

The customs agent looked at Hagen.

"Hagen Baptiste Jessime Dubois," Hagen said.

Taft and I stared at him.

"What?" he said.

"*Four* names?" I said.

The customs agent was having none of our banter. He interrupted with a snarl. "Where you from?"

"Lovat," we all said.

"Came over on the *Gamble*?"

"Yes."

"Here on business?"

I leaned in. "Hagen and I are here to see the sites. Taft is working with a security firm on Lovatine business. I believe it's listed as—" I winced as I said the name Hannah had chosen. "Guardian Security."

"This says you're also working for Guardian Security, Mister Bell," The agent shook the pages in his hands.

"It does, but I recently stepped away from my position."

"Why?"

"Injury," I lied. Well, sorta lied. Half-lied. I pointed to my face. It was an easy excuse.

The customs agent narrowed his eyes. "What happened to your face?"

"Fell down a flight of stairs. Didn't have my sea legs yet. I'm used to caravan work and—"

"Fell?"

"Yeah. One hell of a tumble." I made a hand gesture as if I was trying to explain, but the agent made a dismissive wave, and I stopped.

"Seen a doctor?" the agent asked.

"Just a bonesaw on the *Gamble*," I said. It had been a quick trip. She had given me low-dose painkillers and told me to ice it. "Was hoping to visit one of the Victory doctors I've heard so much about."

The agent leaned back and tilted his head. His scowl deepened. He held that pose for a long time. My breathing sounded heavy in my ears. My skin went clammy. There was no valid reason for me to go inside. If I was rejected, I could go back to the *Gamble*. But a part of me didn't want to be turned around. Hagen's enthusiasm had infected me and I was eager to see this city of canals.

Then the agent was gone.

I stepped back. A knot caught in my throat. The yellow-clad figure from the wasteland was *inside* the booth. Its pale mask regarded me with slow, almost serene movements. It clutched its hands together in front of its chest. The robes billowed in their slow-motion dance, filling the small booth, making the mask and hands look like they were floating in a sea of yellow fabric. Then one of the long hands flashed out and slapped against the glass. I jumped, my own hand going to my chest. The long fingers spread and I could hear them rubbing against the inside of the window.

Taft's steady hand was on my back. She hissed in my ear. "Wal, what's—"

"All right," the agent said. The sound of a mechanical stamp repeated three times. *Cha-chunk. Cha-chunk. Cha-chunk.* He slid the customs paperwork across the counter, along with three golden ribbons. I blinked, confused. The yellow figure had disappeared as quickly as it came. The customs agent remained where he had always been. He looked the same: brown skin, red hair, stern expression, tired eyes. His voice came out in a practiced drone. "Please stay with your escort at all times and wear your visitor ribbons where we can see them. Failure to do so will…"

It was hard to focus on the words. The world around me wavered as if distorted by a heatwave.

"You okay?" whispered Taft as Hagen thanked the agent and took our paperwork, pinning a ribbon to his chest.

I nodded. The custom agent regarded me suspiciously. I tried to straighten myself as best I could. Forced a smile I didn't feel. Told myself to pretend nothing had happened. It was tough, but I managed.

"Let's go," Taft said, and together we followed Hagen past the customs booth and into a plaza beyond. He passed flimsy ribbons to each of us. 'Visitor' ran down the length of each ribbon in block Strutten, blue ink against the gold.

A silent Protection officer in all black disengaged from a line along the walls and followed us. Their face was obscured by the sleek black helmet with a reflective black facemask. Still reeling from my encounter with the yellow-clad figure, I hardly gave our new shadow a second look.

"What happened back there?" Hagen asked in a whisper. His eyes darted over his shoulder toward our new friend.

A huge sign had been erected above the plaza. It read: EMPRESS, and below it QUEEN OF THE TERRITORIES. Signage had been set up to greet visitors and direct them toward specific districts. Security forces were present here as well—standing along the edges, watching everyone, faces hidden.

"I need to sit down," I said. My head was swimming.

The three of us made our way to a wooden bench that faced out to the artificial bay. The hard wood slapped against my tailbone as I sat. Our shadow stood a little ways off, hands clasped behind their back.

The stink that had plagued Lovat was present here as well, though a fresh breeze kept it at bay a little better than the narrow confines of Lovat's warrens. Funny that this was the time I noticed it.

"What happened?"

"Saw the yellow-clad figure again," I said. My mouth was dry. I had a difficult time forming words. "Only for a moment. It was in the booth. Like it had replaced that customs guy. It touched the glass and then"—I snapped my fingers—"it was gone."

"The wasteland again?" Hagen asked.

"No, this was different. It was more like…" I thought about it. "Like the gargoyles. Appearing. Disappearing. I've never seen them replace a person, though. That was…" I couldn't finish my sentence. A shiver traveled down my spine.

"Oh, Carter's cross," Taft grumbled.

I held my head in my hands and rubbed my eyes. A headache was coming on—I could feel it. My brain was still struggling to wrap itself around the break in reality I had just witnessed. It replaced a *person*, entirely replaced him; it was unnerving.

"Mister Bell? Mister Bell! It is you!" The voice was friendly but it sent ice running through my veins. It was out of place— wrong somehow. An intrusion.

I looked up to see Samuel Danforth step in front of me, flanked by two men—humans, in dark suits. They looked more like outfit enforcers than charity workers. A pair of Victory shadows moved behind them as well drifting to stand next to our own, who hadn't moved since I sat down. Danforth wore a dark-blue suit, which highlighted his yellow visitor ribbon. Above that, and pinned to his lapel was a small circular badge, the red lotus mark of the Camalote Group on a white background.

"Hi, Mister Danforth," I said, not feeling as cheery as I sounded. "Just get in?" I didn't want to talk. I just wanted to figure this out.

"Me? Oh no. No, no, no. I came over earlier with Connie. She's all snugged away in her rooms at the Saanich Hotel. Preparing for her meetings. Exciting stuff! Your people are there with her. I stepped away to get the lay of the land. Was heading to a neighborhood called"—he snapped his fingers—"what was it called again?"

He turned and looked at one of the two men who flanked him.

"Dunsmuir, sir," the suit responded, his voice flat.

"Ah, yeah, Dunsmuir. Dunsmuir! This is a remarkably organized city. And clean!" He whistled. "Nothing like Lovat." Danforth chuckled, paused, and regarded me with an inquisitive look that shifted to one of concern. "Hey, what's this I hear about you stepping away from Guardian Security?"

I stood and stretched. My head throbbed but I forced an embarrassed chuckle and ran my hand through my hair. I was glad I changed my shirt. I'd have looked a mess otherwise. Danforth's ceaseless talking eased me. I smiled at him.

His eyes went wide as he saw the left side of my face. "By the Firsts, man. What happened."

He absently touched his own cheek as he stared at me.

"Took a tumble," I lied. "Slipped on a stair and…"

I gestured, spinning one hand over the other.

Danforth winced. "Oh, I'm sorry. Awful. Just awful."

"Just cosmetic," I said.

"Well, it's quite the shiner."

"I'll be okay."

"Just tell people 'They should see the other guy,'" Danforth laughed.

Taft, Hagen and I joined him, but I wasn't feeling it. My mind went to the cultists. *They really shouldn't*, I thought.

Danforth snapped his fingers and waggled one at me, his pinky outstretched along with it. "You know, why not seek out the services of Empress's medical facilities? Some of the best in the Territories, it's said."

"Yeah," I nodded. "Heard the same."

Danforth gave me a politician's smile and a concerned nod. Both felt disingenuous from one angle but sincere from the other. The guy had a way about him—a trustworthy skeeviness. He was a paradox. Politicians, man. "Well, I must run. You rest up. Watch where you plant those feet. Hopefully, in a few days, you'll feel better."

"Thanks."

"I'll be seeing you around, Mister Bell."

He reached out and clapped me on the shoulder. His steady hand wrapped around my bicep for the briefest of instants. At that moment—the most inopportune of moments—I felt the pull. It rushed at me like an oncoming monorail. The heat from the broken sun baked my neck and shoulders.

I glanced at Hagen and then Taft, my eyes wide. Hoping they'd see the panic that was beginning to flood me. A hot wind tickled my neck and mussed my hair. Danforth's smile widened as he turned. I slumped back down to the bench as he and his two men stepped away. Gritty sand scoured my cheeks and the smell of an old dead city was in my nose.

Taft's broad face loomed in my vision. Behind it floated a concerned Hagen. But they were fading. Gone to gray, along with the green city behind them. The world was stretching, flattening. There was nothing I could do. Everything drained of its color, and then the wasteland took me.

TWELVE

The vastness swallowed me. I was a speck in an unknowable and immense expanse. Eerie howls drifted on the hot wind that tussled my hair. The sound sent a corkscrew shiver down my spine and goose pimples across my arms. I was back.

This time, though, there was something different. This time I didn't feel the bench. I didn't see my friends leaning down to check on me. Taft's hand had been on my shoulder, but the pressure was gone. I couldn't hear the clatter of traffic on the Empress boardwalks. I couldn't hear the shouts from the boat pilots or Danforth's shoes on the boardwalk in front of me. My reality was not binary; it was singular. That other was quickly becoming fuzzy memory, drifting and disappearing like a half-remembered dream. I was *here*. No half measures, not this time.

The sky above was devoid of clouds. There was nothing around me. The land was flat—the horizon a perfect line. No mountain, no hills, no slopes. The only blemishes were the nearby crumbled ruins and the distant wreckage. This was a vast nothingness that stretched everywhere and nowhere, and I stood at its center.

Somewhere distant a coyote howled. I looked around me and saw no dogs—not even their shadows or silhouettes. No gargoyles. No strange yellow-clad figures. Past travels had lasted mere moments—information exchanged, and then I had been whisked away.

But something had changed, and that difference was everything.

I began to walk. My knee was no longer stiff and painful. My face didn't hurt. Small blessings. The land passed beneath me. Endless mudcrack, tiny islands with edges curled inward. They crumbled to dust under the weight of my heavy roader boots.

What was this? I wondered. Where was this? When was this? My assumption had always been that it was all visions—either the foggy glimpse of a far-flung future or the echoes of a distant past. Like I was some oracle expected to prophesy. Now I wasn't so sure.

This wasteland felt *real*. I couldn't deny it any longer. The ground beneath my feet felt as substantial as the crumbled gravel of the Big Ninety—or so I thought. Here I could dig my toe into the ground, watch the dust lift around it. Here I could smell the sulfur and taste the ash. Here I could listen to the wind and the distant howls. Maybe I was always here? Perhaps Lovat and the Big Ninety were the dream?

My walk continued. The sun beat down. I was wearing a red keff, faded from use but soft and thick. I pulled the cloth up over my head and tucked it beneath the collar of my jacket, wearing it as a hood. It partially kept the broken sun and its heat off me.

I needed a drink. My mouth was dry. My throat ached.

Nothing changed. Time was funny here, impossible to track. The sun never moved.

My shadow splayed out before me, drifting before disappearing and then emerging on another side. Sometimes it doubled, often it tripled, occasionally it would quadruple. Four shadow Waldos with me at the center like I was a damned windrose. Once they swirled around me like the eye of a storm, the shapes of my arms and legs drifting inward like I was in a constant tumble.

Only the passing ruins marked my progress. They'd fade in from the horizon, small black stains against the sky. Then they would rematerialize and color would flood into them—usually the faded browns and amber of ancient dust, sometimes a ruddy red, and once a granite gray. Then they'd cloud past, silent and impassive, and disappear behind me.

I didn't know where I was going. Only emptiness lay behind and the city ahead. Unlike the ruins, it grew no larger. No matter how far I walked, I drew no closer. But it was there. The bones of a dead city I supposedly knew. One I supposedly loved.

Then there was the old familiar scent on the air. I had grown up in the shadows of volcanos. The Territories burned with them. There was nearby Takobia with its small summit crater. Smoking Mountain to the south. Angry Kulshan, far to the north of Lovat, always rumbled and smoldered. Hellgate to the west was built atop an enormous fissure that some people suggested was connected to the Aligning. Lovat, always hungry for electricity, drew its power from the massive Talol Geothermal Plant, constructed in the pre-Aligning world atop the hollowed out remains of a volcanic caldera. There were many more, and all had the same smell: sulfuric ash.

I pulled the keff close to my mouth, shielding my inhalations from the drifting particulates that floated around me like sad snow. The keff, loosely woven, did little to help. I coughed, and my mouth grew more parched.

"He... is coming... ming... ng..."

The voice took me by surprise. It came like an echo. A distant whisper caught and distorted by the wind. I could hear it as clear as if it had been breathed into my ear.

"...you smell it on the wind... ind... d..."

An old conversation. A memory from another world, yet also from this one. My neck cracked as I tried to locate the source. But I saw nothing. What did I expect? This place was off somehow—*wrong*. Nothing worked here the way it worked in my reality—my original reality. That dreamy place I considered home.

I tried to imagine the faces of my friends. Ground myself in names I remembered. But recalling that world was becoming more difficult. The people there were ghosts. Fleeting shadows.

"...not of our bloodline... ambition... bition... ion..."

It echoed off nothing, but it echoed. The words reverberated inside my head and slammed against brain and bone. Gooseflesh rippled down my arms and across my back and chest. I knew that voice—Ashton's voice, but it was distorted, warped like an old jazz recording.

I continued to walk. How much time had passed? Hours? Days? Did I have any other options? I didn't know if there was anything more I could do—anything more I *should* do. Walking was what I did. Guiding was my occupation. I could read the land. I could see the dangers ahead and react well before they became a problem. But here? Here I wasn't so sure. Here I didn't know how the weather worked, how the sun worked. Did this place even have a moon? How could you navigate without stars, or landmarks, or the familiar?

"…the first of Firsts… my grandfather… father… ather… er…"

The ground was hot beneath my feet. The horizon grew darker—just slightly, but yes, darker. It shimmered like the edge of the world was aflame. I didn't stop. I walked, machine-like, toward nothing in particular and yet toward everything. If I stopped, it would end. I'd die here. Somehow, I knew that was possible. I had to keep walking.

"I'm not going to stop," I said, to no one.

But something heard. Something reacted. I could feel it buzz through my skull. The sun warmed. The land rippled—not heat ripples, but as if it was the sea. It undulated, forming waves of dust that cascaded in the distance, throwing up black clouds that were driven by the wind.

I walked. The ground beneath my feet was as solid as ever. The echoey conversation continuing its play through my mind in half-whispers and partial words.

"I'm not going to stop," I said again. My voice cracked. My tongue was thick, my body hot. Sweat rolled down my face. My eyes burned, stinging with sweat and strained by the constant sun. Reality withdrew from me. I could feel its disgust as I walked atop its skin. But I trudged on. Moving forward with a purpose.

Shapes formed in the distance. New shapes. At first, I dismissed them as hallucinations. But they were persistent, unyielding. They weren't the broken blocks of ruined monuments, but something more comprehensible. As I continued to walk, the shapes grew into defined forms. Buildings. They were buildings. The heat made them waver like a mirage, and I saw their reflections in the hardpan. But they were there. They were real.

They weren't much to look at. Shacks mostly, all a single story. All were unadorned, with flat roofs and tiny opened windows cut into the walls. A few ruined shutters hung next to them and rocked in the wind. A rock-ringed well sat at the center.

A well.

By the Firsts, a well!

Water!

If I'd had the energy, I would have run. But I was barely keeping upright. It was all I could do to keep moving. I stumbled forward, the end of my walk in sight.

More time passed.

The village drew ever closer. There were fifteen buildings. A few of them were low-slung and barnlike, but most were pockmarked shanties. Wooden walls had faded, bleached into a dull gray by the relentless sun. All faced inward toward the well like it was a monument. Perhaps it was.

When I entered the town, the wasteland grew silent. The wind stilled. The echoing conversation faded. The coyotes choked on their voices. The only sound here was my boots on the ground and my ragged breathing. When I reached the well, I collapsed against it.

I could smell the water below, the scent crisp and minerally.

The rope on the well was new. I pulled, feeling a weight resist me. It took the last of my energy, but I managed to draw the bucket upward. Falling to my knees, I cradled it.

Water. It was filled with water! Beautiful water!

With my hand as a cup, I pulled it to my mouth. Slurped, then submerged my face. The water cooled me instantly. I sucked in big gulps, swallowed. It rushed down my throat and filled my stomach. When I pulled my head out, I inhaled a deep lungful of air. Smacked my lips. I felt reborn, alive once more. With a whoop of celebration, I upended the bucket over my head. It soaked my keff, ran down my face, my beard. I wanted to laugh. I felt like crying.

I dropped the bucked back into the well. Heard it thud against the sides and then splash in the water below. Leaning back against the rock wall, I closed my eyes, breathed, and tried not to dwell on everything happening to me.

Exhaustion settled in my joints. Grinning, I raised a hand and lifted a middle finger at the thing beyond the horizon. A small but defiant act, one I felt I had earned.

"Well, you're mighty different from the last one."

My eyes snapped open. A man loomed above me, hands in his pockets. He was facing me, his back to the horizon.

I awkwardly lowered my hand and squinted up at him. Should I run? Was this a fight or flight scenario? There was a time I kept to a code—bizarre little rules I manufactured to keep myself safe on the trail—a system I had dragged with me into the city. My haphazard rush to the well had violated a few of them, and those mistakes had allowed someone to get the drop on me.

"Ain't your enemy, if that's what yer thinkin'," the man said, reading my mind.

He stepped a bit closer, squatted down. He was ancient, sallow faced, with a large aquiline nose and wild eyes. He reminded me of Ashton—not the Ashton from before, but the broken old man. Like Ashton, much of his cheeks and chin were covered by a wild beard that had knotted and clumped. Splotchy tattoos, simple circles long faded, were drawn above his eyes, two on each side, another centered on his long forehead, and one lower, so it rested between his eyes. The tattoos were the faded blue of ancient ink and had gone soft at their edges, resembling birthmarks or bruises. He wore a wide-brimmed straw hat with a shallow crown, dirty overalls, and nothing more. Even his feet were bare, the toes dry and cracked, the nails thick and as yellow as the ruins. I expected him to smell, but he didn't. If anything he was devoid of odor.

"Who are you?" I demanded.

His shoulders shook with a silent laugh.

"Don't remember." The man had a soft voice—kind, with a slight accent I couldn't place.

"Where am I?"

"I call it The Empty. Suppose it has other names. But that's the most fittin' now. What do you call it?"

"The Wasteland," I said. Realizing, at this moment, I was giving this world a name.

He clicked his tongue. "'Suppose that's fittin' too."

He said nothing more, just squatted in front of me and watched me stare. He seemed friendly enough, but so far my interactions out here had been with Firsts and gargoyles, so it was a bleak comparison. I hadn't run into friendly people.

After a moment, the man pulled a pack of cigarettes out from his overalls' chest pocket, pulled one of the white sticks free, tapped it on the back of his hand, then lit it with a match he fished from another pocket.

"Smoke?" he offered, holding the smoldering cigarette toward me. "It's tobacco, not that sour stuff."

I shook my head.

"Suit yourself," he said. He observed the pool of water that was quickly being absorbed by the ground around me. "Good water here. Clean. Cold. Never runs out. Nope. Never." He gazed over his shoulder, staring toward the horizon with a bemused expression before turning back to me. "Say, you hungry?"

I was and said so.

"I got food. Canned stuff, mostly. But it's fine." He offered a hand. I stared at it for a long moment before I accepted. He helped me off the ground, springing back like an anur and landing with a little bounce.

"Thanks," I said. I wasn't sure what else to say.

"Just being neighborly. Follow me."

We crossed the open space that surrounded the well and ducked into the larger of the shanties that faced inward. A strange set of glyphs were carved above the door. A language I didn't recognize. Below, in Strutten, someone had scrawled

'Umr at-Tawil in fading capital letters. They weren't words I knew—read more like nonsense. We passed beneath.

The inside was as odorless as its occupant but was filled with a variety of objects. A table and chairs. A bed with clean linens. Shelves stocked with canned goods in brightly colored tins. A stove. A sink. Posters hung on a few exposed walls, faded paintings of landscapes mostly. Mountains and hills, once bright green and lush—a fantasy in a place like this.

The man busied himself at his shelves, whistling softly as he pulled down one can and then another. After he had selected a few cans, he proceeded to grab a pair of pots that he set on his stove.

"Long time since I seen a Guardian," the man said. He was rocking a can opener over the lids of several cans and dumping the contents into the pots. I watched him in silence for some time, this strange old man eking out his existence in the middle of nothing. How was this possible? Who was he?

"What did you mean when you said I was different from the last one?"

He stopped staring at a pot of sliced carrots and turned and looked at me with a puzzled expression. He almost looked offended at the question.

"Yer a Guardian, ain'tcha?" he clicked his tongue, then mumbled something else in a language I didn't recognize.

The title was a millstone around my neck. What was the point in lying? This man knew the answer even before I confirmed it.

"Yes," I said.

"Well, you ain't the first. And you're sure-as-shit different from the last."

"Who was last?"

He paused. Looked up at the ceiling before responding.

"A woman," he said. He waved the spoon to illustrate his point. "Different than you'd expect. Big dress. Mound of hair. Pale, as if her skin ain't never seen sun. Prim and proper-like on the outside. Like she had stepped off some stage from before the Aligning. She had these fiery eyes, the sort that'd stare into your soul." He snapped his fingers, laughed. "She was a quick one. Before you ask—don't remember her name. Bad with names." He paused and thought about that before adding, "Bad with a lot of things."

Something inside me flipped. Pieces connected, clicking together like magnets. There had been *another*. I vaguely recalled Ashton mentioning someone else. At the time I had ignored it. But this strange desert dweller had stirred up the past with the same carefree indifference with which he was now agitating the warming neon-orange carrots.

"What happened to her?"

"You ask a lot of questions, hamiya," he said. "Eat first. Then we can talk."

We ate in silence. The man wolfed down his food and watched me with his wild eyes. Our meal was canned carrots, canned green beans, and rubbery little sausages that came from, where else, a can. I couldn't remember the last time I ate. When you're starving, any meal is the best meal you ever ate.

Once he had finished, the man pushed away his plate, leaned back in his chair, let out a satisfied belch, and patted his stomach. Then he lit another cigarette and watched me as he smoked.

"Thanks for the food," I said, eager to get to my questions.

He waved my comment away. "Neighborly."

"So, about the woman…"

"The last Guardian? What about her?"

"Who was she?"

"I told you, I don't know. Don't remember it all. She was quick, though. Quicker on the uptake than you are. Realized what she was earlier. Realized what she could do." He tapped the side of his head with the fingers holding his cigarette. "Drove her mad, though. Always does. Yer kind ain't supposed to happen. Hard for your feeble minds to comprehend shit like this."

He was talking in riddles, statements I didn't fully grasp because I didn't know the history behind his words. He knew this. I could see it in his wild eyes. But he wasn't about to clue me in. Was this a game for him? Should I feel rage? I didn't, but I couldn't help but wonder.

"So, who are you?"

He laughed at that. "I'm me, son. All I've ever been."

"What do the words above the doorframe mean?"

"Words?"

"The Strutten. The glyphs. 'Umr at-Tawil—"

He waved a hand dismissing the question. "Graffiti."

I considered challenging him, then decided better of it. Hagen would have known. Samantha as well. A pang speared my heart—for a moment I missed them. But something deep inside me told me that they didn't exist. They were all in my head. Figments of imagination—nothing more. That hurt, like a part of my heart had torn free. I was alone and adrift in a sea of shifting sand.

My next question came out wooden. "How do you live out here?"

The man frowned and looked up at the ceiling, his head bobbing back and forth as he considered my question. Finally, he leaned back and spoke. "I scavenge, mostly. Not the dead city, mind—nothing there. No one goes there. Not anymore."

"Other settlements?" I asked.

"You could say that. What is it you do?"

"Caravans," I said, my old candor coming back. "I work as a caravan master."

"Long time since I've seen caravans," he said. He clicked his tongue again. "Long time. You run circuits? Privately employed? Take freelance work?"

"Little of this, little of that."

"Honest living, caravans." He looked wistful for a moment, staring at the glowing end of his cigarette.

"It is," I agreed. "What happened here?"

He smiled. "Not like this back home, is it?"

"No," I admitted. I realized, as I spoke the word, I was acknowledging that the other reality existed and that it was somehow as real as this place. Warring paradoxes. A break inside me widened further, yawning open. It was impossible to separate facts and fiction. But I couldn't help it. Somehow, for a brief instant, I knew I was in Empress as well as here. I was just shut off and cut out.

"Not yet," he said with a dreamy air. "But it came close once. Damn close."

I squinted at him and considered what he was saying. Was he talking about the Aligning?

He waved a hand. "They happened. We happened. Us? Doesn't matter. They used this place up. Sucked it dry. Drained it of life. It's what they do, what *he* does. It's what they've always done. Once finished, the hunger only grows. Then they turned their eyes elsewhere, other times, other worlds, other existences. They push through. Little at first. Then more. Eventually the walls break. Eventually they come through. Then they spill forth, and the cycle continues." He wheeled a finger around in the air.

I blinked at him, beginning to comprehend what he was saying. The Aligning. The Firsts. The previous Guardian.

"Carter's cross," I croaked.

The man took a slow drag from his cigarette and blew swirling patterns into the dead air above his head. Then his eyes met mine, and he smiled a sad smile. "Maddening, ain't it?"

THIRTEEN

I began to call him Tawil—stealing his name from a portion of the Strutten graffito above his door frame. It was easy enough to remember and calling him 'the man' didn't sit right in my head. He was adamant he couldn't remember his name. The name suited him, and he didn't seem to mind.

It was impossible to tell Tawil's age. He could be sixty, he could be a hundred—hell, he could be a thousand. It was clear Tawil was old. Very old. He claimed he had lived in the village his whole life. Watched the world change around him, as mountains slowly disappeared and forests petrified. Watched as the water was drained away and then vanished entirely. Somehow his village had remained, one small constant as the world around him shifted and fell until it was lost to time.

I moved into a shack near his that had more glyphs above the door, below more Strutten—a single word I didn't recognize: HAMIYA. It was the name he called me during our first meal. I didn't know what it meant. But I figured as long as I was here, this was where I belonged.

Inside the space was much like Tawil's house. Shelves, stove, bed, table, posters. Like his, it was remarkably preserved. Untouched by the Wasteland. The posters here were different. Where his were landscapes, mine were tourist advertisements for cities. The words were unknown to me—familiar but alien. Not quite Strutten. The posters showed brightly colored images of what I assumed were Lovat, Syringa, Hellgate, and even Bridge-town, but there was something off. They were wrong, somehow. Different names, slightly altered skylines. A blue sky burned above each city. There were no levels. No flooded ruins. No wide deserted streets. Smiling people—humans, specifically—promenaded down boardwalks, below clocktowers, and beneath skyscrapers. Among them were odd black smudges. I tried to rub them away, thinking they were stains, but they were a part of the illustrations. They were hooded figures. Gargoyles.

When I asked Tawil, he waved a dismissive hand, a trail of cigarette smoke tracking the motion in the air. "No need to fear the gaunts. They can't touch ya. Not really. Been lost since the death of their master, cloakin' themselves in mourning garments and the like. Not much more than parasites now; cling to whoever would take 'em. They deal only in shadows and whispers. That ain't much in the way of currency."

As far as I could decipher, he had a point. But I didn't want to look at them. I pulled the posters down, rolled them up, and stuck them beneath my bed where I wouldn't have to look at them. I forgot them and made the house my own.

I slept in the bed, ate the canned food off the shelves, used the restroom. For a while, it all felt normal. Boring, but normal. Like Tawil's, my house was well stocked and amply provisioned.

After a few days, I notice that the shelves never ran dry. I'd take a can from the shelf—peas, say—and count the remainder. One. Two. Three. Then I'd prepare my meal, eat my food, and return to the shelve to find four cans of peas. Four when I was sure there should be only three.

At first, I ignored it. Just a miscount. But it happened again. Then again. Then again. That sort of discrepancy can eat at you. I felt half-mad already, and this just pushed me closer to the edge. Was I wrong? Had I miscounted? For days I continued to count the cans. One. Two. Three. But then, later... *four*. My mind disagreed. No. There had always been four cans. There would always be four cans. But I knew that was incorrect.

I slept fitfully after that. Most mornings, I woke from dreams of a flooded city crowded with people. Around me, the Wasteland, the village, and my house continued immutable.

Tawil had no answers. He just repeated what I already knew as fact. "There should be four," he'd say, bored. "Was four. Always four. Don't worry about it."

But I knew it was a lie. Attempting to put it out of my mind didn't help. It lingered. It gnawed at me, slowly eroding my sanity. I was a creature of this reality—a man of the Wasteland. I should accept what I saw. But didn't what I see matter? Wasn't my truth reality? Or was reality governed by something else? Maybe *someone* else. Tawil perhaps? Another First? That monster on the horizon? The idea made my head ache.

At first, I was sure I was only an annoyance for Tawil. Me, with all my questions, and him, used to a life of seclusion, solitude, and silence.

With nothing better to do, I began to assist him in his scavenging. At first he ignored me. I'd tag along, trudging behind him in the hot sun. He'd approach one of the ruins, and the eyes in the shadow would disappear. Then he'd find a hole and descend into the bowls of the Wasteland like a miner. I waited outside until he emerged with a sack full of scrap.

This continued for a few days, until eventually I grew bored of waiting and I followed him down. After that he began to warm to me. Each trip was an echo in my memory, as if I had done this sort of work in another life. Collecting something for a merchant, and complaining to a friend that salvage in the Territories had thinned in the last century. There was something I had sold. Something special. Something to help people. I worked with... with... I couldn't remember. What was the Territories, anyway? It was all fuzzy, a half-remembered dream, playing havoc with my mind.

Together, in the chambers below the wastes, Tawil and I would scavenge relics from a bygone world. Some items Tawil would have me keep, others he'd discard. He was particular, and it was impossible for me to make sense of how he chose. A broken shovel was a must-keep. But a toolbox full of tools wasn't worth his interest.

"Need things to trade," was all he'd say, though I never saw anyone but him, let alone a trader. I never saw him do much except wander off to scavenge during the day and eat canned food at night.

Tawil slept a lot. He had no books. No instruments. He didn't sing. We had no entertainment of any kind. Hell, did he even masturbate? I doubted it. Sexual drive and desire seemed alien and separate from his existence. It felt uncomfortable just thinking about it.

Occasionally I'd catch him staring at the posters on his wall. He'd get a distant look in his eyes. One you could interpret as sorrow. When pressed, he'd always wave away my questions. "Just thinkin', I suppose."

I uncovered nothing more about my predecessor—the pale woman with a quick mind. Tawil had nothing more to offer. Said he couldn't, that it wasn't the time, or that he had forgotten. Much of his meaning was vague, drowned in his eccentricities. Past, present, and future all blended in a weird knot that was impossible to unsnarl. The tattoos on his face seemed to drift as he spoke. He'd ramble on about strange lands I'd never heard of. He'd talk about the fragility of the mortal's condition. When he really got going, he'd speak at length of 'ultimate gates' and 'silver keys' in a way that made them as immense and unknowable as the Wasteland surrounding us. He'd mention his family, mostly his children, describing them as perfectly healthy or hideously monstrous or somehow a combination of both. He struck me as sad. Lonely.

Scavenging was how we connected. In those moments, our lines of communication cleared.

Each ruin was an entry point into substantial cavities located beneath the sand. We'd clamber over the rock and descend into pits filled with bizarre and broken mazes. After some time, I began to recognize the shapes. Beneath the hardpan were pockets of buildings swallowed by the Wasteland, so ancient they had become stone and earth. Some had held against the pressure of the world bearing down on them. Others had collapsed, their treasures lost to all but someone willing to wield spade and pick.

One time we were scavenging inside a favorite location of Tawil's, an old office building—remarkably well preserved despite the cataclysm that had buried it and the time that had worn it down. Cubicle walls gone to stone crouched in a mundane grid. Inside each were metal desks that had rusted into heaps, filled with crumbling documents that turned to dust when touched.

While poking around in one of these desks, I gashed my thumb on a nasty metal curl that had peeled back as I yanked open a drawer.

"Carter's cross!" I cursed. I brought my thumb to my lips and sucked, wondering if that was the right course of action. It was a small gash, but everything down here was so old and rusty. Rust in a wound can lead to lockjaw. I wasn't sure how I knew that.

Tawil popped up over a cubical wall, grinning. "I know him!"

"Who?" I was too slow on the uptake; my expression had to show my confusion. Tawil's smile only widened as he grew eager to explain.

"Carter. Randolph Carter. Long before he was killed, shame that. He's a nice fella. Has a depressed streak, though." It was always hard to follow his change of tense. In Tawil's mind, Carter *was* and *is*—dead and alive. That sort of contradiction would have just fractured me further. But he took it in stride.

"So… he's dead?" I ventured.

Tawil narrowed his eyes and studied me. His forehead stretched taught, turning his round tattoos into slight ovals. "Here, absolutely dead. Elsewhere?" He gave an exaggerated shrug.

When I pressed him further he didn't answer, just went back to digging through a pile of trash and ignoring my questions, never once asking about my cut. This was typical. I never got a straight answer from him.

Time was funny here. The Wasteland had no day or night. It was always bright. Always hot. Always impossible to tell time. We slept when we were tired, ate when we were hungry. Any natural rhythm distorted, broke in a way that's hard to explain and even more difficult to comprehend.

Tawil had no name for what had happened here. There had been no society to band together to decide on a name: *Apocalypse. Aligning. Catastrophe. Disaster. Trouble.* Nothing. To him, it was just the passage of time. Just Tawil, his village, and the world around him slowly changing into something unrecognizable.

"Punishment," Tawil said one day and out of the blue. We were deep beneath another one of the unremarkable ruins, along an equally unremarkable expanse of dry and cracked ground. We had dropped several stories below the earth, using makeshift ladders to descend between caverns. Tawil was looking for something in particular, but said he wouldn't know it unless he saw it.

Which meant I stood around holding a flashlight as Tawil picked through the trash.

"Pardon?" I asked.

"Punishment," Tawil repeated. "Why I'm here. That's why. It's a punishment."

"For what?" I didn't know what else to say.

He turned, smiled, his blue tattoos folded between wrinkles. "Failure, most like. Perhaps treachery. I'm partial to that—at least in their eyes. But I don't remember. All dust." He smacked the side of his head with the heel of his hand as if knocking memories from his head. "All dust!"

I could tell he was trying, in his way, to tell me something personal and important. Something he was desperate for me to understand. But it was always as if we started at the end of a conversation rather than the beginning. I was getting the punchline without the context.

Then it hit me.

"Tawil," I said. He had taken to the name. "Are you an avatar? Were you a First? I mean… a Founder."

His eyes widened, then narrowed, widened once more. I wasn't sure how he'd respond. He looked over his shoulder, then around the dark room. Finally, a smile broke the tangle of his beard, and he breathed out as if he had been holding in a tension I hadn't been able to see. "You're understanding."

He laughed and clapped me on the shoulder. It was infectious; I laughed as well.

"What happened?"

"Carter," he said.

"Carter?" I asked.

"Yes, Carter. It was his choice, really. I was only there as a locksmith."

Before I could respond, the ground around us vibrated. The vibration was small at first, like a monorail passing, or the rumble of a heavy wain over loose shale.

The old man didn't respond. He just looked around. I could tell he was holding his breath.

Another rumble shook the room. I could feel it in my boots. It shuddered up my knees. Lovat was no stranger to quakes, but it had been decades since the last. This wasn't a natural tremor. It was the steps of a giant. Dust filled the air.

"What—" I began. Strong vibrations cut me off, grew more intense. Junk fell from the walls and clattered on the floor. I held my arms out to brace myself, fighting to maintain my balance. I coughed and squinted into the dust.

"What's happening?" I managed.

"Angry," Tawil looked toward the passageway and the ladder that led to the surface. "Someone's upset."

A gargoyle blinked into existence not an arm's length away— tall conical hood, the black robes, the stilted cadence of movement. A shiver traveled down my spine. I froze.

"You were not to speak, outer one," it hissed.

Tawil stepped back. His face, usually friendly, turned angry, lips pulled back into a malignant sneer.

"You were to stay silent," said another gargoyle as it flickered into existence behind me. They were indifferent to the shaking. Robes billowed and moved as they always had—seamless fabric, living fabric, twirling, twisting on an invisible wind.

"I'll not listen to a gaunt," Tawil growled.

"Serve your penance," said a third.

"You vermin."

"Silence!" The first again.

Tawil spat and launched himself at one of the gargoyles. I expected it to disappear or to reach out and through him, but instead he caught it with his shoulder. With a high-pitched keening it slammed into a wall with a thud and vanished. The old man spun to face the others, his shoulders hunched forward, hands curled into knobby fists.

Then we were alone again. The gargoyles had gone.

"We need to go." Tawil's voice was low.

Sand streamed down into the cavity as a fresh round of quakes shook the space. Tawil led the way, running in the dark, arms raised to shield his head, me close behind him.

The world cracked. A rumble, a roar, and the passageway collapsed behind us. Rolling gouts of dust and sand eddied around us as we fled. Rushing dirt spooled around my ankles, trying to trip me up. I was grateful that here my knee wasn't hurt, that I could run, really run.

The ceiling fell just as we made the first ladder. When we reached the second, the floor gave way. The last section was solid stone but it rippled beneath our feet. We were a hundred yards or so away from the final ladder. Both of us sprinted. What else could we do?

A gargoyle blocked our way. Tawil growled and lashed out at it but the creature flashed away before his fists could connect. Another materialized near me, not moving yet somehow keeping pace with me. I slowed enough to throw a low punch. My knuckles connected for an instant and the thing vanished. Another closed in. I tried to grab it. I had fought these things before. I knew I could hurt them. I could fight. But they flickered away before my fingers made contact.

Tawil hit the ladder first, clambered up all elbows and knees. I turned, hand on the ladder as I looked back at the collapsing ruin. More gargoyles winked into existence. I could hear their tittering laughter beneath the thundering.

Shadows and whispers ain't much in the way of currency.

"Come on!" Tawil shouted from above. "Climb! Climb, hamiya!"

I climbed. The light from the broken sun poured down golden but unfamiliar. Climbing through it felt like climbing through liquid, each movement ponderous. Time slowed. My arms and legs dragged. I fought against the downward pressure.

My arms and hands were numb from the vibrations; my legs ached from the climb. The dust gagged me. The ladder slipped and pitched to one side, nearly throwing me off as the ground below began to swallow it. My eyes burned and watered. Tears streamed down my face. Gravity pulled at me. The churning ruins spiraled below. My hand slipped and I scrambled for purchase.

My fingers wrapped around a rung. I heaved and threw myself upward.

A hand reached down through the viscid light. My escape. I grabbed for it, felt Tawil's fingers wrapped around mine. I felt a pull as he heaved me upward—it was like traveling between worlds. I burst from that underground pit like a man emerging from the water.

I flopped to the hardpan and pushed myself up. My shoulders ached. My legs shook. The Wasteland still quivered, but the angry energy was dissipating.

I began to laugh, but the laughter quickly faded into a choking cough that drove me to my knees.

"No," Tawil wheezed. "No. We don't kneel. We stand. *Stand.*"

The old man gripped my bicep and lifted me to my feet. My legs were weak, but I stood. I stood as my friend instructed me. My breathing came heavy. I was angry but satisfied. I was still alive.

Tawil gagged. Coughed. He was covered in dirt and grime but he was grinning. His eyes flicked from me to focus on the horizon. He made a rude gesture at the shape that moved beyond.

"You cold son-of-a-bitch!" Tawil shouted. He stepped forward, hands balled into fists, arms stiff. "You idiot bastard! You blind fool! What did you expect? Victory? Here?"

He whipped his hat off his head and slapped it against the ground, hooting and hollering like he had just won a war. "You can't kill me. You can't kill yourself!" He let out a wild cackle. "Not here! No, no! Not now!"

FOURTEEN

The warm beer felt good on my dust-ravaged throat. We were in Hamiya House, sitting in two of the kitchen chairs, staring at one another across the table. We were covered in dust, our hair stuck up at odd angles. Occasionally one of us would chuckle as if we remembered an old joke, and then we'd return to silence.

Neither of us had said anything on the walk back, just trudged through the heat. It took hours to get back to town.

Tawil had followed me into my house. I had offered him one of my four beers.

"Used to lower these into the well," said Tawil. He turned the bottle over in his hand. The label was faded, but the word 'Aforgomon' was legible below his long fingers. "Cool 'em down a bit."

A cold beer would have been even better than a warm beer, but I was still shaking from the pit collapse, and at that moment I didn't give a damn if the booze was warm or cold.

Tawil leaned back, took a slug from his beer, and then pointed at me with the bottle. "You figure it all out?"

I looked outside. "We going to piss him off again, talking about this?"

A shake of the head. "Can't reach us here. Won't let him."

He didn't explain what it was that wouldn't let him. I decided not to question that particular bit of insanity. At least not yet.

"I know you're a First," I said. "A... *Founder*. I know that thing beyond the horizon is as well. And I know I'm stuck here."

"Well... this place is real." Tawil rapped on the table with a knuckle.

I nodded. The pain in my throat was enough to confirm that the Wasteland was very real. There was a glimmer in the old man's eye. "But so is the plane you come from."

I took a nervous swig from my beer, trying to hide the confusion that I knew was playing havoc with my expression.

"You're a man of two worlds, Guardian." Tawil held up two long fingers, then leveled them at me.

Ashton had said that. It was more than just a clarification; it was a confirmation that my world—the Territories—was real. I should have felt relief, but the fracture inside me didn't close. It was one thing to hear confirmation of what my mind shouted at me. It was another thing to understand.

My memories of the Territories blew in like dust on the wind. People I knew—friends, family. Food I had eaten. Landscapes I crossed—the mountains, the scablands, the deserts. Even as they came into my mind, they were foggy and tough to recall. Other memories jostled with them, memories of this place and other memories I would have sworn weren't mine. Another thrum of madness I didn't feel like prodding at this moment. You don't kick a nest to get rid of the bees.

Tawil went on. "You're here and you're there. For me, it's always been part of slipping from one plane to the next. It's different for you. You're here *and* there simultaneously. You feel one world at a time, but you exist in both."

I felt sick to my stomach.

"The gaunts are in a similar state of fugue." He stretched the last word out as if it was awkward on his tongue. "Been dragged along for too long. Stretched 'em thin, see? Drove 'em mad. Ain't use for much, messages, watching. Humanity is different. You're tougher. Raw. You're survivors."

"None of this makes any sense," I said. My head hurt.

"When you were marked, a part of you was placed here." He took another swing of beer. "Soul. Essence. Pneuma. Whatever you want to call it. It needs a body." He waved a hand at me. "So it got what it needed. Whatever worshiper tagged you probably had no idea what they were doing."

I thought about my missing tattoos and my good knee. Was this body here some sort of copy? Both my knee and the tattoos had happened after Peter Black had marked me. The whole thought experiment unnerved me. My skin began to feel uncomfortable—unfinished.

"It was Cybill," I said.

"Who is Cybill?"

I described the creature I remembered: the tentacles, the beak, the eye.

Tawil shifted uncomfortably. His fingers played against the brown glass of the beer bottle. "I know her. Know her well. I know the form. Not the name. She and I…" He paused. Then shook his head. "It doesn't matter."

"Peter Black—Pan—her husband. I transported her body to my city. He named me her Guardian."

"Her husband?" He asked it with a bitterness he didn't manage to hide.

"That's what I was told."

"I see." Tawil's expression darkened. For a long time he stared out the open door. "Her essence was here. When he performed his ritual. Her body, her true form, had been lost in your existence, epochs ago. When this… Black named you Guardian, it must have split your soul. You needed to be connected to her in both planes. So a part of you is here. It always will be. But a part of you is still back there. Back home, where you come from."

He swallowed more beer and was silent. Again he stared outside, lost in thought. Though his lips were closed, his jaw worked as if he was speaking to someone.

For a while, I said nothing. I could see a cloud of pain pass over him. There was a connection between him and Cybill— that much I could tell. All his swagger and ease had vanished, and what filled the gaps was something broken, something lost. Something entirely different.

"Is that what happened to you?" I finally managed to ask.

A smile formed on his dry lips. The corners of his eyes crinkled. "I think you know what happened to me. Don't you?"

The words poured out of my mouth. "You were killed here. At least a part of you was. Your avatar—the man I'm sitting across from now—was trapped, while the other part of you, the real you, is someplace else."

We regarded each other in silence. What was the real form of this kindly, tattooed old man? It was hard to imagine him as a monster.

"How'd I do?"

He shrugged. "Close enough."

"My world?" I guessed.

Tawil shook his head. "No. There are more planes of existence. Many more."

"How many?"

Tawil smiled but didn't say anything. He took another drink.

"Is Ashton here?"

"Ashton?"

I tried to describe the man—then began describing the monster I had fought on Level Nine. The squat body, the ugly face with the lolling tongue and narrow slit eyes, the matted fur.

"Oh," said Tawil, interrupting me. "I know him by a different name as well. Unpronounceable in your Strutten. Yes—he's here. Somewhere." He waved a hand. "Though where I can't say. It's a big place, this."

"How does this all work?"

"That"—Tawil laughed, then paused, tilting his head as he considered my question—"is a complicated thing to describe. Each plane's different. Stranger than the last. We've found your reality... *difficult*."

"My predecessor," I said, unable to suppress a smile. "The other Guardian. She stopped you. Stopped them."

"Set us back considerable. Thousands of years. Hell, tens of thousands. Ain't never experienced a setback like that before. Scattered us. Took generations to draw our numbers together again. It broke me." He gestured toward the Wasteland outside. "So, I quit. Walked away from it all. Perhaps more of Carter rubbed off on me than I realized. Fascinating man, that Carter. Sixth of humanity. Twelfth of your world. Ain't often I see one of your kind willing to risk themselves for knowledge." He clicked his tongue and shook his head, beaming. "Ignorance is a far easier path."

He went quiet, and for a moment I didn't ask any more questions. This jumble of information was going to take me some time to untangle. I had so much more I wanted to know. Who was the creature in yellow robes? How was he connected to all of this? What did Ashton's warning mean? What was coming from the west?

I set my bottle on the table and met the old man's eyes. "Can I get back?"

Tawil's shoulders shook in quiet laughter. He drained his beer and smiled. "You never left, Waldo."

FIFTEEN

My eyes ached but wouldn't open. I coughed, then gagged. Something was in my throat.

"He's coming back," said a voice. Tawil? No. No, it wasn't. The desert air wicked sweat off my neck, yet at the same time there was a cool breeze that tickled my skin. I couldn't remember the last time I felt a cool breeze. Behind it came the familiar undertones of the King Tide stench.

"He's coming back."

What did that mean? Who?

"Wal, can you hear me?" It was a voice I should recognize.

"About time," said another in softer tones. "Thanks, doc."

I tried to sit up but felt a hand against my cheek. Something was stuck in my throat.

"Easy," said someone else. A woman. Taft? Hannah? Not a voice I recognized. Was this the Territories? Had I shifted again?

The lids of my eyes felt weighted with lead, but I finally forced them wide. The bright light made me wince. The world was blurry. White and gray with mint-green undertones. It took a second for the visuals to reach my brain.

The Wasteland was gone. The scorching sand had vanished. Tawil, the village, Hamiya House—all gone.

Where was I? I tried to sit up again.

"I said easy," the unknown voice said. The obstruction in my throat was removed. I gagged, then gasped. Shapes moved. Colors shifted. Forms began to emerge—people, walls.

"She said easy." That voice had to be Hagen. Who was *Hagen?*

"She did." Wensem. That was his voice.

"My head hurts," I wheezed. My tongue was slow and awkward. I cleared my throat and winced at the pain. "My throat…"

"There's our fighter." Hagen again. I still couldn't make out their features. Did they not understand me? Frustrated, I tried to lift my arms but discovered they wouldn't move. They were bound, strapped in place.

"Doc thought it was for the best," said Wensem. "You were thrashing about for a while. Best to make sure you didn't hurt yourself."

"I don't understand," I said.

Hagen was nearest me; I could see his single horn rising in his tangle of hair, his narrow features, the reflection of light against the glass of his spectacles. He swam in the blur and shook his head.

"Can you understand me?" I asked. My lips weren't working right. Was any of this real? The world drifted around me, slowly coming into focus. Doubt began to worry at the back of my mind.

"Best not to talk," said the woman's voice. "It'll take a bit before your faculties return. Tongue included."

I swore, and that made everyone laugh. So at least some communication was working. Around me, the room sharpened. Wensem and Hagen emerged from the cloud. They both looked disheveled. They flanked my bed, standing at either side.

A small umbra doctor leaned over me, her eyes glowing a brakendale yellow as she studied me. She loomed in close. Old reactive memories fired inside my mind, but my body didn't move fast enough. I jerked my head to one side, and pain flared inside my skull. I let out another curse, which only drew more laughter. I was a performing circus act—see the Amazing Waldo! He can barely speak!

"Feisty," said the doc.

More laughter. I let out another string of curses, and this time the room went silent. Glances were traded. People were beginning to understand me. It's not so cute when you can hear the anger tainting a curse.

"Sam's not here, Wal," said Hagen.

Samantha? What was he talking about?

"Just me and Wensem, I'm afraid. She's back home. Remember?"

I blinked.

A cup filled with cool water touched my lips. It was like the well in the village all over again. I drank greedily, finishing one glass and then another.

The rasp in my throat loosened. My voice returned. The sluggishness fell away, and I became more alert. As this reality began to feel more tangible, the Wasteland began to fade.

"What happened?" I asked, my voice a thick slurry. This time I was sure everyone understood.

Hagen stepped forward. "You collapsed. You saw Danforth, remember? Then you slumped to the bench. You looked at Taft and said, 'It's happening' and 'I can feel his call.' Then you passed out. Empress Protection freaked out. Called an ambulance. They dragged you here."

I didn't remember speaking.

"How long?"

"Two days," said the umbra.

Dammit. I blinked, stunned. Hadn't I spent months in the Wasteland? The difference ran havoc with my mind. For a moment, my mind and body felt decoupled. It was hard to remember what Tawil had said and what I imagined him saying. He had given me so much information. Told me more than I had ever guessed, and still I was like a ship without a sail, adrift on the water with no land in site. There was so much more I needed to know about. So much more I didn't understand.

"Worlds. Founders. Others," I mumbled. None of it made any sense, but I said it anyway. How could I explain this to my friends? Two worlds, a fractured soul, and so much more.

Hagen looked at Wensem. I could see their concern.

"Where am I?"

"Rithets Hospital," said the umbra. "In Empress. I'm Doctor Hae."

"Can you untie me?"

"You just woke from a deep comatose state, Mister Bell. I'd like to be sure—"

"Please," I said.

"I don't—"

"It'll be fine, doc," Wensem said.

Grudgingly, the doctor untied my hands and undid the cuffs at my ankles. When she had finished, she stepped back and stared at me with her brakendale gaze, clutching a clipboard to her chest. Tendrils of black essence drifted from her exposed head. I couldn't read the expression on her shadow-black face, and her eyes didn't betray her.

"I think you need rest," the doc said.

"I just spent two days resting," I lied. I held up my hands. My tattoos were all there. Their existence made me feel better. I clenched my fists, then unclenched them. A wave of exhaustion overtook me. I wanted to sleep. Clearly, when I traveled, I wasn't sleeping much on the other side. Good to know. I looked at the doctor. "Can I talk to my friends?"

She gestured at the pair as if saying *Go ahead, they're right here.*

"Alone."

"Ah," she said, turning to leave the room. She paused near the door and added, "I'll be back to check on you in ten minutes."

When the door closed, I rubbed my wrist and looked from Hagen to Wensem. I had so much to share, but I wasn't sure where to begin. The strange connection between the *Black Book,* Danforth, Shoalta Amaia, and Magnez? My traveling? My split existence? Instead I asked, "How's the job?"

"By the Firsts, Wal." Hagen's mouth hung open. "You've been in a coma for two days, and your first question is 'How's the job?'"

"Roaders gotta get paid," I managed. "I have a business to run, in spite of—" I waved my hand in the air.

"Security is fine. But the reason for this little trip to Victory? Not well," said Wensem. He grimaced. "It's been tense. That Danforth guy has become a pain in Lovat's side. He pissed off Victory. They threatened to withdraw the accords, close the city. Now they're currently refusing to send an ambassador to Lovat. The whole thing is up in the air."

"Carter's cross," I groaned. Camalote tended to throw their weight around with a sort of arrogance that grated on people's nerves. They had the ideas. They had the money. They knew what was best. Some of Lovat's poor refused their help outright because of that attitude.

"Maybe I'll just slip back to the Wasteland," I said. "Until this all blows over."

Wensem scowled, and Hagen breathed out in a huff.

"That was a joke."

"Not a funny one," said Hagen. "We're worried sick."

"I'm fine," I said, swinging my legs off the bed and placing my bare feet on the tiled floor. I pushed up, and nearly collapsed as my knee cried out in pain. Hagen rushed to my side. I waved him away, using my arms and the bed to lift myself into a standing position. I had been operating in the Wasteland with two good knees for so long that I had forgotten the pain that accompanied walking on this side of reality.

"Dammit, Wal," Hagen said. "Take it easy."

"You going to tell us what is going on?" Wensem had folded his arms and stood watching me like a stern father. He knew better than Hagen not to rush to help me.

"I don't fully understand it myself," I said. "But I think I'm getting closer."

"How so?" Hagen asked.

"I met someone else on the other side. Not the creature in yellow, but another—a man."

"A man?"

"Well, sort of—he's a man now. A former avatar of another First," I explained.

"Like Ashton?"

I poured myself another cup of water and drank. The cold felt terrific against my throat.

"How much longer is the *Gamble* going to stick around?" I asked. I took a few shaky steps forward. Stretched my legs, working out the kink in my knee.

"They're planning on leaving in a couple of days. They have that King Tide celebration to make," said Wensem. "Castaigne is beside herself. She's trying to get this whole issue settled before the Council of Captains takes their boat and leaves."

"That could be trouble," I said.

Wensem nodded. "I've already started prepping the crew. If you hadn't woken up, I'd be meeting with Hannah to go over watch schedules for the return trip."

"What if Castaigne fails?" I asked. I turned and paced back toward the bed. I was feeling stiff all over, but better.

"Then she'll be coming back with us, and she'll probably murder Danforth for screwing it all up."

"Yikes," I said. That didn't bode well for Magnez's mayoral administration. Peace with the neighbors had been a big part of her campaign. If this leaked, and I was confident it would, then it'd be a public embarrassment. There were those on the city council who would relish the opportunity to drag her over the coals and sow mistrust with her constituents. Politics is always ugly.

"What's his deal anyway?" I asked, turning and heading back. My knee was still tight, but it was feeling better than it was before. It was strange coming back to a wounded body, after tromping around in the Wasteland uninjured. I suspected that shift was partly to blame for the dissociation I was feeling.

Hagen sighed. "Camalote wants more transparency from the Victory government. In particular, they want census data—they claim it's essential for their work. Something about allocating resources and knowing how much to send. Victory isn't interested in sharing that information. Camalote isn't used to hearing no."

I groaned, and Hagen stepped forward. "That was a reaction, my friend. Not a cry of pain." Wensem chuckled behind me. I turned and looked at my partner. "Maybe I should go and talk to Danforth? Have him ease off."

"I've tried," said Wensem. "He didn't listen to me."

"Maybe he's a speciesist," I said. "Like O'Conner."

"I don't think so," said Wensem. "Didn't strike me that way. I think he's just bullheaded. I mean, the man does work for a charity."

"Lovat's foremost charity," Hagen said, his voice turning up with a slight affectation. "Wait, you plan on going now?"

"We only have a few days," I said. "He's always been friendly enough to me. Maybe he'll listen."

Wensem shook his head. "The doc said you should get some rest."

"I was resting," I lied as I looked around the room. After I'd spent so much time in the open vastness, this room felt claustrophobic. I wanted to do something. The issue with Castaigne and Danforth was a good excuse for action. A goal. Empowerment. Returning, separating myself from the monotony of the Wasteland was energizing. I was in Empress. A vibrant place full of wonders I hadn't experienced.

"Where are my clothes?"

Wensem pointed to a series of drawers nested into the wall behind my bed. I pulled it open and saw all my clothing, freshly laundered and folded neatly inside, the uncomfortable shiny shoes resting on top. I didn't relish putting those back on.

"You going to tell us what happened?" Wensem said.

"Same thing that always happens," I said, pulling off my smock. Hagen flushed and turned, clearing his throat in an attempt to cover his shock. Wensem chuckled, and I joined him. I was used to caravan life. Modesty and privacy on the trail were nonexistent. Changing in front of friends or strangers never bothered me. Hagen's world was a bit stiffer, a bit more formal. He wasn't used to the road.

I dressed, and as I dressed I talked. I described my most recent trip to the Wasteland as best I could. Spoke of the city beneath the hardpan and the woman who came before me. I didn't delve into the discussion with Tawil toward the end. I'd explain that another time. Distilling months of experience into a few moments meant I had to shed many of the details, details that were already fading fast. It was strange—the other side always felt fuzzy and unreal. Moments ago, I would have told you Empress wasn't real, that my friends were possible figments of my imagination. Now, Tawil sounded like a fabrication—a legend passed from traveler to traveler, the particulars growing thin with each retelling.

"Samantha will be fascinated," Hagen said, his voice awed. "Hell, *I'm* fascinated. This affects so much it's hard to wrap my head around. Scripture, creation myths, science, our perceptions. This is both a confirmation and an eruption. The story of the Aligning alone…"

I looked at Wensem, who hadn't said anything.

"Protection?"

"Outside. They let us wander inside alone, but the moment we move down the street they're behind us."

I nodded. It made sense. "Danforth?"

"Saanich Hotel. Up the hill. Castaigne is there as well, along with most of the crew. What're you planning?"

I wasn't sure. It would have been a lot easier if Protection had just ejected Danforth, but life was never that convenient. Danforth had some connection to the Wasteland. I was pretty sure that his touch outside of the Custom's House had sent me traveling. I'd need to be careful.

"Want to talk to him. Maybe he'll listen to me. Camalote isn't running security here, we are. He came along. We let him as a favor, right? Well, then we can retract that favor."

Wensem nodded, but I could see he was still mulling the idea over.

"Danforth will be pissed," Hagen said. "And with him, Camalote."

"Maybe," I said. The prospect of seeing Danforth again was already making me nervous, and nothing in me relished the idea of going up against Lovat's largest charity, but I was here to make sure Castaigne was safe. Her failing in her goal would compromise that safety. "Their interference could cause chaos back home. I might be a lot of things, but I'm a loyal Lovatine. I love my mess of a city. I want to see it succeed." I looked at Wensem. "Any problem with me tagging back in?"

"You sure you're up to it?" Wensem hadn't stopped studying me.

"I feel fine," I said. "Little groggy. Bit stiff. Otherwise—"

Doctor Hae returned at that moment, a tendril of black mist marking the trail as she moved into the room. It shifted in hue—like the umbra back on the *Gamble*—turning into a vibrant yellow that matched her eyes before dissipating.

"What are you doing out of bed?" she demanded.

"Checking out," I said.

"Like hell you are. You were in a coma not more than two hours ago—"

"I appreciate the concern. But I'm not staying," I said. "Really. I'm fine. I feel fine. Hungry. Bit stiff. But I'll be okay."

"Mister Bell, I really—"

"We'll be with him," Wensem said. "And your security forces."

Dr. Hae shook her head. "I cannot allow this to happen. You were completely catatonic less than an hour ago. Anyone in your condition should be monitored by medical professionals. I—"

"I recover quickly," I said.

"He'll be fine, ma'am," Wensem echoed.

I turned and looked at him, our eyes met, and he gave me a slow, even nod.

I really hoped he was right.

SIXTEEN

Saanich Hotel sat in the center of Empress. It was immense, constructed from flat gray stone and sporting a copper roof that had oxidized to a mossy green. There was something castle-like about it despite additions that softened the fortress motif: peaked gables, pointed cupolas, and railed widow's walks that would offer stunning views.

The hotel was an expansive three stories, and at its center was a tall clock tower that rose above the covered entrance. The building sprawled lazily across a small island of stone that lifted from the ocean and separated the hotel from the hurried canals, crowded markets, and busy boardwalks below.

Places like this didn't exist in Lovat. There space existed at a premium, even among the elevated levels. Back home, you could fit twenty-thousand people on a rock this size and have room to spare. The Saanich reveled in its expanse. Rolling green lawns bordered by hedges extended across the grounds. Shadowy Victory Protection forces waiting for their charges lingered along the edges of pathways. Oaks and maple trees loomed over the yards, their branches still bare. A line of thick pines formed a natural barrier between the hotel and the city beyond. If it wasn't for the towers rising above the trees, you could almost imagine yourself in a forest setting.

I let out a low whistle. "How much does a night here cost?"

"Hundreds," said Hagen. "Of course, that depends on the exchange rate between Lovatine lira and Empress huards."

"Whatever it is, it's more than we could afford," said Wensem. Together we walked up to the entrance and nodded to the porter, who wore a purple jacket so dark it was nearly black. He pulled the door open for us and ushered us in with a bored, "Welcome to the webbed."

The inside reminded me of every elevated tower in Lovat. Far above were overly ornamental ceilings, the edges framed with vines and leaves in relief. Everything was white, even the leather furniture scattered in small clumps across the pale wood floor. Huge crystal and glass chandeliers sent glittering sparkles across the room. It was beautiful and also absurd.

"I'll wait down here," said Hagen. He moved to one of the couches and flopped into its overstuffed cushions.

A long dark counter occupied one side. Behind it black-suited staff milled about, marking in ledgers and lifting the handsets of telephones and speaking into the mouthpieces. Wensem and I both made our way toward it.

"Can I help you?" asked the woman behind the counter, a maero with fish-belly skin and dark hollows around her eyes. Her thin lips were set, and her eyebrows arched as she regarded me.

"Guardian Security," I said. The name still felt weird. "Need to talk with Sam Danforth."

"Mister Danforth doesn't—"

Wensem leaned forward. Pulled a card from his shirt pocket and showed it to her, a false smile on his crooked jaw. "I will call on the Ambassador if I need to."

The maero woman looked at the card, then at him, then scowled. After a heartbeat, she stepped back and regarded the two of us for a long moment before she breathed out, "Mister Danforth is in Suite 301."

"You folks have a lift?" I asked.

She smirked at me. "No."

No lift meant stairs. And stairs meant… *dammit.*

The doctor had been right. I should have rested longer. I was paying for it now.

Wensem was patient, which says a lot about him. He'd wait at each landing as I puffed my way up and fought to pretend as if everything was normal. Meanwhile, the bones behind my knee would scream and shout in their way. There were pops, and I would have sworn I heard the grinding of bone on bone. The last several days lying in bed had given the joint time to seize up, which made the stairs an excruciating exercise. With each step, I told myself it'd get more comfortable as I used it. I was not a medical professional. Do not do what I did.

Three stories took me more than ten minutes. But when we emerged in a white hall with the red carpet, my blood was up, my brow and shirtsleeves slicked with sweat. I was ready for an argument. Also a vermouth. Perhaps both?

It didn't take long to find Danforth's suite. Wensem knocked.

An umbra answered the door, glowing white eyes peering through the slit. For a second, my heart seized. Umbra. White eyes. The black space beneath the *Gamble*. The cultists.

I went as rigid as a statue, then caught myself. There was no reason to stress out. This umbra wasn't the same person who had attempted to murder me. For starters, this one presented as female.

"Ah, Misters Bell and Ibble." Her voice was husky, cold, and impersonal.

The door closed. There was the sound of a chain, and then it swung open again. We entered.

"Thank you," I said.

The suite was enormous. Room for five families easily. Maybe a small manufactory. One wall was all glass, and it looked out at the forested rock and the towers beyond. Ancient leather furniture was everywhere: large brown couches, sleek brown day beds, and overstuffed brown chairs. Bar carts stationed near each were all covered with bottles of colored liquor and the accoutrements necessary to mix cocktails.

"Nice place," I said to no one in particular. "Camalote front the cash for a suite like this?"

"Mister Waldo Bell and Mister Wensem dal Ibble, sirs," the umbra called out. Her voice rose an octave as she spoke. Then she nodded at the two of us and disappeared behind a hidden door built into the wall. I kept waiting to see a hue shift in the smoky effluvium that drifted from her body, but no shift came—just inky black dissipating into nothing. A hole in reality wrapped in a suit.

"Nice place," I repeated. How many more rooms branched off from what I could see? While we waited, I made my way to a cart and picked through the bottles, uncorking and smelling each. Most of the liquors here were unlabeled, which required a reliable sense of smell.

"It's eleven in the morning, Wal."

"So?" I replied. I was hungry. Liquor would help curb my cravings. I drew a small bottle of vermouth from the collection, uncorked it, and poured myself a glass. There wasn't any ice, but I made do. It was sharp and sweet and laced with botanical complexity. I generally liked my vermouth chilled, but I didn't usually drink from a bottle this nice.

"Want anything?"

Wensem waved a dismissive seven-fingered hand in my direction just as Danforth emerged from around a corner. He was in shirtsleeves, his suspenders draped around his thighs, and he was wiping shaving cream off his face with a hand towel. His hair was wet but combed precisely along the part.

"Thought you had stepped aside for medical issues, Mister Bell," Danforth said. There was a tension in the way he moved. He was wound tight. Even I could see it. A politician's grin stretched across his freshly shaven jaw: all teeth, no emotions. My mother would have described it as a 'liar's grimace'—but she had been in politics longer than me. I was new to all this.

"I'm feeling better," I lied, and swirled the vermouth in my glass.

"Interesting." Danforth's smile never faltered. He watched me in silence for a moment. His eyes met mine. "I'm glad to hear it."

His expression was friendly, but his tone didn't sound glad. I didn't respond.

"Found the liquor, I see," he said. He walked to the bar cart nearest him and poured two fingers of whiskey. "A man shouldn't drink alone." He raised the glass in my direction and sipped, hissed slightly, then made a smacking sound with his lips. "So, why are you here? Want to talk ausca championships or the upcoming jai alai season?"

"As fun as that would be, this is more of a professional call."

He smirked as if he understood that already, brushed the front of his shirt and stood up straighter. "Ah, then how can I help Guardian Security?"

I cleared my throat and began. "I'm sure you're aware there've been some issues surrounding the accords."

"I am," Danforth nodded. "It's not unexpected. Lovat and Victory have been at odds for generations. The threats toward caravans who get too close to the wall, the harassment of shipping vessels, and then there is the alleged shuffling of the poor from their shores to ours. We expected a bit of tension."

"There's also your demands for the census data," I said. Danforth's smile faltered, just slightly.

"I wouldn't call them demands, more... requests," Danforth said. For the first time since he'd entered the room, he glanced away.

I looked toward Wensem, who was already looking in my direction. "Time is limited. The Ambassador has requested that you bow out of future meetings."

"I beg pardon." Danforth's casual demeanor shifted. The plastered smile that had been so constant fell away. He blinked rapidly. His mouth dropped open for a moment. Then he quickly recovered. His expression hardened. His brow furrowed. "Connie sent you?"

"Not exactly. There's been some… uh, security issues," said Wensem. We had cooked up the lie during our walk from the hospital to the hotel. It would be simple. If pressed, we'd tell him there were threats made against Camalote—him specifically. We'd tell him that his presence meant the Ambassador was unsafe. To keep her safe, we'd have to exclude Camalote's representative. It was vague enough that it would be impossible to confirm. It got Danforth out of the Ambassador's meetings and put the blame on us, rather than on her.

Danforth held up his hand holding the glass; a few fingers splayed outward. His head shook, ever so slightly. "I can't believe what I'm hearing. Security… issues?"

I nodded. "Afraid so. We've started receiving threats. External threats. Nothing confirmed, but enough to put us on edge. We decided it's better for everyone's safety if future meetings are just Castaigne, her immediate staff, and the Victory emissary and their staff. Now, I know it's not ideal—"

Any semblance of calm shattered. Danforth's face twisted.

"Dammit!" The tumbler in his hand spun through the air and shattered against the wall. A few specks of whiskey spattered against my cheek. Danforth was shaking his head in wide exaggerated motions. "No! No. You can't do this. I am allowed access. I must have access. It's *essential!* Magnez gave Camalote access and I"—he tapped his chest—"am Camalote's representative."

I raised my hands. "Look, we don't—"

"You can't do this! You cannot push us out." Danforth was angry. He began to stalk back and forth, shoulders hunched. "Camalote was granted exclusive—"

"I know," I said. "I know. I know. I'm not trying to push you out. We don't want to do this, but the safety of the Ambassador is our duty, and with recent threats, we have to make the call."

"Bullshit." He waved a hand and then pointed at me. "You're lying. There are no threats. This is a secret summit, by the Firsts!"

"Mister Danforth," said Wensem. He used his fatherly tone, the sort of voice he'd use with his son. It didn't work.

"No threats! Only lies!" snapped Danforth with a wave of a hand. He collapsed into an overstuffed chair and quieted for a moment. His hands folded, index fingers steepled. For a time he sat there, unmoving. Wensem and I watched in silence. Then, after a time, Danforth looked up, eyes ablaze. He glared at me, then Wensem. His fingers untangled from their twins, and he pointed at the two of us, swinging back and forth. "What's going on here? What are you two up to? Who do you work for? Is this a power play? Some scheme of Magnez's?"

"We serve at the request of the Mayor and the city," said Wensem. Most people couldn't read his impassive expressions, but I had known him long enough to see it clearly: Wensem was concerned.

Danforth scoffed. "More bullshit. More lies. Waite didn't say anything about a breach."

Wensem caught my eye and his eyebrows arched. Waite was an old name in Lovat, ancient. The family elevated—their number unknown. Normally, Waite could mean anything. The name was plastered all over the city. There was Waite Fishing, Waite Financial, Waite Caravans, Gum, Auditorium, Fronton, Hotel, Garage, Athletic Club, Haberdashery, Apartments, Lifts, Parking, and on and on. A monorail stop, a park, and a warren bore the name. But, at this moment I knew what Danforth meant: Waite Security and Protection. WSP. The family's private intelligence agency.

Legends swirled around them like smoke. If Camalote was private, than WSP was downright secretive. Their movements and operations were myths. Half the caravan companies in the city spoke of them as spooks. Brutal. Efficient. Cold. Calculating. One didn't interact with the WSP so much as react to the WSP. If they were talking with Danforth, then there was already trouble.

"Waite?" The name fell out of my mouth.

"Waite. The WSP. Camalote doesn't go anywhere without a disclosure team." He narrowed his eyes. "What's going on here? What's your angle? It's not Connie, is it? It's you..."

"The only angle we have is the safety of the Ambassador." The best lies are seasoned with truth. "That's why we're here. That's what we were hired to do."

"I want to see evidence of the threats. How did they come? Letters? Telegram? Telephone?"

"We're still investigating," Wensem lied.

Danforth shook his head. "Lies. More bullshit. You think we care?" He crossed his arms. "We won't let the Magnez Administration bully us around. We—" He stopped himself. His eyes narrowed to slits.

"Look, we're all appreciative of Camalote's charity work, but we can't let you attend. The risk—"

"Bullshit." Danforth waved a hand and pushed off out of the chair. "No, we—"

He caught himself. Glowered and then went silent.

This wasn't Lovat. This was Empress. None of us had any power here. That meant we had to rely on the thin veneer of civilization we constructed before we left home. I was counting on that. There was no quick communication between Victory and the city. Telegraph lines didn't connect the two. He was as cut off as we were, which meant he could be manipulated.

"I don't want to be disrespectful, Mr. Danforth. But we're doing this for your safety as well. We're here for the security of the entire delegation. If we see or hear anything that puts you in harm's way—"

Danforth crossed the room and drew close to me. His peppermint breath flowed across my cheeks. I could smell his shampoo—chamomile and lavender. Smell his aftershave—tobacco and clove. Gone was the politician grin, the haughty arrogance, the genial greetings. Something ugly had taken over. Something twisted.

A slight buzzing tickled the back of my skull. A broken sun beat down on my neck. Instinctively, I stepped back, eyeing Danforth up and down. The buzzing receded as I put distance between him and me. Clearly, he had some connection to the other reality; something about him could set me off and send me traveling. I really didn't want it to happen again. Tawil was a fine enough fellow, but the Wasteland wasn't a place I wanted to spend more time exploring. Man of two worlds or no, I vastly preferred this one.

Had this been his plan? Waylay me so he could screw up the accords? Maybe I was overthinking this.

"You don't want to make enemies with us," he said, his voice low, the words forced out from behind rows of gritted teeth.

"Not here to make enemies," I replied. People invading my space tended to put me on edge. I hope I sounded strong. "We're here to keep people safe. Keep Lovat safe. That's all."

Danforth breathed out a cloud of peppermint. "We have the reach. We have the resources. We have the connections. We extend into places you cannot even begin to fathom, you little shit. We can make your pathetic life"—he paused, looked at Wensem—"*lives*... miserable."

"Here I thought you were a charity," I said, smirking, pretending at confidence.

There was a moment or two when my words hung in the air. Heavy, like an acrid cloud of campfire smoke or the wretched smell that'd washed in with the King Tide. Danforth tried to remain impassive, but his expression shifted. He was close enough I could see the shift. Cornered animals had similar expressions. Angry offense became panicked defense.

"Darla!" Danforth shouted. His eyes never left my own. He hadn't moved. His face remained inches from me. "DARLA!"

The umbra woman materialized from behind the hidden door. She tilted her head as if waiting for instructions. Danforth looked from her and to me. His smile returned, although this time it was cruel. His eyes were chips of flint, drained of warmth. "Please show Mister Bell and Mister Ibble the door. Our conversation has concluded." I could hear him choke on his pleasantries.

Silently we followed. Neither of us turned.

Darla opened the door to the suite and waved us through. Wensem passed beyond without incident, as is his way. But for me, for a moment, I paused hand against the frame, my shoulders hunched, my knee as annoying as I was about to be. I grinned. Turned. Looked back at Samuel Danforth, standing in his shirtsleeves, liquored up, suspenders handing at his sides.

"See you around, Samuel."

Danforth said nothing, but as the door swung shut, I caught his liar's grimace return.

SEVENTEEN

Y**ou're** supposed to be the clever one. The talker. The salesperson. The schmoozer. By the Firsts, Wal!"

A seven-fingered fist lanced out and broke a weathered placard advertising low-interest payday loans. A few more punches followed, shattering what was left of the sign.

"Hey! Hey! Stop that right now!" our Protection shadow shouted. He ran down the alley, arm outstretched.

Wensem huffed, raised his arms, and stepped away from the sign, nodding. The shadow slowed, then stopped.

"Sorry," said Wensem. And again, "Sorry."

There was a moment where the officer didn't move. Then he slowly backed away, his posture rigid, clearly tense but allowing us our privacy if not solitude. My partner leaned against the brick wall, shoulders moving up and down like the swell of the waves.

A few Emperian pedestrians stopped and peered down the alley at us three. They each wore the popular collarless jacket I saw around the city. Empress fashion apparently favored the austere and simple. Their eyes were suspicious, their mouths set. They didn't say anything, just watched.

"What happened?" Hagen asked after the shadow had withdrawn. His words tumbled out as he stared at Wensem's rage manifesting. Most people didn't see him like this. They always saw the calm and collected maero. But Wensem's a slow burn. It builds inside him, and when he erupts... watch out.

"Danforth's an asshole," I said, shrugging. "We've dealt with his kind before."

Wensem spoke around gritted teeth. "Asshole or not, we still have to work with him. He's Camalote."

"What happened?" Hagen repeated.

"So," I said, replying to Wensem, not Hagen.

"So? So!" Wensem's blue-gray eyes snapped open. "Do you realize the pull they have politically?"

"I hear a lot about Camalote. I see the advertising on the monochromes, I read them in the papers, their name runs across the tops of budget telegrams, their posters are everywhere. Hell, I feel their heat as I pass below their blinking neon signs. But I never actually see their hand at work."

Wensem had leaned against the wall, his head back. His chest was rising and falling. He hadn't expended the rage inside him, but we didn't need Protection coming down on us. Not right now. My eyes flicked to our little audience. Most of the citizenry had dispelled, but the Protection officer still watched us intently.

"Ease up," I said.

He didn't.

"Wen." This time I reached out and put a gentle hand on his shoulder. "You'll bring Protection down on top of us."

His blue-gray eyes looked at me. His lips folded and unfolded as if he wanted to speak. Finally, he pushed off from the bricks with an expression I recognized. "Camalote does good work."

"So I hear," I said. I wished I had a cigarette. It'd have taken off some of the edge.

"Why pick a fight?"

"Technically, he picked the fight. He's the one ruining the accords."

"What the hell happened?" Hagen asked again, exasperated.

"Okay. But you egged him on." Wensem pointed at me. "Why?"

"I'm tired of the elevated in the city thinking they can just push people around. Besides, I've never seen Camalote at work. Hear a lot about it. AZAH runs stories all the time. The monochromes, too. Never see it. Have you?"

Wensem thought about it, let out a heavy sigh, and slumped against the wall. His long fingers pulled absently at his thin neck. The pedestrians drifted away.

"Exactly," I said, squatting to face him. I had to keep my right leg extended. My bum knee didn't like the squatting position. "It sounds all well and good, but what have we seen? There are Charity Children swamping Level Three through Five. I watch people drop lira into the coin slots all the time. We're told they build all these wonderful things, but where are the clinics, shelters, and food banks? Camalote claims they fund them, but it's easier to find a bonesaw in Level Two than a clinic."

"The city's a big place." Doubt flooded Wensem's voice.

"There are no Camalote Action Committees, no Camalote Conversation Meetings, no Camalote Offices."

"I've had Camalote Community Liaison come by Saint Olm," said Hagen. He frowned and fiddled with the spurs along his knuckles. "Usually asking for charity, thinking about it."

"Exactly. They're great at raising money. But where does it go?" I let my words hang. "So, yeah. I have my doubts. And then when he starts threatening us? Says WSP is involved? Look, I didn't want to pick a fight, but he started it. I just doubled down. You see the way he corrected himself? The way he pulled back?"

"He clearly wanted to say more," Wensem said.

"Now I wish I had ridden up with you two," Hagen said.

"Hell, Waite-whatever-the-damn seems creepier by the day despite the campaigns trying to pitch the organization as some benevolent do-gooder, and they're in tight with Camalote. For a charity that claims to have Lovat's well-being in mind, they seem absent from the day-to-day conversation, don't you think? What have we been shown versus told? What have we read versus seen? I'm tired of being told things. I want evidence, and you should too."

"By the Firsts, what the hell happened?" Hagen nearly shouted the words.

"Danforth didn't take it well," I said, turning to look at him.

"Clearly," Hagen said.

"Threatened us, the company, everything." Wensem rubbed his face.

"Damn," Hagen said. "Threatened. Huh. Like how?"

"Outfit-shit," said Wensem. "Bluster, mostly. But the subtext was there. We do what we want. You can't stop us. We have the money. We have the reach, yadda yadda yadda." He mimicked a talking mouth with his hand. It works well enough for humans, but maero, with their extra digits, have the mimicry down to an art form. "Thing is, I think they can. I think they do."

"You sound like conspiracy theorists," Hagen said. "The Camalote Group is a part of Lovat's bedrock. The org is older than the damn city."

"He did threaten us," I said. "That was true."

Hagen laughed. "What are they going to do, run ads against you? Big posters of your face all over the monorail stations, papering the alleys?"

"Be easy enough to make my face known," I said. I tapped on the cheekbone below my black eye. "Remember, Ash's followers aren't too happy with me at the moment."

"So why aren't you worried?" said Wensem. "The good graces I got from the whole blockade action will eventually fade. If you've made a public enemy, it won't exactly line up contracts for us."

This was the crux of it, the real reason his anger had boiled over. Wensem had a family to think about. Bell Caravans had made great strides in the last few months, and this business with Danforth threatened to ruin it. Kit's writing hadn't exactly taken off, and Wensem didn't want to see our livelihood dwindle. We'd lived through lean times before, and neither of us was eager to relive it.

"I want to get a message to Magnez," Wensem said. "Try to head off any damage from Danforth."

"How?" I asked.

"There're messenger services that run from the docks. They can get a message to a networked telegraph station," Hagen offered. "I saw a few near the Customs entry. Not far from where Wal had his little incident. It's not ideal. Might take a few days."

"We'll be heading home in a few days," I said. Looking from Hagen to Wensem.

"True, but I think we need to move quickly on this," Wensem said. The concern was evident in his eyes. He turned to Hagen. "Can you show me these messengers?"

"Sure," said Hagen.

"I'm starving," I said. "Haven't eaten in what? Two days? I want to find some food. Want to just meet with Hannah and Taft at the embassy?"

Hagen paused, he looked at Wensem, then down at his feet before turning back to me. It was easy to see what they were thinking.

"I'll be fine," I said. It was a phrase I had been using a lot recently.

"You just got out of the hospital, Wal," said Hagen.

I sighed dramatically.

"He's right," said Wensem. "We can't let you wander off by yourself."

"Look, I'm cranky and starving. I just woke up from—" I flicked my fingers above my head as if that described it. "—I need to clear my head. I need to find food. I need to stretch my legs."

"I'll come with," Hagen said.

"You know where the messengers are," I said.

Wensem's face remained stoic. "I can probably find them on my own, Wal."

I looked over my shoulder. The Wasteland was there, but it didn't pull at me. If anything, I got the vibe that it was intentionally ignoring me. As if my presence offended it somehow. How to explain that? "Nothing's going to happen."

Hagen shook his head. "No argument. I'm not letting you out of my sight."

I looked from Hagen to Wensem and then back again. Nothing I was going to say would change their mind.

"Fine," I said. Then, quieter, "Fine."

Wensem nodded. "Get something to eat and I'll see you both at the embassy."

EIGHTEEN

Empress stretched out before us, offering up her sights and sounds as we took to her streets. The embassy sat upon the mountainous island that rose from the water northwest of the canals. It'd take us an hour or so to walk directly there, but my stomach was growling, and I wanted to explore the hermit country's capital.

"If you see a rare book shop, let's stop," Hagen said.

"Works for me."

We took our time. We wandered the raised avenues that ran at canal's edge, poked through some shops, and passed into several arcades. My bruises drew the occasional glance, followed by a quick look elsewhere when our eyes met. The attention was always from a severely dressed Emperian human or a glowing-eyed umbra with wispy color-shifting brume. Why hadn't I seen that before? Perhaps it was unique to Emperian umbra?

The last few days had been a cavalcade of experiences, and as we walked I found myself dwelling on Tawil. Was the old man still hunting for salvage below the sands of the Wasteland? Had my disappearance disturbed him?

You're a man of two worlds now, Guardian.

What did that mean? My body—well, *a* body—was clearly in both places. Here I slipped into a comatose sleep when I traveled. What happened on the other side? I used to always wake in what felt like the same place. But that was before I began to interact with the Wasteland. Would I awake in the Hamiya House or would everything reset, and I'd be back to where I had always started?

I puzzled over this as we walked along a bridge that connected two canal-side arcades. We passed beneath an outer arch and into the interior. It reminded me of home. A roof above me instead of a sky, the streets draped in shadow. It made me feel better.

Shops lined the walkways, and a few clusters of people congregated in the buzzing light of blue and white neon signs. A liquor store, a tattoo parlor, a fortune teller, a bodega, a shoe repair shop—Victory, for all their secrecy, was more like us than they realized. You could plop this anywhere in the span and it'd fit right in—perhaps it was all a bit too clean.

"There!" Hagen nearly shouted, which drew a few looks. He pointed toward a rickety old shop with tall double doors painted black and flanked by windows hatched by diagonal muntins. A sign above the door read THE ARMITAGE in raised Strutten letters painted gold. Behind the windows I could see stacks and stacks of books. Not really my scene.

"Let's go," said Hagen. "The libraries of Victory have been lost to Lovatine researchers for generations! This could be a find."

"Or it could be just another musty bookstore," I said.

Hagen rolled his eyes. "Another musty bookstore has saved your life a time or two."

"I really need to get some food."

Hagen's expression fell a bit. Then his expression brightened. "How about you grab food, then come back here and fetch me. Then we'll go to the embassy together."

"What about leaving me alone?" I could see the fever in his eyes. The draw of the stacks.

"Just get food and come back here."

"I won't be gone but a few moments," I said.

"I'll see you soon."

And, like that, Hagen passed through the Armitage's twin doors, leaving me by myself on the streets of Victory.

The crowds this deep into the canals weren't as thick as those near Customs. Again, they were mostly human, with a smattering of umbra. My clean suit helped me blend in, though it was still far too casual compared to the stiff jackets the Emperians wore. I took one last glance into the Armitage before wandering off. Hagen was already deep in conversation with the man behind the counter—a human mirror of him, well dressed if not a little threadbare, lanky, wild hair, dark features, bespectacled. I had fully intended on just finding food and then coming back in an hour or so—any sooner and I'd be stuck standing around forever.

The Protection shadow had begrudgingly gone with Wensem, leaving Hagen and me all alone. It was not nice to feel like I was running from something or worrying about someone. I was sick of cells, tired of hospitals, and done with wastelands.

"Hey," I said, leaning toward a group of three teenagers. "Speak Strutten?"

They were all humans with dark hair and skin and the thick stocky frames of ausca players. They could have been my cousins. They wore school jackets over button-ups. One was wearing his shirt open, and beneath it was a black tee-shirt bearing the logo of a band—Sempronius Blaesus, written in angled Strutten with a snake crawling through the characters. They all looked at me.

"Yeah. Whole city does. Where you from?" one of the kids asked. He spoke Strutten with a soft accent I had come to identify as Emperian. "What happened to your face?"

"Lovat," I answered. "Got in a fight."

They exchanged murmurs and expressions of awe.

I didn't let them dwell on it too long. "I'm looking for a place to eat. Got any recommendations?"

"Abdul's place a few blocks up has pakora and the like," said the kid in the band shirt.

"There's the bakso place across the street," suggested another.

"Bakso?" I asked.

"Meatballs, basically. They're good."

"Real good," said band-shirt.

"I'd go there first," said the last.

My stomach grumbled in anticipation.

"Just a few blocks up?" I asked. Nods followed. They gave me directions and a few recommendations that made my mouth water. I thanked them and left.

Each block in Empress was a small artificial island. Where back home everything was chaotic and haphazard, here each island specialized in fulfilling a specific need; it was rigorous organization in civic form. Some of the island-buildings were full of apartments and surrounded by hundreds of moored boats. Others were places of business. A few, like the arcade, were full of shops selling all manner of goods, while others focused on production and manufacturing.

Bridges spanned the canals in between. They raised and lowered as larger boats passed through, and crowds of pedestrians would bundle together behind a swinging gate and then shuffle across en masse when the bridge reopened.

The bakso shop was named the very original Best Bakso, and it was where the teens had said it would be. It occupied a corner spot inside another arcade lined with food vendors. I took a seat at the bar and ordered bakso ayam isi telur from a jolly little old lady who nodded in approval. The name of the dish wasn't in a language I recognized, but I was confident that, like back home, it had its roots in some ancient pre-Aligning civilization. I made sure they were the extra-large meatballs stuffed with hardboiled eggs—something the schoolboys recommended. She assured me they were.

When my order came, I devoured it. The kids were right; this was *good*. The noodles were tender, the broth salty but not overpowering. The bakso itself was fantastic—it had a stiff and snappy bite, with a lot of meaty flavor. The addition of the egg added a strong umami undertone. I ordered a second bowl of just regular bakso ayam and a side of shrimp satays drowning in peanut sauce. How long had it been since I had anything substantial? The *Gamble* perhaps? Before that?

When I finished, I paid with lira, much to the chagrin of the once-jolly proprietor. Her smiled faded into a scowl, but she pulled the cash across the counter. I apologized and explained that I hadn't had time to exchange them for Emperian huards. Her expression suggested she wasn't interested in forgiving me. Regardless, her meatballs were phenomenal.

Now agreeing the name Best Bakso was fitting, I left the shop and the food arcade. By this time I had almost forgotten about Hagen lost in the stacks back at the Armitage. Did I need to go back? I was sure he'd be there for hours, and exploring Empress without Protection was a welcome distraction. Besides, Hagen would find his way back to the embassy eventually. Before heading deeper into the city, I swung through the pakora place to grab a snack for the road.

I ate the pakoras (also fantastic) as I walked along the canals. Clouds had rolled in while I had been eating, and their heavy gray bellies hinted at rain. I didn't let them bother me and found myself munching happily and enjoying the sights and sounds of Empress.

What would the city be like in a storm? The walkways were all a good ten or twenty feet above the water, for the most part, but I knew swells could go higher than that. Here the majority of the city lived along the waterfront. Back home only the poor and downtrodden did—the elevated rarely spared a thought for their neighbors, and storms always wreaked havoc with Level Two.

I considered this as I drifted. Eventually I emerged into an open square that sat alongside a wide swath of water in which a collection of boats of various sizes bobbed.

Sometimes being alone in a crowd is therapeutic. It was nice to sort through my mind. Empress became a background— white noise.

My pakoras gone, I tossed the paper container into a waste receptacle. Across the plaza was a small coffee cart, and I considered whether to buy a coffee now or wait until I had met up with Taft and Hannah. As I pondered my choices, the woman at the front of the line turned.

My breathing seized.

She wore her brown hair differently. But I recognized those dark eyes and red lips. Emotions clattered around inside my chest. They fought with the surreal feeling I was still experiencing from being back in this reality.

This couldn't be real. This was some aberration. Some glitch brought about from my shifting between worlds.

My heart hammered inside my chest. My neck and back broke out in a cold sweat. Feelings urging me to run, jump, and laugh as I shouted her name were beaten back by common sense. Protection didn't seem keen on allowing public disturbances— that wouldn't fit into the orderly ideals of Victory.

Her.

Here.

Of all places.

Thoughts of Hagen, the embassy, and wandering Empress disappeared, overwhelmed by memory and loss and the odd joy of rediscovery. I wanted to shout. I wanted to scream! Ten minutes from now or ten minutes earlier and we'd have missed one another, drifted through the city never knowing how close we were. The mystery of her would have remained just that— a mystery.

She turned and, coffee in hand, walked down a street that led away from the plaza and between two apartment complexes.

I couldn't believe it.

Essie Cove was in Empress.

NINETEEN

For a moment, I didn't move. Essie. Carter's cross! ESSIE. I blinked, hoping my eyes weren't betraying me.

Last time I saw her, it had been a mess. She had kicked me out of her apartment and disappeared. Never explained. Never as much left a note. How she got from Lovat to Empress—and during the height of the riots—I had no idea. The *Gamble*? Some other means? She didn't know I was here. But why would she?

Admitting I still had feelings for her came easy—even from far away, the knot of emotions twisted painfully inside me. There was no denying what I felt. Then again, maybe I needed to ignore that. Maybe I should stay where I was and let her live her life. The conflict in my head was a jumble of confusion and heartache.

But I had to know. I had to make sure she was okay. That overpowered everything.

I moved as quickly as my knee would allow, something a bit faster than my regular walk, trying not to appear too desperate. Hoped I wouldn't seem rushed or flustered. As much as I had thought about Esther the last few months, I had allowed something in myself to move beyond her. Or at least I believed I did. I had made terms with the strangeness of her disappearance. She had her reasons. She had secrets. Everyone deserved privacy. Everyone deserved a choice.

But emotions can wash away convictions. Everything disappears beneath their swell.

"Excuse yourself!" said a woman as I crashed into her. She had been busily hurrying across the plaza. I had been so tunnel-visioned I hadn't noticed. She scowled and I mumbled an apology but kept moving, hardly seeing or hearing her curses.

As I hobbled along, I kept telling myself the same things over and over. I was just going to check on Essie. If she wanted me out of her life, I would leave willingly. I just needed to make sure she was okay.

Essie turned left at the end of the street and onto a boardwalk. Beyond were several large tugs floating in a small island port. Somewhere a bell clanged, and music rumbled. It took me a full minute before I cleared the corner. I nearly missed her passing out of the crowd and up a ramp that ended in an intersection of catwalks.

The light was beginning to dim as the sun set. Essie didn't slow. I wanted to shout her name, but I was pretty sure her anonymity was important. So I kept my mouth shut. The ramp did a number on my knee—ramps always do, but they're better than stairs. When I started across the catwalk, I found myself slower than I had been on the boardwalk below.

The climb had closed a little distance. Essie was closer, but not close enough. I found myself hoping she'd stop, browse a bookshop, or visit a newsstand. Something. Anything. Enough to give me time to reach her and say hello without shouting her down. It was strange being so close and yet feel a gulf away. My stomach did little flips, nerves mostly, wondering if our meeting would upset her.

I half expected a buzzing to begin. Now would be an inopportune time for the Wasteland to whisk me away. It enjoyed doing that. I could flop here on the catwalk until someone found me as I drank beer with Tawil while he spoke in riddles and any memories of me meeting Essie faded into a dream-like fog.

Not once did she look back. Essie moved like a woman intent on a mission. She crossed a bridge, and I followed. She took a ladder, so I did as well. She passed beneath a sign encouraging Emperians to STAY VIGILANT, and I did too.

We were up among the signs. Latticework and cables were strung everywhere, keeping glowing tubes aloft—a myriad of signs advertising products or blustering up support for Victory. Lights danced before my eyes, blooming and fading as tubes clicked on and off. They formed temporary auroras of refracted lapis and sea greens that shifted to fiery oranges and blood reds before dying into deep plums, and then the sequence repeated. Clouds of color. Blooms of light.

For a moment, my rational side won out.

"Hey!" I shouted.

She didn't stop. Didn't even turn to see who was shouting.

"Hey!" I yelled a second time. Louder and with more force.

The few people who braved these heights paused and gave me a once-over before they decided I wasn't worth their time and moved on.

Essie slowed, then briefly stopped. She looked over her shoulder. I smiled, moving a hand to my chest and opening my mouth to shout, "It's me!" but I never did. Her skin shifted in hue; she became a part of the aurora. Our eyes locked. Once again I was ready to fall into those endless pools of darkness. But there was no recognition in her gaze. I was no one—a ghost in the crowd.

My stomach dropped in freefall.

My words caught in my throat. I gagged, then coughed.

When I looked up, her back was to me. She was moving away.

Maybe I looked different? The suit didn't help, but that was presumption—a fool's hope. I had the black eye and the bruises from the cultists, but that wasn't enough to make me unrecognizable. I cleaned up a bit for the Magnez job, cut my hair to a respectable length, trimmed my beard. But, I still looked mostly like myself. It's not like I had shaved or gotten any new tattoos. I was the Waldo Bell she knew: dust-brown skin, dust-brown hair, and dust-brown eyes.

Road boy.

But, road boy or not, Essie hadn't recognized me. Her gaze had passed through me. It pained me watching her turn and continue on her way. My heart ached as if it was being torn out yet again. To her, I was just one other person in a city calling to a friend or hailing a rickshaw. Not worthy of her attention.

Carter's cross, it *hurt*.

Even when she had thrown me out, I hadn't seen that expression in those eyes. She hadn't been mad; she had been *scared*. I had been a connection she couldn't afford.

There had been pain at that moment of separation. Her expression had burned into my brain. The rejection had been born of necessity—it hadn't come from anger, hate, or suspicion.

It wasn't a fear of me, but fear of the man following me. Argentum had become the wedge. If only she knew he had been a fraud. If only she had learned what I had learned.

Her fears made sense. She was worried the Society of Collectors would tie me to her, and it was apparent that she didn't want them finding her. That was over now. The Collectors hadn't cared a lick about me. She had nothing to fear.

Stunned, not sure of what else to do, I mechanically continued to follow. Any other plan for that afternoon was lost to the haze. My brain challenged me, pushing against this reality and driving me quietly mad.

Essie crossed the bridge, and so did I. She descended another ramp, so I followed. I made no effort to hide. I wanted her to know I was here. I wanted her to see me. I wanted to have a conversation.

What had she done? I never found out. Why were the Collectors after her? I didn't know. She once told me things at home were tough, but she had never elaborated, and I had never pressed for more information.

I had so many questions. Perhaps this new security joint could offer Essie protection. We had money now, would have more from this gig, I could pay the Collectors off.

It wasn't fair. It never is. Emotions can charge you in ways you don't understand and take you into places you can't fully control.

When I made it to the bottom of the ramp, Essie was far ahead of me, disappearing between other pedestrians. If she knew I was tailing her, she didn't show it. I was so in my head and lost to my thoughts that I nearly missed her ducking down an alley.

A light rain began to patter on the boardwalks as I turned into the alley. The lighting here was darker than along the canals. No neon illuminated the gloom. Only old and flickering sodium lamps cast golden pools beneath opaque hoods.

There was no silhouette walking away from me. There wasn't even the echo of boots on pavement. Beyond a cluster of closed fish stalls standing sentinel, the alleyway was abandoned.

I rubbed my eyes with the heels of my hand and blinked. Maybe I just missed something. Perhaps something had clouded my vision.

Essie wasn't here.

"Hello?" I called out. I got no answer. "Esther? You there?"

Unsure of what to do, I took a few shaky steps down the alley. Before I had seen her, I had a clear plan. Now, everything was muddled and muddied. My realities were collapsing in on themselves, and it created a cascade effect. The alley, the floor, the rain—it all felt illusionary. My world was becoming distant mirages that pull at my subconscious, tearing at my sanity with claws of doubt.

Breathe. Just breathe.

I ran through my options. First was to find an Empress Directory Agent, see if a residence was listed. I doubted that'd reveal much. Essie was on the run from something, and she was no fool. Esther Cove might not even be her real name.

The buildings above could be offices. Perhaps Essie was upstairs? Maybe there were apartments mixed with the office space? It was the antithesis of Victory's appeal to order, but you never knew. I could check with the front desk. Conceivably leave a message with the building's security.

That didn't sit right either. If she lived here, she'd have gone through the front door, not the back.

My third option was to wait, see if she showed. Looking up, I could see a multitude of catwalks connecting the buildings on this island with each other. It'd be easy to pass between them. It only made finding Essie harder. A lot of entrances and exits. Easy to miss someone.

The last option was the worst; I could stake out the plaza where I first saw her. I loathed the very idea. Odds are she passed through there occasionally, but I had no assurance. It could be a waste of time, and I only had a day or so—

I ran my fingers through my hair, lost in thought at my choice when a hand grabbed me by the collar and jerked me roughly into a small alcove hidden behind a pool of sodium light. A knee hit my stomach. I moved to double over. But before I could, I was thrown back against a wall. Flashes of the attack on the *Gamble*. Shovels. Names. Curses. I expected to see one of the cultists: the dimanian, the white-eyed umbra with the black-to-pale-to-translucent miasma, perhaps all of them.

The back of my head smacked against cement. I saw stars and blinked to recover.

I'm sure I made some pitiful sound.

Something distant rattled around in my ears. Someone was talking. Speech slurred. Accented. Strutten and something else. A hand—my own, I think—gingerly touched the back of my head. When I brought my fingers around, they were fuzzy. The tips glistened a dark red.

"I just. I think. I can. I a—"

A forearm fell across my windpipe. I had to stand on my tiptoes to inhale. I was dead. I was stupid. This had been a trap. A lure to bring me to this abandoned alley and—

A small silver blade hovered just below my eye. The light caught its edge and gleamed coldly in the early spring night.

"Move, and I cut you." I didn't recognize the voice.

I made a gagging sound. It took another half-second before everything came into view.

Beyond the blade was a terrified-looking Esther Cove, jaw set, the deep pools of her eyes thoroughly black—bottomless wells of shadow. Her chin quivered slightly. Emotions ran riot through me. But I did nothing. I just raised my hands. Her dark eyes narrowed.

"Okay, you bastard. Who the hell are you? Why are you following me?"

TWENTY

E ssie—it's m-me—" I managed.

Her eyes narrowed to black slits. A security light blazed down from above us, casting us in white-hot light that shadowed our eyes.

"It's me," I repeated.

I pointed with my raised hand at my face and tried to put on an expression of friendliness that probably looked manic. My voice collapsed into a wheeze. I could barely breathe with her knife against my throat. By the Firsts, she was strong.

There was no recognition in her narrow eyes, only suspicion and fear, maybe a little confusion. There was nothing of the Esther I remembered. This was a stranger.

The pressure of her forearm lightened. I managed a hitching breath. She was still holding me in place, just allowing me to breathe.

"From Lovat," I said through a rasp. "Don't you remember?"

"Lovat? You're Lovatine? Ess is in Lovat!" the woman said. The slits blossomed as her eyes widened. She gasped and stepped back, and I collapsed, sliding down the wall into a sitting position and running my fingers through my hair. I gulped a few lungfuls of air, happy to still be alive but only more confused.

My broken mind began to run through alternatives. Maybe Essie wasn't real. Maybe, like this whole reality, she was a figment of my imagination. Maybe she had never been real. Maybe it was all a projection?

She loomed above me, now encased in shadows, the white light a small sun above her. She still held the knife out, but thankfully not up against my windpipe. It looked like she was quickly losing interest in cutting me open.

"Esther—" I began, then caught myself. "You're not Esther Cove. Are you?"

She stepped back, slipped the knife into her jacket, and pressed against the opposite wall of our little alcove. "No. No, I'm not. Bones"—it was spoken like a curse, but not one I recognized —"you saw her, didn't you? You saw my sister. You saw Ess."

She slid down the wall. We faced each other across the small alcove.

"Yes," I said. "Yes, I did."

Did I? My voice sounded so sure.

I began to notice subtle differences now. This woman had a slightly fuller face, but you'd never see it unless you knew this wasn't Esther. She had sharper cheekbones, but not severe enough to stand out. Her lips were red, but nowhere near as red as when I first noticed her in the plaza.

"I'm Olivia," she said. "Esther's my sister. Who the hell are you?"

She told me to call her Liv.

We sat outside at a cafe along the boardwalk that ran along the outer edge of Empress's most northern inner harbor, in a neighborhood called Nelthorpe. We sat under an awning and slurped chicory sweetened with sugar and nibbled on sweets made of wafer, icing, and melted chocolate. Liv had said they were good, and she wasn't wrong.

For a long time we stared out at the rain that disturbed the surface of the harbor, occasionally sparing a glance at one another that lingered until the other caught our stare and turned away, embarrassed. I'm not sure how long we sat that way. A long time. Two strangers feeling each other out.

The likeness was uncanny, but there were subtle queues that made me realize this wasn't Essie at all. This was a different woman, despite what my eyes were telling me. It went beyond the physical. The way Liv held herself. The way she sipped her chicory. The awkward way she would start to speak and then close her mouth and look away. Esther had been bolder, which was probably why she had no problem pulling me into bed and later throwing me out.

"Sorry for following you," I finally said. "Didn't mean anything by it. I can understand how it comes across. I just… thought you were your sister."

Liv held up a hand, closed her eyes. Absently, she wiped her nose on the back of her hand, sniffing quietly. When she opened them again, a sadness had seeped in—a deep and abiding emotion, something that had weighed her down for a long time. It made me feel like a heel.

She took a deep breath. "What did she do to you?"

"Kicked me out of her apartment."

"You lived with her? Romantically involved?" she asked.

I nodded.

"Figures," Liv looked away. Grew quiet.

"What?" I asked. The word felt like an anchor on my tongue.

Liv's scowl deepened. "She disappear out of your life too?"

I blinked. Stuck by such a direct question. For a moment I was speechless. Then words began to form. "Yeah. She did."

"So you saw me and thought I was her."

"Pretty much," I said.

"And here we are."

"Here we are."

Liv sighed, her shoulders slumping in a way that reminded me of her sister. It was strange, almost surreal sitting across from her. My stomach was doing somersaults and my throat was tight.

I didn't know this woman, but the words came unbidden now. "Essie never explained why. I had gotten into a little trouble, and I told her about it. She flipped. Threw me out. When I came back later, I found out she had left her job, moved out. Left the city, as far as I know. Felt wrong trying to track her down. But when I saw you here—"

My voice trailed off with my thoughts.

"What'd she do? As a job, I mean."

"Waitress," I said. "Diner called Cedric's. It's how we met."

"Waitress… bones," said Liv. She gave a humorless chuckle. That word again. *Bones*. Clearly held some significance in Victory.

"Fine enough work in the—"

"I'm sure it is," said Liv. "But she…"

Her voice drifted off. She looked out over the harbor at the boats bobbing in the gentle waves, their hulls shimmering in the rain. When she looked back at me, there were tears in her eyes. "I miss my sister, Mister Bell."

"Call me Wal," I said.

"I miss Ess, Wal. For years I've had no idea where she's been. Where she's lived. If she's dead or alive! Up until now, I assumed the worst. No letters. No contact of any kind. Just silence. Just damn nothing! And now this?" Her fists clenched. "I apologize if I come across as a little overwhelmed."

I spread my hand. "I miss her too. I'm happy to share what I can. Fill in the holes."

For a long time she looked at me, as if she was sizing up whether I was the person to whom she wanted to spill her soul. I could see it in her eyes. I did little to dissuade her. I couldn't— she looked too much like Essie.

Finally she spoke. "Ess and me are twins. Identical twins. I'm sure you can see that." She gestured to herself, then drew her shoulders forward, embarrassed, and looked away. "We were best friends… once. Hell, closer than best friends. She was my reflection. We loved the same books, listened to the same music, watched the same serials, shopped at the same shops—bones, this sounds so superficial. You have any siblings, Wal?"

"No," I said. "Only child."

"Then you'll understand even less. Typical siblings are part best friend and part rival. Twins… aren't, or at least we never were. I was older by a full minute. That can be a big deal for some twins, but for us it never was. If anything, we celebrated each other. There's a connection between us that goes—*went* even deeper than typical siblings experience. It's hard to explain. You hear about "soul mates," but that isn't accurate. Not really." She looked away, then back at me. "This probably sounds insane."

"No," I said. "Actually, it sounds refreshingly normal."

"You seem like a nice sort," she said. "What happened to your face?"

My hand went to the bruises. I felt shame and embarrassment, not just from being called out by a stranger, but for being called out by a woman my brain identified as Esther Cove. "I work security."

Her eyebrows raised, like Essie's and yet nothing like Essie's. She brought the conversation back to her sister. "So you met her in a cafe—"

"Diner," I corrected.

"Diner," she returned. I heard a little sarcasm.

I nodded. "We flirted for a bit. But it was always silly stuff— jokey. My old man does it all the time. I probably picked it up from him. It's harmless. The wait staff reciprocates, probably expecting big tips, usually getting them. Anyway, it started like that, but it quickly evolved into something else. I knew we both felt it. Our gazes lingered too long, our smiles were too wide, the laughs came too naturally. You know?"

"She take you home with her?" Liv asked, with blunt bitterness.

"In a way." I shrugged. "She found me late one night looking out over the water, not far from Ced's. We smoked together on an overlook, talked, then got drinks, talked some more, got more drinks. One thing led to another..."

Liv shifted and frowned. She clearly didn't like hearing about my sexual escapades with her sister, no matter how simplified.

"I liked her a lot," I said, ending the story.

Silence again. I could feel her eyes on me, but I didn't look over at her. I let my gaze wander to the lights of the submerged city below the waters of the harbor.

"I can tell," said Liv. "Can hear it in your voice."

"Yeah?"

Liv didn't say anything for a long while. The rain had slowed, but heavy drops still spilled from the awning and onto the boardwalk. When she turned to look at me, I could see an edge of hostility in her posture. "You're not the first, you know? Dennis. Julian. Osvald. There have been many before you. So many fools who get caught up in her cyclone."

"Cyclone?" I said. The dumb part of me said I should have felt jealous, but I didn't. If anything, I was relieved. I wasn't sure how much truth I was hearing from Liv, but the way she said it made me feel less alone. We might never be friends, but there was a connection here, a solace. She felt it too. I could see it in her familiar eyes.

"When we got older, our priorities changed. We went to Victory University in Empress. I wanted to study archaeology, and Ess, she wanted to study forensics. They matched—in their way. I thought it was perfect. I could see us working to piece together mysteries of the ancient epochs. Forensics was a new course, but it had roots in archaeology."

"What happened?"

Liv quieted for a bit, her eyes meeting mine only for a moment before looking away. She was clearly weighing the pros and cons of telling me the details.

"You don't have to tell me," I said softly.

She turned to face me and the expression on her face reminded me of Essie's the night she threw me out of her apartment. Dark umber eyes filled with a mixture of anger and fear, lips drawn tight, shoulders hunched forward. My muscles went rigid as if bracing for an explosion. Liv huffed and looked away toward the window, but really she was gazing into her past. I recognized that gaze. I'd worn it many times.

I leaned back. Giving her space.

After a bit the tension drained out of her. "No," she finally said. "No. I'm sorry. I've just been keeping this bottled up for so long... It dredges up old memories. Old feelings I thought were long gone."

"This is weird for me, too," I said.

She nodded, wet her lips. "Where were we?"

"Something happened at University," I said.

"Ah, yes. *Elenor.*" A sharp bitterness entered her voice when she said the name.

"Who is that?"

"Friend of *hers.*" She took a drink. The emphasis had been on the "hers." Liv looked away, and then back at me. "A rival of mine, I suppose. Elenor was what Ess aspired to be. We were shy kids. Elenor oozed personality. We were timid. El had an air about her that reeked of authority. She skipped class, ignored Protection, beat up boys and girls alike. She wasn't any bigger than us, but she was tough, bold, *confident.* We lived near campus, in an apartment building four floors above the water, and El ran the floor. I sometimes think Ess was in love with her."

There was a lull in the conversation. Liv looked into her empty cup of chicory, then up at me. "Why am I telling you all of this?"

I spread my hands, gave a small shrug. "I'm happy to listen."

"Maybe that's why. Maybe I'm tired of holding this all in. Mom won't listen. Dad no longer cares. They're both older generation—Victory stood for purity in their time. They don't like the idea of Ess running off with a foreign girl. You... you've experienced this, in a way. Whatever *this* is." Her mouth formed another sad smile.

"We don't have to keep going," I said.

"No. It feels good to let this out. Freeing. Even to the strange man who chased me through the neighborhood." She laughed softly and gave me a wink.

"Elenor was foreign?"

"Lovatine," said Liv, with an edge. "One of yours."

I couldn't suppress the chuckle. "Sounds so silly when you put it that way."

"How do you mean?"

"Empress feels familiar," I said. "Sure, it's canals and boardwalks where Lovat is lifts and levels. Empress is artificial islands, and Lovat crawls across a natural archipelago. But there's a lot here that reminds me of home. You have your own nuances. Including some great food we're lacking. But I think we're more similar than we are different."

Liv thought about that for a long time, then nodded, the sort of nod you give when you're coming around to an idea.

"So Essie ran to Lovat," I said, pulling us back to the past. We could remain strangers in the present. I owed her that much.

Liv nodded. "Something happened. We never got a clear answer. Protection—I'm sure you've met our local constabulary."

"I have."

"Yeah? Well, they came knocking one weekend, asking for Esther's whereabouts. When I came around the corner, they thought I was her. They had no idea we were twins. Four of them rushed in—knocked my dad aside. He ended up with a concussion. They dragged me to questioning.

"It took two days before I had convinced them I wasn't Ess. Two days of pleading. Two days of pain. Two days of wondering why my sister would put me through this." Tears reappeared in the corners of her eyes. She wiped them away.

I tried to look away, but something in me realized I shouldn't. She needed strength from someone. Even me. So I matched her gaze for gaze and wondered what it was Essie had done and what had happened to Liv.

One of those questions was quickly answered.

Liv frowned and held up her hands. She brought both pinkie fingers together, and I could see instantly that both had been severed at their midpoint.

"Protection did that?"

"Two days and the equivalent of a finger," she said.

I winced.

"I hardly notice anymore," Liv said.

It was hard not to react, to offer a hug or reach out and squeeze her hand. I like to fix things. I like to help. To complicate matters my brain still recognized her as Essie. But to her I was a stranger. So I sat still and felt terrible because of it.

"I hated Ess for years. Took a decade to get over. Now I've moved on," Liv said. "I don't dwell on her much. If I do, it just makes me sad. Not angry. Not really."

"What happened to Elenor?"

Liv scowled. "Last I heard, the bitch was running guns in Lovat. Started calling herself by a new name."

"What name?" I asked, trying to be casual.

"Elephant."

TWENTY-ONE

ey, buddy. You gotta go."

"Huh," I said, looking up. The voice and the nudge had pulled me from my daze. The lights in the cafe were dimmed to the color of old amber, and my cup of sweet chicory had gone cold.

"We're closing up. It's eight." He tapped at a watch, and I pushed up from the table. My right knee cracked, then popped and sent a bolt of pain up my thigh, reminding me of its existence.

"Sorry," I mumbled. My head was swimming. Liv had been gone for over an hour, gone home to wherever home was in this city. We had said our goodbyes. Shook hands. It was as awkward as you'd expect. She looked so much like her sister.

But by then my mind had been racing. *Elephant.* I almost couldn't believe it. Always helpful Elephant. Of course she was connected. She had her hands in everything in the lower levels. Why not this as well?

"We open tomorrow at sunrise," said the clerk. I smiled, nodded, and left. Who closed down a cafe and returned the first thing the next morning? Pitch addicts, maybe. Did Victory even have pitch addicts? If it did, I hadn't seen any.

Stiff and reeling, I stepped from the cafe and into the chilly night air. My limp got more pronounced as my leg woke up. The cold from the enclosed harbor slapped at my cheeks and forced a somber dose of reality into my lungs. My friends would be worried sick. Hagen would wring his hands. Hannah would be downright livid. My crew had an inherent distrust in law enforcement—one I shared. Being in a strange country, I doubted that anyone had gotten Protection involved. But it wouldn't surprise me if they were out scouring the canals.

The rain had faded away, but moody clouds above whispered of more to come. The moon struggled to pierce the gloom and gave the sky a bleak, washed-out appearance that cast the canals in indigos and cobalts. The early spring air was cold, and with the chill came something familiar. The wretched aroma that plagued Lovat was now present here in Victory. Must have rolled in with the rainstorm.

It wasn't as pungent nor as sharp as back home, but it was here, a base note that mingled with the evening's bouquet. A pair of Emperians hustled down the side of the canal, handkerchiefs over their noses. So this wasn't just some phantom sensation dredged up from a tired and broken mind; Empress had begun to stink.

The citizenry's response amused me. We were used to foul smells in Lovat. There the stink penetrated the cement, crept into your pores, and leached into the water pipes. Only the highest levels avoided the general reek from the scrape and span. But the lower you went, the more the scent of the city lingered. When something as foul as the smell rolled in, most of us just took it in stride. Only when it reached the rich did it become front-page news.

Unlike Lovat, Victory was closely connected to the sea. It wasn't a city stacked as much as a city expanded. Most of its inhabitants moved on its canals at sea level walking along the shorelines of the artificial islands. When I first arrived, the ever-present smell of seaweed and salt had been invigorating. Now the air was corrupted by a perfume of ancient decay.

I rounded a bend, now only a few blocks from the bridges that connected one island to another, and noticed Protection was out in force. They lingered on the corners, side-eyeing anyone who caught their attention. A few were watching a group of Emperians huddled near the window of a closed monochrome shop. Black and white bubble screens flickered behind the glass as it displayed a news program that caught the attention of passersby, who had stopped to stare.

I moved closer, being careful with each step.

A gargoyle materialized in the group.

I stopped. Blinked. The back of my skull began to buzz. I heard the distant winds of the Wasteland.

The black hood rose from the crowd like the hub of a wain wheel. The thing wasn't looking at the monochromes at all. Unlike the crowd, it was facing me, arms at its sides, the robes billowing and passing through the legs of the people around it. No one noticed.

I took two deliberate steps in its direction. The creature tittered—the irritating laugh sending a shiver down my spine. When I blinked again, it was gone. Leaving only the gathered crowd and the flashing monochrome.

The thoughts came one after another. *Gargoyles. Here. In Empress.* That didn't mean anything good.

"What's happening?" I asked a tall woman standing near the back of the crowd. She turned, sized me up with a raised eyebrow, and was clearly unimpressed by what she saw.

"Trouble. Trouble's out there." She waved a hand behind us, in the direction of open water. Then she pointed at the screens. "Something's happening along the islands."

It took a few moments to process what I was seeing. A camera passed over pale oblong shapes scattered across a tangle of sticks. Then the view switched to another shot. This was closer. The white shapes were the hulls of boats encrusted with barnacles and rust. They were lying among an entire forest of felled trees—white corpses against the gray-black funeral pyres.

The glass window obstructed any sound from the reporter at the scene, but the man was clearly bothered. Unlike most reporters he was disheveled and dirty, his hair sticking up at odd places. The large mic in his hand quivered—and it wasn't just the bad signal. He was frightened.

As the broadcast continued, I realized this was high up in the mountains. Occasionally the camera managed to work in a blurry shot of a hillside or a distant landscape far below. I had heard of rogue waves being able to level forests like that, but those occurred along the shoreline. This was nowhere near the shore.

Rosalia Mountains flashed in bright-white letters across the bottom of the screen.

Gasps rose among the crowd, a few panicked cries.

"Bones of Kuranes!" someone said. "They're five hundred feet up the mountains."

"How the hell—"

"Whole town, gone. Just like that."

"Ain't never seen a windstorm powerful enough to do that!"

"Ain't no wind, ya coot."

"Who could drag boats up there like that?"

"Ain't no one dragged them neither."

As more discussion broke out, deciphering information became more and more difficult. That said, I agreed with the general sentiment of the crowd. What exactly was happening, and how had hundreds of boats ended up among a flattened forest in the Rosalias? This, coupled with the recent arrival of the gargoyles, made my blood run cold.

I turned and looked at the tall woman. She was chewing on the back of her thumb and staring at the monochromes, one arm wrapped around her waist.

"End of days," she mumbled. "A new Aligning."

It hurt to swallow the lump that formed in my throat.

TOOO LAAAATE!

The hiss thundered in my ear, followed by an echoed cackle. They rode on a warm desert wind that made my stomach lurch. The taste of bile was sharp on my tongue, and with it I felt a fury rise inside of me.

I spun, eyes wide, fists balling. There was nothing. Just the entrance to the footbridge that connected canal to shoreline.

The crowd was stirring itself up. Some people suggested heading to higher ground. Others thought they should move away from the sea, abandon the city and the islands altogether.

A few Protection officers were studying me from the other side of the bridge, heads tilted, faces obscured.

The woman next to me was staring at me, a look of concern on her face.

"You okay, son?" she asked.

The crowd was oppressive all of a sudden. I stepped clear without responding. Breathing in rapid breaths of air. Trying to stop my head from swimming.

I walked half a block before I saw another gargoyle. This one was beneath an overhang, still some distance away, a black form against the blue night. Its head tilted as if it was watching me, but when I stepped in its direction, it disappeared, flickering out like a staticky signal.

Cowards. They always cut and ran before I could get hold of them. And I could—they knew it. I was a man of two worlds, as Tawil would say. My reach extended well beyond my own realm. This was my reality—a duality that threatened to drive me mad, but it saved me from them. Gave me the ability to fight back.

TOOOOOO LAAATE, GUARDIAN!

Again it roared, and again I spun. I was a block from the crowd now, but I could see the tall woman watching me. A few people had broken off, while others still stood watching the broadcast, their faces bathed in the flickering light of the shop's monochromes. For a moment, they looked normal—then, for an instant, they were all gargoyles. A cluster of hoods packed tightly together.

I stepped back, and the gargoyles flickered away.

My palms felt sweaty. I reached for the reassurance of my gun, and my hand met only air. It wasn't here—the contradictions of its existence were too much to bear. A buzzing formed at the back of my skull and hot wind rolled across my shoulders, a sun—a sun not in my sky—beating down upon me. Pain flared in my head, and my mind broke as the two realities conflicted with each other. Sand was beneath my feet. Then pavement. Then sand again. Each step changed the world. Each breath created a hurricane. I gripped my head with both hands and tried to shut out the pain of paradox.

Not now. Not now! I needed to focus! *FOCUS!* I clutched the side of my head.

Then my world—Empress, the Territories, everything— snapped back into place. Sweat had soaked my shirt, and I shivered in the chill of the night air. The cold sharpened my senses and dulled the ache in my head.

Gargoyles followed the Firsts. If they were here, that meant—

TOOOOO LATEEEE!

This time I ignored the voice. The next block was a blur, the one after that much the same. At the end of the third block, another bridge beckoned. It arched from the streets and walkways along the canals and across a broad stretch of water to a long quay that ran parallel to the shore. A collection of stern narrow buildings sat across an open plaza—the remnants of a former port that had been converted into a block of taverns and restaurants. The lights inside made the windows glow a warm gold.

I crossed quickly, stepping from the bridge and onto the waterside plaza. As my foot touched the quay, a loud wave crashed against the breakwater. It shook the structure ever so slightly. Seawater rushed over the edge and pooled around my shoes.

A few mumbles of concern rose from those moving through the plaza. It was odd to get such a powerful swell this far into the city—the canals should work as a reef. My breathing grew shallow, and I slowly turned, looking back from where I had come.

A gargoyle stood in the center of the footbridge. Its robes billowed, moving as they had in the Wasteland, with that strange underwater motion. The blank face was as expressionless as ever, its head tilted to one side as if it was curious. The moment felt like a lifetime. Neither of us moved. We faced each other like a pair of gunfighters.

My breathing came in ragged huffs, and I ground my teeth together and tongued the inside of my lower lip. Then the creature began to move. It was part step and part drift, but it came toward me. The few people out on the bridge this night didn't react. They moved like the creature wasn't there.

I knew better. I didn't move. Didn't react. Just watched. Hands at my side, my fingers twitching.

Near the end, it stopped. The long head tilted back, and it slowly raised its draped arms, the black-clad hands outstretched. There was a flash of lighting, and something else stood where the gargoyle was.

Membranous wings, like that of a bat, stretched from its shoulders in herky-jerky motions. It had a narrow blank face with a sharply pointed chin framed by horns that curled inward like mandibles. The hands were lengthened by elongated fingers tipped with talons. Behind it, I could see a barbed tail whip back and forth like an eager cat about to strike.

Above me thunder rumbled. The roll ripped the night sky and echoed off the canyons of the canals. It was louder and more ominous than any thunder I had heard before. A few people around me cried out in surprise. I turned and looked up as if drawn to the sky, the gargoyle behind me forgotten for the moment.

Above Empress boiled a ceiling of turbid clouds that devoured the moonlight. Deep within the darkness, lightning flashed and cracked. More thunder rolled from the bursts. In that brief a moment I saw something, and my breathing hitched.

A dark form moved against the clouds—vast and unknowable. I stepped back, nearly stumbled as my tired mind processed what I was seeing. The mountainous penumbra of head and shoulders turned as if noticing Empress for the first time. Vast branches of shadow drifted from the head, writhing like enormous feelers. An uncountable number of sinister eyes glowed from within that shadow beyond the clouds like a myriad of small suns. For a moment, the monster and I faced each other.

Then the lightning was gone. The monster was gone.

All that remained was suffocated moonlight from behind the clouds.

Rain spattered my face. The stench was even stronger now.

TWENTY-TWO

Chaos greeted me when I arrived at the embassy. The building was an old gray brick affair, covered in ancient ivy and climbing vines and lit at the corners by canister lights embedded in the ground. Its roof was the dusty green of tarnished copper and mostly lost to the evening's gloom. Nearly every light inside was on, and the glow spilled from the panes, illuminating the ground outside. People hurried about in a fevered tumult. I could hear shouts and the clattering and thumps of objects being moved around. The whole building quivered with activity.

Had they also seen the thing above the city?

Around me, rain pelted the landscaping, adding a constant rush that dulled most sound. I kept expecting a rain-soaked gargoyle to leap from the shadows or appear like a specter before me. None came. Every time lightning flashed, my head jerked upward and I expected to see… whatever it was I saw. But each time I was disappointed.

No. Relieved. I was *relieved*.

A troop of leather-clad Protection officers stood outside the front entrance—twenty of them in total. At their waists, they held nasty-looking repeater rifles with curled magazines. Up until now, any Protection I had seen were dressed casually, but these were in full combat regalia. They still wore their polished black helmets but had added thick armor on their shoulders and chest. They glistened in the rain, and gave me pause at the edge of the embassy's grounds.

I'd run from the quay—sprinted, if you could call my painful lope a sprint—and my breathing was heavy. I doubled over, my shoulders growing and shrinking with each inhalation. My knee felt as if it had been stuffed with hot coals and then stuck with porcupine needles. But I'd had to run. Empress—hell, the Territories themselves were in danger.

One of the Protection officers saw me and broke rank. They crossed the ground and approached me with a black-gloved hand raised, fingers spread—the universal symbol of 'halt.'

"No visitors," came the accented voice, muffled beneath the helmet. They pointed at the ribbon on my chest.

"Where's your escort?" they asked.

"Not a visitor," I said through a wince and deep breaths. The reflection of my own face in the black smoothness of the face mask made me look pitiful. Black eye, scuffs and scratches, hair and beard soaked by the rain. No wonder they had stopped me.

I tapped my chest. "I'm Waldo Bell. I run security for the Lovatine ambassador."

The officer lowered their hand. Studied me in silence for a moment.

"I run Guardian Security. Lovat's mayor, Camilla Magnez, hired us to protect Ambassador Castaigne."

The officer sized me up, then looked over their shoulder and back at me. "Wait here."

I was left standing in the wet and muddy grass as the officer conferred with a pair of their comrades that stood just to one side of the embassy entrance. Rain fell in thick sheets. I counted the excruciating seconds between the thunder and lightning. Each time it flashed, I looked to the sky but saw only clouds. Should I be relieved or worried?

My head still buzzed, but not the way it had before. Now it was a low constant. The other world was distant. Any danger of slipping away was mitigated—for now. I rubbed the back of my neck as I waited. Water ran in rivulets down my face. The Protection officer I spoke with disappeared inside. They reemerged a few moments later, gesturing to me.

Hannah's head appeared around the door. "Where the hell you been?"

"You're cleared," said the officer.

Hannah opened the door for me, and I stepped inside, dripping water on the carpet.

"You look like shit, boss. Castaigne's pissed."

My tongue suddenly felt heavy and clumsy. Hannah stood, her bright green eyes sparkling, her head tilted as if waiting for an explanation. Behind her, people were rushing about everywhere. Most had the business-casual dress and boring haircuts of embassy attachés. Boxes, crates, and briefcases were piled in their arms. They all wore panicked expressions.

It was difficult to even spit the words out. "Did they? Did they see—"

I looked down, staring at my uncomfortable shoes that glistened and leaked dirty rainwater onto the pale carpet.

"What? What are you talking about?"

"Did they see the thing, too?" I waved to the staff, then the ceiling.

Hannah gave me a puzzled look. "The thing? No, Wal. What are you talking about? Carter's cross, come on."

She guided me up a stairwell lined with oil paintings of stern-looking Emperians wearing politicians' suits or leather Protection uniforms. All were men—most with gray beards, sober eyes, stiff backs, and glowering scowls. I climbed slowly, the pain from my rush only adding to the agony, so it gave me time to take a closer look.

At one time these men were probably important, popular even. These paintings were their lasting mark on the world—a monument to their life's work. But to me—to a man who had seen beyond this limited scope of reality—what were they? Ghosts of a dead generation. Echoes, only echoes, like the howl of wind in the Wasteland. If that thing crashed through Empress, these canvas monuments would burn and become a legacy of dust and ash. If the Aligning happened again, the world was doomed.

Hannah was waiting at the top of the stairs, and she gestured for me to follow her down another hall. The upper level was as chaotic as the floor below, but less crowded. We walked down a plush hall with off-white wallpaper and bright golden lights and wall sconces. I left a trail of brown footprints as the rainwater leeched mud from my shoes.

Hannah approached a solid door flanked by two of my crew. Both gave me a nod and a smile. I clapped one on the shoulder.

"Good to see you, sir." One hand clasped my own. The other she held up in a clenched fist. I bumped it with the back of my hand.

"You look like—" She began, her eyes narrowing as she studied my face.

"I know," I said, the words hollow in my ears. "I'm fine. You should see the other guy."

She grinned, and I smiled back before I followed Hannah inside.

"There he is," said Taft. She folded her tree-trunk arms across her expansive chest. "Where were you?"

"I—" I began, ready and wanting to explain.

Ambassador Castaigne cut me off. "What the hell did you say to Sam?"

"Danforth?" The sudden demand derailed me. My conversation with Danforth was a distant memory, meaningless compared to whatever it was I'd seen outside. "Nothing much. Told him we got some threats and wanted him to steer clear of the summit meetings."

I looked around the room. This was an office for meetings. A pair of couches sat on one side near the door. They faced each other across a simple coffee table. On the other side of the room, Castaigne and her assistant stood behind an ornate blackwood desk near some windows. Two leather chairs faced the desk. The walls were bookshelves, and they were mostly empty. A few crates lay scattered nearby, half-full from the look of them.

Wensem stood near the chairs, Taft and Hagen near him. When we came in, Hagen had a panicked look that drained out of him when he saw me enter. How long had he been at the bookstore, lost among the stacks and forgetting about his concern for me? It was obvious he had beaten himself up over it.

Eli Pascal—one of our security people—leaned against the back of a couch. He was a wiry dimanian with sharp features, and looked lanky to the point of fragile. He had dark skin and long black hair that had started to gray around his temples. Despite his delicate appearance, he was as tough as nails. When I caught his eye, he gave me a nod in greeting.

"What happened?" I asked.

"He went to Victory," said Wensem. I could hear the frustration in his voice. "He went to Protection."

"You screwed up." Castaigne pointed at me. "Magnez told you this was a precarious situation."

Rage blossomed and mixed with all the other emotions warring inside me. Annoyance quickly followed. Panic made them all subside. Why were we still talking about this instead of the monster knocking on the city's door? I wanted to throw a punch through a wall. Instead, I bit the inside of my cheek and clenched my hands until my knuckles cracked. *Breathe. Just breathe.*

"They're kicking us out," Castaigne continued. She rubbed her right temple, just behind one of her horns. "Not just me. All of Lovat. All Lovatines. All foreigners. They're closing their borders, their ports. Tonight. The *Gamble's* being sent back."

"How'd he contact them? Why'd they believe him?"

Castaigne held up a hand, looked down at her desk, sighed. "I don't know, and frankly, I don't think I care. There was no threat. There *never* was a security threat. You lied to Sam. He called your bluff. In doing so, you reversed all of the progress between Lovat and Victory. You realize what that means? Do you?"

I did, but I said nothing. The emotions from this screwup were just more coals heaped on the fire that raged in my belly. I still hadn't told anyone about what I had seen and it was gnawing at me. So much chaos: The Wasteland. Danforth. Essie. Liv. Elephant. Gargoyles. That… thing above the cloud. By the Firsts, that *thing*.

Carter's cross. I looked around the room. No one in here knew what was going on! This whole city didn't understand. A First was coming. Perhaps already here and we were rambling on about meetings and summits. All this suddenly felt so petty.

"I need to pack. We're all on the next boat out of here," Castaigne snapped. "I expect you all to leave before me. We'll talk when we're on board the *Gamble* and en route to Lovat. Try to strategize some damn damage control." She shook her head in frustration, sighed, and walked out.

For a few moments, the room was silent. Hannah looked at Wensem, who looked at Taft, who looked at Pascal, who looked at Hagen, who stared daggers at me. I wanted to be the brave, bold leader, but shit, saying anything right now felt awkward and clumsy—like my mouth was full of cotton.

After a few moments I recovered. I looked at Wensem. "WSP?" The name felt heavy.

He nodded. "Pretty sure."

A string of curses fell from my mouth. I wanted to kick something, but there was nothing to kick. Probably for the best. Danforth had become much more problematic than I expected. He had destroyed much more than just an opportunity for my crew and me. He had damaged Lovat's chance of peace with its neighbor, and somehow shifted the blame onto me. Victory was edgy. Telling them about threats was foolish. He knew what would happen. If this was Camalote's strategy, then it was trash. Damn him and damn them.

"Get lost on your way here?" Taft asked.

Interrupting any response I had, Hagen walked over to me, stepping between me and the chuck. He leaned close, head cocked, so that only I could hear his words. "You okay?"

"Fine," I said, low enough that the others couldn't hear.

"You left."

"I got distracted," I replied. "Not intentional. Trust me. It was for a good reason."

His eyes met mine and I could see he believed me. "You're sure you're okay?"

"I am," I said. "I'll explain later."

That last statement appeased him. He stepped back, studied my face, then nodded and returned to his spot near Wensem.

"Well," Taft repeated. "Thought maybe you'd fell into a canal."

I rubbed my face, looked at her, and the rest of my crew. Wensem was stoic. He reacted to setbacks the way he always did, with calm acceptance—outwardly anyway. I knew inside it was eating him up. Eventually, it'd spill over. Eli Pascal looked tired and bored. He occupied himself, holding up a mirror in one hand as he buffed one of the horns that curled from his forehead with the other.

Taft was worried, more worried than I had ever seen the chuck. She rocked on her heels, her cheeks puffing out, forming taut half-spheres. Hagen looked concerned, but he cleaned his glasses on the end of his untucked shirt and waited. He was a guest among the crew—a trusted guest, but a guest none the less—and his posture said as much.

Hannah was livid—like I had expected. If Wensem was the deep freeze, Hannah was the summer storm. She paced back and forth, first next to me then across the room. She huffed and puffed, mumbling to herself.

Pascal disappeared for a moment and then emerged from a narrow doorway I hadn't seen before. He tossed a towel in my direction. It hit my face before I could catch it.

"You look cold, boss," said the roader. "Dry off."

He slumped onto the expensive overstuffed couch. A few strands of his hair hung in the air, then slowly drifted down onto his shoulders as if unbothered by gravity.

"I feel cold," I said, pulling the towel down and drying my face and neck before I started on my chest and arms. Images of boats scattered across mountainsides replayed in my memory. Then the smell. Then the gargoyles. Worst of all, the monster and its multitude of glowing eyes.

Wensem stepped forward. I could see he knew something was going on. Despite that, he remained passive, his relaxed demeanor present even in a crisis. I fed off it and allowed it to calm me somewhat.

"What is it?" Wensem asked. "What's going on?"

Deep breath, I told myself. Ease them into this. There was so much I wanted to say. So much I wanted to tell. But the news about Essie's connection to Elephant had gotten less critical. That could all come later. For now, they needed to know only about the dangers.

"Where to start?" I said.

"Maybe the beginning?" Hagen said.

"No," I said. "I want to, but I can't."

Wensem folded his arms and narrowed his eyes and watched me.

"I saw something. Out there. Something big. Bigger than I've ever seen."

No one said anything. They all waited.

"A First," I said, swallowing the lump that had risen in my throat. "It was a shadow among the clouds. Hell, maybe bigger than the clouds. So many eyes. It—it saw me. Looked right at me. We have to go. Leave. It's coming."

"Firsts are just myths." Pascal's words wavered as he took in the room of solemn faces. His tone shifted. He hadn't been with us on the Broken Road. "Right?"

No one replied. Everyone stared, working through what I had said. Replaying their own memories, running through their own experiences. I stared right back, eyes wide. I had to look manic. I felt manic.

My calm demeanor cracked, and the words began to tumble out of me. "Ash was right. Something is here. It was there. In the clouds. Then it was gone. It was close. Tawil knew. He *knew*!

Tried to warn me as best he could. It was coming from the sea. Somewhere near, maybe close."

West. Look west.

I went on. "I can't tell you exactly. It was huge though, mountainous. Glowing eyes. Face like... shit, I don't know. Somewhere. I was coming back from a cafe, and there was thunder and when I looked up—"

I stopped. Looked at my crew. "We need to go."

"Whoa, slow down," Taft said. She took a step toward me, hands outstretched.

"Ominous," said Hagen. "Concerning. I don't recall a First like that before, Wal—"

"Look," I snapped, interrupting him. "I spoke with Ashton. I talked to him before he fell. He said something was coming. Told me to 'look west.' But there hasn't been anything there. Just sea and mountains and nothing. Until now."

I rubbed my temples. My head hurt. My brain felt fried. "Castaigne's right for the wrong reason. We need to go. We need to go now. We need to warn Empress. Carter's cross, we need to warn Lovat. We need to get out before it gets here. Before it finds me. Before it finds us."

"By the Firsts," Hagen breathed out. "You sure this wasn't just a hallucination?"

I took a breath. Tried to calm myself. "I'm not sure about anything anymore. It was here. There. Wherever. It was physical. But it wasn't exactly corporeal. Shadow and smoke."

Some of the panic drained out of me. If it was a First, here and corporal, it'd be on top of us already. "I saw something, and it saw me."

"Well, we are leaving," said Wensem. "But if it's as big as you say—"

I didn't even pay attention to him. I was on a roll now, my panic rising again as I spoke. "They kept whispering. Taunting me. 'Too late! Too late!' In the Wasteland, and now here. I thought it was just the same creepy shit they always try to pull."

"Creepy shit?" Taft said.

"Who is saying this, Wal?" Hagen asked.

The room went quiet.

"Gargoyles," Hannah said, her voice low. "There are gargoyles out there right now. Aren't there?"

I looked at her. Nodded.

"Aw, Carter—aw, dammit," Taft said. She stomped a foot.

"They're here. Appearing, disappearing. Just like before," I wanted to tell them about the one that had shifted form, but now wasn't the time. "You all know what that means."

"Dammit," Taft repeated. She let out a long string of curses.

Hannah drew into herself and stared at the ground.

"What's a gargoyle?" asked Pascal.

"Robed fellas I told you about." Wensem waggled his finger above his head. "Pointy hoods. First saw them on the Broken Road."

Pascal's eyes narrowed. He nodded but said nothing.

"If they're here—" Taft began.

"—then there's a Founder around," Hagen finished flatly.

Hannah slumped onto the couch opposite Pascal. Her bright green eyes had dulled and were distant. She began to fiddle absently with the stiff fingers of her wooden hand.

Taft looked at me with an edge of concern, then crossed the room and sat next to her. The chuck draped an enormous arm over Hannah's shoulders and pulled her close. The scout stiffly fell against the big chuck, then eased a bit.

"How many gargoyles?" Wensem asked.

"Three. Maybe four." I was feeling calm again. If it was here, we'd know it. So it couldn't be here. Right? "Although who knows? They're not exactly easy to count."

"I need a stiff drink," said Taft. Pascal tossed her a flask. She took a sip and threw it back.

"Anyone else?' Pascal asked.

I raised a hand and caught the flask. Rye whiskey. It burned going down but the warmth help ground me. I handed it to Wensem, who also drank.

"Gargoyles and Founders," Hagen said. He shook his head slowly.

"Never a dull moment," said Wensem.

"There's too much going on here to be a coincidence," said Hagen. "I'm sure Sam would be able to make more connections, but I think—"

"Hagen, I really want to hear what you have to say," Wensem began, holding up a seven-fingered hand. "But Empress isn't going to allow us to have a lengthy confab. So let's get out before Protection decides to throw us out. We can rendezvous on the *Gamble* and hash this out on the way home."

An hour later, we left the canals of Empress behind.

TWENTY-THREE

Victory didn't care about the optics. They implemented their will with cold efficiency. As we left the embassy, we saw that Protection was already beginning to force foreigners from the city. Lovatines fumbling with their visitor ribbons were shuffled from their beds and cast out into the streets. Black-clad patrols went door to door looking for anyone who didn't have national identification. They didn't stop with Lovatines. They threw everyone out—Syringans from Syringa, Spanners from Bridgetown, Hellions from Hellgate. No one was spared. Pleas were ignored. Begging didn't help. Victory was uninterested in dialog.

The banks of monochromes in the store windows were no longer showing news. Now, all displayed the same picture: the crown and sun of Victory on a black field. The words SERVICE WILL RESUME SHORTLY glowed below in thick Strutten letters.

We watched a hotel empty out, its guests scattering. A few kids cried, their parents looking confused.

Protection worked with cold efficiency. Once they liberated foreigners from their rooms and beds, they took up position flanking doors preventing reentry. Occasionally an officer would explain to the confused people what was happening, and direct them to Customs.

Strangely, I saw no violence.

An eerie silence drifted over the canals. The city's heart seized up. The thrum of vibrancy—a city's constant—went silent. The few noises that broke through the stillness were amplified. Conversations above a whisper rumbled like distant thunder. The waves breaking around pilings were a cacophony.

As we moved through Empress, the throngs of people began to thicken, clustering around Customs terminals and queueing up near bumboat launches.

"We should scope out the Ambassador's cabins on the *Gamble*," I said to Wensem.

He nodded. "I'll take my crew. We can nab a priority boat. Meet you over there."

Wensem and his team went ahead.

Taft, Hannah, Hagen and I decided to split up. It would be easier to find a seat as a single as opposed to traveling with companions. We were all going to the same place anyway. I found my ride near Customs.

All of the bumboats were over capacity. Most rode dangerously low in the surf as they crossed the water toward the myriad of vessels that sat just offshore.

From the water, Empress looked as if it was being abandoned —but I knew it wasn't. My gaze kept drifting to the low clouds above the city. Any moment I expected something to descend, but nothing did. The sky had gone quiet, and that made me nervous.

The ride over to the *Gamble* was awkward and uncomfortable. A few people cried, clutching bags to their chests. Others stared blankly off into space, still reeling from the expulsion. Behind me, a baby fussed.

Danforth had called my bluff. If I had just been honest, it was possible all these people wouldn't have been displaced. Victory would have never called an end to the summit. Why they went as far as kicking out foreigners, I'd never know. Perhaps they believed Danforth? Maybe they were worried about violence.

Fear. It all came down to fear. It always does. Fear can make even the wisest sage a fool.

Across from me, a family of dimanians sat together. Two fathers and their small son. He was upset, and they worked in tandem to comfort him, putting on a brave face whenever he'd look in their eyes. A brave face that faltered when he looked away. Their lives would have continued uninterrupted if it wasn't for me. It was difficult not taking responsibility.

Some passengers talked with disbelief and shock about the reports of missing towns and fleets of boats stranded high up the Rosalias. Others questioned if Victory's actions weren't rooted in those unnerving reports. The waters of the western archipelago were mysterious—but they could never be described as dangerous. Accidents happened, but for the most part, the inland waterways were safe. This sort of thing didn't happen in the Territories.

It sounded like the work of a titan, some unreal and mystical force. But if the thing I saw was just a vision, how was it wiping out fishing communities on the archipelago? Seeing it hadn't been like visiting the Wasteland. It was here, even if only for a moment, before it vanished. Why? I rubbed my temples.

It was hard to concentrate. The last few days overwhelmed me. My mind clicked from one event to another, playing through each like a back-to-back serial feature. As I slipped from one situation to the next, my pulse got quicker, my skin went clammy, panic set in. Then I'd push it aside, and a whole new crisis would replace the one before, and the process would repeat again.

This went on for quite some time. Below me the bumboat shifted side to side. I could hear shore birds crying out above the white caps of the waters. I wrinkled my nose as the stink made its presence known over the smell of the sea.

Then I awoke in the Wasteland.

The yellow-clad figure floated in his stained tatters a short distance away. The pale mask it wore was as expressionless as ever, the single hole, black as the void, fixated on me.

The sun beat down upon us. The howl of the wind filled my ears.

This wasn't a full transition. I could still feel my ass on the wooden bench of the bumboat. I could still hear the engines and the family across from me speaking to one another.

My mind tried to establish a reality as truth—either reality—but it couldn't, and the paradox sent me reeling. I collapsed to my hands and knees. Gagged. My stomach flipped as my mind leaped back and forth—*boat, Wasteland, boat, Wasteland.*

A few ruins lay off in the distance, and far beyond them was this world's equivalent of Lovat. Once again, ash filled the air, and the smell of death and decay drifted like an autumn fog.

I closed my eyes and tried to visualize the deck of the bumboat. But when I opened them again, all I saw was sand.

"Stop them." A rasp, like dry paper fluttering in the wind.

The words angered me. I pushed myself off the ground and sat back on my haunches, threw my arms wide and shouted at the creature. "Who? Dammit, WHO?"

I stood up and strode toward him, my boots kicking up small clouds of dust with each impact.

He didn't move, but strangely he was always the same distance away from me. It was like I was repelling him backward with each step.

"Stop them," he repeated again. "Before it's too late."

The yellow-clad figure turned, his whole body dipping to peer behind himself, as if he couldn't just turn his head.

"What?" I began.

But the thing had disappeared.

Tawil appeared in his stead—first as a walking shadow emerging from a heatwave, then gaining definition as he drew closer. He looked even older than when I last saw him. The tattoos on his face were darker, his wrinkles deeper, his hair longer and whiter. How much time had passed here? He carried a shovel and had a rough sack thrown over one boney shoulder. He was still barefoot, his only article of clothing the overalls.

"You're back," he said with no emotion.

"I'm back," I said. "Where'd he go?"

Tawil made an indifferent motion that could have been a shrug. "Not sure how he even gets here. He's been gone a long time. Need a drink?"

"Do I ever," I said.

"Walk with me."

So we walked, striding across the flat expanse beneath a shattered sun. The non-Lovat wavered behind a heatwave, and beyond that was the creature, a writhing mass of something that existed just beyond the horizon. Beyond the world. I could feel it watching me. I did my best to ignore it.

"Did the usurper say anything to you?" he asked.

"'Stop them,'" I said. "Over and over. That's it. Who does he want me to stop?"

Tawil set down his sack and pulled the straw hat off his head. He wiped his brow with the back of his hand like a farmer surveying his land after a hard day's work. "Can't rightly read his mind."

"I saw something." I was certain Tawil was keeping things from me. "Before I came here. In my reality."

"Oh?"

"In the clouds. Above the clouds. It saw me."

Tawil smiled a bitter smile and gave a knowing nod. "The High Priest. He presses."

"He's been the one destroying villages," I said. "He's the one who threw those boats up the mountainside."

"Mere flickers. Rage. His will is there, then"— he snapped his fingers — "gone. Back here."

I frowned. What did he mean by *flickers*?

"But he's coming closer. Isn't he? He won't be pulled back here."

"He won't." Tawil's head dipped, a nearly imperceptible nod. "He's in your world—physically. This isn't Ashton. There's no crossing over. His body, his *form*, it's fully in your world. Been there a long, long time."

"Body?"

Tawil nodded.

"So his mind—"

"Flickers. In and out. In and out. Like the waves. Here. There. Here. There."

"Like the waves..." I went silent for a moment as the idea sank in, dragging me down like an anchor. An imagined sea pressed in, and I felt like I was suffocating.

"No avatar." Tawil watched me carefully. His gaze was hard, his lips drawn. It was a warning, his strange way of telling me this wouldn't be like before. "Eventually he won't flicker. He'll be fully there. The time's drawing close. When he's there, when his continuity is no longer split..."

"He'll destroy Empress. Lovat. The Territories." My words were a rasp.

Tawil tapped one of his long fingers against his lips. "Possible. Very possible. But he's been stopped before. Norwegian fellow, if memory serves. A sailor."

"What's a Norwegian?" I asked.

"Ah"—a laugh—"forgot you wouldn't know that." Wrinkles formed as he smiled. "An old human tribe. Clan? Kinship? Doesn't matter. Long ago. Before your Aligning."

My brow furrowed. "How'd he stop him?"

"Don't remember," Tawil chuckled, then plopped his hat back on his head and picked up his sack. "We have a long way ahead of us. Coming along or you going—"

My world corrected itself right as the bumboat clattered against the side of the *Gamble*. It took some time before I felt right again. Portions of my other reality were interspersed among what I could see from the boat. Wasteland stretched on one side, water the other.

The *Gamble* was part vessel and part sand-scoured ruin. A hot wind swirled with the cool salt-laden breeze. It was as if existence itself was coming apart at the seams.

I looked to the sky and saw no monster.

Slowly the wastes faded. Slowly the world righted itself. I

was getting better at handling these shifts, but the transition still left me sick.

I took a breath, tried to clear my head. Thought about what Tawil had said.

He's been stopped before.

That small phrase had germinated inside me and given me hope.

Most of the other passengers had already departed. I rose and stepped into the queue. Soon I'd left the bumboat behind and had crossed onto the *Gamble's* deck, arriving in the Yallup district.

Wensem was there, just beyond the checkpoint. He wore a suit and tie that had been loosened. His shoes were scuffed. His hair was wild and sticking up in places. He had his hands on his hips, crooked jaw set, a toothpick in his lips. Two of our crew were with him, standing to one side near a bulkhead and quietly chatting. They saw me and gave a nod.

"How was the ride?" Wensem asked as I approached. His blue-gray eyes continued to watch the line of bumboats streaming from the city.

"Fine," I said, taking up a vigil next to him. People moved around us. "I slipped a bit on the way over. Not a full shift or anything. I'm fine. That yellow-clad figure wanted to whisper nonsense to me."

"Stop them'?" Wensem asked. I nodded. "Was the other one there? The one from before?"

"Tawil," I said. "He was. He warned me about the First—the one that's coming."

"Anything significant?"

"Not that I can figure out." Again I looked to the sky—nothing. "What?"

"He said this new First can be stopped. Has been stopped. Before."

Wensem's expression was drawn, his brow furrowed, crooked jaw set as he mulled it over. But he wasn't upset by what I was saying. If anything, his demeanor eased somewhat.

"You like our odds."

"I do," he replied.

"And you claim to be the level-headed one," I said.

Wensem shook his head. "You've faced three Firsts now, Wal, and you've come out on top every time."

"Two of those I had help. The third… don't know if I can call that a win."

"You stopped Ashton. That's a win."

"Tell that to his followers." I looked around as if expecting the murderous cultists to manifest.

Wensem ignored me. "Can't speak for the rest of the crew… but, *I'll* be there. Say the word."

"Wouldn't it be nice to just be roaders again?" I held up a fist. He bumped the back of it with his own and clapped me on the shoulder. We shifted into a companionable silence and stared out at the rash of bumboats crawling across the water, filled with their cargo of Empress's refuse.

The *Gamble* was more crowded than it had been before. Hundreds of newcomers had come aboard, most returning to Lovat for refuge. They thronged the passageways, stood around in groups, and huddled below overhangs. Many clutched bags. All wore the vacant expression of the displaced.

An unassuming human with a plaid shirt tucked into brown pants was watching me from a corner where one of the *Gamble's* corridors led away from the crowd. He was trying to look casual about it, but I could feel his brown eyes on me, and when our gazes met he looked away awkwardly. I didn't recognize him, but I couldn't shake the feeling that Ashton's followers were watching the evacuation and waiting.

The watcher's whole demeanor was non-threatening, but that was to be expected. These folks could blend in—and that's what made them dangerous.

A pair of Deeperist bufo'anur in sackcloth passed between us. By the view was clear again, he was gone. Great.

Wensem followed my gaze but didn't say anything. Everything was crashing together, and I stood in the eye of swirling chaos. The accords. Victory. Essie's sister. These vengeful cultists. They were all a distraction. Whatever was coming would be here soon, and somehow, I knew it carried the Wasteland.

"I feel responsible for this." I gestured at the crowd.

Wensem scoffed. "You didn't go to Protection. Play the martyr all you like, Wal. But you're not the one who pissed off Victory. That's on Danforth—if he suspected foul play, he should have gone to Castaigne. She was the senior official for this delegation. He skipped by her and went right to Victory. This—" he gestured to the boats on the water "—this is on him. On Camalote."

I watched a fresh boat unload its passengers. My emotions around the expulsion were still sharp, but I buried them for now.

I spoke a new thought before I had fully processed it. "At least this has helped partially evacuate the city."

Wensem's crooked smile reappeared.

"Castaigne aboard?" I asked.

"Not yet. Waiting to escort her up top," he said. "The executive berths are clear. Pascal's up there now."

"Oh, yeah. A berth," I said, thinking aloud. "Wonder if I can nab my old spot."

"I wouldn't even try. Everything has doubled or tripled in price—lodging, food, the slots. The sharks smell blood in the water. The *Gamble* is gouging these people, and the Council is letting them and collecting their cut."

"Shouldn't that be illegal?"

"Maybe in Lovat. But out here…" He didn't finish his sentence.

"I hate this boat," I said.

"The Council sees this as a business opportunity." He made a disgusted face. "Just stay with the crew. Don't ask for permission, ask for forgiveness."

"That one of your Dad-isms?" I said.

"No, those usually involve a curse or two. Look, if they give you any problems, just set Taft on 'em. Hannah and Eli will vouch for you. That said, I doubt the crew will give you much guff. The beds up top are nice. Worth the risk."

The mention of Taft sparked another question. "Everyone else here?"

"Seen Taft and Hannah—they're above. Ain't seen Hagen."

"I'll head upstairs," I said. "Find a bed."

"Hey, Wal," Wensem said, catching me right as I was about to turn and leave. I stopped and looked at him. His eyes were the colors of the sea. "I meant what I said—I like those odds. No matter what shit we've gone through, I'm glad to be in your corner."

"Thanks," I said and left him standing dockside on the aft end of the *Gamble*.

Moving through the *Gamble* was never easy. There were only a handful of lifts, and they only held a handful of people. The stairwells were the primary means of vertical navigation, and the narrow spaces were always clogged with bodies, even on typical days. But now, with the added refugees, that usual slow crawl became glacial. A two-minute climb became ten, then twenty, then thirty.

Along the way, I noted that *Gamble* stewards were out in force, armed with hooked crowbars that they carried openly. It was a show of strength, a display of security, and a warning for anyone who was considering causing trouble. The few who did were quickly dealt with and dragged away—probably to the brig. I felt safer back on board with the stewards around.

Thirty minutes after leaving Wensem, I found myself making my way down the length of Yallup and crossing the bridges into Kaleetan. The central neighborhood was packed with all manner of civilians. Most wore the confused and shocked stare of the recently displaced as they wandered through the shops. I shouldered through the crowds, making my way to a central stairwell that'd lead me higher.

It was in that crowded corridor that I ran into Shoalta Amaia. She was carrying her blue duffle clutched in both her claws. I don't think she noticed me at first, and when I called her name, she jumped and nearly dropped the bag.

"Shoalta, good to see you," I said. Together we stepped to one side between a teapot vendor and a tee shirt shop. "Sorry for the fright."

"I-I'll be f-fine," said the kresh. She clutched a claw to her belly.

"Did you enjoy Empress?" I asked.

"Didn't disembark. Victory doesn't allow aquatics," she said. Her voice was distant, and she stared at the crowd with a confused expression. I frowned at the overt speciesism inherent in that sort of rule. It smacked of O'Conner's vile evangelism. Perhaps it was best we were all leaving Victory behind.

"Besides, the shoal never leaves," she said. "Shoalta in particular. This vessel is our home—our church. This journey, we focused on preparation for the King Tide celebration on the return trip."

"When does that start?"

"Soon as we're within sight of the city. During King Tide's Ebb." She spun slowly and took in the crowd moving around us. "Where did all these people come from?"

"Victory closed the borders, ejected foreigners. It's a mess," I explained. "The *Gamble's* well over capacity now, and we're not done. You should see the main deck—it's packed, and there are a lot more boats incoming."

She said something that sounded like a curse, in a language I didn't understand.

The additional people clearly displeased her. She was already distracted. Now her confusion drifted toward concern. "Too many. Much too many."

"What?"

She turned, looked up at me. "Thought you were returning to Lovat another way? Told you this boat wasn't safe."

I looked around. With people everywhere, Ashton's cult would have a much more difficult time clubbing me and dragging me below. My mind went back to the watcher near the checkpoint. The thought of them trying anything here in a crowd forced me to stifle a nervous chuckle.

"I don't understand. What's funny?"

"Nothing," I said, clearing my throat. "It's nothing. But finding another way isn't really an option for me. Not now."

"Mister Bell—I must urge you. Please seek another form of transport. Another boat. Abyss—walk if you have too. Please! It's not safe here."

There was an urgent aspect to her tone that gave me pause. Her black eyes were wide and very serious. She kept looking away to stare at a child or teenager. Her beak worked slowly— nervously. She clutched the blue bag as if her life depended on it. Maybe it did.

"This isn't about my attackers, is it?" I asked.

She clutched the duffle tighter. "It's not safe here, Mister Bell. The *Gamble,* it's—"

Now she looked away. Swallowed. The fleshy folds of skin on her beak quivered as she glanced at me and glanced away. It was a particularly avian motion.

"What's going on?" I asked, feeling slightly nervous. It was habit to glance around us, and as I did I caught another human male watching me. Our eyes met—my heart thrummed—but the contact was lost as a crowd of maero passed between us. When they had cleared, he was gone.

I was overreacting. Seeing devils lurking behind every bush.

"I need to go," she said.

"Shoalta, please."

She ignored my words. "Sorry, Mister Bell, I need to go."

"Amaia."

She paused and looked at me, her black eyes glistening, her beak drawn and severe. I extended a hand toward her, wondering if her touch would send me into the Wasteland again. I didn't care. She was afraid. I could help.

My hand never found her shoulder. The Shoalta vanished.

TWENTY-FOUR

My coffee had grown cold. I drank it anyway. I was sitting in the room where my crew berthed on the trip to Empress. It was an ample space by *Gamble* standards—long and narrow, roomier than some of the casinos on the decks below. Funny how even here on the *Gamble* the separation between the haves and the have-nots was clear.

Six bunkbed-style berths ran along one wall, split by pairs of lockers. A narrow corridor filled the space between the beds and lockers and the exterior wall. A sink with a mirror sat at one end, an exit door at the other. The walls here were beige, and what light came in entered through narrow windows that ran along the edge of the ceiling on the external wall.

Taft lay on a lower bunk near the entrance, using one of her arms as a pillow. Hannah leaned against the lockers, just past Taft's head. I sat in the room's lone chair near a small counter occupied by an ancient kettle and a jar of instant coffee. My right leg extended out before me. My knee was killing me from the climb. I should have queued and taken a lift.

This room connected to a short hallway that led to the executive berths—spaces that had once been a wheelhouse, now converted to fancy apartments that overlooked the upper deck. The location allowed us easy access to Castaigne's quarters.

We were discussing Shoalta Amaia. I had told both women about her odd behavior, how she disappeared, and how uneasy it left me. One more worry in a series of them—where did it end? I hadn't even been able to process the information from Liv that connected Essie to Elephant. My mad rush to warn my friends and then our expulsion from the city had been a whirlwind. This endless leap from one calamity to another had to end. I needed it to end.

"No," said Hannah, answering a question of mine. "Strange is an accurate descriptor. You say she was adamant that you leave?"

"Yeah," I said, scratching my beard and taking another drink of cold coffee. "And it wasn't about the cultists who assaulted me, either. I thought it was at first. But there's something else going on."

"Ain't this boat basically a church for them?" Taft raised her eyebrows.

I nodded.

"Think it's connected to all of this?" Hannah said. She shifted and folded her arms across her chest.

"What do you mean?"

"The First, the… " she paused. Took a deep breath. "The damn gargoyles. All of this."

I sighed, set down my coffee, leaned forward, and rubbed my face. "Maybe I should go down to the chapel. If she's there, I can talk with her."

"If she'll talk," Hannah said.

"It'll be on her terms," I said. "In a location I know is more comfortable for her."

"If you're going down there, I'm coming with you," Taft said. "I'm not having you walk around on this boat alone anymore. The shoalta might not be concerned about the cultists, but I am."

"Me too," said Hannah. "I agree with Taft. Don't much care for you going below without an escort."

"It's basically Guardian security," Taft said with a wry smile. She pushed herself up from the bunk.

Hannah laughed, then laughed harder after she saw the expression that crossed my face.

"I hate you two," I grumbled.

The chapel was darker but otherwise much as I remembered from my previous visit in my shovel-addled state. A few candles burned near what the Reunifieds would call the altar, but the rest of the room was swathed in gloom. Only a few gray slivers of light managed to sneak their way past the murky portholes and into the interior. Unlike last time, the floor wasn't covered in a thin layer of seawater—a state I commented upon.

"Only do that for services," said the shoalta who had been leading the proceeding last time I was here. He was large for an anur, his head nearly coming to my shoulder. He had a broad mouth and dark bulbous eyes—a cross somewhere between frog and fish. He introduced himself as Shoalta Sander and urged us all to call him by his given name and drop formalities.

He regarded the four of us: me, Taft, Hannah, and Hagen, whom we had picked up on our trip down here. Being a religious-antiques dealer, he had been more than eager to visit the chapel and meet the clergy who served here on board the *Gamble*. Deeperism, in general, fascinated him.

"Any of you believers?"

"'Fraid not." Taft shook her head.

"Reunified," Hagen said.

"What brings you to Our Father of the Obscured Atoll? We hold daily services in the mornings. Are you perhaps interested in joining us for the King Tide's Ebb celebration?"

"You allow visitors?" Hannah asked.

"Certainly! We encourage all souls seeking guidance and harmony to join us," said Sander. "Deeper is a kind and benevolent—"

"How do you light bonfires down here?" Hagen interrupted. "I can't imagine the council allows fires to be built inside the *Gamble's* hull."

"They do not," said Sander. He was smiling and clearly comfortable with all the questions. "But they do allow us to light a controlled burn in special braziers on the uppermost decks."

"Mighty kind of them," I said.

"It helps that Captain Jurer is a member of our little congregation. It's a celebration, and this year's King Tide has been most fortuitous." He spoke as if the Territories had been blessed.

I was reminded of the smell that permeated Lovat, the stink of death and decay that had ridden in with the King Tide. I knew the faculties of the aquatic species processed olfactory scents differently than us land-born, but even they seemed bothered by the odor. If that had come in with the tide, I wasn't sure how anyone could find it serendipitous.

"Expect big things?" Hannah asked.

"Indeed. It is, after all, a new age." He spread his hands as he said it. "Deeper's time has come."

A slight shiver drifted down my spine. Sander hadn't meant the words to be ominous, but to my ears that's exactly how they sounded. "We wanted to talk with one of the ministers here."

"Oh?" Sander asked. "Who?"

"Shoalta Amaia," I said.

Sander's face fell. "She's not here right now. Haven't seen her since services."

"Something the matter?" Hannah asked.

The shoalta tilted his head and regarded the four of us in silence for a drawn-out moment. Then he turned away and walked over to a small shelf located to one side of the altar and busied himself with the knickknacks scattered on top. "I shouldn't discuss it with outsiders. Especially those who are unshoaled. No offense intended."

I turned and looked at my friends. They each were regarding the shoalta with varying expressions—understanding but also eager to explore my concerns as well. I widened my eyes at them and nodded with my head toward the exit, a give-me-a-minute gesture that thankfully they all understood. The three of them slipped out into the passageway beyond, pulling the hatch half-closed and leaving Sander and me alone together.

I cleared my throat.

"Where'd your friends go?" Sander asked, turning.

"They're giving us a little time to talk," I said. "Amaia helped me out, I'd like to return the favor. When I saw her last, she seemed... *distracted*."

"She's lost her way," Sander nodded. "Quite lost."

"How so?"

The anur turned and walked over to me, rubbing at his neck with a webbed hand. His bulbous eyes drew back into his head, and their lids narrowed as he regarded me. "She helped you out, you said?"

"I came seeking refuge, and she offered it to me."

"Ah, so you were our interloper," Sander chuckled. "A few of the shoal told me about you coming in, followed by those stuffy Eibonians. What did they want with you?"

"Eibonians?"

"That's what they call themselves, yes," he nodded. Then he repeated his question. "What did they want with you?"

There was a flat honesty in the way he asked his question. An interest, assuredly, but laced with concern, the sort that many clergy show for their flock—or in this case their shoal. I weighed my options and answered him. "They think I killed their god."

His eyes slowly rose. "Did you?"

"No." It wasn't precisely accurate, but I didn't feel like I was lying either. Their god still existed—just elsewhere, if Tawil was to be believed. What remained in Ash was a broken shell.

"Who are you, exactly?" Sander asked.

"Name's Waldo Bell," I said. "I'm running a security outfit on board. Maybe you've heard of us? Guardian Security?"

Sander sighed and shook his head, then looked at me and spoke. "Amaia lost her way. I would have never thought she'd have been one of the unfaithful. She had been so earnest in the beginning. So eager."

"A believer," I said.

"Exactly," said Sander. "She had quickly risen up through the Lovatine shoals. There was even talk of her taking over in Destiny, heading up her own shoal there for a time. I liked what I saw. It might not look like much, but among the Deeperists, Our Father of the Obscured Atoll is a prestigious posting. I requested that she be transferred here."

I looked around. There was a presence to this space. It was unlike any other chapel I had stood in—it felt more connected to the sea. It wasn't fussy, it was useful. It wasn't here to show the glory of some ancient deity, it was here to serve. In a way, it matched the sackcloth robes the Deeperists wore—simple, effective, and symbolistic. I was used to houses of worship being grand affairs—gilded palaces like Saint Mark's or Shepherd's Rest.

"There's a schism that runs through Deeperism," said Sander. He motioned for me to follow, and together we moved over to another side of the altar where four wooden chairs—as simple as their surroundings—stood. He sat in one and waved me into another nearby.

"Sects. Our faith was long persecuted by Reunifieds and Hasturians, later Curwenites. It made some of us angry. Vengeful, even. This was long ago, before the reforms and before the faith's militant factions were silenced. At that time, traditional Deeperists rejected the demands for violence. We see ourselves as a benevolent shoal. Others—"

He sighed, then continued. "They chose a more volatile form of faith. Called themselves the Dead Dreamers. Fool dreamers, more like. They preached that Deeper, in all his glory, was coming to lead his faithful into a place of leadership as kings and queens, the inheritors of the world. Conquerors. Their worship was through action, not celebration—fighting with nonbelievers in Deeper's name."

"You think Amaia is caught up with these Dead Dreamers?"

"I have my suspicions," said Sander. "For example, she's been adamant we skip the bonfires for King Tide's Ebb. Called it 'conceited pageantry.' I told her it was tradition! The young don't care for tradition—the militant young especially. Would she listen? No. She demanded that the summoning be stopped."

He huffed and crossed his arm across his belly.

"Summoning?" I asked. Old memories of black rituals in deep places sent a chill along my neck.

Sander clucked his sizable tongue. "We call it that out of convention. It's little more than a traditional ceremony at this point. Like singing Birthday Greetings to a newborn. But we believe it's an important ceremony. It's our way to show Deeper that we remain faithful. He will return at his own time. Our sacraments and feastings won't matter on that day. He doesn't need us. We need him. Amaia knows this. Even in her rebellion she knows this. Why it suddenly bothers her now, I don't understand."

I scratched my beard and studied the old anur. "When I spoke with her after the services, she talked only of kindness and charity. I don't know her as well as you do, but that doesn't seem like the Amaia I know. At least not the version I've seen."

Sander rubbed his chins and grunted as he considered what I said.

I went on. "She was adamant that I leave the *Gamble*. Encouraged me to find another way back to Lovat. Any idea why?"

"Those Eibonians perhaps? One mighty shiner they gave you."

"No," I said, pulling on my jacket and hoping it distracted from the black eye a bit. "She mentioned them, but there was something else going on. They were an easy excuse. That's why I came here. I was hoping to talk to her further."

"When I see her next, I'll tell her you called."

"I'd appreciate that, Sander."

We shook hands and rose together. I headed for the door, where my three friends waited.

"Oh," I said, turning back as I thought of one more question to ask the shoalta. Sander paused and smiled, bowing his head slightly as if giving me permission to speak. "What's in the blue duffle she carries?"

"Blue duffle?" He said, rubbing his chins. "You know, I don't rightly know."

I explained the conversation to my friends as we walked back.

"This whole thing is strange," Taft said. Then she laughed. "Stranger than normal, I mean."

"Who is Deeper, anyway?" Hannah asked.

We were passing through the hull of Kaleetan and moving through a series of chambers towards a stairwell. Before, this area had been dark and largely abandoned. Now, with the influx of refugees, even this dank spot was filling with passengers. Golden lights glowed from recesses as people found a place to laager and make themselves comfortable. It reminded me a lot of Lovat's lower levels—the low light, the dampness, the sound of the sea.

"There's conflicting stories about Deeper," said Hagen. "The Reunified Church believes it's a modern name for an ancient pre-Aligning deity. A fellow called Dagon."

"Pre-Aligning?"

"Yes, the most ancient of ancient earth history," said Hagen. "We're talking tens of thousands of years old. The name Dagon shows up in Reunified scripture. He was commonly believed to be half-man and half-fish—so it's easy to see how he'd be associated with the anur in particular—or any of the aquatics, really. One of their own."

"So what's the conflict?" Hannah asked.

"Well. Dagon is only one suggestion. The other, uh—hits a bit closer to home. For us anyway." He glanced at me and cleared his throat before continuing. "Some scholars believe that this being is a Founder. That he's largely responsible for uplifting the aquatics' ancestors to sentience during the Aligning."

"Wait," said Taft, ducking beneath a long hanging pipe. "What is uplifting?"

"It's like a guided metamorphosis. Controlled evolution. The changing of a species' capacities and intelligence through outside influence. That sort of thing," Hagen explained. "The theory held that many of the aquatics were little more than animals, but something happened during the Aligning that helped them evolve. They all gained intelligence and free will. They became the people we know today."

"That sounds sketchy," said Hannah. "Unethical."

"Understandably. This theory was initially proposed by a cephel scholar named Tampter—he wrote a whole treatise on it. It occasionally gets mentioned whenever the Deeperists show up in the papers. It always seems to cause a little chaos."

"How so?" I asked.

"The treatise was written nearly two hundred years ago. Either way, people like to argue over some of his terminologies. They all have a speciesist bent to them. Some think it's a translation issue. Others feel it was intentional. Some think it was a difference in language. The problem stems from the way he refers to his fellow aquatics. He uses the term 'spawn' as in 'spawn of Deeper.' You can imagine how well that goes over."

"Stairs are this way," I said, ducking through a hatch and into another chamber, where small canvas tents had popped up like mushrooms. Families of all shapes and sizes sat near the tents' mouths.

"That's—" Taft's tone was concerned, and she drew the word out.

"Disendowing?" Hagen suggested.

"I was going to say gross. Maybe dehumanizing, but doesn't really work for the aquatic species," Taft said.

"I feel the same way. Most scholars bristle when it gets mentioned. Hell, Conrad O'Conner has used it in the past as a reason for humanity to reject the aquatic species," Hagen said. "But the theory remains, even if the bigots picked up on it."

We gingerly stepped our way through the tents. Navigating the space was taking some time, with so many people everywhere. I was able to relax a bit—there's safety in numbers. The Eibonian cultists would be fools to try something in this crowd.

"This fellow—this First—have a name other than Dagon?" I asked. "I somehow doubt he was called Deeper."

Hagen nodded, then made a choking noise, a half-bark and half-gargle. Then he laughed. "See, I can't do it justice. It's not a name we can really pronounce. Like most of the Firsts, his name is impossible to say properly in Strutten. A cephel's vocal apparatus can get closer than we can."

"Let's just stick with Deeper, then," I said with a cold laugh. "Here's the stairs."

I lifted my right foot and planted it on the first step, not looking forward to the brief shout of pain that would follow. Behind me, a voice rang out through the crowd, and it stopped me in my tracks.

"Well, well, well…"

I turned. I knew that voice. My stomach flipped.

A dimanian with massive curling horns and an umbra with glowing white eyes stood a few paces away, arms folded across their chests. The dimanian was smirking and glaring at the same time—a mix of expressions that made him look off-kilter. The umbra was impossible to read, the blackness of its head and neck like a null space in reality. The occasional wisp of smoke drifted from its head before dissipating in the air.

"If it isn't Waldo Bell," the horned man said. "I heard you were back on board."

"Fancy seeing you down here again," the umbra said. I could hear the sneer in his voice.

Taft, sensing their intent, took a step toward the pair. They immediately dropped their arrogant poses and stepped back. The enormous chuck's fists were balling, and I could see her mouth opening. She'd have probably gone further if I didn't hold her back with a well-timed hand on her shoulder. The big woman understood the signal. She froze in place and said nothing.

"No shovel this time?" I asked. "Been seeing your lurkers the last few days. They aren't subtle."

"Didn't intend to be." A sly smile.

"Bold of you to come without a weapon."

"Too crowded," said the umbra cultist. He looked at the people around us. A few had taken notice. Sensing the emotion in our small standoff, they moved closer, the way crowds always do. "At least for now. We're just here to talk."

"Why wait? Let's do this and be done with it," Taft said, throwing her arms wide. "I'll happily kick both your asses."

"Found friends, I see," the dimanian said.

"We'll go to the authorities," Hagen said.

The dimanian laughed. "Go. You have no proof. No evidence."

"What do you want?" I asked.

"You made a big mistake returning to the *Gamble*," said the dimanian, stepping closer. He smelled like peppers and sweat.

"Big mistake," the umbra echoed from behind him.

"Ashton will be avenged. Know this."

"Ashton is gone. I saw him leave."

"No." The dimanian said, his voice low and cold. "You killed him. You *murdered* him! You are not worthy of speaking his name."

"Let's go," I said to my friends, and I turned and began to climb the stairs. The others fell in behind me.

"You made a big mistake," the dimanian growled even as I walked away. "You won't leave the *Gamble* alive, Bell. I promise you this. I promise—"

I didn't hear the rest.

TWENTY-FIVE

A storm rolled in as the *Gamble* took to the waves and slipped away, leaving Empress behind. The two tugs that pulled the heavy vessel rode low in the surf, their hulls glistening with seawater. The extra passengers and cargo had slowed down the boat down considerably, and the two tugs struggled to get the *Gamble* up to speed.

Wensem and I had watched the sunset to the west in silence from the upper deck of the boat. After the light had faded, we stood side by side in the darkness, saying nothing but understanding each other better than we could ever put into words. When we broke from our view and turned east, we could see the glow from Lovat reflecting against the rainclouds. Strange how Empress was so close yet felt a world away.

Wensem took one of his walks. I stayed with the crew, taking a turn at watch with Hannah in the middle of the night. We didn't speak much. Both of us sat on metal chairs flanking the door that led to Castaigne's quarters. It was tedious work. There were few people about, but the rumble of activity from below could be clearly heard—music and laughter, mainly, as well as the plinks and plonks of gaming machines.

The Ambassador had acknowledged our presence but spoke very little to us. I didn't see Danforth, but I knew he was on board—him and his goons. He had requested a transfer from Kaleetan to Yallup, and the Captains had granted his request. It was a smart move on his part. If I saw his face again, I'd be hard-pressed not to knock his ass out.

"What's the plan?" Hannah asked toward the end of our watch. She let out a yawn and stretched until her spine popped.

"About the cultists?"

"Among other things."

I rubbed my face and looked at her. Her green eyes were heavy with lack of sleep, and her dark hair was tousled in places. Her lips were set; the old toughness had taken root.

"That guy sounded adamant," she said. "You believe him?"

"That he'll kill me?" My shoulders shook in a silent laugh. "No. Not really."

"Taft thinks you should lay low. Stay on the upper decks with the rest of us. Easy to keep you safer up here."

"Yeah," I said. "She has a point."

"You're not going to do it, are you?"

"I'm still trying to figure out what's up with Amaia," I said. "It bothers me. I know Shoalta Sander thinks the summoning is all for show, but I know a First is still lurking. We're still Castaigne's security team. Amaia seemed to have a premonition about the *Gamble*—one I didn't like. We still have a job to do, and keeping Castaigne safe is a part of that. If whatever is bothering Amaia threatens the Ambassador…"

I let my sentence drift into silence.

Hannah stood and stretched. "Why not talk to the Council of Captains? Maybe they can help."

"You really think so?"

She nodded. "This is their boat. If there's trouble brewing, they should know about it, right?"

I considered that. Hannah had a point. Perhaps she was right and we should get the *Gamble* involved.

Late the next morning, Wensem and I called on the Council of Captains.

The board room where I had met them looked the same. The same small windows provided views of the rain-soaked islands that slowly passed. A constant drizzle had begun to fall and the cloud cover had dropped, allowing for less than a mile of visibility. The tugboats were ghosts in the haze.

Captains Chen and Jurer sat at the central table. The maero captain, Shelna wen Oshen, leaned against the wall behind them, silent and placid. Chen motioned to the seat across from her, and we sat.

"How you liking your quarters?" Chen asked. There was a slight tension beneath her cordiality. My past transgressions had not been forgiven, even if I was allowed up top.

"The *Gamble*'s a fascinating place," I said. I opened my mouth to elaborate but closed it again. Did I want to tell the Captains about the Eibonians? What would that accomplish? I'd just anger them further if *Gamble* security came down on them, and the Captains wouldn't be able to do much despite the threats. The *Gamble* had its own rules, but Lovatine Law was cagey about threats at best, and Ash's followers had a presence in Lovat as well.

"We heard about the failure of the summit," said Chen.

"We're trying to determine what this means for us," said Jurer.

I hadn't even though of that. The *Gamble*'s bread and butter was the trips between Lovat and Empress. If Victory was closing their borders, that meant they were losing their route. With nowhere to go, the *Gamble* might be forced to become more of a fixture in the harbor.

"There's always Bridgetown," I said.

Shelna and Jurer exchanged dark looks.

"Why'd you call?" Shelna asked.

I ran my hands through my hair and dove in. "I think the *Gamble* might be under threat. That concerns me. A threat to the *Gamble* is a threat to the Ambassador."

Chen sat forward. "What kind of threat?"

"We're trying to figure that out. But it felt foolish to keep this to ourselves. The safety of the *Gamble* is important for our client as well as all of us. I'd hate to have something happen."

"How'd you find out about this?"

"I was warned," I said.

"By who?" asked Shelna.

Wensem leaned forward. His steel eyes met Shelna's gaze and glinted. "For the personal safety of this individual, it's imperative their identity remains a secret."

Chen bristled and her mouth opened, but before she could speak I was already talking. "Once we uncover more, we'll share everything we know. But until then, it would be smart to tighten security around the boat."

Jurer leaned back and smacked his fleshy beak. "I've been saying the same thing to my colleagues. The influx of refugees has increased incidents in some of the casinos and taverns. I'm happy to welcome them, but we don't know who we let on board. Not really."

"Desperate people do desperate things," said Shelna. She pushed off the wall and collapsed into one of the chairs and swiveled it back and forth with her long legs as she talked.

Chen shook her head. "There's been some fighting. Not anything premeditated, mind. Mostly disagreements over space, queues, that kind of thing. Hardly enough to warrant double shifts."

"Everyone's on edge," I said. "Some of those people had lived in Empress for a long time. It's devastating to be thrown out of your home."

"So you look into this threat. Then what?" Chen asked.

"Let you know what I find," I said.

"What do you propose we do until then?" Chen asked.

"What Wal said. Increase security," said Wensem. He folded his hands in front of him on the table. "Checkpoints on the stairwells and elevators. You could restrict access to VIP levels as well. That'd help us out a lot."

Chen rubbed her temples. "We're tight-staffed as it is—"

"Use us," I said. "Let us help you."

The captains exchanged looks. Finally Shelna nodded, followed by Jurer. Chen watched in silence, her chair swiveling slowly to the left and then right.

"Well, Denise?" said Jurer.

She let out a huff and waved a hand.

"Do you see this causing a problem with the celebrations for King Tide's Ebb?" asked Jurer. "The shoal would like Castaigne to be our guest of honor at the celebrations."

King Tide's Ebb. Amaia had mentioned it when we discussed the refugees coming over from Empress. Would she… no. No! That was insane. She was clergy—a servant, not a killer. But the thought lingered, unspoken but pricking away at the back of my brain.

"I'm not sure," I said.

"It's a big deal," said Jurer. "Thousands come on board for the summoning. If you think anything might disrupt the celebration, let us know immediately."

"We will," said Wensem.

Jurer leaned forward and tapped the table with a claw. "We'll send word to Kepler. He handles the security work on board. We'll let him know he's to work with you on security concerns."

"One other thing," I said.

"Yes?" Chen said now exasperated.

"We'd like to develop a plan. In case something happens."

"Explain," Chen said.

"Let's say there's a crisis. We need a way to get the Ambassador off the *Gamble* safely—because of the nature of her position. We're concerned about her among the population that would be on board the lifeboats."

"Why is this our problem?" Chen asked.

"Didn't say it was," said Wensem. His voice had gone from cold to flat and impassive.

"There's *Greedy Three*," said Jurer.

"By the Firsts, Eeoshi," said Chen. She threw her hand into the air. "Can't you keep that beak shut?"

"It's plenty big for us," said Jurer.

"What's the *Greedy Three*?" I asked.

Chen said nothing but shot me the same nakedly angry look she had thrown at Jurer.

"Our private Captains' yacht," Shelna explained. "It's tied to the starboard side of Kaleetan."

"Nice name," said Wensem.

Shelna flashed an evil smile. "Sometimes, the best way to quell rumor and gossip is to just embrace it as a joke."

"You'd let the Ambassador use it?"

Jurer nodded. "I'm fine with it."

"I as well," said Shelna.

Chen folded her arms across her chest.

"Oh please, Denise," said Jurer. "It's not like we couldn't fit a few more on board. Quit being selfish. The name's supposed to be a joke, remember?" He turned back to Wensem and me. "It's large enough. We'd be glad to have her."

"Should something happen, we'd just want you to take the Ambassador to Lovat. Wouldn't use it otherwise." I held up my hands. "I swear. Only in case of an emergency."

"Fine," said Chen. She sighed. "You've been such a model passenger. So, fine. Why not?"

TWENTY-SIX

The tugboats continued their relentless grind toward Lovat. Weighed down by passengers and cargo, the *Gamble* was moving slower, and the return trip was expected to extend beyond four days to as many as six, according to her captains.

Life on board continued as normal. People ate and drank and gambled. Lira flowed from pockets and into the clanging machines. Lines at watering holes were out the doors as eager patrons waited to fill barstools as soon as they were empty. Tensions were high, but the increased security presence put most passengers at ease.

Atop the Chee, the members of Our Father of the Obscured Atoll began to erect the necessaries for the King Tide bonfire, hauling big timbers from somewhere below and stacking them into a pyramid shape atop an enormous brazier. We could see the construction from the windows of our cabins. I had expected the rain would put a damper on the festivities, but the Deeperists didn't seem too bothered by the endless downpour. If anything, they reveled in it.

When I wasn't on duty, I spent most of my time with Hagen drinking long blacks in Shantak Coffee and talking over what he'd found in the *Black Book* and probing my memories of the Wasteland. Getting to the café made me nervous. Moving around on the boat put me on edge. I expected to turn a corner and meet the flat of another shovel, but every time I found my way to Shantak unmolested.

Occasionally, as I walked the *Gamble's* corridors, I'd swear I felt someone watching me. I'd spot a pair of eyes turned in my direction, or catch the glare off a pair of spectacles. It was enough to catch me off guard and make me look again.

Most of the time the watchers disappeared when I turned in their direction. Only once did I recognize one of them—the big dimanian with the curled horns. People milled about him, but he never moved, never came closer, just grinned a long, almost languorous grin. It was impossible not to read the threat in it. I've seen enough nutcases to understand what was cranking inside his skull.

Ash's words echoed around in my head. *You stirred up my followers. You should be careful.* I had disregarded the warning at the time. Hindsight and all that.

The dimanian wasn't stupid enough to attack me here, not in this crowd. But he wanted me to remember his threats. He was no wolf, he was a vulture. He'd be patient. He'd wait.

For now, the crowd kept me safe, and the persistent threat from the Eibonians was enough to keep my mind off thoughts of Essie, Elephant, and that creature I'd seen behind the clouds.

Hagen was a welcome distraction. Together he and I tried to piece together the mysteries of the Wasteland and discover its connection to myself and the Firsts.

"I'm pretty sure Tawil is right," he said one day over a steaming long black. "All the signs are similar—the forms are different, but that's not too surprising. Different realities call for different adaptations. Lovat might be a weird place, but if you walk around the city with wings you'll attract attention."

"What are you saying?" I asked.

"I'm saying the gargoyles are most likely these 'gaunts mentioned in the book. Actually, their full name is 'Nightgaunt.' The robes, the hoods—essentially they're disguises. A new form for a new reality, new plane, new existence."

I swallowed a mouthful of coffee and laughed. "'Nightgaunt' sounds like something a kid would come up with when playing adventure games."

"Like 'gargoyle' is any better?"

For a moment all that I could do was stammer. "But they watch—silent, like—" I stared at him. He hadn't been with us on the Broken Road. "You know what? Never mind. Who's the guy in yellow?"

Hagen closed his notebook and waved a hand. "No idea. He's not in there."

"Yellow robes, weird mask, whenever he shows up he's floating and there's ash in the air. I smell sulfur."

Hagen nodded. "You mentioned. Many times. But there's nothing like him in the *Black Book*. Deeper? Absolutely. Ashton?

Sure. Shit—Auntie Mason? Indeed. But this yellow fellow?" He smirked at the rhyme. "No idea."

"Ashton called him a pretender," I said. I picked at someone's carving of a cephel on the table. There was something carved in jagged Cephan below, but not anything I could read. Three spiky horizontal lines laid out vertically, like the swell of cresting waves. Not the usual form, which generally featured a horizontal bar with four descenders twisting in various directions. "What do you think he meant?"

"I'm assuming he meant that it was an illusion, something to make the yellow-clad figure seem like some kind of claimant."

I shook my head, not following.

"Usurper?" he suggested.

Again, nothing. It didn't ring any bells for me.

Hagen must have read my baffled expression. "Really? That means nothing to you?"

"Look, I don't know—"

He waved a hand, cutting me off mid-sentence. "You need to read more. 'Usurper' is an old term. Pre-Aligning, really. Keep in mind this is all speculation."

My hand whirled in a go-on motion.

"We don't have monarchies anymore, not in the Territories at least." Hagen's voice slipped into a familiar lecturing tone. He folded some of the old parchment of the book over and spoke as he searched it. "Usually, within a monarchy, the crown—the symbol of authority—some cultures use staffs, others scepters, doesn't matter—anyway, it's passed down from parent to child. Blood to blood. Usually firstborn to firstborn. To call someone a pretender means someone is falsely claiming they are a part of a bloodline or that they usurped the power of the true ruler."

"You think this guy is trying to be some sort of king?"

"A king in yellow?" Now Hagen laughed. "Maybe? I doubt it. The Founders don't really behave like royalty—at least, not royalty we can understand. A hierarchy, certainly, but with more standard familial roles. Father, mother, son, daughter, grand-kids. Uncles, aunts. I could see how they'd want to protect their bloodline. Family calls to family—or whatever constitutes as family for them." He tapped the spurs on his knuckles absently. "All that said, it seems like he's on your side. He *was* warning you, after all."

"I'm not willing to accept he's on my side," I said. "Not yet."

Once you see how assumptions get people killed, you begin making fewer of them.

I thought of Ash and his former disciples. We're all useful until we're not. It's easy for the powerful to discard followers. That's a relationship that only goes one way. History is filled with this lesson. Fall in line or suffer the consequences. I hadn't sworn any allegiance to this usurper, but I wasn't about to let him make me an instrument, no matter what he was plotting.

"What about Tawil? You said he was a Founder?"

"I think he's indifferent to all of this," I said. "I think if he wasn't trapped where he's at, he'd be just as keen on a showdown as any other First. He's one of them, after all. On the outs, maybe—cut off from his true self—but still one of them inside. Like Ash."

Hagen leaned back. "He said you exist there."

"Yes."

"And yet you're here."

"Yes."

He drummed a knuckle spur on the table. "You said you brought the Judge from over there. That you pulled it from the holster and it appeared here?"

"I did. It did."

"That connection is—" a spreading of hands cut his sentence in two "—unusual."

"What are you getting at?"

"Could you pull *other* things from over there? Objects? Experiences? Weather? Like—hear me out—your leg. I mean your knee. Could you dull the pain here by somehow connecting to or, like, tapping into the healthy one in the Wasteland? You said it was fine over there, didn't you?"

"Uh," I said. Not sure what I wanted to say. There must be something to Hagen's theory, even if the idea made my mind feel like mushy neon carrots.

"Forget it."

"No," I said. "You're not off-base. I've been thinking about that same thing myself on some level."

Hagen blinked, as if stunned I had even considered the idea. "You realize how crazy this all sounds?"

I breathed out. "You realize how crazy it sounds to think I punched Ashton? You realize how crazy it sounds to know I can see gargoyles in my city and no one else can? Do you realize how crazy it sounds to feel vibrations from others and... and... not—"

Bingo. I snapped my fingers. "Oh, oh, *oh...*"

"Wal?" Hagen's eyebrow raised. It was something Samantha did when she was intrigued. "What—"

"*Amaia.*"

My friend sat forward. "The kresh Shoalta?"

"Yes," I said. "Dammit, yes! Hagen, you're a genius!"

Hagen stared at me blankly. A bashful smile crept across his face.

"She's been there. To the Wasteland. *In* the damn Wasteland. By the Firsts, Hagen! She's been there! Shit, she's spoken with Tawil. It's why I feel…" I waved my hand behind my head. "It's why… Carter's cross!"

I pushed myself away from the table. Hagen rose as well.

I had the find the Shoalta.

Hagen refused to leave my side. Like Hannah and Taft, he was adamant that I wouldn't be caught alone by Ashton's worshipers. Strength in numbers and all that. I barely noticed him as I stalked my way down the corridor towards the stairs, my knee popping with each step.

Crowds of people hemmed us in from all sides. I could smell the stench of unwashed bodies and rancid breath. It was still a sweeter perfume that the stink that rolled in with the King Tide. What had Ashton called it? *The fragrance of a corpse-city.*

The descent down a single deck took nearly fifteen minutes. What would happen if there were a true emergency here? This boat was dangerously overcrowded. If a fire or worse tore through the decks, hundreds—maybe thousands—would die, if not from smoke or flame then from the press of bodies. Panic could kill in a place as tightly packed as the *Gamble.*

"We were already crowded on the trip over." Hagen had noticed the problem, too. "This is getting ridiculous."

"People bring cargo. Cargo takes space."

"Space is at a premium."

"They letting people on the top decks?"

Most of the top levels were still devoid of anyone but the high rollers and the Deeperists preparing for their ceremonies and bonfires. From a security standpoint I was grateful—it made protecting our charge easier. But from a humane standpoint, I had my doubts. Charity isn't just acknowledging a problem, it's doing everything you can to fix it. That takes grit. Which is something most people don't understand. You have to get uncomfortable. In my experience, most people hate feeling discomfort.

Comfortable people don't change the world.

We were in the queue waiting to descend the stairs. It was taking a while. The slow progress was easy on my knee, but now, driven as I was to find the Shoalta, I was growing irritated with the wait.

"Level Two isn't even this crowded," I said. Bitterness leaked into my tone.

"We'll get there," Hagen said, ever the pleaser.

I gave him a scowl.

When we finally emerged onto the main deck, we broke away from the stairwell and I turned toward the port side. No; I corrected myself. Navigation on the *Gamble* was confusing. Back home in Lovat, the warrens never shifted. But here on the waves, left and right, forward and backwards changed.

The *Gamble* never turned around. When they returned from Empress, the towboats disconnected from the Chee and then connected to the Yallup. That meant the aft end became the forward end and port and starboard flipped. Addresses tended to be listed with clarifiers such as Outbound (toward Empress) or Inbound (toward Lovat.) The tea shop where I had talked with Amaia was on the main deck of the Yallup's Outbound Port side, which mean on return trips it became Inbound Starboard.

"Dammit," I cursed, correcting myself and pivoting on my bad knee, which let out a silent painful screech.

"Where are we going?"

"A tea shop," I explained.

"They had tea at Shantak," said Hagen.

"We're not going for the tea. We're going to find the Shoalta."

I turned and pushed through the crowd.

The trip toward the (now) fore of the Yallup took another fifteen minutes. Even in Lovat, the distance would have taken no time at all. Most people complained about the crowds back home, but the streets of Lovat felt downright roomy compared to the *Gamble's* decks.

The bells and clangs of the pachinko parlor were audible before we arrived. A crowd of mostly kresh stood along the little exterior rail, sipping tea and babbling at one another in their native tongue. I looked for the shoalta and didn't see her among the crowd.

"She's here?"

"If not here, then down below," I said. "I rolled the dice."

"Wal, we'll never find her—"

"Patience," I said, and kept pushing through the crowd.

Hagen mumbled something but continued to follow. The crowd parted, allowing me to duck inside and into the turmoil of the pachinko parlor. The smell of cigarette smoke was heavy on the air, masking most of the florals from the tea. Lights blinked, bells rang, and whistles howled. The clatter of ball bearings was constant as players either dumped them into the machines' hungry maws or collected their winnings.

The room wasn't enormous. Heck, it wasn't much bigger than my place back home. A tiny counter stood by the entrance with a bored kresh proprietor behind it, hardly giving the human and dimanian a glance as we entered.

The rest of the room was dominated by four rows of machines. Each was occupied.

I took a step to one side, peering down one row, then another.

Shoalta Amaia sat near the corner, her hood up, a claw feeding bearings into the machine before her. A cup of tea steamed from a small cup holder mounted to the machine. I imagined it smelled like rose and brakendale.

"There," I said.

Even the narrow rows were crowded. I had to push through. When I got close, I called out. "Amaia! Amaia, it's me."

She turned, her eyes wide.

"We need to talk," I said.

"No. No, we don't."

She abandoned the tray of ball bearings and rose quickly, moving past me and through the crowd along a corridor that ran along the back of the room.

"Amaia," I said.

Hagen broke away from me, moving around the machines in an attempt to head her off.

"Miss," he said, pushing up his spectacles. "I really think—"

Her left claw flipped out and smacked him in the stomach. Hagen blinked in surprise, then doubled over, wheezing. Kresh might be small, but they're heavily muscled. They can whip their boney claws out fast, and when they strike, it packs a wallop. Hagen was lucky she had aimed high. Any lower and he'd be in considerably more pain.

The shoalta slipped past my scholar friend and out the door, getting tangled up in the crowd outside.

"Go after her," he wheezed.

"But—"

"Go! If she talked to the yellow king, then you need to talk to her!"

I left him in the parlor. Amaia had just broken free of the mass of people and was rushing aft toward the rear of the *Gamble*. I wouldn't lose her this time. She was hiding something, had been since the moment we met, and something inside me told me I needed to find out what. That the fate of Lovat—perhaps all of the Territories—was at stake. She was a part of it.

For a moment I lost her as she slipped through a group of bufo'anur. But my skull continued its hum. The hot desert air pulled at my skin, and I could feel the heat from a broken sun.

I was close.

"Leave me alone," Amaia said. I heard concern in her voice, not fear. She was worried. Not about me but about something else.

Failure, unacceptable.

The word hissed in my ear. A gush of dry wind.

She cannot fail. It was the yellow-clad figure's voice.

"Amaia, let's talk about this!" I was shouting now.

"No!"

We were racing through the deck, passing casinos, poker halls, hotels, brothels, taverns. Neon and glowing signs whipped by as I ran, turning the deck into a kaleidoscope. I didn't slow. I matched her pace. Every once in a while I caught her glaring at me from over her shoulder, then she'd turn and continue her retreat.

"Amaia, we have to talk!" I shouted.

The reply was angry. "Not now, *Guardian!*"

I staggered to a stop. My head jerked back as the base of my skull continued its thrumming vibration.

Amaia also stopped. The crowd around us melted away.

Slowly she turned, her arms dangling at her sides. She was twenty or so feet away—a few more and I would have lost her. A few people stopped, grew bored, and continued on their way. Others moved around us, some giving us strange looks. We stayed still, facing each other like gunslingers.

The Shoalta was only half my height. Her heavy salt-stained robes hardly moved, despite the constant breeze that moved through the decks. Her hood had fallen back, and the small shoalta stared at me in stunned silence. Her V-shaped mouth hung open in shock. Her eyes were wide. Slowly, her claws rose, coming to her mouth but doing little to cover it—a human gesture, one that didn't work as well on kresh.

"Then I'm right." My words were a whisper. "You know."

"Oh, Deeper," said the kresh. She closed her eyes and rubbed the top of her head. "Oh, deep, dreams, and darkness."

After a heartbeat I took a step toward her. Then another. She didn't move, just stared at me with those wide black eyes. In a few more moments I was in front of her.

She looked up at me. Breathed out a long sigh and extended a bony claw.

I took it and—

TWENTY-SEVEN

Together we stood in the wasteland. Flakes of ash eddied around us like snow caught in a gyre. It took a moment for my eyes to adjust from the blues and pinks of the *Gamble's* decks to the dull parchment world before me. The dry desert air blew as hard as ever, but now it felt colder than before, as if winter had come to the barren landscape. A shiver ran across my shoulders and down my arms and spine. My skin puckered with goose pimples.

What were our bodies doing back on the *Gamble*? I felt the pull between worlds—a fear of danger, coupled with the faith I had in my friend. I was sure Hagen had caught up with us. He'd keep us safe.

I looked down at the kresh shoalta. She smiled up at me. The expression stretched out her fleshy beak. Amaia released my hand. Stepped back and regarded me with a quizzical expression.

"You knew," she said. The fact we stood in another world didn't seem to faze her. "How?"

"Same way you did," I managed. My stomach was still reeling as my equilibrium attempted to recalibrate to the shift. I tapped the back of my head, slumped back and down into a sitting position, my right leg extended more out of habit than need. There was no pain here. Here my leg was fine—if here even existed.

With me sitting, Amaia and I were nearly face to face.

"For me, it's here." She pressed a hand to her belly.

Around us was nothing. I'd half-expected to end up in the village, but we were back among the endless flatness. A few squat ruins hunkered nearby. Further out were the bones of towers. Outside of that, there was nothing else—no gargoyles, gaunts, or whatever the hell I was supposed to call them now. No figure in rags. No shadows. No Tawil—although he was probably around. He was always around.

The monster looming beyond the horizon remained, though. Vast. Enormous. But even those words felt insufficient. It didn't seem to bother Amaia. She didn't even give it a second glance. Following her lead, I remained as calm as I could, despite the unease of being back here, in this false reality that now felt more real than home.

"Who selected you?" she asked. "As Guardian."

"Fellow named Peter Black." I saw no reason to lie. He was dead, after all.

"And he failed?"

I nodded.

"So he unknowingly put you on your course. Interesting." She tapped her beak with a claw. The tone of her voice told me that she believed me but was withholding something too. "What do you see here?"

"A wasteland," I said. "*The* Wasteland. On the horizon is a city, much like Lovat, but ruined—shattered. Beneath our feet are more ruins. The further down we dig, the deeper they go."

A smile, or what I interpreted as a smile, small but genuine. "So you met the other one."

"Who?"

She laughed. It was light, almost lyrical. I had spoken with kresh before, but rarely for long and never heard one laugh. They tended to avoid humans, and vice versa. "Tawil, I believe he calls himself here. Though the *Black Book* gives him other names: King of Orbs, the Lurker." She waved a claw. "Auntie Mason knew more of them." There was something in the way she said it—more she was keeping to herself.

"Are the names important?"

She laughed with her whole body this time, then sat next to me and patted my knee with a claw. "And you call yourself Guardian."

It was as much a question as a statement. I spread my hands in an apologetic gesture. I'd never been much for book learning. I stumbled on the truth more than discovering it within the texts of ancient tomes. Maybe the answers were already in front of me and I was too stupid to seek them out.

What did Mom always say? *Convictions are fickle, truth eternal.* Something like that, anyway.

"He is harmless. But for other worlds." her voice drifted off. She looked out over the Wasteland. "For this one…"

"I don't understand."

"We're not meant to understand. Yet consciousness demands knowledge. It's an inherent desire—an instinct, but we're bound within fractured realities. Our reality is but one shard of the fractured whole. The space between—therein lies the truth. What we perceive as rainbows are glisters of something far grander. We see color and cannot comprehend the colors between the colors—the spaces between worlds. They're out of our reach. Well—" She turned and looked at me, smirked, then looked toward the horizon gesturing with an extended claw. "To most of us, anyway."

"So we're the special ones," I said with a laugh.

She smiled with me and nodded slowly. It wasn't a nod that confirmed my statement, but also not one that rejected it outright.

"Are you like me?" I asked, the words clumsy in my mouth. "Are you also a Guardian?"

"No. No," Amaia shook her head. "I'm nothing like you. You are hamiya. I am mutaealim. You protect. I travel to obtain knowledge."

"Mutaealim," I repeated the word, butchering the pronunciation. "So you're a seeker."

"Something like that," she said. "You're not a spiritual man, are you, Mister Bell?"

I shook my head.

"Then this will be harder for you to understand. I came here looking for validation. But instead I saw another way open before me. Another door, another journey. I didn't choose this path, mind. I thought I'd remained wedded to the deep, dreams, and darkness."

"What does that mean?" I asked.

A laugh. "Sorry. It's… Deeperist verse. A reference passed down in the oral tradition of the faith. It's what we call Deeper's realm. The old city. The drowned city. The dreaming city. The dead city."

"Look West," I said, the words coming out in a mumble. "Who is he? Deeper, I mean."

The two halves of the fleshy beak pressed together and her eyes narrowed. I wasn't sure what to make of the expression. "A Founder. A First. Like Tawil—and like him, he has other names. So does his home. All, perhaps many, are considered holy. Sacred to some. Profane to others. We dare not utter them. That said, most are unpronounceable anyway. Especially in Strutten."

I nodded but said nothing. What could I say?

Amaia didn't wait for a response anyway. "I don't believe you're an evil man, Waldo. I think you have Lovat's interest at heart."

"It's my home," I said. "Rough edges and all."

"Then—" She looked away, growing silent.

Ash lightly fell on us. The smell of sulfur permeated the air. Still, I didn't move. It was the wrong time to move. Amaia had convictions, and saying or doing anything would prevent her from speaking them.

When she spoke, it came out in a whisper. "My heart is in conflict. A battleground. I feel adrift, but I cannot reject what I know to be true merely to accept a world view that makes me comfortable. I see those reports on the monochromes. Destruction. I've smelled the stink that washed over our city.

The stink of death. It doesn't make sense. It doesn't match what I was told when I joined the faith."

I turned and met her gaze. It was difficult for me to read any emotion in her ink-black eyes, but I could hear it in her voice. Like calls to like, and her feelings matched my own. She processed them differently, but she was experiencing the same decoupling I was. Navigating the spaces between worlds was ruining us.

For her, it was her faith at stake. For me, it was my reality. She believed her faith unshakable. I believed in my own stability. It's always hardest to lose what we hold most dear.

"Deeper is supposed to be benevolent. But I do not see benevolence. I do not see charity. I do not see acceptance. But I was taught that—I believed that. I still believe it," she said. Her words were assured, but she didn't look like she believed them.

"I grew up believing in what I could see," I said. "The trail before me, the creak of a wain, the sound of wind passing through the trees. In Lovat, it was the feel of the cold air, the sound of the crowds, the smell of the carts. But I've seen things now—things I couldn't explain."

I paused. "I touched what I shouldn't have been able to touch. I'd conjured what I should never have been able to conjure. Fought what I never should have fought. It makes sense here." I waved around us, disturbing the falling ash. "But it doesn't make sense *here*." I tapped the side of my head. "It's getting harder for me to piece everything together. It all comes in fits and starts."

She was watching me. I went on.

"I think I'm on the *Gamble* to stop Deeper. I don't know what's going to happen, but I think that is why I am there. Here. Wherever."

Her expression was severe. I said nothing more, just sat in silence.

The Shoalta blinked at me. Had I expected her to resist? Was she the type to lurch into action, come at me with claws bared?

"He wants me to stop the ceremony," she said. There was a finality to her words.

"Who?" I shook my head, trying to make sense of what she said. "How?"

"He looks in from outside and understands the pattern in ways our mortal minds cannot. He moves in our world through an avatar but is too far, so he called to me. He sees the beginning and the end."

With a shock I realized that she was talking about another First.

"Amaia, who?" I asked again.

Her face was expressionless, the black eyes looking nearly lifeless as she spoke. "The Golden One. The Goodly Shepherd. The King in Yellow."

Each title tolled inside me like a clanging bell. *The pretender.*

As if his name had summoned him, the creature was suddenly there—off in the distance, a narrow form in hooded and tattered yellow robes. He didn't move, but the robes swirled about him in slow motion. Was he watching us? The idea unnerved me. My skin prickled.

"It's him," Amaia said. "He called to me. Reached out, found me, spoke the truth. He has people back home, people in Lovat—more than we realize, so many more. Friends—friends in places you'd never expect. He plays the great game as well, but from another side."

"Who is he?" I asked.

Amaia looked up at me. I could have sworn there was amusement and pity in her expression. "You don't know? Waldo, that's Hastur."

TWENTY-EIGHT

Pain seared hot, burning through my head like fire. A spasm followed, my back arching as saliva filled my mouth. The name tore through me. Reality ripped and reformed. The image of a burning upended torch seared against the inside of my skull. Golden light overwhelmed. Something similar yet altogether different from our sun. It was the light of a distant star—corrupt and tainted. I found myself writhing on the sand as the pain and the bright golden light faded from my eyes.

Hastur.

The Cold Shepherd.

The King in Yellow.

I was on my knees, spitting and gulping the hot air, when the sound came. It started low and slow but soon rose in intensity. A sound eerily familiar ripped through the air around us, a forlorn moaning that rent the sky and silenced the wind. I couldn't help but shudder. Old memories of older trails sickened me. Gooseflesh prickled across my skin.

"He called to me, and I answered," Amaia said. She was unmoved by my pain. "He's how I can slip between worlds unmolested."

There was a profound reverence in her voice that told me her allegiances had shifted. She didn't worship Deeper. Not any longer. The Shoalta had become Priestess. She worshiped someone new. Some*thing* new. Hastur.

The name tasted of ash, even in my mind, and I had to spit again. He was still there, against the horizon. Pale yellow rags whipping in the wind. The distant First stayed well away from us. It reminded me of when I had first seen the gargoyles— the nightgaunts—on the Broken Road. Always watching, never daring to come close. Oozing that foreboding sense of menace.

"You answered? Amaia, it's a *First*. One of the Founders. He's a monster," I said. My gulps of air had made my voice weak, and it wavered and cracked.

"No. He wants what's best for Lovat," she said. There was a fervor in her voice, a deep fire. Passion. She glowed with it. "He told me. There are others. So many others. The stars are right once again. The Founders awaken. Deeper is just one of many. If we can stop Deeper, then the shepherd will be able to return to his flock. A glorious procession from sulfur to salt. Hastur has chosen Lovat. He will become a generous and kindly king. He will make the city his seat. Don't you see?"

I scrambled back, rolling onto my haunches, and then rose. My legs wavered, my head pounded.

She looked toward the distant figure and her posture shifted as if she was pulled in his direction. Then she turned to me and eased back. Her eyes were still deep pools of shadow, even here in the Wasteland.

"Amaia," I said, my voice soft as I stepped toward her. "What did you do?"

"I pulled some strings. Managed to meet with the Outfit. They helped me."

"The Outfit! By the bloody Firsts!" I ran my hands through my hair and rubbed my eyes with the heels of my hand. Of course Elephant was involved. Why wouldn't her hands be in this as well? That woman wouldn't help a zealot just out of the kindness of her heart. There had to be something in it for her. She had made a tidy sum off the riots. She had an angle here as well. I could sense it.

"They were eager to help. They understood. Hastur will bless them, despite their past sins."

"What did they do? What are they going to do?"

"They gave me what I needed." Amaia drew away from me now, seeing something in my eyes that she didn't like. Rage? I felt rage. Hate? That was there as well. But I thought I had control. We always have less control than we think.

"Stop the ritual," she said. "Keep Deeper from returning."

"With what?" I demanded.

"I don't like your tone," Amaia said. She took several shuffling steps back from me, her claws held out before her in a guarded position.

"I want to help," I said. "I want to stop Deeper too. But I need to know what we're dealing with." Did she believe me? It was impossible to read her expression.

"No," she said. "It is handled."

She looked away.

"It's not handled," I said. I crouched and enjoyed that the motion was pain-free. "I can tell. Amaia, Elephant is dangerous."

"I don't know this Elephant," she said. "I know of Fress and Allard. That's all. They are faithful men."

Allard. That name rang a bell. That wasn't the name of the bok—he was Hank. Was that the other goon I had met? The dimanian? It had only been months, but it felt so long ago.

"I don't know Fress, but if—"

"You aren't a believer. You don't see what's at stake."

"I know enough," I said. "I've faced down a few Founders in my time. Deeper isn't the forerunner. There have been others. Hell, he's not even the second. They're monsters, all of them."

"Tawil," she spat.

"Broken," I snapped back. "Alone. An avatar without his... his..." I waved a hand in the air "connection to... whatever. It doesn't matter. They're dangerous."

The former shoalta curled her claws and glared at me through narrow eyes.

"Amaia," I said, stepping toward her.

"No."

Then she was gone.

She had completely disappeared. Like before.

I turned to look toward the distant figure—but he was gone as well. Instead, a long lanky form was plodding across the hardpan toward me, boots kicking up small clouds of dust that drifted on the ceaseless breeze. He covered the distance quickly, and I found myself once again looking up into the tattooed face of Tawil.

"Oh," he said. "You again."

"Yeah," I said, pushing up from my squat to stand again. Out of habit, I dusted my pants. "Me again."

"You ain't the one who called," he said.

"No," I agreed. "I'm not."

"Was it the dimanian?"

"The dimanian? There's a dimanian who comes here?"

"Yep."

"No," I said. How many people visited this terrible place? But before I could ask, Tawil was readying another question for me.

"The little lady, the uh… kresh, I think they call themselves kresh now. Was that her?"

"Shoalta Amaia," I said. "Yeah, it was her."

"Fervent one, that. Good servant. Shame she ain't on our side."

"*Our* side?" I raised my eyebrow at him.

"My family's," he said, and gave me a wink and flipped off the thing on the horizon. "Want a beer?"

Condensation dribbled down the side of the bottle of Aforgomon. A strange moment of peace. I knew I should be worried about my body back in my reality—after all, Shoalta

Amaia and I had traveled from the middle of the crowd—but it seemed so distant now. I touched the bottle with the tips of my finger and felt its chill.

Tawil had once told me he cooled these in the well, but until this moment I had only drunk them warm. They were better cold. I slumped in my chair and stared at the bottle, watching beads of sweat grow larger as they trickled down the side and mixed with their siblings before adding to the tiny lake at the bottle's base.

For his part, Tawil continued to busy himself at his stove, humming. It was an old blues number from Saint Broonzy I knew as "Mean Old World." Not one of the saints I was totally familiar with, but a number I remembered my mother singing. Occasionally Tawil would dip a wooden spoon into a pan, taste whatever he was working on, then toss an empty tin into the trash.

On declaring he had finished, he turned and set before me a plate of long spaghetti pasta covered in a steaming red sauce that smelled heavily of onion and garlic. On top was a single meatball the size of my fist, and atop that was a dusting of white cheese. My stomach growled in excitement.

"Hope you're hungry," Tawil said.

I was, and I said so as I cut into the meatball and devoured the pasta. I had been starving, and up until then I hadn't noticed. Unusual for me. Too distracted. I wasn't sure what was real anymore. Reality had taken on a sheen I couldn't describe.

When we finished, I rose and gathered the dishes and put them in the sink. As I turned to face Tawil, my mind was running through a smattering of questions.

"Grab me another beer, would you, Wal?" said the avatar. He waved a long hand toward a bucket on the floor near the foot of the stove. Two beers bobbed slowly in the cold water, waiting to be opened and drunk. I noticed there were four fresh ones on the shelf behind them. I drew the pair out of the bucket and replaced them.

I freed the metal cap from the mouth and handed the open beer to Tawil. He nodded at me, then took a long draw and smacked his lips and then his flat stomach. "I like a little exercise after a heavy meal. Let's take a walk."

We walked across the desert, which was now devoid of any ashfall and substantially warmer than before. For the first time I realized that it never collected on the ground. Only dust, mudcrack, and hamada remained. The sun had melted it away as if it was snow.

The heat beat down on us. It used to be unbearable. Now it felt familiar. Give me the Big Ninety, not this wasteland—but at least I no longer stood here in fear. Hell, the beer was keeping me more relaxed. Tawil strode next to me, his long legs having an easier time navigating as he wandered across the wastes.

"How much do you know?" I asked.

He smirked and took another swill of the beer he'd brought with him. "Enough. I was already acquainted with the particulars. I usually am."

I ignore his last comment. "Then what should I do?"

He looked at me, and for a second the tattooed blue discs on his face moved together, joining before separating. Then it was as if they hadn't moved at all. I found myself doubting my own eyes.

When I blinked, they had returned to their permanent locations. Maybe the beer was getting to me.

"Do about what?" Tawil asked.

"Deeper. The yellow king—Hastur. All this." I gestured with my bottle toward the open space before us. A few broken ruins sat within walking distance, the ruined city even further.

"There's so much more, Wal."

"Don't follow."

"Look around."

The now-familiar buzzing flashed along my head, neck, and spine. At that moment, the desert of the Wasteland fell away—and now Tawil and I stood in a far different place. The blast-furnace heat was gone, replaced by a pleasant twilight breeze. No broken sun hung in the sky, and no moon had yet risen. The sky was dusty blue fractured by shades of coral pinks and dark lumps of shady purples toward the horizon.

We stood on a grassy shoreline that ran forever in both directions beside a shallow lake that stretched to the horizon. A garden lush with life was at our back. The sounds of strange keening filled the air, part birdcall, part mammalian cry. The air was sweet with the fragrance of flowers—so strong I could almost taste it. Countless flowers bobbed among the water plants that covered the surface of the lake. Small islands of floating vegetation, starred with blood-red flowers, rose from the plants. The colors here were lively and bright, a reminder that the broken sun hadn't baked the color from this world.

It was beautiful.

I looked at Tawil, and he looked both different and the same. Younger somehow, the crevices and crags of his brown face softened. The blue orb tattoos that stained his cheeks were darker, more refined. It almost looked like they were floating in front of his face.

A wave of dizziness came over me. I blinked and shook my head. Then sat and stared—feeling my ass settle against grass, hard sand, and the decking of the *Gamble*.

Three realities. Three.

How many were there?

Tawil must have sensed my thoughts. "Many realities, but one only is beginning to show the signs of our interference."

He gestured toward the lilies. At first I didn't understand. This wasn't the ruins of the Wasteland. This place pulsed with life, beautiful and abundant life.

Then I noticed what he was indicating. Coal-black smoke drifted from the centers of some of the water lilies as if a lump of red hot-coal smoldered within them. It was an unnerving sight—ugly smoke emanating from something so pure and beautiful. I shuddered involuntarily.

"Reality is a funny thing," he said.

We were back in the desert. The hot sun baked my neck. I was on the ground and rose, my legs wobbly from the sudden transitions.

Tawil smirked, kicked at the dust beneath his toe. "You're always going to be here, just as you'll always be there."

"So I'm not just of two worlds," I said.

"No," Tawil said with a sad smile. "Not quite."

"How many?" That feeling of unreality wavered through me. I was decoupled and adrift. A runaway wain.

"As we drift, so you will drift. You can thank Peter Black for that."

"How do I stop it?"

He shook his head. "Ain't nothing you can do about it. Best make peace with that."

Make peace. It was an odd thought. I stared at the city—or what remained of the city— and then looked at the thing beyond and shuddered. This was a land of nightmare. The thought of this being my home as much as the Territories sent a wave of panic careening through me. It wasn't what I wanted to hear.

Tawil continued. "As for the other bits—way I see it, you have two options." He raised a long finger. "First option. If you stop the ritual, the High Priest—this Deeper, as you keep calling him—will fail. But that yellow bastard, he of the smoke and ash, the self-made king in his tattered robes, he'll succeed."

"The shoalta's belief in him is misguided," I said.

Tawil took a sip of beer. "You'll be trading one problem for another."

For a moment, the folksy air was gone. There was a warning in his tone, coupled with a venomous disdain I hadn't heard from him before. His own gaze followed mine, his jaw set, his eyes hard. Together we stood and stared out across the flat expanse at the ruined city.

A flock of something rose from the bone of the dead city, lifting into the air before heatwaves obscured them and they melted into sky. They must have been enormous, whatever they were.

"And if I don't stop the ritual and stop the Shoalta instead—what happens then?

"I think you know," said Tawil. His voice was still tight, but some of the charm had crept back in. He looked toward the ruin of the city.

"Then the High Priest will succeed, and Hastur will fail," I breathed out slowly. I thought of the boats scattered across the mountain side and the stories of missing fishing villages.

Tawil jerked and scowled at the name. The beer sloshed in the bottle as he tipped it back. In two gulps he finished it and sent the bottle hurtling into the distance. It fell end over end, arcing toward the city, and fell out of sight. I didn't even hear the glass shatter.

"Don't much care for that name," he growled. "Never liked hearing it before. Don't much like hearing it now. The sisterhood and their songs are lost to the dust of this world. As they should be."

"What about that other place?" I asked. "The Garden."

Tawil didn't answer. Together we maintained a silent vigil staring out across the vastness to the ruined city.

The broken sun was low and red. It never set here. Why would it? It would only dip and give the desert that pre-twilight feel where the shadows grew long and the light turned the color of wine, hinting at a night's coolness that would never come.

I took a swig of my own beer, then I held it out and stared at it. Broken crimson sunlight glittered inside the brown glass, sending bloody shards of light dancing inside the bottle. Wish we could get this back home. It was good. Malty, but still refreshing.

A sigh escaped my lips. What was I doing? Standing next to the abandoned avatar of a First wasn't the time to discuss beer profiles. I let out a long breath. "Ain't much of a choice."

"Seldom is," said Tawil as he took another drink. Then he repeated himself, softer. "Seldom is."

TWENTY-NINE

No hospital this time. No brig. No nurses. No friends sitting around a bed staring down at me with concerned expressions. The room was dark. I heard heavy snoring—Taft, it had to be. Someone let out a soft fart, followed by the rasp of nails scratching skin.

A meager light played in beneath colorless scalloped shades. The room was quiet, but I could hear muffled music, laughter, the occasional scream—the sort that was impossible to interpret. It could be excitement or distress. The vibrations of choppy sea against a distant hull rattled my backside.

I still felt Tawil's hand on my shoulder. A friendly gesture. I smiled at him, nodded—and realized I was smiling and nodding at a dark bulkhead wall. My brain spasmed at the shift. I blinked a few times, trying to clear the Wasteland from my vision.

And my knee ached. Always lovely when pain is the anchor that helps you hold fast to reality... well, *a* reality. Why couldn't it be a pleasant sensation?

The transition was smoother this time. I didn't feel sick to my stomach, nor did I feel like my equilibrium was thrown off.

I sat up, ducking just in time to keep myself from smacking my head on the berth above me. I peeked over the edge. Hannah slept peacefully, the blanket pulled to her chin, her chest moving in the rhythmic slowness of someone adrift in deep sleep. I was still in my shirtsleeves and slacks—even more rumpled than before—but my shoes, jacket, and tie were lying next to the berth, near my small trunk.

The thought of slipping my feet into the tight leather shoes repulsed me. I wish I had my boots. The job had become something else—something bigger and more important. I had a decision to make, and I damn well didn't want to make a decision in uncomfortable shoes. Not that I had much of a choice.

What day was it? Hell, what time was it? How long had I been out? There had to be some way of telling, but I was still so new at slipping between the Wasteland and the Territories that I wasn't sure.

Could Tawil help me? I considered turning to ask him but knew if I did, I would somehow be pulled back. Right now, I couldn't handle that. I didn't have much time left to act.

I looked at the six berths that were filled: Hagen, Taft, Hannah, and three of the security crew. No Wensem. No Pascal. They and the others must be on duty. I considered waking my friends, but I needed to know where things stood. Whatever happened, I'd need my crew ready and waiting. We still had a job to do.

I pushed through the cabin's door and into the hallway, squinting at the bright light. Wensem and one of the crew flanked either side of the door, hands at their sides, their suits as wrinkled as mine.

"Oh, you're awake," said Wensem, his voice toneless.

I yawned—couldn't help it. "What day is it?"

"We're a day out from Lovat. You've been asleep for about twelve hours."

"Carter's cross," I growled. Time was inconsistent between realities, which made figuring out the shifts even more confusing. "Time?"

"Three in the morning," said Celina Dewire, the human woman standing opposite Wensem. She had worked with us a few times. I liked her, though we rarely interacted. I could see the tension as she sized me up. Clearly, she wasn't on my side.

The hallway was abandoned, but the muffled noise was only slightly louder out here. Impressive insulation. Say what you will about the *Gamble's* crowded passageways, they treated their high rollers well.

"Where's Eli?" I asked.

"Patrol," said Wensem. He narrowed his eyes at me. "What's up? You got something on your mind."

"Hm? Oh, yeah," I said. "Yeah."

Wensem's expression was all concern, but he hid it well. I doubted Dewire noticed—she had already made up her mind about me. I considered saying something but bit my tongue. No need to provoke her. Not now.

"Have the bonfires started?" I asked.

"Tomorrow night, after we arrive," said Wensem.

"Celina, think you can handle watch alone?" I looked to her, and she gave me a curt nod. "I need to talk to my partner."

Lovat glowed in the distance. Millions of lights lit the night sky and burnished the clouds above the city—the living version of the corpse city in the Wasteland. The body made whole.

At night Lovat was most alive. You don't see stains in the darkness. You don't see her injustice. You don't see her depravity. Her selfishness. Her arrogance. Night is the city's cloak.

Even from miles out, the city sparkled against the water, a gleam upon the waves that reflected her evening attire in jeweled facets. How many souls dwelled inside those levels? How many people struggled to live among the stairwells and lifts, automats and diners, directory agents and collectors?

The stink was back—that sickly sweet scent of rot and decay. It had been muted in Empress, and I'd almost forgotten it. This close to Lovat it was stronger. Now I knew what it was—the harbinger of that First I had seen in the sky. I wrinkled my nose and shuddered.

Beside me Wensem stood, stoic and silent. He let me look out over the water. Didn't press me. We stood on a narrow walkway that arched beneath the forward-inbound penthouse that had once served as a pilothouse. A stiff breeze cut at us. No one was here. The high rollers had long since abandoned their thousand-lira buy-in tables and returned to their beds. Gaming would continue anew tomorrow.

"Danforth is preparing to go to the Mayor," said Wensem. His voice startled me, though I knew he didn't mean it to. I had been so lost in my thoughts, I had forgotten about the comfort of having him standing next to me. "Camalote will probably support him."

"Think your message got through?"

He spread his hands with a 'who knows' gesture. Honestly, Danforth was the least of my worries at the moment. I looked over at my partner. "You believe in fate?"

"Fate? Wal, Danforth could *ruin* us. Our crew is near mutiny. And you brought me out here to ask if I believe in fate?" His voice was calm, but I could hear the edge in it.

"Answer the question." I leaned forward against the solid rail. Wondered briefly if it had been replaced and, if so, how many times. The sea was not kind to metal.

"No," said Wensem. "I don't believe in fate. I don't believe in luck. I believe in family and honor."

I said nothing for a minute, just watched those distant stars that were my city. "Five years ago, I'd have agreed with you. Now I'm not so sure."

"What do you mean?"

"I mean I've faced three Firsts in a handful of years. I'm pretty sure I'm about to face my fourth, one way or another. All this because I received some so-called boon assigned to me by a mad cultist. If that isn't fate, then I'm not sure what is. Hard to ignore it either way.

"That kresh is involved—Shoalta Amaia," I scratched the back of my head. "She touched me when I confronted her, and it sent us both to the Wasteland. We talked. Parlayed, more like. I learned more about her. About this."

I waved a hand. In typical Wensem fashion, he didn't say anything, just waited.

"This goes well beyond a rogue Deeperist," I continued. "She's been working with Elephant—indirectly as far as I can tell, but the Outfit is certainly involved. Elephant didn't seem to give a damn about Ashton or the blockades. It's all business to her, which makes me think they have other motives. All I know is Amaia's been coerced into stopping the bonfire ceremony for King Tide's Ebb, and they're helping her."

Wensem's expression hardened. "They wouldn't care about the fires."

"No, which means there's something else going on. Elephant is somehow connected. The shoalta mentioned one of her goons—Allard, a dimanian. I met him once. He was her contact in the Outfit."

Wensem chewed his lower lip and pondered this information.

For a long moment, I watched him. Unsure how much more I should reveal. "There's more. A lot more."

He looked at me, his blue-gray eyes sparkling in the light of distant Lovat. I opened my mouth to speak, but the words didn't come. They felt stuck in my throat. To be perfectly honest, I'd yet to process everything I'd learned in Empress.

Wensem must have sensed this, because he reached out and placed a big seven-fingered hand on my shoulder and gave me a friendly squeeze. Urging me on.

The dam broke, and the words tumbled from my lips. "Essie—the woman I met at Ced's—she was somehow involved with Elephant. Knew her in Empress. Went to university together. Something happened. Don't know what. They ran off to Lovat and—"

"Lovers?" I could hear the hesitation in his question.

I stopped, thought about it, then shrugged. "Friends, certainly. Maybe more. I'm not sure. When they left Empress, Essie disappeared. Her family lost track of her. Mind, I heard this all from Essie's identical twin—an Emperian woman named Olivia."

"You never talked much about Essie," said Wensem. "I got the gist of it, but still…"

When he'd gotten back from the blockade, neither of us had taken time to explain everything that had happened. Life had been a whirlwind. I only knew bits and pieces from the blockade and he knew little beyond what had happened with Ashton. How would I begin explaining Essie to him? When this was over, I decided then and there, we'd rectify that.

"Not sure how to tell it—if I'm being honest. This traveling… the slipping between realities. It's messed me up." The words were difficult to say. My throat hitched. My eyes watered. It wasn't easy to admit weakness—especially not to the strongest person I knew. Made me feel like a screw-up. "Everything's starting to run together. It's hard to tell what is where." I looked toward my city. "Maybe the crew is right. Maybe I'm not cut out to Master anymore."

Even now, I could feel the Wasteland's pull. How did I explain that to him? How does one describe that they don't feel cold because they're also standing in a baking desert? That they could be hit here, but not feel it because they were also elsewhere? It was a symptom—the result of being torn in two. And it was slowly destroying me.

Ashton's voice echoed in my head. *You're a man of two worlds now, Guardian. That might not be easy to comprehend, but you'll either figure it out or go mad in the process.*

Wensem shivered, then slumped onto the deck and patted the space next to him. "Sit."

I dropped and settled next to him, then looked up. Our view had disappeared, but we could still see the stars. Always the stars. We were also out of the wind—well, *this* wind. I still felt another breeze, one I pushed from my mind.

How many times had we done this around how many fires? I couldn't count the moments, but each of them swirled around inside my head as memories—flickers of the past, some nearly forgotten, others as sharp and poignant as if we were still there.

"Why don't you start at the beginning," he said.

"Okay," I said, the words tight in my throat. I took a breath that was cold and crisp, hot and dry at once.

"All of it," he said.

A long pause. I swallowed.

"Okay." Then again, "Okay."

So I began. I told him *everything*, starting at the beginning of this journey. I talked about traveling between realities. I spoke of Tawil. I told him about Liv and her story about Essie.

I explained my relationship with Ash back in the city. I described my encounters with the shoalta, talked about what I knew of the Deeperists and Our Father of the Obscured Atoll. It was hardest to explain the tearing of my mind, but I tried. I fought to keep my emotions in check but couldn't stifle the hitch in my throat. Wensem listened in the way he had that drew the truth from anyone. He nodded in the right places and hummed with encouragement, never interrupted. I told him what I could in the best way I could. When I finished, we were both staring at the sky, our knees up, forearms balanced atop each of them.

"Carter's cross," said Wensem after a long moment of silence. A few more curses followed, but none with force. He sounded awestruck. "That's—"

His voice drifted into silence. I couldn't blame him.

The light of a single shooting star burned across the sable sky, its colors shifting across the spectrum as it rushed to its death—white then silver, silver then gold, gold then blue, blue then orange, and orange fading to aquamarine. Then it fizzled and the sky swallowed it before it could reach the edge of the railing—our artificial horizon.

"It's a lot to keep track of," I said.

"You trust this Tawil fellow?"

I considered that. "No," I finally said. "But I believe him."

"I wish Sam were here," he said.

Something inside of me tightened at the mention of her name. Old emotions stirred.

"Me too," I admitted. My voice came out weaker than I had expected.

"Hagen is good with books and all, but she's good with people." He sighed and lightly thumped the back of his head again the bulkhead. "How the hell would the shoalta get help from the Outfit? Aboard the *Gamble*, I mean. It's not like they could threaten the Council of Captains."

"They might have a soldier on board," I offered.

Wensem shook his head. "No, impossible. What's an Outfit soldier going to do? Weapons are illegal here, everything is checked, no one gets a bag on without—"

My hand shot out and I slapped him in the chest with my palm. He was too level-headed to react, but his face swiveled in my direction, the crooked mouth breaking into a smile. He knew something in my memory had been triggered.

"What?"

"Shoalta Amaia!" I said, grinning as the pieces fell into place. I should have seen it. But who would have expected much from a kresh? Much less a holy woman. She was the perfect mule. Suddenly I loathed and respected Elephant. She picked her marks well.

"Her *bag*," I said, remembering the blue duffle Amaia carried—her anxiousness moving through security. It should have stuck out to me. It was an aberration—a bright blue aberration, nothing like the sackcloth, luggage and ancient salt-stained leather trunks hauled about by most Deeperists. The scuffle on the docks had distracted everyone, myself included. Amaia had disappeared, taking her bag—and whatever was inside it—on board.

I scrambled to my feet, forgetting my knee was still messed up in this reality. A lance of pain burst up my leg, and I had to support myself with the rail so I wouldn't collapse. But I couldn't sit still. "Carter's cross, Wen! Carter's damn cross. It was all right there and I missed it! She brought something with her. A duffle. It was a blue canvas duffle. She was stopped at the gate, but a scuffle at the dock distracted everyone. She disappeared. Didn't think much of it at the time." I smacked my forehead. "Damn it all. Never even registered."

"Who'd suspect a kresh?" said Wensem. He knew the answer. No one.

"No wonder they chose her," I said. She had tried to warn me. Told me to stay in Empress and find another route home. She wasn't talking about Ash's cultists—she was talking about what was in her duffle.

Wensem rose. Lovat didn't seem any closer, but I knew it was. It had to be. This whole ordeal had an endgame, and it would play out right on my city's doorstep.

"What's in her duffle?"

All manner of things rolled through my head. Guns. Knives. Hell, explosives. Whatever it was, it was enough to smuggle on board—enough to stop the *Gamble* for good.

"Explosives," I said. "How else would this work out in the Outfit's favor? They want to stop the *Gamble*, right? Take away the competition. What better way than to sink the boat. Do it during the bonfires. Remember how the Captains talked about taking great care to make sure they were safe. It'd be easy enough to blame the celebration on the Deeperists. No one would assume otherwise."

"Wal, if this boat's in danger—"

"No wonder *he* chose *her*," I said.

"He? I thought Elephant—"

"No."

A bewildered expression came over his face.

"I mean, yes. But also no. Hastur. As in the Hasturians' Hastur. Elephant is just a tool. He's the guiding force. In… the other place he convinced her—Amaia. She's working for him. She's a Hasturian, or something more—a zealot and true believer."

Wensem gave a long whistle, the sort he'd give on the trail when we were in danger. "Another damn First."

I nodded. "We're stuck in the middle of a feud. Hastur is on one side. Ash, Cybil, Curwen, and whatever is out there—" I nodded with my chin towards the aft of the *Gamble* "—are the other side. Tawil made it really clear he doesn't like him, and I can only assume the feeling is mutual."

"But I know Hasturians. They ain't—"

I raised a hand. "I doubt they know. At least I doubt many of them know. Trust me, I've been mulling that over as well. Look at the Deeperists. Think they understand what it is they worship? He recruited the shoalta. She found the Outfit. Here we are."

Wensem ran his hands through his hair and nodded.

"Here we are," he repeated.

THIRTY

Celebrations are in ten hours. The *Gamble* actually stops off the West Lovat point above a flooded Deeperist site known as the Looff Fields," I explained, pointing to a spot on a crude map Hagen had drawn earlier. "Many aquatics will be below celebrating, while others will join in the festivities above. Ferry boats will bring over more revelers from West Lovat. I'm sure the refugees and passengers will start departing then. It's going to get chaotic in that back-and-forth traffic."

"Why wait until the celebrations begin?" asked Hannah.

"The bonfires are going to be the excuse." It was a guess. "Once they're lit—"

"Blammo," said Taft softly.

I nodded.

"Can we get Castaigne off the boat?" asked Pascal.

"We're going to try," I said. "But I'd like to do it quietly. If people catch wind of her leaving before tomorrow, it might spark a panic. Plus, if the shoalta hears, she might set the bomb off before the celebrations."

"Can't they just arrest her?" asked Hannah.

"Perhaps," I said, looking at Wensem. He rubbed his chin and nodded as if he understood what I was thinking. Amaia has disappeared on me more than once, and I knew how. She could trigger her own shifts to the Wasteland. That gave her a distinct advantage. She'd be hard to corner and even more difficult to lock up.

"Wensem and I are going to go talk with the council. See if we can't figure something out. At the very least we're going to tell them what we suspect. Then we'll speak with Castaigne and explain the situation."

Hannah gave a low whistle and shook her head.

"What?"

"Danforth will be hanging around. So will Waite."

She was right, of course. Danforth hadn't left Castaigne's side since Empress. He'd no doubt put our concerns on ice while using his station to further his agenda. If I was right about the explosives, then the ambassador's life was in very real danger. Now wasn't the time for social maneuverings. I hated politics, and this sort of glad-handing backstabbing bullshit rankled me.

"That's a risk we'll have to take," I said. But I could feel my emotions slipping into my voice. My expression might have been confident, but my tone hinted at trouble. I could see the crew react. It was subtle—a tick of the eye, the bite of a lip, a rub of the back of the neck.

"What do you want us to do in the interim?" Taft asked.

"We need to scour the *Gamble*. Look everywhere for Amaia and her bag. Maybe we can find her bomb before she uses it."

"One duffle bag in this whole damn boat?" Hagen had pulled off his spectacles and was cleaning them on his shirt. He squinted through a lens at me. "Tall order, Wal."

I spread my hands. "We don't have a choice. Either we stop the shoalta and interrupt her plan or a whole lot of people are going to die. We're Guardian Security, and we need to do our damnedest to make sure we keep people safe. It starts with Castaigne, but it extends beyond the Ambassador."

The crew shifted with nervous energy. Each taking their cues from the others. No one said anything.

Wensem clapped his hands. "You heard the boss, people. We're going to find that duffle and stop the shoalta."

I rubbed the back of my head and looked at my crew. The nerves were still there, but they had a purpose now. They stood a little straighter. Their eyes were a bit more focused. The malaise and distrust that had settled over them for the last week were dispersing.

"Taft, Hannah, and Pascal—you three take point. Split the rest of the crew up into teams. Each team take a neighborhood. Start at the top and work your way down. I mean all the way down, people. Kick the beams."

Last time I had spotted the bag, it was in Amaia's arms. She didn't have it in the Wasteland. I doubt she just left it lying around—but we needed to do something, and looking for the duffle was a start.

"What if we find the kresh?" Pascal asked.

"Watch her and come find me. She'll be hard for anyone else to pin down."

Once again Wensem and I were ushered into the captains' board room at the top of the *Gamble*. The lights of Lovat, sparkling through small windows, were brighter and closer now. I straightened my tie, the knot loose but manageable. I had to look a sight. I couldn't remember the last time I had changed, much less bathed. So much for the elegance of a suit.

You could see the faint outline of the city's edge perched above the bay and the haphazard hook of the West Lovat peninsula that formed the harbor. The two massive tugs that pulled the *Gamble* struggled against their lines, making one last momentous effort before they cut their engines and helped *Gamble* settle offshore for the Deeperist festivities.

When we entered, none of the captains rose from their places behind the long table that dominated the room. None of them said anything or extended an offer to sit. They all regarded Wensem and me with cool indifference.

"What now?" Chen's dark eyes flashed with emotion: annoyance, anger, frustration. It was late. We had roused them.

"We have a problem," I said. "We need the *Greedy Three*."

Chen laughed. The sound was bright and loud and affected. It made her co-captains wince and pull away. It stopped almost as quickly as it started, and the silence in its wake was as loud as the laugh.

"No—and besides, Danforth says you're the problem." Chen nearly snarled the words.

Of course he had been here. Of course he had spoken with the captains. The man was a plague.

"Danforth is a liar," Wensem replied. His voice was cold, his words clipped. Gone was his soft drawl. He was all business. If Chen noticed, she didn't react.

"It doesn't matter," I said. "It's not good. This is bigger than Danforth and his little games. Bigger than the Ambassador."

Shelna wen Oshen, the quietest of the captains, leaned forward. Her seven-fingered hands curled together, index fingers steepled into a point before her lips. There was a sigh from Jurer, and he wiped at his beak with a claw before waving it in my direction.

"Go on then."

I explained what I knew, up to a point. I reserved my opinion on Danforth and the WSP. I held back a few details regarding the Outfit and their connection with Amaia. It was better these three think this threat was the work of a rogue agent rather than a constructed plot. That could come later, when the LPD and the Mayor could be involved. For now, we had little evidence—only the word of a disturbed former shoalta.

Besides, the *Gamble* was its own operation, with its own security force. They had a lot in common with the organized criminals that made up the Outfit. If they suspected Outfit involvement, I was reasonably sure a not-so-subtle turf war might break out in Lovat's sub-warrens. *Gamble* versus Outfit.

Fights like that matter little to the middle or upper classes, but they hurt the poor. I couldn't do that to my city.

I finished, and we stood in an uneasy silence across from the three captains. It was Chen who finally broke the silence. "So let me get this straight. You propose we quietly evacuate the *Gamble*, right before King Tide's Ebb—all because of a single individual's random threat."

"She threatened to sink the *Gamble*," I said.

"Bigger and more dangerous people have tried." Chen laughed. "That didn't work out so well for them. It's impossible to smuggle anything on board, let alone a bomb. We check everything—by hand."

Chen let out another mocking laugh, and this time Jurer joined her.

"I managed to get a gun on board," I said, my voice flat.

The laughter died instantly. The captains exchanged glances. Wensem stiffened next to me.

Chen was already shaking her head before she began to speak. "This is ridiculous. Danforth was right—you're spooked. You failed, and now you're jumping at shadows. You realize how many people live on board this vessel? How many people think of the *Gamble* as home? Do you understand how big King Tide's Ebb is for this community? You already got us kicked out of Empress. What more damage do you want to do?"

Was that where this was heading? Profit was worth the risk?

"Does it matter?" I said. "If lives are—"

"There are industries kept afloat because of our cargo," said Jurer. "Thousands that rely on our return from the islands. And the Deeperist shoals believe this boat is holy. We're happy to oblige them."

Shelna rubbed her fingers together, and the three captains exchanged grim expressions.

"All the more reason to keep people on board safe," I said.

"No evacuation," Jurer said. "Too much at stake."

"No *Greedy Three*," Chen added. She steepled her fingers before her lips. "Permission denied."

"What the hell do you have planned?"

"Trying to figure that out," I said through gritted teeth. We marched together down a corridor toward another hall that would eventually empty us out onto the *Gamble's* highest promenade. I was trying not to punch a hole in the wall, and so far I had succeeded.

Those three assholes knew the dangers. They knew Castaigne's profile. It wasn't enough that the summit had failed—now I had to figure out how to get the ambassador off a floating high-security casino before the boat itself was blown to hell and back. They hadn't left me with many options.

Above us one of the corridor's lights flickered, then popped and went silent. The hallway around me dimmed as the dull panels surrendered a little more color to darkness.

Wensem's voice hitched as he spoke. I could tell the slow volcano inside him was on the verge of eruption. "We're supposed to see Castaigne safely to the Mayor's Office. Upon return. Those were her orders."

I kept walking, not sure if I was in the mood to respond appropriately. I was no politician. I was a caravan master—and somehow, and for some reason, the world's damn Guardian. That meant it was my duty to stop Amaia.

"Wal!" Wensem said, exasperated. "Castaigne. City Hall. Orders. *Wal!*"

I kept moving—still saying nothing, not sure if I could even if I wanted to. The *Gamble* shifted beneath my feet. My knee moaned as my balance corrected itself and added extra pressure to the right side of my body. Damn boats. Damn captains. Damn waves.

"We're supposed to see Castaigne to City Hall," Wensem repeated for the third time.

Then a thought struck me.

"Guardian Security," I managed to growl. The thought became an idea and the idea a plan. It bloomed inside my mind, and my anger subsided—well, somewhat.

"Not us. Not you and me." I waved my hands as I spoke. "Guardian Security. That's what's in the contract. Hannah and the crew can escort the ambassador to City Hall. They're as much Guardian Security as we are. It's a simple job at this point. We just need to get Castaigne off the boat. Then I focus on Amaia."

I took a few more steps before I realized Wensem wasn't following me. I turned and looked at him, expecting some verbal chastisement. "What?"

Wensem stood a few strides back, beneath another flickering light. His suit was as disheveled as mine. It hung off his lanky frame. He looked tired, cheeks hollower, eyes sunken, but a smirk was on his crooked mouth. It broke into a smile as he spoke. "Since when do you read contracts?"

I rubbed at the stubble on my face and managed a weak laugh.

"Something I'm trying out," I said. "What do you think?"

Wensem snorted and shook his head as he closed the distance. "What are we going to do?"

"Way I see it, we have three things to do. First, we're going to find a ferry bringing over revelers and offer that pilot an absurd amount of money to ferry Castaigne and everyone else to the Port of Lovat. Second, I'm going to find Amaia. Third, I'm going to stop her."

Wensem sniffed and put his hands on his hips. "Okay," he said. "I think we can work with this. But, Wal—"

"What?"

"I'm not leaving you here."

"I don't know what's coming," I said. "I can't promise it'll be safe."

"I don't care."

"This could be worse than Humes Tunnel," I said, thinking about the fading monstrosity I'd seen against the clouds in Empress. "Worse than the Broken Road. Worse than—"

"I don't care," he repeated.

"Wen—" I began.

"Shut up, Wal."

THIRTY-ONE

Revelers of all shapes and sizes flooded the *Gamble's* main deck. We moved through the crowd slowly and purposefully, allowing our group to be jostled but never letting anyone penetrate the ring we had formed around the ambassador.

She was tired of the trip, and even more tired of my presence. Convincing her to get her off early had been simple enough. Learning that I was going to stay behind had only been a bonus. In times past, I would have been offended, but there was too much going on for me to take her wrath to heart.

Danforth was with us, along with a few of his goons. They dressed like him, besuited in dark wool lined with deep red silk that, if real, was worth enough lira to feed a family of anur for several generations. As far as I knew, there were no silk farms in Lovat. Real silk had to be imported, and it most certainly cost a fortune.

A majority of the aquatic species were represented in the crowd that had come aboard for the celebrations. Eight-limbed cephels, squat anur and their hulking bufo'anur cousins, and of course the kresh with their strange fleshy beaks and spindly claws. I even saw an enormous bok in the sackcloth robes of a faithful Deeperist, its long lizard snout extending from beneath a shadowed hood. My heart seized until I realized the red scales on his maw made him unfamiliar to me. He wasn't Elephant's goon. Deeper hadn't just found disciples in the water dwellers. Humans, dimanians and maero in sackcloth also moved among the newcomers. The *Gamble* was already crowded before we began taking on revelers. Now she felt overloaded.

A long line had formed for those wanting to disembark. The *Gamble* was adamant about security. Anyone leaving had to go through the same security checks as those coming aboard. Winnings needed to be reported. Bags were checked. It kept the gamblers honest, I suppose but the bottleneck made the main deck a mess.

"This is taking forever, boss." Hannah's voice in my ear.

"Don't I know it."

There was the ringing of bells, and the Deeperists in the crowd cheered. Three bells. Three hours until the festivities started. That and the checkpoint delay had me feeling nervous. Amaia had wanted to stop the ceremonies. I doubt she'd wait until they were half-finished. She was too touchy for that. She'd act fast.

"So what's your plan, Bell?" Danforth asked. I didn't even turn to acknowledge him. "Stand here for the next four hours? That's a lot of time in a crowd."

Some of his own crew—WSP goons?—laughed. Nasty laughs. Mocking laughs. Laughs that would settle into matching liars' grimaces. He was right, and I hated him for it.

"WSP would have—"

"Shut up," said Taft. Danforth said something, but I couldn't hear him over her question. "Plan, boss?"

I looked up at the ceiling. Thought about the three captains sitting up there, smug as could be. My teeth ground together as I made up my mind.

"The *Greedy Three*," I said.

"No, sir," said the guard. He wore the *Gamble* dress uniform. White pressed linen pants. Dark blue sweater. One of those little sailor caps that up until this trip I had only seen on babies and in old paintings. The *Gamble* had its own ranks, and I didn't know what the little coin-and-star insignia on the left side of his chest meant—but he spoke with authority. A leader, then.

"Know who this is?" I asked, thumbing over my shoulder.

"Don't rightly care," the leader said. He tongued at a space between his teeth and looked down his nose at me with a bored expression.

"This is Ambassador Castaigne of the Lovat Office of the Mayor," Danforth said, stepping forward and shouldering past my guards. His mouth split and his teeth sparkled as crow's feet crinkled the corners of his eyes.

"Ma'am," the man said, and touched fingers to his cap.

We had made our way here quickly from the main deck. The *Greedy Three* was accessible in a middle space, between the enormous holds below deck. It reminded me of an entresol in Lovat—the sort of place where a joint like Cedric's operated. A between space, not meant for ordinary folks. The Ambassador had snorted in disgust as we stepped out of the main hall and took a narrow passage toward one side of the *Gamble*, where a small room opened onto a portal that led to a gangway that extended to the yacht named the *Greedy Three*.

"We're here for the *Three*," I said. I chinned toward the porthole behind the leader.

"*Three's* for cap'ns only," he said, dropping most of the word. "You don't look like any of 'em."

"Not today, son," said Danforth. "It's a security risk for us to wait in that crowd out there. We can't do it."

I could see the *Greedy Three* beyond the open portal. Its hull glowed in the fading light of day, further reminding me of how much time we didn't have. Upstairs, bonfires would soon be lit and revelers would begin their call.

Where the *Gamble* was clunky and lumpy, the *Greedy Three* was long and sleek. It reminded me of a knife. At one time it had probably been a pearlescent white, but generations of disuse had stained its hide a ruddy green. Barnacles clung to it at the waterline, and a few crewmen moved about on the exposed deck. Still, compared to most of the vessels that operated out of the city, it looked downright new.

Black smoke rumbled from its engines.

"They're nervous. *Three's* idling. Keeping it handy just in case we're right." Wensem's voice was a low whisper. I gave a nod I hoped was imperceptible to everyone but him.

There were six crew. None armed with anything more than their crowbars. Typically, it'd have been more than enough to protect the captains' private vessel. But I was confident my crew could take all six. Carter's cross—Wensem, Hannah, and I could do it with energy to spare, and I have a bum knee.

It's one thing to carry a crowbar, it's another to be willing to use it. Most of these guys were paid to stand around and look menacing. *Looking* menacing and *being* menacing are were two vastly different things. Wensem might have looked like a gangly spider, but I didn't know a better fighter. Hannah was tough as leather, and she'd only gotten tougher since the Broken Road. And Taft—well, her punches hit like a runaway ox.

Six kids with demolition tools didn't stand a chance, and I could tell by their agitation that they were starting to realize this. Besides, between us, Danforth's gang, and Castaigne's crew, we were nearly triple their number.

"Jeff, call up," the guard said. His eyes broke contact with us. A stupid mistake, one I could have taken advantage of if I was an asshole. Thankfully for him, I wasn't an asshole. Not right then, anyway.

"No, Jeff," I said, extending a hand and pointing at another guard who had begun to break away. I hoped it was Jeff and not just a fidgety sailor. The man froze. "You really don't want to do that."

The leader sighed and slapped his palm with his crowbar. "Sir, please."

If he thought it was menacing, he had overplayed his hand. His rolling eyes and puffed-up stance showed me how nervous he was.

"Look," I began, spreading my hands in the friendliness gesture I could. I didn't have time for this. "Here's how it's going to go down. I can give you a bunch of money, and you can look the other way. Then we can get the Ambassador on the *Three* and off the boat. Or—and here's the second and *only* other option—we'll knock you senseless. Throw you into the water. Leave you for the cephel rescue swimmers and still get the Ambassador on the *Three*."

I'd made myself clear. The leader stepped back. He looked from me to Jeff to some of the other guards.

"How much?" he asked.

"By the First," said Ambassador Castaigne. She stepped forward, her exasperation clear in her voice. "I will personally give each of you a thousand lira if you let me borrow that damn boat for the next few hours. The last thing on earth I want to do is spend another damn minute on this rat trap."

"A th-thousand?" said the leader.

"A thousand," I said. "Each."

Wasn't my money.

"Fine," said the leader, this time not bothering to look at the rest of the guard. There was an awkward shift in their posture. That had been too easy, and I suddenly knew why.

"Fine by me. Us. So—can we come with?"

Pay your people well, despots.

Most everyone boarded quickly. The crew was eager to leave. Only Pascal looked back as they disappeared down the gangway. Even the *Gamble* guards had gone, excited for their promised paycheck.

Hannah, Taft, and Hagen hung back with Wensem and me. "That was too easy," said Taft.

"Way too easy," said Hagen.

"We could use some easy," said Wensem. He leaned out the porthole and eyed the sky. "Getting close to dark, Wal."

Time was wasting. Amaia would be somewhere close. I could smell smoke from the bonfires.

Hagen shifted the bag on his shoulder and hefted the *Black Book* in his arms. He had volunteered to remind behind, telling me I needed someone with 'esoteric expertise.' Whatever that meant. Right now, he looked anxious. That made him a liability.

"I'm worried," Hannah said. She had her wooden hand on the rail and her real hand against the outer skin of the *Gamble*. The waves had picked up as the passengers boarded the *Greedy Three*, but nothing too outrageous.

I'm trailborn—I don't read waters. But I can read the sky. Black clouds were coming in from the southwest, and before them they pushed rough seas—harbingers of a coming storm.

I'd be lying if I said that didn't make me nervous.

"You should worry," Wensem said with a grin and a playful elbow into my bicep. "Wal's an idiot."

It was an attempt to defuse the tension we all felt, but no one laughed. Even Wensem rubbed his arms afterward as if warding off a chill. Despite our thin smiles and half-hearted chuckles, we all felt it. The clouds were the vanguard. Something was coming, summoning ritual or no.

"I don't like this," Taft said. "Too many unknowns. Too many loose threads. They all lead in different directions. Threats against Castaigne. Threats against peace. Threats against you, Wal. Not to mention the threats against King Tide's Ebb. Maybe I should stay."

We could use her strength. She looked back toward the yacht where Pascal stood at the foot of the gangway. He waved a hurried hand in her direction, beckoning her to descend.

"No," I said. "We need someone to deliver Castaigne to the Mayor's Office so we can get paid. Hannah, you're a partner. Taft, you're an associate. You fulfill our contract. Doorstep to doorstep. Be sure to give the crew their bonus. They deserve the extra twenty percent."

"Guess we're stuck on a tiny boat with Danforth," Hannah said with a long groan.

"At least it's a short ride," I offered. Hannah's expression told me my words hadn't been a comfort.

"We can handle it," said Taft, slapping Hannah on the back.

"If Danforth gets out of hand," Wensem said, his voice flat, "throw him overboard."

We all relaxed. Even Hagen managed a laugh at the thought of the perfectly pressed Danforth sputtering in the saltwater, suit ruined, hair plastered against his forehead, mouth ballooning as he spat brine and sucked in air. He'd be safe, of course. There was a myriad of shorelines to swim too, and the cephel rescue swimmers didn't let anyone drown. Not in the shadow of Lovat.

"Still," Hannah said, the word drawn out. A punctuation mark that darkened the lighter mood. "There's something wrong. Something we're not seeing. I felt this way before."

I knew what she was referring to. Could see it in her eyes. It prickled my skin.

Hannah rubbed her arms again. I knew what she was thinking about the Broken Road. Wensem, Taft, and I traded glances. Imagined a forest of bodies. Imagined sounds crashing in the sky—not thunder but something else, something wicked and wanton.

"I don't know what there is to see," I said. But something in me told me I was missing something too.

"Let me switch spots with Hagen," Taft offered. She looked at my bookish dimanian friend and gave him a 'no offense' shrug. "Hannah can fulfill the contract without me. Let me help."

Hagen turned, looked over the water, and after a few dry gags turned back to me, sadness and a little fear in his expression.

"You don't need to stick around," I said. "You've done enough. Carter's cross—more than enough."

He looked longingly toward the *Greedy Three*. "I want—"

I heard passion in his voice. A Dubois passion. The wracked breathing of true bravery. A willingness to risk it all despite the cost. Despite his fear.

For a moment, I imagined his sister standing over his shoulder, nodding at me, dark eyes flashing, a slight smile on her perfect lips. That damnable knowing smile—the one she always gave me before she spoke the truth of my innermost feeling and left me exposed and floundering. Infuriating woman, Sam. But the right kind.

I missed her more than I ever had. What would she do? How would she face this? I wanted nothing more than to talk through this with her. I loved Hagen, but she was my rock. She was wisdom. She grounded me. This trip, Elephant, Essie, the Wasteland, Amaia, the Ambassador, everything—Samantha Dubois would have had answers. She'd drag me kicking and screaming back to reality, and I'd love her for it.

Hagen stared at me in silence, the single horn that sprouted from his head tangled in his curls, his spectacles askew. It was part of his charm. He smiled a Dubois smile—one at that moment I refused to risk.

Outside, the city shimmered, a sparkling crystal shell, twinkling hot and white in the descending darkness. The vibrant echo of millions of souls manifested in light and steel and cement.

I knew what I needed to do. Time to make some decisions without someone else's influence.

"Hagen," I said. I placed a hand on his shoulder and gently squeezed. He relaxed. "Go."

Hagen Dubois hugged me, one horned hand slapping my back with brotherly love.

"Don't be stupid," he whispered. "Remember the warnings. There's more at play here than we can see."

He released me and hefted the *Black Book* as an object lesson. I leaned away, feeling the buzzing but not wanting to slip into the Wasteland. Not right now.

"Go with Hannah. We can handle this." I smiled. "Taft, yeah. We could use you here."

The chuck nodded.

Hagen rubbed his chin, then his neck. He looked at the sky, then at us. He was always terrible with goodbyes. He teared up when he gripped Wensem in a handshake and began to quietly cry when Taft embraced him.

"Carter's cross," she said as he pulled away. "We're not going away forever."

"I know," he said, slowly backing down the ramp. "I know."

Hannah's expression darkened. She looked at me in silence for a long time.

"Go," I said, my voice low.

Hannah hugged Taft and Wensem before she embraced me. The hug was long and tight and hurt my neck. I had to pat her on the back before she released me.

"Be careful, Guardian," she whispered.

"Get Castaigne to City Hall," I replied. "Make sure she pays those *Gamble* boys. Keep the crew happy."

Wensem's seven-fingered hand rested on my shoulder and squeezed, not just out of companionship but for comfort.

Hagen was already descending the deck. I thought of Sam and for that moment something deeper inside me strained. Hannah released me, then turned and followed Hagen.

"See you soon." Hannah lifted a hand in farewell.

More than anything, I wished she was right.

THIRTY-TWO

Together, we stepped out onto the exposed top deck. Below my feet, the *Gamble* quaked. Woodsmoke filled my nostrils, pushing back the heady stink that had suffused the air as we slipped deeper into Lovat's shadow. Laughter, music, shouts, and happy cries reverberated off the deck. Sounds of celebration—King Tide's Ebb had begun.

Three enormous bonfires crackled and popped like slow chains of firecrackers. The smallest was at the front of the boat, the largest toward the rear, closer to the deep water.

Confetti rained down from the rising levels of West Lovat just off the *Gamble's* inbound Portside. Far above, hundreds of people occupied small balconies at the city's edge, shouting and singing and throwing streamers that fluttered down to the deck.

"Either of you ever attended a Deeperist celebration before?" Taft asked. I heard a smacking sound and turned to watch her blow a bubble of gum that she popped loudly.

Wensem shook his head.

"No," I said. "You?"

"Nope. Hoping someone would give us some direction."

My eyes scanned the crowd. Looking for a sign of Amaia and her small blue duffle filled with powerful Outfit-supplied explosives.

Nothing jumped out at me. Nothing would. Amaia was no fool. She wouldn't leave an explosive where just anyone could find it.

"Direction?" said a small voice from behind us. "Advice?"

Shoalta Sander waddled forward in his way, a stein of some foamy beverage in his webbed hand, his fleshy lips lined with suds. The mug reeked like seawater but mixed with a sharper and more pungent odor. He bobbed to the music that rose from below, a mix of styles—songs I couldn't place. I could hear allusions to the work of the jazz saints that soaked the cement and iron of the city, yet there was something else there—a nod toward another time or place. I had never heard them before, and they made my skin crawl. Supposedly they sounded better several fathoms below the water.

If the sound bothered the crowd, they didn't show it.

"Hello, Shoalta," I said, giving him a slight bow. "Happy King Tide's Ebb."

"And to you as well, my boy! Who are your friends?"

"This is Wensem. You've met Taft. We're looking for Amaia. Seen her?"

He scratched behind an eye and thought. When he shook his head, his jowls quivered.

"Ain't seen her since set up. Tried the sea cider?" He hefted his tankard. "It's good this year."

"Never had a taste for it," I said. "What did she help set up?"

"Why, the far brazier. The largest of the Ebb Fires. Deeper's Call!" He hoisted his sea cider and spilled half the tankard on his salt-stained robe and let out a drunken laugh. "She is, after all, a Master Shoalta—despite our differences. It is her honor." He pointed past the nearest fire to the enormous blaze erected atop the open deck of the Chee.

From this distance, I could make out a shadowed stack of cordwood assembled into a large pyramid inside a metal basin. It burned ferociously. The flames ate at the wood, and hot coals had begun to fill the enormous metal bowl.

A hot breeze carried from another world. A rush of wind. A whisper. The scent of ash and death. At that moment I was sure I knew where Amaia had placed her bomb.

Amaia wanted to stop the ceremonies. An explosive planted beneath the brazier would blow it sky-high. Sander had said it was important. He had named it Deeper's Call. In Amaia's mind, snuffing out that bonfire would stop the ceremonies.

Except I knew it wouldn't stop anything. The ceremony was an exercise in futility. Sander had said as much, they did this more out of tradition. Whatever was coming—this Deeper— would come with or without King Tide's Ebb.

The Outfit thought this would sink the *Gamble*—what else would they think? In their minds, Amaia wanted to stop the vessel. But neither party had been transparent with each other. The boat wasn't ever Amaia's target. It was the ceremony. It had always been King Tide's Ebb. It had always been Deeper's Call.

"I know where the bomb is," I said.

My eyes were locked on the far fire and the rapidly collapsing pyramid of wood.

Both Wensem's and Taft's heads snapped in my direction. If Sander had heard me, he didn't react. He took another swill of his sea cider, then belched.

"Beneath Deeper's Call. On Chee."

"You sure? If we're wrong about this..." Taft's voice drifted silent.

"I'm not wrong," I said.

I gave Sander a nod, and we rushed down a set of stairs down to the roof deck. My knee hurt so badly I had to use my arms to help swing my body down each step. The pain was constant now. I could just manage walking, but if I kept this up, I wouldn't even be able to do that. I hoped the knee would hold out long enough.

The crowd on the roof was in high spirits. Paper confetti cascaded down around us as we pushed through the throng. Everyone had turned out—King Tide's Ebb wasn't just for Deeperists. Clearly many of the revelers were here for the party. Groups danced and sang. Some cheered and clapped along. Bands played impromptu sets. All manner of people from all over the city were celebrating. Most clutched steins or bottles of cider. Maybe it helped cover up the putrid smell that now permeated everything.

We passed choirs. We moved through dance lines. We raced around soap box preachers and crossed through groups of mourners gathered to grieve the passing of close friends who had missed the celebrations. We struggled through the crowds that packed the high-roller cocktail bars in their shaded pink-lit cubbies built around the center points of each neighborhood.

It took longer than I expected, but eventually we stepped from the Kaleetan to the Chee and found ourselves standing before the enormous bonfire.

Waves of heat wafted from it. I broke into a sweat even standing several feet away. A few half-drunk acolytes tended the flames opposite us. They took turns to poke and prod the fire and occasionally throw a fresh chunk into the inferno. The crowd here was thick. Most wore the sackcloth robes of Deeper acolytes. A human shoalta I didn't recognize was reading from a book to a small group. One of his hands raised. While some here carried drinks, most were dead sober and lost in the ceremonies. This was the fire of the faithful—Deeper's Call was erected for the true believers.

The glow reflected off the Chee's bridge—dancing waves of vivid oranges and vibrant golds in the dark glass of the *Gamble's* captains' quarters.

Wensem crouched and peered beneath the brazier. His head tilted and his eyes narrowed. "Something's under there."

"I'm the smallest," I said. "I'll go."

I peeled off my suit jacket and handed it to Wensem. Few paid us any attention.

Taft crouched. "Tight squeeze."

"It's going to be hot." Wensem reached out and touched the decking—then pulled his hand back quickly and gave me a concerned look.

"I can handle it." The inside of the brazier was still mostly empty. It'd get far hotter as the night went on and more coals settled against the metal. Any later and this might have been impossible. Plus the deck had been coated in a granular material that kept people from slipping in inclement weather. It had to be somewhat heat resistant as well, or else the captains wouldn't let the Deeperists throw this party.

My stomach was a lead weight, my heart a rhythmic drum, my body prickling at the thought of burns. Ignoring all of these things, I dropped to my stomach and slipped beneath the brazier.

The deck below the massive metal bowl was hot, but not so hot as to be unbearable. That was changing. Best not linger too long—it wouldn't get colder. The heat made the air thick and sultry. Beads of sweat ran down my face and dripped to the deck where they quickly evaporated. Soon they would sizzle.

Above, I could hear the dull roar of the fire crackling, and the occasional thrum of wood on metal as a half-burned chunk collapsed. Each time the deck shook. The air wavered around me, and the hot air was heavy in my chest, but I pulled myself deeper.

As I closed in on the object, I began to realize it wasn't a bag at all, merely a drum embedded in the decking and serving as the center point of balance for the brazier. Decades of abuse had dented it, making it look lumpy from afar. It was no blue duffle—it was no bomb.

My heart sank. This hadn't been Amaia's plan at all.

Vibrations reverberated through the deck. I could see dancers' feet beyond the brazier's edge, and beyond them Wensem's shoes and Taft's boots.

Don't linger. Too hot. Leave—I had to leave. The scent of burning hair was pungent. The hot air was slowing down my thoughts. I turned quickly, my shoulder connecting with the metal. The heat sizzled through my shirt and the pain forced me down, a barrage of curses pouring from my mouth.

I didn't dare reach back despite the pain. Fear of scalding the back of my hand forced me to stay low as I scrambled back towards the fresh air beyond the brazier.

Another vibration shook the *Gamble*, this was much larger than falling wood or dancing feet. Did we strike something? My sweat steamed away, and my skin felt strangely dry. If I stayed here any longer, I'd burn more than my shoulder.

The trip back didn't take long. Mere seconds. I stayed low using my arms and one good leg to propel myself across the deck. Taft and Wensem grabbed my arms, and I was pulled from beneath the inferno, into a crowd of dancers holding hand to claw, claw to tentacle as they encircled the fire and chanted in a language I didn't understand. Faces blurred past, mouths agape, eyes wide. We jostled through the ring and stopped along the edge.

The shoulder that had connected with the metal throbbed. My hands hurt. My lungs felt heavy. The air beyond the brazier felt frigid. The sudden shift from hot to cold had sent prickles along my skin. I pressed through the dancing ring, causing a few shouted complaints that were swallowed up by the chanting and singing. Another shudder vibrated through the *Gamble's* hull.

I began to shiver. My arms and shirt were steaming in the air. Sweat continued to pour from me. Without the constant heat, it began to soak my shirt and pants, which only added to my discomfort. A cephel reveler drinking and dancing around the fire slapped me on the back and laughed a clacking laugh before stumbling away.

Taft and Wensem were staring at me. Taft's mouth hung open.

I felt fine and said as much. Taking my jacket from Wensem, I pulled it on, easing it carefully over my shoulder and then tucking it tight around my torso. My shirt was ruined; it was smudged and marked with black soot, and now thoroughly sweat-stained. It'd never gleam white again—not that I cared much. I'm not cut out for suits.

"Wasn't under there," I managed through chattering teeth. The frustration of failure bubbled inside me. I wanted to kick something. I wanted to scream. Instead, I just shivered.

"Wal, your hair," said Taft. "Your face."

I reached up touched my scalp and felt the unevenness of my hair and where strands had singed together. I didn't need to look at it to know it was a mess. The palms of my hands were red and raw—they felt hot and tingly. My face felt the same. I had to look a mess.

"You feel those vibrations?" I asked, looking around but seeing nothing.

"No." Wensem gave me a puzzled look. "Where's the bag?"

Another vibration clattered beneath our feet. I spread my hands towards the deck.

"I felt that," said Taft.

"What is it?" Wensem asked.

Whispers filled my ear, followed by a low buzzing at the back of my skull. My head snapped around, looking for Danforth or Amaia. A strange shadow played across the top of the Chee's topmost deck. For a second, I thought it was a bok or a bufo'anur—but that couldn't have been right. Neither grew that big. Gargoyles? No. I hadn't seen any of their kind on the *Gamble*.

Then I realized I wasn't cold anymore. A warm wind had caught me, and it wasn't coming from the fires, distant Lovat, or the surrounding sea.

As the desert faded in around me, Tawil's tattooed face materialized out of the dissipating world, his head thrust in my direction, his eyes bulging, the blue discs on his skin collapsing as his wrinkled face swallowed them. Instinctively, I stepped back, feeling both sand and decking beneath my feet. A dull headache blossomed. The pain from my burns and the ache from my knee all were gone in an instant, but I could feel them lingering on the edges of my perceptions.

"By the First," I said. "Don't do—"

"No time," Tawil nearly shouted, his long arms extended toward me. Carter's cross, he was fast. Long fingers wrapped around my biceps and he squeezed. I struggled for a moment but threw him off and stepped backward.

We were in the village. Standing near the well. West from here I could see the broken Lovat, and beyond the horizon the monster. It was moving now, but not in the ponderous shifts I'd seen before. Now it thrashed about, its massive continental arms twisting and writhing. But there wasn't rage or irritation in those movements. It looked elated.

Ash began to fall.

"What—" I nearly shouted. I coughed, dusted the ash from my shoulders. "What do you want?"

"No time! No time!" Tawil was pacing, looking west, shaking his head, and then looking toward me, over and over. There was something in his panic that sparked panic inside me. Up until now, even in the collapse of the buried building, he had been calm. Now I saw raw emotion.

Tawil was worried. Tawil was scared.

This time I stepped toward him. He took an instinctive a step backward and scowled at me.

Hastur's presence was heavy in the air. The dusting of ash was a clear enough sign. But Tawil cared little about him. He was worried about something else—worried about the excitement of the monster beyond the horizon.

"Tawil," I said.

He mumbled. Stumbled, caught himself, and spun to face me. "I can't keep you here. Not again. I can't shade you from him. Not any longer."

"What are you—"

"He's here. There. Your world. There and here. It won't be like before. He's not coming. He's already there. Fully there. Wal, be careful. Wal—"

Another vibration shook the *Gamble*.

"What the—" I began. I almost fell, reeling from the shift from one place to another. That had to be my fastest trip to the Wasteland yet. My stomach flipped. I bent over and was sick on the deck.

Taft and Wensem were still across from me. Revelers danced their ring around the fire behind me. I rose, wiping bile and saliva from my mouth with the sleeve of my jacket.

"I was just there," I said. Feeling the panic surge anew. "I spoke with Tawil. Something's here. Something has come. We need to—"

I wasn't sure what I was going to say. I had no plan, no strategy. At this point, I was in the dark. Acting on instinct alone.

"BELL!"

I turned and saw the Captains standing nearby, all three of them. Chen and Shelna flanked the bellowing Jurer, their eyes chips of flint in the darkness. Jurer's claw was wrapped around the handle of my revolver, and the black gaze of the Judge's barrel was aimed directly at me.

I raised my hands and stepped back gingerly. Taft and Wensem were doing the same. The crowd, now in a fevered adulation of worship, barely noticed the drama playing out at the edge of their bonfire's light.

"You took it!" Chen shouted.

"Where is it?" Jurer demanded.

Shelna was silent as always.

It was clear what they were upset about.

"The *Three*," said Jurer. "You took it by force."

"Who told you that?" I made an expression I hoped would read as innocent.

Jurer waved the gun at me and shook his small head as if I had disappointed him.

"We watched it pull away, you dolt," Chen said.

I lifted my hands and took a tentative step toward the three captains. The black mouth of my revolver was aimed at my chest. Jurer's cheek worked as he nervously aimed the gun at me. This was dangerous—much too dangerous. Jurer's claw had curled around the trigger. The wrong move could cause him to spasm, leaving me a dead roader.

Then I stopped.

Were my eyes playing a trick on me?

I blinked, trying to clear what I was seeing. My brain refused to acknowledge what my eyes were declaring as truth.

Behind the captains, just off the *Gamble's* aft, the horizon was going black. Stars winked out as a shadow swallowed up the light of a billion years.

I thought of the Wasteland. I thought of the creature on the horizon. My step forward became a step back—my mouth went dry.

"Carter's cross," Taft said.

With a juddering slam, an enormous mound of flesh the size of a building crashed into the *Gamble's* deck. The captains and a few bystanders were thrown clear. A brazier tipped then collapsed, spilling a bellyful of fire-orange coals. The sound of moaning steel and tearing deck plate rolled like thunder as the impact traveled outward.

Ears ringing, I forced myself to stand up. Screams had begun in earnest now—natural sirens born from chaos. The deck below me quaked. The mound of flesh glistened beneath the moonlight and reflected the loose bits of broken fire. It took a moment for me to understand what I was looking at.

It was a hand.

An enormous hand.

And its owner was rising behind it.

THIRTY-THREE

The behemoth rose from the waves. Great gouts of water poured off shoulders the width of city blocks. Small waterfalls surged from lakes that formed and then emptied as flesh unfolded.

The stink was overwhelming. My eyes watered. Tears flowed down my cheeks.

It was horrible to witness but impossible to look away. My legs gave way beneath me, and I stumbled, then crashed back on to the deck.

The shouting and screaming disappeared beneath a throaty bellow that emanated from deep within the huge chest. It filled the sky and echoed off the pitted facade of Lovat. I pressed my hands to my ears, which did little to muffle the hateful roar.

The enormous hand lifted from the deck as it pushed off from the *Gamble*. The crater it left behind was a mass of twisted metal and pulped bodies.

The release sent the boat into a violent rocking motion. I grabbed onto what I could, wrapped my fingers around something cold and metal and hoped it'd hold. For a moment, I was in free fall. Then I slammed into the deck as the *Gamble's* buoyancy threw it back.

Burning logs were thrown clear as the Deeper's Call broke free from its base. The metal bowl slid and banged against a bulkhead, then careened across the deck. It traced wheels of sparks as the last bits of flaming char caught the wind. Several revelers disappeared beneath it as it smashed through the guard rail. I never heard it hit the water.

Still the creature rose—higher and higher. Coruscating forked lightning silhouetted the thing against the clouds. A loud rumble of thunder followed on its heels. It echoed off the wall of Lovat.

From his back a pair of enormous vestigial wings expanded. Membranous flesh pulled taught and reflected the city's lights with an oily glow. The wings were too small to carry a creature of this size and bulk. One wing crashed into the outer edges of West Lovat. Windows shattered, walls erupted, and floors collapsed. Those who had gathered to watch the King Tide's Ebb were thrown or knocked from the edge. Clouds of dust rolled outward. Like a corrupted confetti, lumps of jagged cement, ragged broken bricks, and slivers of glass rained across the cratered deck of Chee.

The destruction didn't faze the monster. Screams didn't draw his attention. There was an instinctual quality to his actions—less conscious, more bestial. The creature shook himself, and water flew from crevices in his skin. Slowly he turned and regarded West Lovat, then refocused his attention on *Gamble*.

He was a mountain of flesh and muscle. His massive belly slumped low, the bottom touching the water. His skin, the color of deep ocean water, carried scars, pustules, and pockmarks. Bone-white patches the size of boulders marred limbs and elbows and ran in splotches across his belly. A cape of kelp hung from his arms like ragged vestments.

His head was a writhing mass of fat tentacles and long feelers that twisted and curled from the lower part of his face. Countless bulbous glowing eyes of various sizes blistered the skull. They crackled with light and glowed in the moonlight. Narrow irises split the half-spheres, almost ranine—not dissimilar from anur eyes.

This was Deeper. But not the god Deeperists believed they worshiped. That Deeper was merely a dream. A fanciful tale. A false narrative. A myth that allowed the truth to disappear under the waters in the post-Aligning world.

What now stood off the shores of West Lovat was the true Deeper. The First. The Founder. The High Priest that had come to bring about a New Aligning.

Rain began to fall. Big heavy drops splashed across the deck, plating in tiny watery explosions. It was warm, the first warm rain of the spring, but it brought no comfort.

Man of two worlds or not, I was nothing compared to this titan. Curwen had not been this big. Neither had Ashton. Cybil never had a chance.

What I saw now was something wholly unlike any of the previous monsters. This beast was awesome and terrible in his vastness, cold and uncaring in his disregard. He observed the boat that settled in the sea before him as if it was a plaything—and how could it be anything else? Even the guns of Lovat had no chance against something like him.

The immense gaze fixated on the *Gamble*. The tentacles on his face squirming, stretching out, and then curling in like fiddlehead ferns. Was he looking for something? Tasting the air? I shuddered, feeling the madness creep deeper inside my skull. This... thing, this creature shouldn't be. It shouldn't be possible.

"Wal!"

The enthrallment faded. My mind still reeled, but the sound of familiarity had broken the spell, at least temporarily. A hot wind caught my sanity and blew against the stench that the First had dredged up from below the sea.

I turned toward the voice, scrambling to my feet, slipping in blood and seawater.

Taft was several feet away, near the torn guardrail. She had her sizable arms wrapped around a rusty iron stanchion that supported a small deck covering. She was soaked and bleeding from a cut above her eye. But she was alive, and she was pointing at something.

"There! Look! Look!"

I followed her finger, twisting at the waist and turning toward the former spot of Deeper's Call. Burning logs were scattered on the deck. Most of the supports had given way or been torn free. The central drum was severely bent and looked like a sagging pipe. Around it, a few revelers were recovering and climbing to their feet despite the *Gamble's* rocking. They blocked my view for a moment as they gawked and then collapsed to their knees, arms stretched up in reverence.

"The drum!" Taft was shouting.

And for good reason.

Inside the drum was Amaia's blue duffle.

THIRTY-FOUR

Deeper took a swipe at the *Gamble* even as I began to move. It all happened so fast. The impact of the hand sent me sprawling, my cheeks and hands rubbed raw as I slid to a stop on the grit. The boat listed toward the port and began to spin, sagging. Metal groaned as it spun. It was probably taking on water. Who knows how long it took for a vessel like this to sink. Minutes? Hours?

A roar above set me in motion again. I pushed off the deck, my knee—

My knee both ached and yet did not ache. Blowing sand obscured my vision, and like the grit on the deck it rubbed my cheeks raw. I coughed against the dust. The Wasteland was trying to embrace me. The Wasteland was angry.

Waldo, hide!

Amaia's voice? Tawil's? Wensem's? The heat here was overwhelming. Sweat rolled down my face and mixed with the tears from my watering eyes. It stung my bleeding cheeks. The warm rain and ocean spray of cold, early-spring seawater disoriented me. I felt nauseous, as if the desert was a ship adrift in rough seas.

I was in two places at once, doubting the reality of both. I stumbled. My head buzzed. I clasped my hands to both sides of it and tried to shout, but nothing would come. My tongue felt leaded. My body was like an anchor, holding me down. I was drowning in madness, and I couldn't shut it out.

Waldo!

Damn ghosts. I looked up, seeing the broken sun in the endless midday of the Wasteland and the enormous beast looming and lit by the glow of the evening lights of West Lovat.

Hide!

The deck was twisting below me. The desert cracked. The world shook in violent laughter. "No!"

HIDE!

Dammit! Not now!

N—

Night. Damp. Cold. Nausea. Headache.

My hands were still pressed against my head. Here my knee ached. The smell was overpowering—stinging, like potent onions. I sniffled, choked, and then gagged.

My back was against a bulkhead not far from the shattered rail. Seawater was running all around me, hurrying toward the edges of the twisted decking. The sky was empty save for the storm, but I could hear the beast somewhere behind me. In the distance, the lights of Lovat still sparkled. Across the wide bay, the north side of the city drifted past.

Lightning arced across the sky, tracing jagged white lines across my vision. Another convulsion undulated through the vessel. I heard shouts of terror and screams of pain.

I struggled to my feet in time to see movement out of the corner of my eye. Ducking, I pressed myself to the bulkhead, half-expecting to see another vast hand taking another swipe at the boat. Instead there was a traffic jam of bodies, some attempting to scramble down a stairwell while others fought to climb topside.

My mind struggled to comprehend what I was seeing.

They had gone mad.

"Praise be! Oh, praise be!" There was a manic quality to the voices.

"Deeper has come!"

"Glory! Glory!"

"It was promised! Brothers! Sisters! Lift up your praise!"

A few of the fleeing revelers turned, empowered by the celebratory cadence of the newcomers. A few shifted, as if realizing their folly, and became worshipers. Some dropped to their knees, their sackcloth robes bundled around them as if they had melted into the decking. Others babbled in unknown tongues; some mashed their teeth together in enthusiastic mania, their glossy eyes rolled back becoming orbs of white. Many more shouted chittering praises. They stretched their arms toward the monster and joined a worshipful chant that carried upward from lip and beak.

Wensem emerged near the stairs, not running away but trying to help the injured, passing people down into the arms of others. He pushed at a manic Deeperist that stepped in his way. The man's elbow landed in the face of one of the injured, and Wensem sent him flying across the deck with a shove. My partner's pale skin was bruised and scratched, but outside of being thoroughly soaked, he looked none the worse for wear. Maero are—after all—hard to kill.

I checked for my chuck and found Taft clinging to her pole. Her expression had grown darker in the last few moments, and she was mumbling to herself. Most likely curses. No one could curse like Taft.

At the end of the boat, Lovat kept drifting past. Deeper was out of sight. Somewhere to my aft—or the vessel's aft, or its fore. Whatever. It didn't matter. None of that mattered. He was behind me right now, and that bought me a little time. Mere moments. But I could use moments.

I hobbled across the deck to the drum. Plucked the duffle from the inside. I could feel the weight of it as I pulled the shoulder strap over my non-burned shoulder. A shiver danced up my arm.

In a former life, before serving as a brazier stand, this drum must have been a vent. A metal lattice sat just inside its mouth and would have prevented anything more substantial than a coin from dropping down into the hull. It made a handy shelf for the bomb. It was an ingenious hiding place. We'd have never found it if it wasn't for Deeper.

Wensem was arguing with someone for blocking the stairwell. Toward the end of Chee, the bulk of Lovat had slipped into view. Soon we'd complete our spin, and once again face the creature.

"Got it!" I shouted, knowing my friends would understand.

The voice had been right. *Buy some time. Hide.*

Deeper knew me—I knew him. We were drawn toward each other in a way I still can't explain. Bewitched in a way. We could never avoid one another. Not forever. We each knew that. And we hated the other for it.

There was a shoving match that Wensem quickly won. A light touch on my shoulder turned me around to face a gasping and still cursing Taft.

"This belongs to you, boss," she said through heavy breaths. She held out the Judge. The big gun was wet. I doubted the reloaded cartridges in its cylinder would fire, but I took it anyway. Its weight felt good in my hand.

"Thanks," I said. I lifted the bag.

"That the duffle?"

"The very same," I said.

Taft nodded and glanced upward. The monster was coming back into view, looming over the starboard side. The *Gamble's* aft pointed toward West Lovat, its fore towards the north. The creature's feelers floated all around its skull, and the mass of glowing eyes was half-closed like a pitch addict riding a high.

"Ugly's lookin' for something."

"Me," I said, hearing the echoes of the warning from the Wasteland. "He's looking for me. Come on."

The Chee's promenade was mostly open—or mostly flattened. But there was cover in occasional places—twists of metal, small shelters not yet smashed. The end of the deck that lay toward the rest of the *Gamble* was mostly intact. The high-roller bars would make for decent shelter from a First's prying eyes.

"Come on," I said and nodded towards the shelter.

Once, the plastic above us had been clear, but generations of rain and salt had coated it in a gummy black that hid us from above—at least visually. The bars constructed here had been cocktail-focused, and most of the bottles and glassware had jumped their shelves during the last hit. They now lay on the floor in a serrated and pungent wreck. A pile of four-legged wooden barstools was clustered in a mass along the back bulkhead. A few panicked people—passengers, not Deeperists—huddled in a corner, their finery disheveled, their hair a mess. Blood marred their clothes and faces. I could hear them crying.

Dropping the duffle behind the bar, I rushed to the group—two dimanians and an umbra.

"You need to go," I urged. "Go! Get off the *Gamble*. Hell, risk the rescue swimmers. Just get off this upper deck."

None moved.

"Now!" I shouted as frustration boiled over. They scrambled to their feet, arms raised like I was robbing them. I herded them toward the open deck, being careful to stop just at the edge below the cover, out of Deeper's sight.

"Go! Go!" I urged.

They continued on, hands still above their heads as they made their way toward a stairwell.

"Wal, we got bigger problems!"

The bomb. No time to linger. Taft was behind one of the bars. The duffle was atop it, zipper open. I careened back in and grabbed the bag as the boat rocked.

Inside the duffle were wires, metal tubes and chambers, and a few other bizarre attachments I hadn't seen before.

"That's military-grade. Syringan." Taft gave a low whistle. "Ain't seen ordnance like that in a long time."

The boat quaked beneath us and both of us looked around, expecting another brutal hit. But none came. Apparently, the First was content shaking his feelers and occasionally letting out a sky-shattering roar.

Sirens from Lovat had begun to mix with the din—more chaos, this time from Lovat proper.

"Know how it works?"

"More or less. Chemicals, I think. Timer breaks them open and they begin to mix. That starts a slow chain reaction. Then— *blammo*." Taft mimed an explosion with her hand. "Timer's set by the amount that gets mixed, I think."

I looked at the live explosive in my lap. "How long do we have?"

Her eyebrows rose. "Don't know. Not long. What time is it?"

"Hour 'til midnight," I guessed.

Taft scratched her cheek and then pointed at me. "Bet we have an hour."

"Can we stop it?" I asked. Throwing it over the side wouldn't work. Chemical bombs could function beneath the water, and this close to the city there were thousands of innocent people living in submerged suburbs below. Dropping a bomb on them from above was barbaric—but we couldn't keep it on the boat either.

Taft shook her head and tapped between two empty containers mounted on the outside of the explosive. "Doubt it. Once the chemicals mix, it's going to happen. The biggest question is when."

Revulsion welled up in my throat, riding a wave of panic that spread from my belly. A low moan escaped my lips. I looked at the creature half obscured by our cover, then at Lovat, then at the duffle.

Too many fraying threads. Too much at stake.

I was coming apart.

"You found the bomb," Wensem said, bursting into the space beside me. He leaned over and peered into the duffle with us. I nearly jumped out of my skin. I hadn't expected it.

"We did," I said. "It was under the brazier. *Inside* the drum. If that thing hadn't knocked it free…"

"Can you stop it?"

"No," said Taft. "Chemical."

That was enough for Wensem. "Damn. What if we dilute it?"

"It's sealed," I said.

"Break it open," Wensem half-suggested and half-asked.

"Think Syringan military didn't think that through?" Taft snapped. She waved an open hand toward the duffle. "You want to take a hammer to an explosive?"

"How much time do we have?" Wensem asked. His voice was distant now. Distracted.

I stared at the bomb, not comprehending the shift.

"Probably an hour," Taft guessed. "Maybe less."

"Good," Wensem said, his voice fainter. When I looked up, I saw he had pulled away and was staring out to the open chaos. "Pack that away. We got new problems."

My eyes followed his. Eerily familiar figures had begun to materialize across the ruined upper deck.

THIRTY-FIVE

One was joined by a second, then a third. They materialized suddenly, with no sound or flash or motion. They flickered into existence like dying lightbulbs. I blinked but the figures didn't disappear. It wasn't some trick or vestige of another reality. They were here. In this place. On this ship. And they just stood there. Motionless.

"Are those—?"

"Yes, dammit," Wensem muttered.

A dozen of them stood on board now, all of them appearing as quickly and quietly as the first. I had never seen shamblers this close. Most of my experiences had been from a distance, watching herds of them meander and scavenge across the rolling plains of the Territories, bumping into thistle and shrub.

Up close it was clear they were humanoid, seemingly sexless, with misshaped heads that sprouted from their shoulders. Their eyes were bulging and wrinkled, like dried prunes—most people believed shamblers to be sightless—but I could see that they glowed. It was a subtle luminescence, not as bright as umbra eyes, but easily detected against the night. Their skin was an ashy gray that skewed black against the darkness; it hung loosely from their limbs but stretched taunt across belly, breast, and buttock. Their limbs were long and irregular, with large hands composed of random fingers that twitched and spasmed.

It took a few moments for the worshipers to realize shamblers stood in their midst. They all stood awkwardly, straight-backed, swaying slowly like a drunk pretending to be sober. Their shoulders rose and fell, each breath a telegraphed event. They just stood, as if waiting.

"Oh, Carter's cross," Taft swore. "Shamblers?"

"This is bad," said Wensem. He was nodding. "Real bad."

I cracked my knuckles, thinking about the duffle and the explosive inside it sitting on the bar at my back. Wensem drew a pendant from a chain that hung about his neck—a small circle with two arching lines at its center. He kissed it before dropping it below his collar. I hadn't ever seen him do that before.

I thought about the expanse of smoking flowers that Tawil had shown me—the connection of all things. How did these things fit in? How did any of this? Any of *us*?

The worshipers nearest the edge scrambled away from the new arrivals, compelled to escape. Some who had fallen now crab-walked backward, resorting to the most primitive locomotion. One darted to the port edge and leaped overboard—choosing the mysteries of the sea instead of the things now flickering into reality around us.

"This is what we faced at the blockade," said Wensem. "This is what that bastard O'Conner summoned."

There was a hushed moment where nothing happened.

Anticipation built.

Held.

Then broke.

In a sudden unison, a surge of activity, the shamblers moved. These were not the slow-plodding shamblers of the empty plains. They shuddered across the deck with terrible speed, descending on those nearest.

A thickset human man in a sackcloth robe was the first. He was on his knees, arms extended upwards and eyes closed as he shouted prayers.

His prayers couldn't stop the shamblers' onslaught. Hands came in at a blur. Cries of praise became horrific screams of pain. The face of one of the things buried itself in his thick neck, and a bloody struggle followed.

The mangled corpse collapsed to the deck. Dark blood mixed with the standing seawater.

Panic burned like a wildfire through the people on the exposed deck. Shamblers jittered past the initial carnage and began to attack more people. Some disappeared and reappeared as they moved. It gave them a shuddering, zoetropic effect.

Taft had withdrawn and was stamping on one of the fallen barstools. There was a crack of wood, and the stool fell apart. The chuck bent and pulled up two of the wooden legs, tossing a jagged leg to Wensem who caught it with his broad seven-fingered hand and considered it. Taft gripped hers like a bat.

"You ready for this?" she asked.

Two shamblers paused for a moment near the mouth of the covered bar section. The hanging strings of pink lights flickered, which made their gray flesh crawl and their grins bloody. Their pruney eyes fixated on us. Their smiles widened—stretching beyond anything that should be physically possible.

Bravery is fear conquered—and at that moment, I knew fear. A First, bigger and meaner than anything I had ever seen, now loomed above, and at its beck and call was an army of creatures that, moments earlier, I'd believed were docile herbivores.

A few years earlier and I'd have been one of the folks fighting to flee. Now I realized the foolishness in that. Cybill had toughened me. Curwen had hardened me. But after Ashton, something had changed. Something in me had calcified. My reality was a turmoil, but I no longer cared. Not now. I doubted myself, my world, and my reality—but I didn't question my duty. Not anymore.

I was Guardian.

The city behind me was my home, the people in it my neighbors. No matter how rough around the edges, it was a place I loved—a refuge from the trail and the harsh world of the Territories. Sure, it changed. Sure, it never remained comfortable, but that was its nature. It's what made it home to misfits like myself. Lovat never judged, and Lovat always welcomed you back. If that wasn't worth fighting for, then what was? If I didn't stand, who would?

"What are you thinking, Wal?" Wensem asked. I could hear the concern that laced his question.

"We stop that thing." I pointed up.

"How?" Taft asked.

"First, by stopping these things," I said, waving my gun at the two shamblers.

"Ain't much of a plan," said Wensem.

"Rarely is," I replied, giving him a stage shrug.

The shamblers had grown bored with our banter. They howled like wolves and then loped toward us, arms flopping, mismatched hands splayed wide as they reached out for us. I lifted the Judge. Pointed at the closest, felt my heart surge with strength, and pulled the trigger.

Click.

Tried again.

Click.

Again.

Click.

Dammit! The cartridges had to have gotten wet when the gun went skidding across the sea-soaked deck. New rounds were rare in the Territories, and reloaded rounds weren't watertight. Time to improvise.

Heart pounding, I flipped the revolver—grabbing it in mid-air by the barrel. Gnarled hands strained toward me. I stepped inside the creature's reach and swung the gun like a hammer. The grip connected with one of the bulbous eyes and I put my weight into it. The orb burst. Viscous liquid spattered my hand and forearm.

The thing howled as its feet slipped on the deck. It pulled back just in time to receive a crack on the side of its head from Taft's makeshift club. It grunted, stumbled. Disappeared and then reappeared.

A stream of black muck dribbled from the destroyed eye. It took a dazed swing at the chuck, who deftly danced out of the way and then lowered a shoulder and slammed into the thing. Taft had to outweigh it three to one. The monster's howl became an animal bleat as it was flung across the deck.

The second shambler rushed past—an icy presence that sent a chill through my bones. What *were* these things?

Taft had crossed the deck and was striking the first shambler with swing after swing. Her lips had pulled back into a grimace. Each blow was accompanied by a heavy grunt of exertion. A crack of wood against bone carried through the covered shelter, followed by a shriek as the thing tried to ward her off. She didn't relent.

Taft had this covered. I turned in time to see Wensem dispatch the second shambler with ease. Unlike Taft, my partner had used the stool leg as a spear. It had now skewered the second shambler's head, and the thing stumbled around in shock, occasionally sputtering out of existence before flickering back. One of its malformed hands beat weakly at the spear, but before the offending object could be removed, it collapsed.

Wensem spat at the corpse, then struggled to pull his make-shift spear free.

"At least they die easy," Taft said through heavy breaths. She stepped beside me.

"How'd you face them before?" I asked Wensem, who was glowering in disgust at the gory end of his spear.

He glanced at me, then back at his improvised spear. "They didn't stick around too long. Would always flicker in and out, like a bad monochrome signal. Stole some people. Ate some others. Threatened the Breakers." When he looked at me again, his eyes had gone from gray steel to black iron. "So I went after the source. These things are called. Directed. Stop whoever is doing the calling and you'll choke off their arrival."

The *Gamble* was slowing in its spin. The open deck was still chaos. Bodies lay everywhere. Shamblers rushed about, some struggling with those who were willing to fight back. Others had their faces buried in the stomachs of corpses. Blood slicked the uncovered surfaces. I expected to smell sweet iron but could only detect death and decay. It was everywhere. It was in everything.

The smell drew my eyes from the horror toward the monstrous menace beyond. From our cover, I could see Deeper—or part of him. His stomach and chest, his arms. A few feelers from his chin. Bile burned at the back of my throat. There was something so wrong about that creature. So alien. So impossible.

I grabbed a stool leg from the pile and tucked the Judge into the waistband of my pants. Wet cartridges did me no good, and while I'm reasonably good with my fists, I wasn't sure how well my two-worlds brawling skills would work with shamblers. They were entirely from this plane. Somehow I knew that. Sam and Hagen would be proud.

The First, frustrated with my absence, roared and then pummeled the Chee. The initial blows were lighter. Corpses scattered. The *Gamble* rocked, and we had to grip each other to stay standing.

When nothing changed, the assault grew stronger.

In a rage, Deeper sank his building-sized fist into the captain's suite. Deck collapsed on deck. Metal folded into metal. The superstructure warped into impossible shapes.

This time, no amount of help could keep us on our feet. The blow knocked everyone, even the shamblers, to the deck. A roar filled the sky. Thunder and lightning crashed. Rain saturated the deck. The smell of death and decay grew stronger. The *Gamble* moaned, and I could hear snaps and pops from deep within the hull. The vessel listed like a boxer growing exhausted, its starboard side tipped toward Deeper's belly.

When the monster pulled back, the whole ship lifted as jagged pieces of metal hooked themselves into the meat of the enormous hand. Deeper shook the appendage, and thick black globules the size of chuckwains spattered across the decking. The gore sizzled, burning holes into metal before hardening into an obsidian-like mineral.

"Ugly's mad," Taft growled.

A roar, louder than the last.

I covered my ears, but it didn't help. The sound penetrated my bones. Shook my very soul. We writhed on the deck until the voice quieted.

The fist came down again.

Then again. Each time the *Gamble* whimpered. It wouldn't take much more of this. It couldn't.

"Real mad," Taft added, her voice a resonant shout above the cacophony.

More shamblers were appearing now. Occasionally one of the creatures would turn and tilt its neckless torso up toward the

First as if in awe. Wensem had gone after the source, and I was pretty sure we'd need to as well.

An idea struck me. It was deranged, but it *might* work.

"The bomb," I said.

"What?" Wensem was getting to his feet. He managed to put his long legs under him just as a shambler flickered next to him. He cracked it across the side of the head, then kicked it in the chest, a kick that sent it sprawling into an overturned table.

"The bomb," I repeated. "Climb the big guy. He's big enough. Look at him—he's like a craggy rock face. I'll stick the bomb in that mass of tentacles, maybe shove it down its throat, then…" I mimicked Taft. Grinned, even. "Blammo."

The chuck's grin mimicked my own. "Blammo."

"That. Could. Work." Wensem spoke each word between swings. The shambler at his feet wasn't moving.

The duffle still sat atop the bar. The jostling hadn't thrown it free.

The bag felt warm in my hands, as if at any moment it could rupture and take half of Chee with it. I hooked it over my shoulder using the long strap.

"It's looking for me," I said. "So we expose ourselves. Try to draw it to attack. When it does, I scramble up." I couldn't believe I was suggesting this.

"And if it crushes you?" Taft asked.

"It won't," I said. "I'm wily."

"Shamblers are going to be a problem." Wensem shook his stick at the dead creature at his feet.

"We can handle problems," I said, looking again at the monster above us. It shivered. Once he finished with the *Gamble*, Deeper would undoubtedly turn on the city. If he turned on Lovat, he'd kill millions.

I had to kill him first.

THIRTY-SIX

The three of us emerged from cover and out onto the wreck that had once been Chee. Blood slicked the deck. Corpses were sprawled everywhere, some missing parts, others looking more like torn and bloodied rucksacks. Shamblers roamed about, some of them devouring the flesh of the dead, others pursuing those who remained.

I stared up at the great monster—Deeper of legend. His nest of eyes fixated on the *Gamble* and, after a brief moment, on me.

"Hi," I growled.

Taft and Wensem broke away and engaged some shamblers. But I moved on, crossing the open deck and keeping my eyes fixed on the creature above. A large shambler turned and came toward me, flickering out of site before appearing in the space between us. Then it disappeared again. Judging the creature's pattern of movement, I began to swing the Judge, hammer-like. When the shambler reappeared, the grip collided with its stupid grin.

There was a throaty crack, followed by a sound like air being let out of a bladder. Misshapen hands rose to feel at its face, a decidedly humanoid gesture. Wrinkled eyes stared out at nothing. It showed no rage, no emotion of any kind. Black ooze dribbled from its mouth, and I could see part of its jaw had shattered. The manic grin never faltered. It flickered out of existence without so much as a sound.

I spun, expecting another attack, but no attack came. The shambler didn't reappear.

Wensem and Taft were holding their own. Broken carcasses of shamblers now joined the bodies of their victims.

Those still here drew away, leaving me exposed and in the open. Far above, Deeper paused in his rage. He held his arms up, building-sized hands curled into building-destroying fists, and stared down his expansive chest. Our gazes locked. The tentacles that hung from its face stilled.

Founder and Guardian—a standoff I'm familiar with.

Part of my mind screamed. Sanity slipped further away. I could feel something tearing inside of me. But I shoved all that aside. I was a man of two worlds, perhaps more, but here in this place, I had a purpose. Lovat and her people needed defending. I had been forged for this—if not me, who? If not now, when?

Something struck me.

Bright pain flared across my bad knee and exploded up the side of my body.

I collapsed, grimacing and barely managing a sputtered cry. I hadn't been paying attention. Was it the shambler? I was already moving, rolling away, expecting another attack.

Something heavy struck the deck. When I completed my roll, I finally managed to see my attacker.

"You!" I shouted.

The Eibonian cultist with curved horns stood just to one side, a smug grin on his face. His shirt was torn and dirty. Blood was smeared across his forehead—not his blood, from the look of it. He held one of the security steward's long crowbars. The leather grip had begun to unravel and the hooked tip rested against the deck. Red and black gore dripped from the shaft. He had been fighting shamblers as well.

"I told you, you wouldn't leave this boat alive," he growled.

He hefted the crowbar and moved to strike. Again I rolled. Again the weapon cracked to the deck. A miss.

When I came back around, I glared at him. My knee howled. White-hot bolts of pain seared through my body. The duffle was behind me, the strap still hooked over my shoulder.

"We don't have time for this," I managed through gritted teeth.

The Eibonian tried another swing. I moved, scuttling backward, dragging my leg and just barely escaping. Too close— that was too close. I was too slow. The tip of the weapon smeared a streak of red across my shirt. I kept scrambling, using my good leg to push myself across the deck. My right knee felt dislocated, useless.

The dimanian stalked after me until I collided with a bulkhead that ran parallel with the stairwell that led below. There would be no time to get down the stairs. I could go no further. I was trapped.

"That thing will kill us!" I shouted at him.

"You fool. Haven't you figured it out yet? This boat is the great sacrifice. The High Priest! These people! The servitors! It's all been put into play for this very moment." He stabbed a finger at the ground down to emphasize his point. "Ashton was supposed to partake. He was supposed to meet his cousin here—on this sacred spot! The lines of Nub and Yeg were to reunite. You stole that from him—you stole that from *us!*"

Taft and Wensem weren't in sight. Noises cascaded all around us. Sirens. Alarms. Cries. Shouts. Roars. Metal on metal moaning. The wet slaps of flesh and wood. The dissonance would drown out any pleas for help.

The pain in my knee was unbearable. I had one play. I drew the Judge and leveled it at the Eibonian.

He had more sense than the monsters around us. His eyes widened and he took a cautious step back. His larynx bobbed nervously as he swallowed.

"Where'd you get a gun?"

"Around," I said through gritted teeth. "Drop the crowbar."

It clattered to the deck. He took another a tentative step backward.

"You alone?"

He nodded. "The others fled when the High Priest arrived. I'm all that's left."

I waved my gun at him. "Hands up."

He complied, and in his pitiful state he was looked less threatening. I pressed my back to the wall and pushed off the deck with my good leg, slowly inching my way upward. My breathing came in tight bursts. I was cold but sweating. If I tried to put any weight on my leg, I was sure the pain would make me pass out. The bulkhead kept me steady.

I glanced at the city, then at the monster above. There was no way I could climb up the thing now. I had no way to get up there. No way to plant the explosive.

The dimanian watched me, but his eyes drifted toward a pair of shamblers who busied themselves over a corpse nearby. It was the right distraction at the right time. The wood whistled as it swung. He heard the sound and turned, but it was too late. Taft walloped him across the back of the head. Her makeshift club split in two. My attacker crumpled and lay still. The chaos all around had muffled Taft's approach. I sagged and dropped my arm with a heavy sigh as I slid down against the bulkhead.

"Thanks," I hissed as a new wave of pain traveled up my body.

She rushed to my side, tucked a hand under my armpit, and helped me stand.

"He did a number on you," she said. "Knee again?"

I nodded, shut my eyes, and bent at the waist. I reached out to the Wasteland. For a time, two Waldos experienced the same moment in reality. The worlds around me bent in on each other. Shifting sands and wind-blown waves vied for and occupied the same. The desert wind caressed my face as the cold air nipped at my nose.

Tawil's warning echoed in my ear and hardened me, and I breathed out as the pain subsided. How long I could hold this? How long would my mind let me?

Wensem rushed around the corner, his spear-club still in his hand. He saw me, Taft, and the unconscious dimanian.

"By the Firsts!" he shouted as he rushed to my side. "Wal!"

"Eibonian. Crowbar. Knee," I said, waving my gun at my attacker. "Bastard."

"You shoot him?"

"No. Taft knocked sense into him."

Wensem scowled. His fingers tightened on his spear. He looked at me, then at the duffle.

"You can't climb that like that," he said. "You need a bonesaw."

"I have to stop that thing," I said. "The city, Wen. Lovat. It'll destroy Lovat."

"You try to climb in your condition, and you'll die," Wensem said. "If you die, we all die."

I looked up at him. His steel gaze had hardened—I could almost see the wheels turning behind it. He was right. My mind went back to our conversation at Ced's all those days ago. I wasn't in this alone.

The spear dropped, and Wensem held out his hand. "Give me the duffle bag."

"It's my—"

"Give me the duffle, Wal."

The outstretched maero hand with its extra digits was a lifeline. Wensem knew the risk and was making a sacrifice of his own. He was my partner, and this was a partnership.

I couldn't do this alone. I would be dead if it weren't for Taft. Now it was time to let Wensem help. I slipped the duffle off my shoulder and looped it over his hand.

"We can draw him out," I said. "I'll get him to hit the deck. Then you can scramble upward."

"Don't linger long," Taft warned. "Drop that thing and skedaddle."

Wensem nodded. The fire that simmered deep inside him was beginning to bubble over. It was evident in his posture. In that moment, he reminded me of the warrior I had seen in the Humes Tunnel.

"One more time, my friend," I said.

He set his crooked jaw, slung the blue duffle over his shoulder, and stared upward—his iron-blue eyes narrowed.

"Let do this."

THIRTY-SEVEN

Above the chaos and gore, Deeper loomed.

Taft and I worked in tandem. She hooked an arm around me, lifting me up. I tucked the Judge in my waistband and picked up the steward's crowbar. The tip screeched and banged against the metal of the deck as I began to use it as a makeshift cane. Once set, Taft and I half-hobbled and half-jogged back to the open deck.

Some of the shamblers still feasted on their victims, though a few had disappeared. Others stared upward in an awed and silent vigil, their mouths cracked in bloody, too-wide smiles.

"When you see him move, we need to move." I looked at Taft. "We're not fast enough to dive out of the way at the last moment."

She nodded.

It was time to do this. I waved the crowbar. I shouted. I cursed.

Deeper's nest of eyes locked with my eyes. Its hands lifted. I felt seawater spatter my face and arms. Then the creature roared.

"Incom—"Taft shouted, her voice drowned out by the titanic bellow that shook the world.

I glanced at Wensem, who was crouched in the shadows like a wound spring ready to be sprung. The blue duffle was over his shoulders. There wasn't time to wish each other good luck. But we didn't need to say anything. Our eyes met, and that gaze was everything.

Good luck, my friend.

Taft was already moving. As Deeper's fists descended, the fingers splayed open. The reaching digits blocked out the sky. The High Priest—this destructive giant of a First—didn't want to crush me, he wanted to pluck me from the deck. What would he do if successful? Eat me? Tear me limb from limb? Both?

My legs lifted off the deck as Taft carried me at a run across the deck of Chee.

It was like outrunning a collapsing city block. We maneuvered between a pair of huge fingers. She was saying something, screaming it, but with the monster bellowing, I heard nothing. Fingers descended around us, forming a valley of flesh. The skin was leathery and covered in sea life: starfish, anemones, barnacles, crabs, and other strange creatures. It was like the seafloor had collapsed from the sky.

We emerged from the valley's mouth haggard but unhurt. The roar turned to a howl as Deeper realized we had escaped. The fingers shifted, curled, and then clawed at us. Hooked barbs bigger than wains tore into the metal deck plates. All I could do was stare as Taft dragged us on, putting more space between us and the groping digits.

Wensem sprinted from his hiding space and leaped up one enormous finger. His long limbs propelled him across the back of Deeper's hand even as it lifted from the deck. Wensem was already at the wrist before it cleared the *Gamble*. He drove his wood spear into the flesh, using it to cling to the arm as the First lifted him higher and higher and higher.

He was up climbing with the beast. The monster's bellows quieted, and for a moment the world stilled.

Taft kept going, dragging me with her. She sucked in huge lungfuls of air. A second gigantic fist smashed down. Metal howled, rivets popped and broke.

We skidded to a stop, slipping on the blood-soaked deck and tucking behind the edge of a bulkhead. This position would keep us out of sight for the moment. I collapsed against the chuck. We were both gasping. I reeled, and the world spun drunkenly. In my daze I watched a pair of stunned crabs skitter in confusion across the nearby deck.

Taft had propped me next to the bulkhead. Everything crashed and broke around us. The deck vibrated with each strike. The noises of panic were rising from below. Shamblers shimmered into and out of existence, moving away from Deeper's rage.

"Can you see Wensem?" I gulped air and tried to straighten my leg out.

Taft peaked around the corner. "He's near the elbow, assuming that little fleck of gray is him."

The elbow. Good, he was close. What was it like, climbing that creature? Was the skin as craggy and rough as the hand? I was useless down here—but he had been right. I couldn't have climbed, not in my state—heck, maybe not before. It had to be him. This time someone else had to do it.

Please be okay, Wen.

"Let me look at that knee," Taft said.

I eased it out, and she leaned in, poking and prodding. Chucks tend to know a little bonesaw. It helps with trail work. I winced as she gripped it.

"Ain't broke. Ain't dislocated." Blood was streaked across her left cheek, and her eyes had a hollow look. Some of her hair had fallen in front of her face. "Bad sprain. He got you good. It's going to swell up something fierce."

She pinched and massaged. Pain flared, and for—

Tawil crouched across from me. The desert sand was blowing behind him, turning the horizon the non-color of sunbaked dust. A low keening echoed from beyond the sky, from the great titan that sat outside the world.

"You were supposed to hide."

"I did." The pain was ebbing away. My gasping softened.

He looked at my leg, then at Taft, who was unknowingly occupying the same space as him.

"Good. You're learning. Extending yourself."

What was he talking about? I stared at him as he calmly sketched an oval in the dirt—or was it the deck?—with a stick. Then he drew a symbol in the center—the pupil of an eye, split into three. Around the oval, he drew a hooked shape, and below this, he drew three more circles. The symbol reminded me of graffiti I had seen scattered across Lovat and Syringa. A horned eye.

"Always watching." The stick tapped the drawing. It tinged off the metal deck and kicked up puffs of Wasteland dust.

"We're going to stop him. We're going to stop Deeper." I felt dizzy. The blending of realities slowed my mind. Thoughts crawled with glacial slowness. Even my motor skills felt sluggish.

"You cannot stop, you can only delay." There was a sadness in Tawil's tone. He tapped at the symbol, and as suddenly as before we were no longer in the desert. Now we rested along a green shore beside a vast lake covered with gently rocking water plants. The sweet fragrance of flowers filled the air. No broken sun baked this place, no monster loomed beyond this horizon. Instead, the water was filled with smoking water lilies that bobbed next to islands of floating vegetation starred with red flowers.

I could smell the sulfurous smoke of the lilies. The sight of beauty marred by such ugliness unnerved me. Something innocent had become tainted by something profane. I shook my head, trying to clear it.

Wensem should be at Deeper's shoulder now. Did the First even notice him? Did he run along its collarbone or had the creature tried to dislodge him? Thoughts of Deeper and Wensem and the *Gamble* jumbled together. They might have well have been fiction. The idea of Lovat was fuzzy and malformed. The world I defended was colorless compared to the oversaturated color here in this waterside garden.

I looked at Tawil. The man sitting across from me pulsed with vibrancy. The faded tattoos on his face were sharp and clear and bright blue. For a moment they floated before his face, a tree of blue orbs that drifted like clouds on the wind. He smiled. His mouth and eyes mutated and became keyholes. Somewhere I heard doors squeal open, the rattle of keys, and the sound of locks unlatching.

"What is this?"

I received no answer.

The slap stung, but it pulled me back. Taft was sitting across from me, and she looked concerned.

"Wasteland?" she asked.

I nodded—I stammered something, then shook my head. The world buzzed around me.

"We need to do something. Ugly noticed Wen."

My consciousness returned to my damaged body. The pain wasn't as bright and hot as before. I struggled to my feet, still favoring my knee as best I could. Again I reached out to that other reality. Pulled at myself there but held fast refusing to slip fully across. My pain eased somewhat. I leaned around the corner to size up the situation.

Taft was right. Deeper had discovered my partner.

Wensem was a small spot of paleness against the First's dark body. He'd reached the shoulder, ducking as the creature shifted and twisted, trying to dislodge him. In his rage Deeper spun, and one of the malformed wings again slammed into the wall of West Lovat, dragging through several buildings as he completed his harried pivot. More detritus rained down, along with a few limp bodies.

In a few moments, I knew, Deeper would try to brush him away. I couldn't let that happen.

"Come on, Wen," I leaned forward, wanting to leap out, shout, draw attention away from him.

I was proven correct and it horrified me. Deeper dragged a hand across his shoulder, a gesture not unlike a human dusting off their jacket. My teeth ground together. When the hand cleared the shoulder, the pale spot was gone.

Wensem!

"No! No, no, no!" I moved to rush to the open deck, but Taft held me back.

My breath was stuck in my throat.

I squinted up toward the monster. *Please.*

Then Wensem appeared over the slope of shoulder. Somehow he dodged the stroke. Some way he avoided the dusting. Too close. Much too close. His luck wouldn't hold.

"We need to distract it!"

"What? How?" Taft was incredulous.

"Don't know, but if Deeper's distracted, Wensem can finish the job."

I could see Wensem picking his way across the shoulder. It had to be as wide as Chee was long.

"You want to shout at him?" Taft said. "We won't be lucky a second time! If we try to trick Ugly again, he'll catch us. He ain't a fool."

"We're not going to trick him," I said. I looked back toward the bent and broken decking. My knee felt better. Maybe that was a positive side effect of my mind slowly going insane. But I knew the joint wouldn't perform well. It was damaged here. "We're going to distract it."

I stepped around the corner, the Judge in one hand, steward's crowbar in the other. I pointed the revolver in the air and reached into the Wasteland. I could feel the Judge in my hand there and here simultaneously. I was acting on a wild theory—acting out of desperation.

Here the gun had been soaked, which made the cartridges in the cylinder useless. There they would still be dry. It was chaos in my mind. But, all I knew was that Wensem was in danger. Act. I could only act.

I pulled the trigger as my hair stirred in the hot wind. In both realities the hammer fell—*click*—and…

BOOM!

The Judge's report echoed across the broken surface of Chee and off the edge of West Lovat. It silenced the howling wind from the Wasteland. For a second, the world went silent. Everything stopped.

Wrinkled shambler orbs turned in my direction as Deeper leered. Feelers drifted near his enormous face and stroked his plaza-sized cheeks. His expression was one of deep enmity. A thousand eyes pulsed putrid amber. Hate oozed from the thing like ephemeral pus. The scent of the grave rose around me.

I pulled the trigger again.

Click—BOOM!

Damn these monsters. Curse this colossus. Lovat wasn't down for the count. Not yet. Not by a long shot. Deliver the package, and we were done. Then just wait and hope the charge wasn't set for sooner rather than later.

"Stay here," I said to Taft. I tossed her the Judge. It had done what I needed it to do, but I couldn't linger between worlds. Deeper was here, fully here, and I needed to move.

"What are you going to do?"

"Stay here, Taft." Firmer this time.

Her expression hardened. She gave me a curt nod.

Above, Wensem moved closer.

I limped to an open spot in the decking, still clutching the crowbar. The ruin was apparent. In his rage, Deeper had wreaked havoc on the *Gamble*. It would never recover. Most of Chee's upper deck had been destroyed, as had the tops of the other two districts. A smoking fire burned somewhere on Yallup. Oily black smoke rolled into the air. It drifted around me like a malefic fog.

"Here I am, you bastard," I shouted. I slapped my chest. "Here I am! I'm the one you want!"

A shambler appeared, flickering out of nothingness like a malfunctioning bulb. It swung at me. I shattered its arm with the crowbar. Bringing the weapon around again, I sent the creature sprawling. More of the monsters were moving in my direction.

Some covered the distance by winking in and out of existence. Others chose an ambling run. They all wore the rictus grin, their slab-teeth stained bright red.

I clubbed another shambler. Its mouth shattered. Its wrinkled eyes stretched as it tumbled.

Deeper's nest of eyes watched me. His arms hung limp, fingers and hands lost beneath the water. The tiny figure of Wensem appeared near the nest of tentacles that writhed around the lower half of the prodigious head.

You're close now. Drop the bomb. Run! Dive!

Another Shambler appeared beside me. I jabbed the flat end of the crowbar toward its chest. A misshapen hand batted it away. Another struck me in my burned shoulder. My damn shoes slipped on the deck. I fell, catching myself with my good knee.

A hollow gong sounded. The shambler took a step toward me.

I broke its leg with a second strike. My swing was better than the dimanian's had been. A pitiful mewling tumbled from the shambler's bloody mouth. Then it fell to the deck. My third strike finished it. Black blood spattered my arms and face.

Rising, I shouted up at Deeper. "Here I am! I'm the one you want!"

Its titanic arms began to move.

"I killed your family!" I was screaming. My words came out ragged and raw.

More shamblers swarmed around me. I threw them off, striking this way and then that. Each swing hit something. An arm. A leg. A neck. A head. A mouth. A few of the creatures made contact but I kept swinging until the wave broke and fell back.

Hot desert air caressed my face, the coolness of Lovat invigorated my lungs, and the sticky sweet smell of the water garden worked through me. My body buzzed. In that instant, I existed everywhere—I was stretched between worlds, pulling them all closer together.

And the giant knew it.

I waved the crowbar. "Cybill crushed! Curwen burned! Ashton impaled! What about you? How would you like to die?"

Deeper roared. The sound was louder than anything I had heard before. It shuddered through the decking. Stirred the sea. Shook the city. Quaked the bedrock.

Then, for a moment, it all went silent. My ears buzzed. The world was quiet.

Fists crashed down on either side of me. I was thrown off my feet and slid across the deck.

The Chee broke away, then tilted dangerously. The *Gamble* was dying. It'd be beneath the water soon.

This amused Deeper. He absently slapped the Chee, a predator playing with its prey, and the old boat spun in the water as it sank. The sky above carouseled. The clouds formed a twisting vortex. Deeper's black mass appeared and disappeared as the boat rotated.

The spinning world made it hard to focus. Then a hand lashed out. The vessel halted. Those standing on the deck were thrown off their feet. Debris went flying.

Wensem! I looked up at the huge shoulder. No gray spot there. My eyes traced the line of the collar. Nothing.

THERE! There he was! I caught sight of Wensem's lanky little form as he slipped below the heap of writhing feelers.

A wave of euphoria filled me, followed by a swell of pride. He had done it! Carter's cross, he had done it! We were going to kill this bastard. Deeper was going to die.

Drop the bomb, Wen. Get off the beast.

How much time did we have left? Couldn't be long.

I struggled to my feet.

Deeper's shoulders shook in a silent mocking laugh. Then he lowered its head. His tentacles twisted upward along one side as if he was smirking. Colossal hands reached in my direction. My chest swelled as I inhaled, getting ready. I exhaled, puffing out my cheeks as I sized up my enemy.

Around me, the shamblers winked out of existence.

Wensem still hadn't emerged.

Had something gone wrong?

I imagined him trapped and battling tentacles beneath that overhang of a chin. I could see his crooked jaw set and his gray-blue eyes ablaze as he struggled to find the right place to jam the duffle into.

Come on, Wen. My lips moved but no sound came out.

I held my breath.

"Come on."

Deeper's fingers spread. Descended toward me.

And then the bomb exploded.

THIRTY-EIGHT

A city has no memory. But she's crisscrossed in scars. Change is a wound, and wounds leave blemishes. You can read those scars in a city, just as you can on a person. Old impressions haunt shadowed corners and remind us of all the lives that came before. Tear out an old building, watch the new rise in its place—something always remains—angles, foundations, walls.

People though, people have a memory, and our memory tends to be full of scars.

My city was bleeding. A long line of refugees stretched up the hard-packed gravel of the Big Ninety, a gray-clad mass of people moving through a cut in the mountains. The city lay far behind us. Cheerful birds sang from the tops of pines, and you could hear squirrels angrily chatter at one another through the soft patter of rain.

I walked among them, head down, shoulders hunched, the hood of my leather coat pulled up over my head. Gone were the ruins of the uncomfortable suit and the uncomfortable patent leather shoes. I had traded them away for more familiar gear. I was back in my boots, with my worn keff tied around my neck. We walked slowly, which suited me just fine. I didn't move at any other speed anymore.

Time had drifted since the *Gamble* sank. Uncountable weeks of torment. Days of heartbreak. Hours, minutes, seconds of sorrow.

I felt numb.

I hadn't eaten much. I couldn't. I had no appetite. Didn't have much of anything anymore.

After the bomb went off, Deeper's smoking carcass had collapsed into West Lovat, the gore hissing and spitting from the massive crater where his head and neck had been. The wound his corpse had made was deep. It would take generations for the scar to form. Generations more for the pain to heal.

Cackling laughter from another world echoed in my ears. I pushed it aside. Breathed. Closed my eyes.

In my mind I could still see that hellish sight. A cloud of billowing black dust rising and rolling away from the impact. Floors and ceilings shattering and collapsing, houses and storefronts pancaked flat as the First's body burst through them.

Destruction spread from that great tent, bringing down more and more of West Lovat's warrens.

There was no victory. There was only disaster.

Tens of thousands killed. Tens of thousands more wounded.

Fire had rippled away from the devastation, devouring even more. People died in the inferno. For days an oily black smoke choked the air and the sounds of wailing sirens filled the night. The fire still raged.

No one was allowed inside the fire zone. LPD set up a perimeter. Panicked people clustered at each level, shouting out the names of loved ones. I was among them, pushing at the edges.

Much of West Lovat was gone. Homes and businesses had vanished, leaving only the charred skeleton of the city's superstructure.

Those displaced were left without shelter. The Camalote and the other charities were unable to deal with the influx. Many took to living on the streets, many more fled.

The parts of the city that survived could thank the arrival of the spring deluge for their salvation. The rain poured though warrens, stifling hotspots and beating back the flames. Then storm drains, now blocked by debris, flooded and a new disaster rolled though Lovat's ugly wounds.

The same rain continued to drizzle down around the column of refugees.

"From West Lovat?" The question came from an iron-masked dauger wearing a billowing yellow raincoat and a floppy fisherman's hat. Spots of rust discolored his iron chin. He carried a big backpack complete with a roader's bedroll. Pink and purple lights whirled across the edges of his mask—lights from somewhere else. Lights I saw but couldn't really describe.

I looked at him. Looked over his shoulder at the Wasteland, both there and not, here and elsewhere. I shook my head, trying to clear it and answer his question in the same gesture.

It didn't dissuade him. "I am too," he said. "Lost my boat in the fire and my house in the collapse. Lost an aunt. Only family

I had in Lovat. Ain't nothing left for me now. Figured I'd head east. Seek my fortune in the frontier. Maybe return to my people. Hellgate always has work."

I said nothing. What could I say? How could I begin to say anything?

"You see any of them beasties?"

A long sigh escaped my lips. I shook my head. Harsh desert wind caressed my stubbled jaw. Coyotes howled from another plane I perceived and yet didn't.

West Lovat's destruction wasn't the only reason people were leaving the city. Some left out of fear.

"I have a friend in the fire authority, and he claims he saw shadows in the smoke. Swear this is true. On Hastur's crook!" The name made me flinch, but if he noticed he didn't show it. "I swear! Said they were twisted-looking, he did. Like someone had sewn a cephel child to a bok's neck!" The dauger shuddered at his own description and then laughed, but there was more nervousness than humor in it.

This wasn't the first I'd heard of this. After the collapse, stories had begun to trickle from the ruins. Tales of weird creatures—monsters, some said. The *Ledger* had shared similar reports. All manner of folk claimed to see things with the bodies of a bok and heads that looked like a cephel—Deeper in miniature.

Citizens had vanished. Cops had gone missing. There were rumors that a whole fire brigade had been lost.

Those weren't the only stories. Tales of aggressive shamblers were becoming commonplace. They would flicker into existence, assault someone, then flash away. Caravans were running spooked. Others told worrisome accounts of specters as black as umbras, with long pointed hoods and billowing capes—silent watchers who said nothing but observed everything.

The facade was beginning to crack. Worlds were spilling into one another.

The Wasteland beckoned. I ignored its pull.

It was as if everything I had experienced over the last several years was settling into my city. And here I was, leaving it all behind.

Could I do anything else? The cost had been too high.

"You seen anything like that?" the dauger asked.

I didn't even acknowledge the question. My legs shuffled along, kicking mud and dust in two different realities, my limp pronounced and yet nonexistent.

Where was I going? I didn't know. All I knew was I had to get away. Away from Lovat. Away from her ruined skyline. Away from the machinations of cults and gangsters and politicians. Away from the monsters that stalked the streets. Away from the chaos. Away from the broken city that I loved, that I ached for, that I was abandoning.

His questions unanswered, eventually the dauger drifted away and disappeared into the column of refugees.

There was still too much for me to wrestle with. Too many threads hadn't been pulled. Maybe the silence I'd find in the Territories would give me answers. Maybe I could find solace along the road. I loved Lovat, but I was made for the trail.

I wasn't alone in my brooding. This was a stoic and mostly quiet column. Occasionally a child would ask a parent where they were going, or cry about a lost toy or the comforts of a lost apartment. These were usually hushed, not out of unkindness but from a pain that was still too fresh. A wound that hadn't scarred over yet.

No one wanted to pry too deeply. No one was willing to pick at the scab. Few desired conversation like the dauger sailor. It hurt too much.

In truth, Lovat couldn't absorb the loss. West Lovat was a bedroom community. Many of the city's workers lived there, taking the monorail into the city in the morning and drifting home at night. There were few places for them to go, so they began to pack up their meager belongings and leave.

Some hoped to find work down south, in Bridgetown. Others looked for a future in Syringa or perhaps in one of the smaller settlements along the way, Robbers Roost or Junction City. A few, I'm sure, were like me. Drifting.

My last moments on the *Gamble* had been a blur, lost to the grief that had burned through me in the time since. Somehow Taft had carried me away. Screaming—I remember there was screaming.

It was me. It had come from me.

I could remember what I felt right after the blast. The beast was dead! We had done it! The memory of how I'd celebrated only made my pain more potent. The euphoria and hope that had blossomed had turned in an instant to cinders.

There'd been no miracle.

Wensem dal Ibble, my best friend, was dead.

Thinking it made my throat hurt. Tears welled in my eyes. A deep ache opened inside my chest and my stomach went into freefall.

Maero are hard to kill—until they're killed. Even Wensem couldn't withstand an explosion.

My mind drifted to the small memories, odd little moments that reminded me of him. Smells and sounds, phrases and gestures. The way he'd crack a bone-dry joke, or how the lines around his eyes would wrinkle when he smiled. His kindness. His care for everyone, especially the disadvantaged—a genuine empathy. You don't find that in most folks. Most are too selfish to see beyond their needs. Most wouldn't sacrifice themselves the way Wensem did.

It's so easy to assume that the people who matter to us will always be there—until they're gone. And the void they leave behind? Nothing fills that hollow. Nothing can.

There are other things as well. Things that remind me of what he loved. The way he'd hold his son, or how he would embrace Kit. The stories he would tell with such delight. Slapping his knee when something struck him as funny.

These small recollections are never tied to a single event, but they say more about him than any single account could.

I miss him.

I miss him so much it hurts.

I'm still not sure how Taft and I made it off the *Gamble*. I don't remember. Everything after the explosion is a grief-soaked blur. The authorities were still trying to figure out how many died. The papers and monochrome news shows had been talking about it. Magnez had press conferences. LPD had urged calm. I hadn't had the energy to read or watch any of it. The world was background static—lost to the ringing that still echoed in my ears, and buried beneath the heartache.

The steady heartbeats had developed a murmur.

Sorrow engulfed my shattered world, and I'd let it take me. I'd retreated to my apartment buried my head beneath my moldering pillow. Sleep was spotty. Time passed in fits. I'd wake up in tears, fall asleep in exhaustion. Nightmares were constant, reality broken. I dreamed of Wastelands and green shorelines, of smoking flowers, grinning shamblers— and explosions. Always explosions.

I lived in the darkness, never bothering to turn on a light or open the shades. I didn't check in with the rest of my crew. At one point, someone knocked on my door. They spoke, voice muffled.

I didn't answer. I couldn't.

When I could, I looked for him. For days. Weeks? I don't even know anymore. The monorail to West Lovat was closed, the Lovat Transit Authority had the platforms blocked. I had to make my way there on foot. It took hours, and I when I got there I found most of the warren was closed off. Yellow police tape blocked passageways, and stern officers stood by, thumbs tucked into belts. LPD stopped me when they could, but eventually I eluded them.

But what awaited me on the other side—

Death and soot. Fire and blood.

It didn't matter. I came back the next day. And the next. And the next. I explored the waterfront standing on the edge and waiting, as if I expected Wensem to emerge soaked and grinning, wiping the hair from his eyes. I clawed through wreckage near Deeper's corpse expecting to hear his voice call out from beneath a tangle of wreckage. Days and days. Hoping. Praying. Wishing something had changed.

Nothing had.

Wensem was gone.

The Wasteland beckoned. The gutted bones of West Lovat reminded me of the bones of the dead city. The smell that lingers in this reality carried an odor similar to that of the sun-bleached bones of her twin.

You can only scratch through soot for so long. Eventually, I retreated back to the darkness of my apartment. I answered no knocks on the door. I fought back pulls from those other realities. The knocks came and went. The muffled words drifted away. My pillow grew stained with tears and then sweat.

Toward the end, I went to see Kit.

Telling her about Wensem's death was the worst experience of my life.

I won't put it into words. I can't.

After I left her, shame shackled me. How could I stay? Lovat had become a mausoleum, Wensem's death a wound that wouldn't heal, a scar that would never form. Staying in Lovat would bleed me dry. All I could do was leave.

I left a telegram for Hagen and Hannah, another for Taft. Sam received a letter. They were apologizes, mostly, regret scratched out in ink blurred with tears. They probably didn't make much sense. My stomach still ached in embarrassment. These people deserved more. They deserved better.

A better man would have spoken to them in person. A better man would have faced his friends. But I couldn't trust myself. My mind was broken. I didn't believe anything I saw anymore. I wasn't sure where each step would land. Speaking seemed impossible. My throat was still raw and ragged anyway. Silence suited me. That's what I told myself. I pushed back against the shame. I pretended leaving was the right decision, that it was all for show. I began whispering lies to myself. I tried not to think too much about believing them.

I was of little use now. I didn't need much.

The quiet of the road beckoned.

A broken caravan master with no caravan is a sorry sight. Seemed odd to call myself a roader, anyway. That was a title I no longer deserved. And Guardian? The word left a bitter taste on my tongue. If anything, I'd become Drifter. That was the title I deserved most.

My gear was still in my ruck, and it took no time to clean out my apartment. My landlady didn't even react when I told her I was moving out, just kept smoking as she flipped through her morning edition of the *Ledger*, the headline cruelly reminding me of my best friend's death and my weeks of useless searching. The landlady barely grunted in my direction.

I began to walk. I crossed a span. I shuffled through a caravansary. I ignored the voices that called out to me. It became harder and harder to decipher which reality they came from. Eventually, I found the column. Became just one more refugee.

In moments like these, you go back to basics.

Hands in my pockets, head down, shoulders hunched forward, I walked my painful hobbled walk, unsure of where I was going or why. It was something I needed to do. Mourning my friend. Remembering the better times—the trails we had walked, the caravans we had led, the decisions we had made, the silly arguments, that last drink we shared.

A good walk will clear out any troubles. So I walked.

A city has no memory. But people do. Maybe the wound would heal. Maybe it wouldn't.

It didn't matter.

A hot desert wind blew through that cold spring morning.

I walked.

It's what Wensem would have done.

ACKNOWLEDGEMENTS

Book IV was a long time coming. The scenes in this story were in my head since the opening lines of *The Stars Were Right*, and I'm proud they're now alive and out there. But, as with previous books, I couldn't have done it alone. Hitting the fourth book in a series like this is something to celebrate, and there are so many amazing people I need to acknowledge who got me here.

As always, I have to thank Kari-Lise, my wife and partner, who endured me being me as I wrote this story for the last few years. She read the early drafts, suggested changes, and suffered through the emotional rollercoaster of being married to a writer. Thank you for all that you do, Kari-Lise. I love you so very much.

Thank you to my editor, Jennifer Howard. Coming into a series mid-stride isn't easy, and this book only works with Jen's help. I'm a feral writer in the best of times, and tackling my prose can be daunting. But, Jen's attention to detail, whip-smart suggestions, and kind instruction made this book better.

I also need to thank Christine Nielson for giving this novel its last bit of polish and proofreading. Little details sharpen a story, and Christine helped hone them. I'm glad to have you as a part of this team.

Jon Contino is owed another huge thank you. Once again, he helped me out with the lettering for the cover, and it's my favorite in the series. I felt terrible hiding it for way-too-many years. But I am so excited to finally see it out in the world and in people's hands. It establishes the tone I've always wanted from the get-go. It's the opening stanza in many ways.

Once again, thanks to Steve Leroux and Sarah Steininger Leroux for your encouragement and support—especially throughout 2020. Love you guys. Thanks to Steve Toutonghi for your friendship, advice, and being so excited about these weird little books. Thanks to Josh Montreuil for your encouragement and support over the years—this world wouldn't exist without you. Thanks to Mal Jones and Sarah Meskin for their friendship and fantastic networking skills. Also, thanks to Dave Clark and Rachel Avery, who helped me sort out Islamic translations. Thanks to Adam Wygle for introducing me to both of them. The internet can be a beautiful little place.

Huge thanks to my beta-roaders who offer insight and impressions on this book early-on: Sky Bintliff, Vanessa Garbini, Steve Leroux, J. Rushing, Kelcey Rushing, and Redd Walitzki. Calling you amazing isn't sufficient. You've helped me and this story out more than you know, and I can't thank you enough. You're my caravan crew, and this journey is only successful because of your effort.

And, of course, the last and biggest thanks goes out to you, my readers. We're four books in now—this book only exists because of you. I sincerely hope it was worth the wait. Thank you for writing your reviews, tweeting your tweets, blogging your blog posts, sending the emails, and drawing the fan art. You make it worthwhile.

APPENDIX

The official and ever-expanding Glossary of the Territories
and so much more can be found online at:

KMALEXANDER.COM

K. M. ALEXANDER is a Pacific Northwest native and novelist living and working in Seattle, Washington with his wife and two dogs. *Gleam Upon the Waves* is the fourth book in his cosmic-horror soaked dark urban fantasy series, the *Bell Forging Cycle*. Follow his exploits and stay up to date with his work at KMALEXANDER.COM

ALSO BY K. M. ALEXANDER

THE BELL FORGING CYCLE, BOOK I
The Stars Were Right
THESTARSWERERIGHT.COM

THE BELL FORGING CYCLE, BOOK II
Old Broken Road
OLDBROKENROAD.COM

THE BELL FORGING CYCLE, BOOK III
Red Litten World
REDLITTENWORLD.COM

The Guardian will return in

THE BELL FORGING CYCLE, BOOK V
Through Hostile Lands
THROUGHHOSTILELANDS.COM